THE LAST SUMMER OF HAIR

A NOVEL

PAUL RANSOM

First published by Truth Serum Press, November 2020
Novel copyright © Paul Ransom

BP#00099

Truth Serum Press
32 Meredith Street
Sefton Park SA 5083
Australia

Email: truthserumpress@live.com.au
Website: https://truthserumpress.net/
Store: https://truthserumpress.net/catalogue/

Original hair image copyright © OpenClipart−Vectors
Original scissors image copyright © Clker−Free−Vector−Images
Cover design copyright © Matt Potter

ISBN: 978−1−922427−14−4

Also available as an eBook
ISBN: 978−1−922427−15−1

Truth Serum Press is a member of the
Bequem Publishing collective
http://www.bequempublishing.com/

for Jo Jo

Contents

1   Spring equinox

39   November / December

93   Xmas / NY

157   Another summer

167   Australia Day weekend

217   Another festive season

229   February

279   Autumn equinox

Spring equinox

01. The appointment.

He'll never do it, she thinks. It's another of his famously dramatic gestures. A plot device. His way of keeping our attention firmly fixed. *Look at my shiny new head.*

Christa Marie Bell knows Antonio 'Tony' Timone too well. Or believes she does; and so acts accordingly. Like someone who thinks they have a claim on him.

He was going to be a star, wasn't he?

Before he wasn't.

Now he's a tick off fifty and looking like he has no idea — what, where, why.

Lost. Disappointed. Disoriented.

Thinning and frustrated. Lined and thwarted.

She thinks he has the look of a man finally beaten by the world.

Or is this what she hopes?

His loss, her triumph.

Told you so, Tony.

Christa is convinced she has a knack for emotional truth, for seeing people. Years of clients. Their dramas, deceits, denials. Watching it all unfold in the expansive mirror, like an accretion of murmurs.

Therefore — emboldened — she has quickly arrived at the view that Tony's abrupt homecoming was triggered as much by as yet unspecified disasters as by the events of the past week. Though he offered no obvious clue during their appointment, unspoken motives lurked in his evasive eyes. In every silent beat of his otherwise up-tempo routine. From rounding shoulders and tightening mouth.

She studied him closely in the salon's soft lit mirror. Noticed his gaze. His focus consistently elsewhere. Miles away. Not on himself, which she might have expected, nor on her, which she may have hoped. Just somewhere.

Maybe nowhere.

Nostalgia? she wonders; but then dismisses the idea as cliché. Anyway, Tony's glories aren't the kind you get nostalgic about.

Now, hours later – another working day finally done – Christa has a few moments to herself. She sits pensively in the moulded, black plastic chair he had occupied earlier, hoping perhaps to catch the slow ghosts of his thoughts lingering in the sideways light.

'The poor boy's been cut,' she says aloud, as if to her mirror self.

She thinks of little nicks, gathered over years – accidental snips and stabbings – and she smiles at the audacity of the man.

'That absolutely clinches it,' he had theatrically declared, eyeballing her in the glass. '*This* is the last summer of hair.'

He appeared to revel in the comic and ridiculous bravado of the idea, and together they had joked that it sounded like a good idea for a bad musical; and for the length of a routine haircut, in tiny snatches, it was almost like it used to be. During their previous summer. When he was her willing guinea pig and she believed in everything.

Yet, when he cheerfully insisted she book an appointment six months out, a playful spark had shimmered in his grin. As she typed his name into the system he said, 'Around equinox.' She could not contain her smile.

'You'll never have the balls,' she teased.

His quick and cheesy retort – 'watch this bald patch, babe' – did not convince her. Indeed, she is now certain she saw enough in the involuntary shift of his eyes to suggest his cheerful determination will founder in the usual way.

Christa is confident Tony won't go through with it. It's just not his style.

'You're too vain,' she says to herself in the mirror, flicking her own fashionably groomed hair in lampoon of her one time love.

Then, half a heartbeat later, she is snarling.

'After all, it's your crowning glory, darling.'

3

02. An audience.

It is all too obvious. People are talking. He is used to this. People have always speculated about Antonio. Even his mother used to wonder ... not that *she* was an open book.

Remembering this, he looks into her deep, ambiguous eyes, motionless now in their two dollar frame. Yet still they prise him open, peeling back the curtains, peering into secret chambers.

He is tempted to turn her face down on the heavy, ancient bookshelf. To close her like one of the three hundred or so half read books she had collected over the years, their page markers still in place. But he knows there will be no privacy from ghosts. Not in this house. This town. For this is the domain of memory, the edited and imperfect landscape of incarceration and escape.

Or, as some will doubtless insist, of betrayal.

Arrogance. Downfall.

Tony Timone smiles at his departed mother, wipes a smear of fine dust particles from the glass she now lives behind. He notices his reflection, overlaid on her flattened image, as though their eyes were meeting across time. Across the valley of life and death.

He lets himself believe she would be pleased to have him back under her roof.

This is precisely the kind of poetic notion he has always been attracted to. He can imagine it as a scene in a European art film. As something beautiful.

Around town, he is sure that the reviews of his return – and of his eulogy performance – will be less generous. The talk, he guesses, will run from *about time he paid us a visit* to *what's he running from?* Although not entirely sure where, he senses the truth lies somewhere between. For there is no denying it; he has been spooked, thrown off course, and now, as if in an act of contrived symmetry, he finds himself in his dead mother's living room. About to visit Christa.

He hears again the spectral echoes of Gianna Sofia Timone's rounded maternal tones, so full of obvious, undeclared suffering, beseeching him not to overthink things. She used to hold his fizzing head in her soapy smelling hands and say, 'The world is out here, Antonio, not in there.' And she would make a gun shape with her fingers and hold it to his temples until she felt he had got the point.

He is tempted to regard the play of circumstance that brought him back to the old weatherboard house as a reiteration of that motherly injunction. The part of him that appreciates a well−structured script wants to believe that the decision to return to the bosom of Bravery Bay is his way of letting her know that he has understood her reasoning at last.

The truth is far messier and less saccharine; yet Tony knows how pervasive the reductionist lie of narrative is. He is no longer ashamed to admit that, for as long as he can remember, he has nurtured the private fantasy that his very existence is, in and of itself, a work of fine art. That it will reveal in its passage a form of greatness − a grain of universal truth.

However, the protective lustre of this life−long vanity is now a heavily fissured veneer. The textured, peeling remainder of delusion. Like blackening bags under the eyes, or a softness in the belly that no amount of sit ups will flatten. Or an increasing dread of mirrors. The thinning of not so black locks.

It is the unmistakable death of physical beauty; a treasure, he believes, now slowly ... surely ... being buried beneath the gathering dirt of time. Much like his mother's bones.

For a man who traded on his looks for thirty years, who very nearly won the lottery of fame with a handsome face, this is more than merely sobering. More than a corny crisis of confidence. Indeed, it is fair to say that Tony now wonders who he is. In his more dramatic moments he toys with the idea that he is now the embodiment of the hackneyed, ageing actor trope. Formerly glamorous dreams yielding to the pragmatism of day jobs. Celebrity fantasy to side hustle.

Having pretended to be other people all his life, he now finds himself side stage and alone, without a part to play or the convenience of scripted dialogue. An orphan in the wings. Beauty bleeding into pity.

He rests his mother's picture on the shelf. Swallows down the flood that comes too easily. Normally, he would love a good cry. But not right now.

The old fashioned clock on the wall opposite, with its loud ticks, is urging him to leave.

Now he wishes he had not made this morning's appointment. Yet he knows it would be costly not to show. The gossip would spread like wildfire; and these days Tony is a good deal more pragmatic about the side effects of whispers. More wont to keep certain things under wraps. Not at all like the nineteen–year–old country boy who dreamt of a wider world and did not give a damn if the neighbours prattled.

Besides, he has the whole summer for crying. If that's what it takes.

In his secret heart, he has come back to the Bay in defeat. With youthful promise used up and self–serving myths unravelled. There is little point denying it.

Though he would prefer to have been propelled by a lurid drama of cataclysm or epiphany, Tony knows he was nudged towards this moment in unspectacular increments, by the gentle removal of things and the slow accumulation of detritus in corners. The shock of suddenly seeing, he now understands, is simply the quake of realising that he had, for some time, taken such great pains *not* to see.

The truth will whisper and sigh before it screams, he assures himself, by way of counteracting his recent habit of reproachful monologue. I am not the first to be fooled, he thinks, neither shall I be the last.

And anyway, death is the ultimate truth. Tony accepts this now.

His mother's abrupt departure.

The headshot the agency chose; the one he cannot bear to look at, where even the airbrushing has failed to mask the signs.

Time. Gravity. Entropy.
The magnificently unlikely order
of things collapsing back towards chaos.
Songs devolving to noise.
The remaining hints of erstwhile love in
Christa Bell's flirtatious laughter.
The seemingly impossible youth of the kids
in his screen studies class.
Firm young bodies and untamed ideas.
Handfuls of winter wet soil on the
wooden lid of a casket.
Spell checking the headstone.

The awesome silence of now vacated rooms.
Cold, still air in a house not far from the sea.
A lifetime of objects stripped of ownership.
Coffee gone stale in an earthenware jar.

It is not so much the inevitability of ending that worries him. Rather, it is the long lead time. The sheer banality of decay. Tony has never enjoyed the thought that he might be ordinary.

In the plotline of selective memory, he was five or six when he first imagined himself as exceptional – when he thought he knew for sure that he was *not* the same. For the rest of his school years he clung to this idea. It protected him against the sting of what his contemporaries were thinking and saying. Especially the things he feared may be true.

Then, on the cusp of adulthood, he took his teenage cocktail of self–belief and insistent doubt with him and left Bravery Bay for good. It fuelled his resilience. His determination. It drove him to knock on every agent's door, to endure the belittling cattle call of auditions and to tolerate the permanent uncertainty of life on the road to stardom.

These days, he will admit he was pedestrian as an actor, and that although he could always hold a tune, he was never going to light up the airwaves. Like so many before him, he had stumbled from thespian ambition to campus compromise, better at teaching than doing. Of his alleged talent he now knows … it was his beauty that got him everywhere.

For every serious role, there were countless photo shoots and token hunk walk–ons.

Hairspray, oiled pecs and a smouldering pout – that's what Tony Timone was.

Gay? Straight? Who knew, who cared?

So long as his pretty face shifted units and the sexually frustrated suburban mamas tuned in.

As he prepares to leave the house bequeathed him, Tony wonders if his anonymous admirers were women like his mother. Girls who dreamt of being the princess but ended up as the kitchen hand. People like him. Ambition in tatters. Ground down by the erosive motion of time. Numbed by denial. Wallowing in the slow burning self–drama of capitulation.

Perhaps now I am my own audience, he thinks ruefully. At last.

Then he thinks the better of it. For Tony harbours no sense of injustice. There is, he feels, nothing unfair about his predicament. In fact, it is not truly a predicament. Even its urgencies seem mundane. Little more than the cut/copy spectacle of Western bourgeois ageing.

And now, under his mother's roof, the cool weight of her keys in the palm of his hand, he considers her legendary endurance, and wonders if he is merely being vain.

Though he will never admit it publicly, it was the dumb circumstance of chancing upon one of the ads – his own Photoshopped eyes staring back at him from a backlit poster – that precipitated Tony's current spiral. Maybe it was the glare of being billboard sized, but to him the guy in the hair colour ad looked desperate. Worse than that, foolish. Like the middle–aged dude at the disco.

Students and work colleagues were the first to notice the changes. A kind of distance, like a loss of belief; and beneath the dissolution of interest, something sometimes simmering like rage.

He began to feel like he did as a teenager. Imprisoned. Constricted. He dreamt again of departure.

His young lover noticed too but, like him, she had tried not to. Had hoped it would all go away.

However, with a five figure fee from the ad campaign fattening his account – and a few thousand in accrued leave owing from the college – he knew he had a buffer and that he could survive the uncertainty of letting go and the impracticality of impulse. At least for a few months.

All it took was his mother to confirm the timing. To bring the inevitable moment forward and lure him back to the Bay.

As he locks the front door behind him, he pauses to take in the view from the verandah. From its perch halfway up the hill, his mother's house looks down to the town centre and out across to the white caps breaking on the offshore reefs that once rendered the approach to the bay so treacherous for the old time fishers. He notices the bobbing marina in the sheltered section of the harbour no longer moors barnacled fishing boats. Instead, the gleaming white hulls of pleasure craft are catching the bright springtime sun and the old servo is now four storeys of chic glass and steel. And there are many more solar panels these days. Less rusting roofs. Over it all, the skeletal spire of the new phone tower is rising above the trees.

The scene is a dance of colour and light. Of things as they once were and things irrevocably changed.

Tony begins his downhill stroll with the thought that this could be the first time he has ever left the house without wishing his mother goodbye. Though he senses it too neat an idea to be true, it creates a veil of symbolic importance for him. As a lover of symbols, this matters. It taps into his story of exceptionalism and bolsters the precarious delusion of meaning he continues to cling to.

With his relatively slender figure, V neck t–shirt and expensive shades, he cuts an incongruously metrosexual figure in a town of working men and retired corporates. Farmers, business operators, superannuated sea changers.

This could be a scene from one of the films he used to make his students watch. Or an ad for a fashion brand. Except it isn't.

It's just a balding man going for a haircut. To a soundtrack of birds. The gulls and the cockies. The kookas and the maggies.

A little more than a week ago he had been bidding his students farewell. Reassuring his worried boss that he *would* return. Extricating himself from an unwise and still thankfully secret dalliance. Scared but also relieved.

Today, with the funeral fracas done and the storm of polite commiserating passed, he can begin to settle into what he hopes will be a season of cocooned reappraisal, from which, like the chrysalis, he intends to emerge as a brand new butterfly. With a new beauty to replace the one he is losing to the years.

At the heart of this concoction is an imagined future self. An older, wiser, humbler Tony looking back on a sabbatical summer with wistful satisfaction. As though it were a coming of age drama, with an arc that goes from restive churning to relieved equanimity.

Yet, his investment in these fantasies is waning by the day. The impassive behemoth of reality is asserting its authority creak by creak. Crack by crack. Strand by strand.

> *Yet more hair on the pillow this morning.*
> *The hot, sharp pin of agony*
> *just inside his right knee.*
> *The way he needs to squint to use his phone.*
> *The fact he can't quite recall whether*
> *he said ten or ten–thirty to Christa.*

He pictures her at nineteen. Lithe and loving. Her perfect melon breasts unspoiled by gravity. Her hazel eyes not yet narrowed with suspicion and disappointment.

God, how they used to kiss back then.

She is nearly fifty now; and been there, done that. Kids, divorce, etcetera. Jaded, maybe even bitter. Nonetheless, she was the only one to offer genuine solace when he arrived to tie up his mother's affairs.

'I know what loss looks like,' she had assured him, her voice suffused with both compassion and accusation.

And then she had touched her painted mouth lightly onto his — a little stain of colour left behind.

Tony did not notice it until much later, peering at his tired eyes in his late mother's rust–speckled bathroom mirror. He laughed at the fact that nobody bothered to tell him.

Thinking of it now, he reminds himself not to be complacent, to maintain his guard against the seeming friendship of the locals. Despite the physical reshaping, he senses that not much has changed in Bravery Bay in the thirty years since he fled to the city. The excruciating, small town falseness he first encountered as a child still predominates. Or at least, that's how it seems to Tony.

By the time he has made it down to the edges of the town's picturesque business precinct, and the cute cottages have given way to bakeries and hardware stores, his mind is racing. For it is a predilection of his to extrapolate epic themes from tiny moments. The poetry of homecoming, irresistible after all. He rehearses dialogue in his head. Imagines what he will tell his boss and his new students when he returns to his real life in the autumn. How cutely picaresque it will all seem.

While he waits for his long mac at one of the new cafés in town, he sets himself a task. 'Find a project,' he mutters under his breath. 'Create something.'

Partly, he does this to mitigate a fear of laziness — for which he can thank his mother's tireless peasant ethic — but mostly he is in need of distraction. Because of late his thoughts have taken on a distinctly cannibal bent, as though feeding on the plump comforts of assumption.

The young woman behind the machine hands him his coffee with shining eyes and an armful of tattoos, and he reflexively returns her brightness. 'Didn't you come here the other day?' she wants to know.

'Friday,' he tells her — and he watches as she replays a scene in her head.

'Where you staying?' she asks, assuming he's a tourist.

'Up the hill,' he answers. 'Here for the summer. Or for as long as I can stand it,' he jokes, just to see if she smiles along. Which she does.

Her coquettish, cool chick act is enough for him to decide to make her café his regular stop, even if he *has* had better macchiatos. Tony Timone still has a weakness for flattery. And for the easy beauty of youth.

It is a little known fact that he has never been attracted to anyone over thirty−five.

He estimates the barista to be no more than twenty−two.

A year ago he would have tried. Not now. These days he feels too ugly. Too self−conscious and ridiculous to make such a play.

'Well, see you soon,' he says, feeling every lurch and bumble of his recently amplified ineptitude.

'Sure,' she smiles. 'I'll try and remember your order next time.'

Outside, he inhales the steam from the coffee and sets off to find the hairdresser's. Christa had given him clear instructions but they had become muddled in the fuss of funerals and wakes; so now, he will enjoy a pleasant amble around the town while he searches.

The old pub he remembers well. The Catchers' Inn. With its Edwardian frontage and frangipani−shaded beer garden. The fancy looking Italian restaurant across the road − Via Amore − he knows only from his mother's stories. The boat tour place offering day trips and fishing adventures is new to him. So too the wellness spa and New Age bookshop.

The coffee is finished and the paper cup discarded by the time he finds himself outside the salon. He shakes his head and laughs to himself when he reads the sign.

Equinox. Hair & beauty by Christa.

It has been a long time since she cut his hair. They were kids. Both dreaming of something other. Tony was never quite sure why she didn't run off with him when he left − so he makes a mental note to ask her before the summer is up.

As he is about to enter, he sees her through the window. She is engrossed in her work, moving with targeted efficiency.

Without thinking he runs his hand through his increasingly grey and depleted mane. He neither needs nor particularly wants a haircut. It is Christa he's come to see; or rather, what she reminds him of.

Now that his mother has passed, she is the strongest connection he has to the idea of his youth. To something not so far removed from hope.

The chime rings as he pushes the door, and in a flash Christa Bell's eyes are all over him. For a beat they smile at one another. There is a quick effusive greeting and then, like a knife, Antonio 'Tony' Timone is riven with the fear that he will let her down once more.

03. An arrangement.

Truth be told, Vin Carlyle was more saddened by Gianna Timone's death than her son. Than anyone. She had her flaws but he loved her without cease – and he likes to think she loved him too, in her own peculiar and lonely way.

It has been more than a week and he misses her like crazy. In private, he cries every day; but it is not merely the grief of her leaving, it is a sadness he feels on her behalf. As though she has passed onto him the buried river of her sorrow.

At the funeral he had been unable to tear his eyes from Antonio. Still good looking and graceful in his movements ... but miles away. So distant and vague that he failed to notice the off-putting smear of Christa Bell's lipstick on his face. Vin wondered if he was too up himself to bother caring or whether he was in shock. All he could be sure of was that Tony was no longer the charismatic go-getter he remembered from childhood. He had the look of someone crushed. A look Vin often noticed at the edges of Gianna's broad and motherly smile.

He is thinking about this now as he sits in the cramped, windowless space he uses for an office at the back of the restaurant. All around him: milk crates, cardboard boxes, and towers of take away containers. He is meant to be doing the books, sorting out the pays and finalising the roster, but instead he is staring blankly at the grubby, off white wall in front of him.

> *Numb.*
> *Drifting.*
> *Unsure of everything.*
> *The wife, the kids, the business.*
> *The town, the future, what it's all for.*

He hopes it is simply a phase, something that will fade like the detail of memory. Or just be trampled in the rush of the busy season.

He sighs when he contemplates another tourist–driven summer in Bravery Bay. Good for the takings but hard on the family. 'Daddy's gotta work now,' he can hear his wife telling the girls; and he tries not to linger too long on the thought of their disappointed eyes.

So he does what he always does. Gets busy. Turns the music up loud, makes himself a double espresso and churns through the numbers.

When he is done, he drifts outside for a smoke and a few minutes of sunshine.

It is lunchtime and the light is a deep azure, the rich blue of the late September sky showing the first the signs of fading to the bleached canvas of summer.

Sitting on an upturned milk crate, Vin exhales cigarette smoke with deliberate slowness, and watches as thin snakes slither up past his eyes and dissipate. He loves this little ritual. It is the closest he will ever come to meditation.

Over the years he has had many of his best ideas during smoke breaks.

This time however, he finds himself thinking of Tony, wondering if he is still in town. The funeral was three days ago, so he figures there is a chance. He's probably up at Gianna's right now, he speculates.

On a whim, he drives there.

Pulling up, he is struck by a dense wave of nostalgia. The very shape of the weatherboard house is engraved in his past. So too its cooking smells. Though he can still picture the teenage Tony loitering in the lounge room watching rented VHS videos, it is the countless sounds and visions of Gianna that populate Vin's imagining.

Even though he does not believe in ghosts, he feels a faint shiver pass over him as he climbs the three steps up to the front porch and sees her now untended herb pots. Basil dead, parsley dry, rosemary turning brittle. Her gardening gloves are still laying, neatly folded, on the round glass top table where she used to take her coffee. As though the only thing missing from the scene is her. Like she is simply out to lunch.

Before he can control it, the tide of his sadness pushes silent tears over the brim. Wet streaks snaking their way into stubble. Thus, instead of knocking, he quietly withdraws. Retreats to the safety of the car and lights a cigarette. Quells the urge to disintegrate.

By the time he butts out he has calmed down and is re−thinking the Tony thing. 'Maybe tomorrow,' he says to the house, inching the car forward.

He is barely a couple of hundred metres down the road when he spots Tony Timone walking up the hill.

He looks too cool for the Bay in his trendy gear − and this makes Vin smile. Even as a boy he loved the way Antonio had the guts to be different.

He slows up and cranes his head out the window. 'Eh, Tony?'

Pulling down his shades, Tony blinks, smiles warmly. 'Hey Vinny, mate. How are you?'

'Not bad considering. Yourself?'

Dawdling across the road, Tony extends his hand. They shake heartily before Tony says, 'Yeah, same.'

There follows a few minutes of general catch up − including the awkward mouthing of the standard platitudes of death and grieving − before Vin suggests they meet up for a drink. 'Maybe come down to the restaurant. I'll shout you dinner.'

'You sure? You know I wouldn't expect that, right?'

'Yep. But we're closed Monday, Tuesday in the slow season. So, if you're still round on Wednesday…'

Tony chuckles to himself, raises his eyebrows. 'Planning to be here all summer, as it happens.'

This surprises Vin because, ever since he first left, Tony has made it plain he has no wish to return. In thirty years he has come back once. For two days.

Gianna had accepted his absence with grace. She was, Vin reasons, quite used to the idea of the men in her life letting her down. And anyway, Tony always treated her well when she went

16

to visit him in the city. Bought her nice things. Took her to shows.

'He has to live his own life,' was what she used to tell Vin whenever he raised the topic. 'I don't own him, and he don't owe me.'

Ownership was a big thing for Gianna Timone.

Vin wonders if this is why Tony doesn't seem guilty or devastated. In fact, all Vin can say is that Tony seems unsettled. Weirded out. As for tears...

For a few moments this fuels a righteous anger. A jealousy he finds difficult to acknowledge.

You have no fucking idea what a wonderful woman your mum was, he wants to spit out.

But doesn't.

Instead, he confirms a time for Wednesday, and the two men shake hands once more before Vin drives the short distance home, where his two little girls are glad to see him and his wife is curious to know more about this enigmatic Tony character.

'He was always a bit strange,' he tells her. 'It wasn't just that he didn't fit in or anything, it was that he kinda *liked* it that the whole town thought he was a freak. Maybe he just wanted the attention.'

Vin's wife smiles; not because of Tony but because of her husband's gentle way of trying to understand people. She only wishes he could spare a little more of that loveable quality for her and the girls. Maybe now that the old woman has gone, he will. This, at any rate, is her unspoken wish.

Over the next two days, Vin carefully percolates his memories and impressions. Seemingly random thoughts bubble up, sometimes in the form of revelation but mainly as potential questions for his guest. He wants to know:

Does Tony remember when he first came to the house?
What did he think of his mother agreeing to
'babysit' the Carlyle kid?

*Did he mind having a skinny little tyke
constantly interrupting his videos?
What did the adult Tony think when Gianna
gave Vin seed money for the restaurant?*

He is not so much seeking approval or confirmation – although it *would* be a bonus. It is more that he senses something important might come out. Something about Gianna, and there— fore about him. Or something to address the demons; those that have always hovered on the periphery.

Yet, there is also the thirty year fascination Vin has had for Tony. As a six–year–old boy he had adored his Aunty Gigi's nineteen–year–old son. Looking back, it wasn't just that the older boy had included him in his activities, had let him sit in his bedroom while Christa Bell practised cutting his hair and putting make up on him, but that he had stuck up for him when other kids teased him about his tendency to cry easily, or worse, said mean things about his parents. Then, after Tony left, Vin followed his career. For a while he was a proud fan, until optimism turned to scattered bit parts, a regular job, and an increasing distance.

In the silence of time all heroic gestures are reduced to the embarrassment of common folly.

Vin gets this now – accepts it – but for many years it bruised him. Goaded him like a school bully. Nonetheless, despite a lingering sense of being let down, Vin will always make time for Tony.

Besides, he knows what it's like to fail. He sees it every day in his wife's eyes.

When Tony appears at Via Amore half an hour late, Vin tries to play it cool.

The thin crowd of weeknight diners – locals mostly – cannot help but notice the unusual elegance of the new arrival, let alone his obviously expensive shirt. Vin also observes Tony's smile of satisfaction. It is the same sardonic grin he used to flash back in the day, whenever he knew that people were watching him. This, in turn, makes Vin smile; a reaction he tries hard to hide.

18

By the time the two men are sat in the back corner with a bottle of red and selection of warmed olives, their orders processed, curious eyes are all over them.

Tony is sure he does not recognise any of them. 'In fact I'm kinda wondering what happened to all the old faces,' he is saying. 'Only really seen a handful since I've been back. Didn't know *half* of them at the funeral.'

'Town's changed quite a bit since your day, mate,' Vin reminds him. 'New lease of life since the fishing died. Even got the Chinese out here now.'

For a while the two men reminisce about the Bravery Bay they remember, but after the meals arrive things get more personal, especially when Tony remarks on the unexpected quality of the food. 'Fuck, this is alright, mate.'

'You can thank your mum for that,' Vin replies.

'Well, you obviously learnt well.'

'Didn't really have much choice. She was a hard task master.'

Tony laughs at this. Sits back in his seat. Dabs his mouth with the white linen napkin. Looks into the deep distance. Nods to himself. Says nothing.

Vin is dying to know but holds his tongue.

'She often used to tell me how much she loved working here,' Tony finally says. 'I reckon this place gave her a sense of purpose. Bit of an outlet, I guess.'

Vin jokes, 'She was just making sure I wasn't frittering away her investment.'

'Ah c'mon, Vinnie, you know her investment was in *you*, not the business.'

Though he does what he can to conceal it, this is exactly what Vin has been longing to hear. In his chest, a flower opens, and for a second or so he is all warmth. He tries to close it down but a flicker in Tony's eyes tells him he's been caught.

'You've got no idea how glad I was when you came along,' Tony reveals. 'It's like, I knew she'd be alright and that it would be okay for me to leave. In an arrogant, teenage way, of course. Nothing noble about it. Fucking selfish really ... but even so, I could see how much she loved you. In a way maybe it was my cue.'

The sound of such confirmation is too much for Vin. It borders on humbling. On love.

Part of him wants to gush – so much dammed up drama – but he clenches his fist, screws his eyes tight. 'You really couldn't stand it here, could you?'

'Fucking hated it,' Tony fires back, not missing a beat. 'Felt like prison to me.'

Again, Vin is ruffled, this time by the hard edge of resentment in Tony's voice. Yet, rather than get defensive, he finds the clarity to ask if his guest ever blamed his mother for her decision to stay in the Bay after the accident that killed her husband. His father.

'We could have gone anywhere,' is the answer. 'She could have sold the house and gone back to Italy if she'd wanted. But I guess she didn't see the point.'

None of this surprises Vin. He often wondered why Gianna chose to stay in a town populated by racist rednecks. Mostly she used to insist it was for Antonio. At other times she would hint at more personal reasons. But Vin never really believed any of her explanations. Not fully.

'Do you think she was happy?' he wonders aloud.

'More like stubborn, I'd say.'

Vin nods. 'Maybe she just wanted to make the best of a bad situation.'

'Yeah, that too.'

Tony is about to launch into something when the young waitress arrives to top up their glasses and his attention is immediately diverted. He flirts with her in an almost rehearsed fashion that Vin finds vaguely off putting. But he ignores it and, over the rest of their dinner, they roll through the dot points:

> *Jobs, wives, kids, gigs.*
> *Plans for the restaurant.*
> *Plans for the summer.*
> *What Tony will do with the house.*
> *How Vin will invest the small but worthwhile*
> *sum of money Gianna left him.*

A second bottle of Shiraz is demolished and the two men share a smoke out back after the staff knock off. There is an undeniable warmth between them, as well as an observable distance.

Just before they say goodnight, the conversation drifts back to Gianna. Loosened by alcohol and familiarity, Tony opens up. 'It's funny but ... I don't think she ever had a plan or anything like that. She wasn't the sort to ponder shit, she was just determined, and somehow, she found a way that worked for her. She wasn't *psychological* or *spiritual* or whatever. She just found herself here and kinda bumbled along with it. Like we all do really.'

'Yeah well, she was a survivor,' Vin agrees – and as he says it something dislodges inside him.

Noticing, Tony places a hand on Vin's shoulder. 'There's no great story or meaning, or overall purpose to things. Life isn't an exam. Stuff just happens. Maybe I used to think everything was like a movie but not anymore. It's not scripted or story boarded or anything. We just make shit up as we go along.'

He pauses to look more deeply at Vin. Holds his gaze a fraction beyond comfort. 'All the editing happens afterwards,' he notes wryly. 'When it's too fucking late.'

This is not at all how Vin remembers Tony. The swaggering joie de vivre has gone, even if the penchant for dramatic flourish has remained. 'I don't know mate,' he says, 'I reckon everything happens for a reason.'

At this, Tony scoffs and blows out a long, thin jet of smoke. His eyes fix Vin's once again. 'Between you and me, I reckon that's a fantasy. It's how we *wish* things were, not how they are. Mum didn't end up here because it was meant to be. She ended up here because her fucked up, medieval parents sold her into an arranged marriage.'

The cool savagery of Tony's assertion makes Vin flinch. He remembers when Gianna first confirmed that this was indeed how she came to leave a small village in northern Italy for an even smaller hamlet on the Tasman coast of Australia. Mostly, he tries not to think about it.

A shy teenage girl alone on a boat.
On a rickety bus to nowhere.
Married to a man she didn't know.
Pregnant at nineteen.
Widowed at twenty—two.
Beautiful and doomed.

'Sorry, Vin,' Tony mutters. 'I'm a bitter old fuck these days. Don't listen to me.'

'Nah, you're probably right, mate.'

For a moment both men fall silent.

In the quiet Vin convinces himself that Tony has been profoundly disturbed by his mother's death after all — unaware that the accelerated momentum of his companion's thinking was triggered several months before Gianna's sudden passing. That her death has simply underlined things. Confirmed certain impressions.

All the same, he is both relieved and heartbroken to witness what he believes is Tony's state of shock. For him, it is a re—ignition of his boyhood love.

The direct consequence of this will not be realised for several days. Memories, loyalties and necessities will mingle in Vin's thoughts until it occurs to him. When the idea finally pops into his head he will smile at its neat power and, although he will never tell Tony so, he will feel sure that there has been a fateful alignment of stars.

And even if this *isn't* true, there is something satisfyingly neat about the arrangement.

In time, even Tony will come to acknowledge this.

04. A promise of cinders.

He heard it first from the photographer. On an expensive shoot. The coin sized polish of bare skin on his crown. Almost ten years ago now. Initially, he had shrugged it off. In the mirror it was far from obvious. Front on, his face still looked uncommonly young – high cheekbones, oval eyes, soft and sensual mouth. The black of his Latin mane still shone soft and lustrous. And he was still getting gigs. Not as many, but enough to keep his hat in the ring. To pay for portfolio shots and to bother with the fiddly irritation of creating an online profile.

These days, the circle is more defined; like the creosote plant of the North American desert, where the central shoots die off and the newer ones form an ever larger perimeter. There is now a distinct rim of black hair around a dead white hollow. When he is alone, Tony finds himself worrying it incessantly – pulling at his hair, working it, shaping it over the glaring evidence of genetic disposition.

Of sexual redundancy.

Deep down, he is terrified that if he is no longer considered beautiful nobody will give him the time of day, and that all people will see is a sad middle–aged white man clinging pathetically to the life raft of delusional virility. More than this, he wonders if he will ever be able to look at himself again.

> *What creeping incursions will he spy in the mirror?*
> *Will this emerging ugliness ever be tolerable?*

The logical part of him is less concerned. It's just hair, he says to himself. Better to go bald with dash and pride than pretend not to. No comb over bullshit for Antonio 'Tony' Timone.

No fucking way.

Yet there remains a deep seam of angst that no amount of defiant assertion can touch. It lives beneath equanimity in a dark corner of knowing. Beyond the sensible denials of the educated, middle class professional. In the space where absent fathers, sorrowful mothers and the shivering dread of loneliness lurk. In the emptiness that Tony has always had inside him.

So, when Christa Bell smiles at him in the salon mirror, her painted fingers running over the naked space of male pattern baldness, he knows instantly. The light in her eyes contains flashes of both scorn and victory. There is kindness and good humour also, but Tony is alert to the sparkle of her vengeful delight. He doesn't blame her – but still it stings. Chips a little piece off his heart.

'Getting a little thin up here, pretty boy,' she smirks.

What else can he do but smile and play along? 'I'm an old fart now,' he jokes. 'It's my badge of honour.'

'Honour, huh?' she teases, running her fingers across the evidence. 'Well, you're gonna have to start putting a little sunscreen on your honour before too long.'

As she says it, she leans in closer, pressing her warm, soft C cups against him, as if to say that she still has in abundance what he is fast losing. That she is the beauty now and he is the plain and ordinary one who will be left behind.

Christa doesn't mean to be cruel – or rather, doesn't intend for it to show – but she subconsciously straightens herself to her full height and enjoys the visceral sensation of looking down on him.

There is barely a half breath of silence between them but it is enough. They have both seen it – and now it will not be unseen.

This reminds Tony of the 'tram stop incident'. A few months ago. The first cold night of autumn. He was on his way home from a late dinner and there on the platform, in over–sized high definition print, his magnified face. Although the experience of seeing himself on billboards, in glossy magazines and on television screens was not new, this time it shocked him. Alone in the chill drizzle with a huge replica of himself, he had felt somehow reduced. As though the airbrushed avatar was mocking him. Collapsing the waveform of his vague terrors into something measurable. In his sinews Tony knew he was nothing like the idealised man in the picture; that behind the carefully constructed image an undeniable acceleration was taking place. Age. Ugliness. Uselessness. For what is a fire but a promise of cinders?

That was when the seed was planted.

> *Shave it off.*
> *Don't hang on.*
> *Avoid the unedifying rock and roll*
> *fantasy of fossilised youth.*

Then the tram had arrived with its comforting trundle and ding and Tony had wondered – whilst watching his diaphanous double travel along in the window – if anything worthwhile would remain after beauty.

He still does not know; but something in the playful brutality of Christa Bell's plump sexual toying pulls a trigger. So he says it out loud, if only to make it more real; and he likes the sound of it. 'One last summer of hair and good looks. Six months to let it grow and let it go. And who better to execute the act?'

'God, you're such a fucking drama queen,' she says with a flirty smile.

'And you're the lead actress, so don't complain,' he shoots back.

'Oooh yeah,' she coos. 'In the film you never starred in, huh?'

It is a little below the belt but Tony knows it is true. For his hubris, for his loudly trumpeted ambition, he continues to pay the price in forced humility. The nineteen–year–old dreams that took him from her arms have solidified into the brute reality of her forty–nine–year–old scissor hands. He understands that some form of apology and explanation are likely due but knows that it is neither the time nor the place. Today they just make jokes. Like they used to.

He watches the way she goes about her business and in his frightened heart an ache like thirty years. Spaces uncrossable. Sins etched in the weathered edifice of memory. A river inside him threatens to sweep him away. But she doesn't notice – and he is mighty glad of this.

Later, as she books his next appointment, they laugh at the adolescent melodrama of it. She goads him, convinced this is just another moment of attention seeking noise. Partly, he thinks she might be right. He *does* have a record of vanity and over statement. In point of fact, beneath his flowery acclamations, he still does not trust himself to follow through. On anything.

Yet, as he strides back up the incline to what is now *his* little house on the hill, he has the weirdly calm belief that this time he means it. Like he did when he first hitched out of Bravery Bay as a skinny kid with a cool haircut, one thousand four hundred and thirty—six bucks in an envelope, and a naively optimistic belief in his own talent.

He is turning these things over in his mind when he is waylaid by yet another ghost. Vin Carlyle. His mother's favourite. In his sturdy masculine car. The symbolism makes him laugh under his breath and he wonders if his resolve is being tested.

Maybe I'm over—reacting, he thinks. Perhaps this is nothing at all. Just the bruised ego of an ageing hair model.

When he gets home, he makes his way to the bathroom and peers into the small blotchy rectangle of mirror on the wall mounted cupboard. 'Hey there princess,' he says to himself with gentle mockery. 'You ready to live without your crown?'

It is a brisk night in the Bay and Tony is curled up on his mother's worn but comfortable couch. Her ancient and inefficient bar heater sits glowing nearby as he researches pattern baldness online. His brain sizzles with terms like androgenic alopecia, dihydro—testosterone and minoxidil. The more he reads the less helpful the information seems. Only when he discovers that roughly half of men at age fifty are affected does he log out. Somehow becalmed.

However, the idea that his condition is inherited sends him through the cupboards, searching out his mother's photo albums. He remembers the pictures of his dad she used to show him. Images of a slender, awkward looking man with red toned, outdoor skin and a deep uncertainty smoking in his eyes. A man who had no idea that he would die at twenty—five. Drowned within swimming distance of home.

As Tony turns the now sticky pages of the albums – their clear plastic covers sweaty and rumpled, the artless pictures no longer neatly arranged – he is struck by the tireless undoing of time. Even closed books, things stashed carefully in drawers, will bow to its magnificent, even handed power.

Nothing is hidden from the eye of time.

He laughs out loud. It is the kind of poignant, almost filmic moment he loves. On one hand a ruthless universal disassembling. On the other, precisely preserved slivers. Flat quadrilaterals excised from the mess of life. A graphic novel of nostalgia. Himself, Vin as a boy, Christa as a teenage Goth. And her, Gianna Sofia, growing older in stills. Some that Tony remembers taking, others almost certainly taken by his father.

Yet he does not thumb through this collection for the sentimental thrill of memory – nor even for the exercise of grief – but for a clue to the present. He gathers up all the pictures he can find of Franco Timone and lays them side by side. His guess is that they cover a period of three or four years. His father is young and firm in all of them. Hair as black as black. Indeed, there is a rustic beauty to him.

> *A dumb animal grace.*
> *His unpractised fisherman's smile.*
> *The way his arm is draped possessively*
> *across his young bride's shoulders.*
> *The look on his face as he cradles his baby boy.*
> *His lovely biceps.*

Here, Tony realises, is a man untouched by the phoney revolution of the sixties. Perhaps not even troubled by the Sturm und Drang of romance or the wrenching gravity of anything so strong as love. A man of the soil and the sea. Of sweat and effort and the pride attached to those things. Not saintly. Not brilliant. Not even cruel. And certainly not bald.

In a way, this pleases Tony. Helps him to see how vain he still is. Reduces his disquiet.

Now maybe he really *will* go through with his crazy hair plan. Because by then, he hopes, it will cease to matter. The shock of the billboard – which is really the cold fact of ageing, and therefore of death – will have been placed into its proper context. Like a polaroid. Something to look back on with a smile.

When he lifts his attention from the photographs, he takes in the countless details of the museum he now lives in. The quiet objects, the ghosts of aromas, the tufts of dust in corners. The signs that his mother was still living as though there was no end in sight. This month's mags. Packets of seeds. Ten dollar DVDs on the ceramic topped coffee table. Still unopened. Unwatched.

This gives rise to a thought that has never previously occurred.

He is the last of the line. The only Timone.

In turn, this confers a freedom on him. Unencumbered by family and the genetic egomania it so often entails, he knows that blood, guilt and honour will have no power over him.

This ... and the fact that he is now truly alone.

Even though it feels cramped, Tony sleeps in the same single bed he did as a boy. There is no way he can sleep in his mother's room, so he puts up with the discomfort. As always, his night is broken. Waking and turning dozens of times. Never really settling until the first signs of birdsong. As though their morning music were a lullaby of sorts. An invitation to flight.

This morning however, his brief rest is punctuated by hyper–real visions:

> *His billboard face looming huge and illuminated,*
> *like the image of a great dictator.*
> *The fuss and bother of a photo shoot.*
> *The cute young art director, with his*
> *newbie nerves and desire to please.*
> *The make–up artist hovering – a cloud of aerosol.*
> *The finicky client and the blasé,*
> *dope smoking photographer.*

And Christa, with buzzing clippers.
Hair in rude clumps on the floor.
The art director freaking. Client furious.

He lurches awake, like falling face first into consciousness.

The room is a hard bright surface. Jolting him. There is a second of breathless disorienting confusion, during which he has the time to feel a note of regret, before he acclimatises to the regular beat of the day.

His first thoughts are: Mum, the house, no lectures to prepare.

He takes a long, deliberately slow breath and knows instinctively what the first order of business will be.

Christa.

While he goes about his morning routine – coffee, emails, etcetera – he thinks of her. About their teenage years. How they clung to one another. Boy and girl outsiders. Both different, both ambitious. Like siblings for a while and then, inevitably, as first time lovers. He shakes his head when he recalls how close he came to popping the question.

Though he could simply text her, he opts to walk down to the town centre. He stops for a long mac, flirts briefly with the pretty barista and ambles across to the salon.

She grins knowingly at him. 'Come to cancel, have you?'

'Actually, I thought we might have a proper catch up sometime soon. If that works for you.'

Christa looks briefly away to gather herself before returning her eyes to him. They are afire. Three decades of feeling. Everything from hatred to heartbreak. Warmth to wariness. Tony sees this and offers her an out.

She bites her bottom lip and declines. 'Well, I guess you're gonna need someone to talk to, aren't you?'

'You know how much I crave an audience,' he jokes.

'As long as I don't have to applaud,' she says in return.

'Sure,' he agrees. 'If you don't applaud, I won't perform. How about that?'

'Ah, so the last summer of hair's gonna be a reality show, is it?'

'Yep – and you can vote me off any time you like.'

This excites Christa's vibrant sense of humour. Her laughter chimes out like flares of sunshine and inexplicably warms them.

But she has customers, so they cut it short. He leaves her with a promise to call. There is only the vaguest notion of what might happen after that. For now at least, this suits them both.

05. Ghosts.

The death of Gianna Sofia Timone came with merciful swiftness two Saturdays ago. No protracted illness. Just an abrupt and conclusive heart attack shortly after eight on a cool and blustery morning. Sitting on her front porch with her coffee and her ambling thoughts, watching the ruffled trees and listening to the raucous chatter of gulls and kookaburras. A shortness of breath, a rising, irresistible tide of sharp, fizzing agony and then ...

> *The beautiful, quiet black.*
> *The oceanic compassion of oblivion.*

Four hours later, young Jake Salter had found her face down, and by nightfall the regulars at the Catchers' Inn were observing minutes of silence and proposing toasts in her honour. The whole town knew her story – or thought they did – and had sampled her legendary sauces and soups at Via Amore. She was one of the few remaining constants in a time of accelerating change and uncertainty. The bloody wog woman who, by a slow accumu-lation of familiarity, became a kind of universal nonna.

Though it was a day everyone knew would come, Bravery Bay staggered almost visibly with the shock of it.

Christa Bell was halfway through a cut and colour when the news reached her.

In her heart, Christa acknowledges an unpleasant truth – that there was always a silent, simmering contest between her and Gianna for the affections of Antonio. It wasn't bitter, and it never spilled over, but it had an undeniably sexual timbre. The frustrated passions of the young widow had found an outlet in maternal possession. The sight of a buxom teenage girl on her son's arm had inspired a

31

passive—aggressive spite that never quite went back into its box. Or so Christa contends.

For this, and other reasons of history, Gianna's passing and the inevitable return of her son have thrown Christa off balance. She isn't so much overwhelmed by grief or guilt, or even regret; rather, she is afraid of disinterred feelings. Love, anger, a desire for revenge. The well of her bitterness. But most of all, self—loathing.

In the days leading up to the funeral she found herself hoping Tony wouldn't show. It would have made things easier. She would have been free to write him off without compunction. A thickly drawn line at last. The final crossed off item on her list of ridiculously harboured hopes. A long overdue confirmation.

His appearance – elegiac and understated – had scrambled her senses. The unmistakable signs of time around his eyes. A softness around the middle. A withdrawn quality she had never known in him. Yet still handsome, even fashionable. Obviously *not* from the country. As estranged from the paranoid insularity of the Bay as ever.

Yet he had smiled at her with such ancient warmth. Such instinctive recognition.

Her first impulse had been to melt, to fold herself back into his embrace and to forget that he had ever run away and left her – but it only lasted a few minutes. Her defensive wall soon locked itself firmly back into place; the ring fence of her disappointment freshly electrified.

She does not trust him. Nor any man. She finds their vanity intolerable and their susceptibility to flattery and manipulation weak and stupid.

Life has taught her that it is safer to regard them as little more than occasionally useful beasts of burden. Since her divorce she has treated most of the men who have dared to venture close with little more than impatient disdain.

Even so, she could not keep her eyes off him at the funeral. It was as though age and defeat and grief had bestowed upon him an exquisite and aloof sadness. Only Tony, she thought, could turn the cold, predictable grind of making old bones into something approaching sculpture.

Then there was his eulogy. The other mourners found it tasteless. Worse than lip service. Some were angry. Vin Carlyle looked like he wanted to punch him. Yet it had reduced Christa Bell to water.

On the evidence of this alone, she will allow herself to see him socially. She knows this is breaking the rules, that it may even be dangerous, but there was something in the quality of his voice, in the way he avoided all the expected clichés, that sang to her. His thirty—year—old vanishing act and the nigh Trappist silence thereafter are things she will certainly broach with him ... but first she wants to discover if it is worth her while.

If he deserves it.

✂

Christa doesn't fuss too much with her appearance before her rendezvous with Tony. Just takes a quick shower, brushes her teeth, and gives herself a cursory once over in the mirror before driving the short distance back to town. She knows he will notice. That he will read the message she is sending.

However, she hopes he will *not* notice how nervous she is.

This is not necessarily personal, nor specifically aimed at him – it's more that she has cultivated the habit of not letting *anyone* see beyond the smart brightness she projects. She has paid a heavy price for opening up and is determined not to do so again.

When she pulls up, Tony is out front with Vin Carlyle; both with arms folded against the waft of frigid night air rolling in off the bay. She wonders if they have been gossiping about her, before remembering that Gianna is the more likely topic. She pauses in her car a moment to remind herself to keep her game face on. Not to let Tony's easy intimacy unpick the locks.

Though she would have preferred the $19.95 seafood special at the pub – and maybe a few bucks on the pokies – she understands that Via Amore is the more appropriate choice. And much more like Tony. He was never one for the calloused and salty homophobia of the Catchers' Inn.

Inside, Vin sits them in a corner by the window, perhaps realising they might require the safety of a distracting view. Not that it's much of a view at night. Not at this time of year.

Sitting across the tablecloth from him she realises again how unusually lovely Tony is to look at. Manly without being a block of wood. Feminine without being faggy. His pattern printed shirt, hint of stubble, and subtle breezy fragrance briefly undo her. She flashes knowing, sexy eyes at him and he smirks.

It takes four seconds alone for them to be nineteen again; and they both know it.

'So,' she begins, 'you bored shitless yet?'

'Ah, come on babe, give me five minutes at least.'

'I'm just concerned, is all,' she continues lightly. 'A sensitive, sophisticated, arty type like you in a town like Bravery. There'll be fuck all for you to do round here.'

'I'll find something,' he assures her with a slight dip of the head.

She wants to say 'or someone' but refrains. Far too risky.

Before she can frame an alternative, he smiles raffishly and adds, 'I was thinking maybe I could connect with the local theatre group. Audition for something maybe. Who knows, I might even get a part.'

This makes Christa laugh out loud and eyes turn towards them. In this, she is reminded.

> Tony's vanity has always been tempered
> with self–deprecating humour.
> Plus, he has a knack for getting people to notice him.

Partly she is charmed by this. Partly cautioned. In the closed loop of a small town his haughty habit of teasing people, of taunting them with their narrowness and obvious lack of savvy, will not go down well. It will translate as big city arrogance.

By the time she regains her composure, one of the young waitresses is wandering across. As she nears, Christa cannot help but notice the way she looks at Tony, or the way that his eyes consume her.

'I don't know,' she sidesteps. 'Have you?'

'To be honest, I'm not even sure what 'grow up' actually means. Apart from racking up debt and disillusion.'

She smirks to herself, observing that since he is not only able to accommodate taking six months off work but has recently come into possession of a house, his finances are likely sounder than hers.

Resisting the temptation to dig, she jests, 'Are you saying you don't believe your own hype anymore?'

'Exactly,' he confirms.

'In which case I take back what I said about you not changing.'

Picking up the inference, Tony looks down at the dregs in his wine glass and nods to himself. 'Hey, we both know I was a conceited little shit. I'm not proud of it.'

As if to punctuate the remark, he swallows what remains of the Cab Merlot with a squint and a pucker and Christa takes this as a cue to suggest a change of scene. Though he recalls the adjacent pub with a shiver, he agrees, if only because it offers them the chance to switch topics.

Christa is clearly thinking the same. She does not wish to further indulge his feelings because she does not wish to risk feeling her own. In fact, she is already on the verge of deciding to strictly limit contact with him, and to keep the conversation deliberately light.

Safe.

She favours such caution because she believes intimacy of any kind will end badly for her. She knows exactly where the empty spaces are and is honest enough to admit that he would be the most romantic and obviously pleasing way to fill them.

'Are you really going to stay here six months?' she drills him once they have set themselves up across the road with cold beers and a bucket of gold coins.

'That's the plan.'

'I still reckon you'll get bored.'

He laughs under his breath — suggests that she is acting like she wants to be rid of him. Both detect the irony in this. He looks down. She puffs out her cheeks. They both recall a windy autumn afternoon three decades ago. The heavy rumble of the bus that bore him away.

In response all she can think to say is, 'Maybe I do.'

Far from being offended, Tony concedes that there is an amount of good sense in this. *How dare you crash back into my life.*

Nonetheless, he is not so cool as not to feel hurt. Christa looks at him sideways and intuits this. Each restrains the urge to apologise. Instead, she ploughs coins into a slot and buys time.

He watches her without saying a word. She can feel his eyes, and a little something of his ache. *And* his gathering tiredness. When she looks up from the screen of whirling cards and catches his eye, she suddenly has a sense that he might be as lonely as she often feels.

She watches as he drains his glass and does not resist when he indicates a desire to leave. He is dressing it up with plausible excuses, but she knows.

Because it is the same for her.

This is why – barely five minutes after he has kissed her politely and bid her goodnight – she too is on her way home. To a house as haunted as any dead mama's.

November / December

06. The end of certainty.

It is not simply a familiar room that Jake Salter is packing down for the final time. Nor merely the bag stuffing ritual of expected departure. Even the sentimental ceremony of falsely warm goodbyes is not exercising his attention. For this morning is offering up richer seams of reflection, and 'end of era' clichés are not cutting it.

However, as near as he can tell, this is the end of certainty.

Much as he is glad to get away – to abandon the dark brick enclosure of the Boarders' Hall to the brutal erosion of time, and to consign the narrow, entitled world of his expensive, all boys schooling to the scathing autopsy of history – he knows that he is also leaving behind a cosily bounded world. A life of easily knowable allowances and restrictions; one in which all he was required to do was to satisfactorily appease the expectations of others and repeat, by rote, the lazy catechisms of complacent custom.

Jake was quite young when he realised the violence of ownership could be blunted by mimicry.

He tried it first with his blustering, big–boned father and cocksure older brothers, diverting their suspicion and judgement by aping their vulgarities. Then, during term, he worked the trick on teachers and students alike. Before long he was living almost entirely under cover.

At first it was an unconscious process – animal instinct, survivalist reflex – but over the course of insomniac nights and solitary weekends it bubbled up into teenage resentment, and from there, into a deliberately mocking spectacle of obedience.

In public, he was the blue blazered and pimply marionette of elite private education. Certainly not First XV material, but clever enough to get high grades and follow a respectable and profitable path through university and onto a career that would do his family, his home town and the Old Collegians proud.

But in private ... like an Anais Nin heroine ... a spy in a house rumoured to contain love.

He smiles to himself, snorts knowingly, as he turns his back on the dormitory cell and walks along the echoing, high ceilinged corridor, with its honour boards and triumphal portraits of old boys – the ones who had gone on to play or die for their country on various fields of sport and slaughter, or who made millions and were elected to the bench or the House. Jake knows he will never feature in this gilded parade. He's just not that kind of boy. Doesn't want to be.

Yet – though he exudes an adolescent smugness befitting heroic alumni – he is aware that when he walks beneath the black iron, filigree archway atop the bullish Victorian–era main gate, and out into the hectic plasticity of the twenty–first century, he will be stepping into a future far less predictable than his immediate past. He won't say it, but he is afraid. Afraid he won't ever fit in. That he won't ever be seen. That the universe of books and music that has fuelled and sustained him since childhood won't keep the wolves of the adult world at bay.

He knows he could hide himself away in the family business, maybe even live off his share of the farm when his chain smoking father finally dies, but he believes he would end up hating himself for this. Though he has developed an excellent façade, he is itching to see what life might be like without it.

As he steps over the line, he satisfies himself with the thought that there is now only one more summer – 104 days to be exact – between him and what he imagines will be a form of freedom.

Europe.

The so–called gap year.

Except that Jake has no plans to return – nor indeed to let anyone know this is his intention. Having refined the liberating art of secrecy he is in no mood to compromise himself with anything so pusillanimous as the truth.

Besides which, he has the structured outpouring of his music, into which he channels the undisciplined energies of venting and confession. It is a language of naked yet abstract revelation that nobody else understands. At least not anyone who would wish to exert control over him.

He is thinking of this, laughing to himself, as the Uber driver pulls up. He pictures the bewildered, angry looks of his father and brothers, and the polite condescending kindness of his mother, as he torments them with yet another of his compositions.

'Fuckwits,' he mouths silently, with a deliciously vicious curl of the lip.

A few beats later, as the hired driver cuts into a spine of tightly jostling traffic and begins to prise his way toward the bus station, Jake tempers his scorn by remembering that it is his parents' largesse that has allowed him to assemble the mini studio of equipment that awaits him back home – just as it is *their* credit card that has paid for his plane ticket and funnelled a few grand into an expense account. Though he suspects their generosity will be used against him one day, for now at least he is grateful.

This is not an equivocation Jake would have indulged a few months ago. Though he has been telling himself that *this* hour marks the cessation of certitude, his retreat from one dimensional youthful surety began in the last school holidays.

On a porch.

With a corpse.

He likes to arrive at the station hours earlier than necessary. He enjoys people watching, the random vignettes of coming and going; and he always takes the opportunity to surreptitiously record snippets of conversations and other sundry sounds. But really, it gives him the space to be alone. To let time dawdle, slow as breathing, without the tiresome act of conversation. Without pretending. At home and at school he cultivated a habit of late nights for just this purpose; yet here in the crowded, utilitarian mess of the afternoon, he can wriggle into this niche in full view. Sit with his coffee and muffin, eat his tandoori chicken wrap. Like the silent eye of a thronging storm.

Only the staff and the beggars break his trance.

For Jake, this is meditation. Somehow, in the bustle and whir, the usual monologues are quieted and the defensive drama of persona is switched off. As though the anonymity of the people he watches is a space he can somehow empathically enter.

He is in this lovely daze now. It is a kind of lucid dream, a solid world blurred into a wall of indistinct sound and colour, as if the wires have been re-patched to create a beautiful wave of dissonance. In this disjointed reverie his thoughts flutter. Not in the usual order or typical forms. Rather, like music.

The hubbub morphs into the sound of sharp coastal gusts. Ruffling trees. Shrill gulls. He feels the tug of cool, swirling air. The incline of a hill. His nostrils fill with salt and eucalypt. Grass and decay. The old lady is face down. He touches her frozen shoulder and in an instant he knows.

Until that moment, mortality had been an abstract banality. Death a sanitised and unseen ritual. Now it lay at his feet. In a pool of spilt coffee and stench. A kindly, generous old lady – a woman he worked with during school holidays – bereft of whatever it was that made her her.

Jake is not surprised to be seeing this scene again. It has been playing over in his mind, and sometimes in his dreams, for the last two months. He isn't frightened or appalled by it. Or saddened greatly. Yet it has altered him somehow. He cannot say for sure what the change is, but he knows it is not nothing.

> *To approach the frontier of life and death.*
> *Comprehend departure.*
> *Feel the weight of remaining.*

Then, before he can turn the body over and look into the dead, startled eyes, he is at a funeral, sitting next to his dad, listening to the woman's middle-aged son.

Now his heart is full.

He does not remember much of what was said, only that the man was beautiful in a way he thought impossible for anyone outside a book, and that the quality of his words, the depth and subtlety of their meaning, had brought him to the precipice of tears.

His father had leaned in close and whispered, 'Still a fucken faggot.' Only later had Jake understood that he had meant the man, not him.

Hearing his father's gruff assertion again, feeling his domineering judgement, punctures the languorous drift of his thoughts. Sharpens his focus on the bullying assumptions he has grown up with. On the necessity of escape, and the flood of unknowns it will entail.

Around him, the station thrums. The PA, the people, the rumble of engines.

So easy to get on a bus now. Take a road to anywhere.

But Jake has learnt not to be impulsive. To be calculating. Tactical. He has a plan and he will stick to it. This mode of operating has kept him safe thus far and he is sure it will last another summer. After that … who knows.

This journey, Jake has taken many times. The seven and a half hour bus ride south – firstly through the scrawl of suburbia, then the slicker, straighter smoothness of freeways, and eventually out of the crowds and onto to the snaking coastal roads that will carry him home. He always books a left hand window seat, so he can peer out eastwards and disappear into the distance of the shimmering sea. And even though he is squashed in by both the size and the strong cologne of the shaggy Canadian backpacker seated next to him, he uses his headphones and his practised aloofness to throw up a wall between him and his temporary companion.

For Jake is saving his energies.

For home.
For judgement.
For the grinding formalities and
tasteless excess of Christmas.
For the relentless idiocy of workplace banter.

In his head he is rehearsing his routines. Congratulating himself for the convincing nature of his act. Reminding himself of Europe.

Yet now that his exams are done and he can almost taste the end of his confinement, he is wondering how and why things came to be this way.

Why isn't he like his good natured brothers?
How come he didn't seem to get the same lucky genes?
What is it about him that focuses
his father's ire so unerringly?
How come his mother never says a word?
Why is he such a massive fucking disappointment
to them all?

Though – in righteous moments – he lapses into the reflex of blaming, in his more philosophical moods he ponders their motives with cooler filters. He has read enough to know that *their* attitudes are not *his* fault; yet the prudent counsel of good books has had nothing convincing to say about the real reasons for his family's punitive coalition against him.

It couldn't be his slight, less than robust body, could it? His cack–handedness? Or is it the other thing? That which they will not say aloud.

He is turning these things over, teasing them out, as the bus lumbers through a slow, sweeping arc and the Tasman Sea glitters in the evening light. He knows that he could sheet it all home to fear and ignorance; but somehow that seems an unsatisfactory blanket. An explanation without sufficient nuance.

This is a big thing for Jake. The blunt simplicities of his rural upbringing, and the equally unexamined worldview that have informed his schooling, are verboten to him. Like the bright plastic sugariness of pop songs or the infantile us and them of heroes and villains. Having found sanctuary in bookish, labyrinthine complexity, he is wary of anything offering easy conclusion.

As he leans against the window and percolates these ideas, it occurs to him once more that *this* is why he chose music as his

45

preferred language. And why he was so affected by the son's eulogy at Nonna Gianna's funeral. It was the first time he ever heard a real person – as opposed to a figment in literature or history – speak the beautiful ambiguous truth with such clarity and grace. In Jake's heart, buried beneath an obscuring layer of scorn and intellect, this represents a kind of permission. The allowance of uncertainty. The letting go of the exhausting delusion of control.

Now, for a few exquisite, slow–mo seconds, Jake Salter will glimpse the hidden unity of opposites. Will run both from *and* towards. Will simultaneously embrace and revile the things he craves and the things he dreads – things he is now experiencing as one and the same.

When the moment is over, he will smile broadly at his luminous reflection in the window and enjoy the indescribable glory of emptiness.

Meanwhile, oblivious, the Canadian is sending countless text messages to girls he will never fuck. The bus is taking yet another curve and the bright glare of the day is dissolving into the smoky veil of evening. It is time to stop all this thinking now, he decides, and return his attention to the Tod Dockstader piece playing in his headphones, and onto the enticing idea of meeting the man from the funeral.

'I reckon you two will get along,' his boss had told him earlier. 'He's kinda arty and weird like you.'

It is telling that Vin Carlyle, and not his father or one of his brothers, arrives to meet him when the bus pulls into the bright new service station on the main highway just outside Bravery Bay. Not that Jake minds. Vin is easier to deal with. His only stake in him is that he turns up to work on busy nights at the restaurant. No bullshit about the grand old Salter surname.

Also, Vin strikes Jake as genuinely kind, which is not a trait he is used to; so he is able to deal with his small talk without feeling the need to grind his teeth.

'So Jakey, how'd you go in your exams?'

Confident he has cantered through them, but aware that anything short of feigning nervousness will seem arrogant, Jake rolls out a pantomime reply about being stressed and worried and Vin smiles at him and offers the regulation reassurance.

The trip out to the Salter property – with its classically rambling gaggle of sheds and machinery, and the recently refurbished main house sitting at the high point of an undulating broad acre spread – takes no more than five minutes.

As Vin pulls the car into the long, Norfolk Island pine fringed drive, Jake sees the lights on in the house and, as they draw nearer, the dogs running in the yard; which means that his dad is having one last smoke on the verandah before retiring.

In the passenger seat, the youngest member of the town's pre—eminent family pulls in a deep, calming breath. He glances across at his employer, who looks back at him in a manner which says, *yes, I know.*

Jim Salter is a renowned alpha bully and his teenage son is the black sheep of a proud lineage.

The car swings a broad right into the dusty forecourt, and as it does the headlights illuminate in their clockwise arc:

> *Old tractors,*
> *A clutch of water tanks,*
> *The beaten up 1980s motorcycle Jake likes to ride.*

Then the beam settles eerily on the powerful figure of a silver—haired man, a firm jet of smoke escaping from the side of his mouth.

'Good luck,' Vin says.

'Yeah thanks,' Jake grunts.

'Pop down tomorrow after five and we'll sort out a roster if you like. And I'll introduce you to Tony.'

Jake knows Vin means this as a form of compensation, but it is of little cheer to him tonight. In the few moments it takes him to unbuckle and step out into the cool night air, he has not only recalled the calm, packed up stillness of the school dorm – pillows and mattress stripped, all personalising items removed – but imagined other rented rooms. Ones he will come to know on the

47

other side of the world, far removed from the lumbering patriarch who is making his way across the scrubby lawn and powdery dirt to shake Vin's hand with utterly dishonest bonhomie.

By the time Jake has fetched his bags from the boot he has finally understood where his knack for strategic falseness comes from, and he is looking at his father with more admiration than he can ever remember.

Well fuck me, he is thinking to himself as he stands next to his dad waving Vin off and breathing in second hand smoke.

Who fucking knew?

07. The redundancy of choice.

At first, Tony was quietly amused by Vin's offer of a part time job. It struck him as ill thought out, a result of either sentiment, misplaced obligation, or the optimistic fancy that he had somehow inherited his mother's renowned kitchen prowess. After all, he had not worked in hospitality since quitting his last waiting job at an upmarket French bistrot in the early nineties. Indeed, since leaving the Bay thirty years ago he has barely strayed outside the insular world of the arts. But he had not wanted to insult Vin, so he had accepted, certain that his incompetence would quickly annul the arrangement.

Previously, his plan had been to isolate himself. To linger in the house with his mother's ghost. Reacquaint himself with the museum pieces of his youth. With the décor of her lonely years. The random clutter of cupboards. The abruptly abandoned props of a life. As though to make up for his erstwhile absence by spending time with the relics she left behind.

> *Her collection of DVDs – films he would*
> *never normally consider.*
> *The unread portions of the many books*
> *she started but set aside.*
> *The shampoo, the toothpaste, the home made*
> *passata stashed in the freezer.*

This, Tony had convinced himself, was not so much morbid as a kind of archaeological reconstruction; a form of completion achieved by watching, tasting and touching. A visceral connection that went deeper, and yet was more subtle than the lachrymose sledgehammer of loss or the guilt driven recompense of too little too late. In the river of Tony's heart, this was going to be a slow dance of poetic symmetry. Two acts of solitude. Both one handers. With the house and all its objects at the intersect.

Now, having been at Via Amore for a few weeks, he laughs when he recalls the undergraduate purpleness of it. Shakes his head when he thinks of his still tenacious habit of defaulting to lyrical excess. A tendency so far removed from his mother's skinny, peasant pragmatism. Her survivalist refusal to indulge the layers.

He is thankful too, for Vin's insistence is paying off. The physical distraction of prep jobs – peeling, chopping, fetching, carrying – is sweeping the thickets from Tony's head. Taking him out of himself. Leaving him with a glad kind of tiredness. Giving him the rare pleasure of deep, uninterrupted sleep. Not to mention a little extra pocket money and the intermittent fun of flirting with the pretty young front–of–house girls.

He pictures them whenever he masturbates – their pert little tits, their beautiful uncalcified thighs – and though it is plain a couple of them find him exotic and handsome, and he can readily imagine himself inside them, he has promised himself not to start any more incendiary affairs with girls their age.

Sitting on the front porch, drinking coffee at the glass top table where his mother always began her days, he looks out across the town and the breeze–shivered bay and thinks of hot girls and sweaty kitchens as he contemplates another shift.

It is late November. The sky is a lighter blue. The air drier. The restaurant busier.

Back in his real life, the academic year is over. His students have handed in their final assignments and presented their ten minute films for assessment. (He has agreed to watch them and they await on his laptop. He will get round to it soon. When he can be bothered.)

In the meantime, he will work through another weekend. Just like his students probably will. Like his mother once did. He will deal with the stressed out anger of the chefs, tolerate the cut fingers and hot oil burns, and get a perspiring buzz from the heat and closeness of a busy kitchen. In the rush, he will spare not a moment for self–pitying monologue or over wrought analysis. He will feel tired and sore but, strangely, not old. Not bored. Not alone.

Yet there is one startling, unexpected aspect of it that always engages his reflection. At Via Amore he belongs. Antonio 'Tony' Timone is at last a part of the town where he was born and raised. It is a curious feeling and he wonders what it says about him.

However, the answer to that, like the student films, will have to wait, as it is now time for him to walk down the hill into town.

In his unflattering work gear — daggy, baggy blacks, functional closed in footwear and baseball cap — he starts out into the bright, toasty warmth of the day. As he makes his way in his awful clothes, he reminds himself of the pledge he has made to stop fretting about his appearance, to get over the addiction of his own beauty; and he thanks Vin once more for his ridiculous suggestion.

When he gets to the café with the cute barista — her name, he has discovered, is Rosie — he forces himself not to make any adjustments, enduring what he imagines to be her less than impressed response to his workaday drabness. He knows he could get a free macchiato at work but confronting Rosie's loveliness in his ugly outfit is part of the challenge he has set himself this summer.

She smiles at him and he cringes inside; but after thirty seconds of awkward discomfort he has passed the test once more. He pats himself on the back and proceeds to the restaurant.

In the kitchen the prep list is long. The forecast is for warm, sunny weather and Vin is expecting big numbers. There is an extra girl rostered out front and a new kid coming in later to do dishes. The time will fly and Tony will forget about beauty and ageing and thinning locks for a few hours — and Vin will pop his head in every now and then and forward him a fraternal smile and assure him he's getting the hang of it. The chefs won't necessarily agree, but neither he nor Vin will care too much about that. Because, here and there, both men will think of Gianna and wonder idly what she might say if she could see them together.

His first weekend at Via Amore had been deeply unsettling; in some ways more so than the silence of the house. Up the hill, all the dust had settled in its place, only disturbed at times and in ways of his choosing, but down in the kitchen the miasma swirled in chaotic whorls. Here his mother still moved with the cloudy volition of memory and sorrow. As though her imprint were plastered into the walls, ground into the benchtops, and infused into every sauce. This was Gianna as living, breathing, active woman – as opposed to distant, theoretical mother.

Dry ideas about the locals knowing her better than he did became dense rolling waves of undeniable fact. Not just Vin, the whole crew. The grumpy, pokie-addicted head chef Hank, his super-efficient, bossy sidekick Clarice, and even Kel, the wiry old man Friday who did everything from running errands and repairing fridges to making salads and portioning out antipasto serves. Tony remembered them all from the funeral.

Then there was the food; her influence everywhere. On the menu. In the dry store and in the cool room. On the chopping boards and in the pots.

> *Garlic, butter and bay leaves.*
> *Oregano and basil.*
> *Peas, rice and chicory.*
> *Aceto di vino rosso.*
> *The small, sweet smelling tomatoes she preferred.*

The aromas, textures and tastes were from his childhood, from the cobbled together kitchen at home, from her herb pots and vegie patch – and whilst it had been overlayed with Hank and Clarice's more technical and contemporary additions, the baseline was straight out of Tony's past.

All this, plus sore feet, a stinging knife wound and a nasty, coin sized steam burn on his left forearm, had left him shattered after his first two nights. On the verge of quitting.

It did not help that he was unused to the pace and culture of commercial kitchens. Hank took his stress out on Clarice, who took it out on Kel, who took cheap shots at him. As the dockets came in and the chefs got cranky, Vin's faith in him had started to seem like a costly indulgence.

'Mate, I thought film sets were tense, but that was fucking crazy.'

'You'll get used to it.'

'Hank and Clarice don't seem to think so.'

'Luckily for you *I'm* the boss.'

'Come on, Vinny, there's got to be loads of kids round here who could do this gig. Kids who probably need the money.'

'True – but I reckon you need the outlet more … if you know what I mean.'

Unconvinced at first, Tony has now come to see the wisdom in Vin's ploy.

Although he still finds Hank's jokes painful, his casual sexism even worse, and sometimes bristles at Clarice's automatic assumption that as a man he is somehow inherently incapable of even the most basic tasks, the positives have begun to significantly outweigh the negatives. When the bullying tone of the kitchen lurches into nastiness – as it often does now that the busy nights are busier – he consoles himself with the thought that the low pay and high stress of 'hospo' is something he can walk away from in a blink.

Meanwhile, the distracting physicality, and the fact that his presence appears to give Vin such a shot of satisfaction, are enough to carry him forward. To yank him through the snarls of fatigue and the foggy echoes of late mothers.

'You know it's only going to get worse,' Vin warns him. 'Christmas, New Year is crazy. By the end of Jan we're all pretty much fucked.'

'I guess it's where the money is though,' he smiles in return.

'That's the plan.'

'And after that?'

Vin arches an eyebrow at him, puffs out a quick phew. Pauses long enough for Tony to witness his uncertainty. His amorphous fear. 'I'll get back to you on that one, mate.'

Here again, a reason for Tony to feel both humbled by his employer's trust and determined to repay his inexplicable, lingering loyalty. Because both men have no idea what awaits them at the end of summer. Or rather, both have accepted that for all their plotting and planning, the future remains beyond the frontier of their control.

Tony nods fraternally, swigs off the rest of Rosie's macchiato, and makes his way to the clamour of the kitchen to chop vegetables and think about nothing else.

It is a Friday night and the rush begins shortly after six. Before long, the dockets are seven deep and Hank and Clarice are smashing out covers. The restaurant bubbles with happy chatter and chilled jazz. Ceiling fans whir, cutlery and glasses click and chink, and steam shooshes from the coffee machine … yet Tony can't quite lock himself into his usual trance of action.

Because there's the new kid – who he watches carefully from the corner of his attention. An ebony–haired boy with a mouth so dark it looks painted, and long, slender fingers. Back from his posh school in Sydney, back to his holiday job, moving with a rehearsed speed that doesn't quite hide his underlying clumsiness. Joking with Hank and Kel like one of the boys but clearly not meaning it.

This, it is confirmed, is the Jake who found his mother.

Tony tries to concentrate on his job, his occupied hands, but something is burning keenly in him tonight. A desire to know. To see through this young kid's eyes.

For Tony never saw Gianna after the fact. The reality of her passing was a Saturday afternoon phone call, followed by a week of drama around funerals, long service leave and the abrupt jolt of homecoming.

He remembers the sound of Vin's voice. Brittle, deadpan, dazed. 'Hey Tony, it's your mum.'

Then, by the time he had made it across the miles to Bravery Bay … a locked up house and a highly lacquered box. He couldn't look. Just couldn't. So he left her in her sealed container. Packed away.

It seemed fitting that way. He had, after all, effectively abandoned her for what he thought was a bigger, brighter world. What right did he have to claim her now? To sit on the untouchable pedestal of noble, filial grief?

All that week he had felt like a sham; and when he stood at the lectern for his oration and looked out across the rows of locals

– neighbours, co–workers, bowling club buddies, a couple of his long dead father's fishing friends, the ones who lived – he could feel that the distance between him and them was as wide as the sea.

Since then, Tony has speculated about the precise nature of such distance. Presently, he believes it's the space between who he wants to be and what he really is.

> *The ocean of fantasy.*
> *The expanse of denial.*

Consequently, as a result of split focus, he scalds himself badly with boiling water. Within seconds the skin on the back of his hand is yelping and reddening. Hank laughs and advises him to run the burn under cold water for a few minutes. Clarice lectures him about proper technique. The new kid is the only one who appears to care. He doesn't say anything or act it out in an obvious way, but Tony observes it in a tiny movement of his eyes. In the quarter second his breath is suspended.

There is definitely *some*thing about that boy, he thinks, as he rushes to the staff restroom, leans against the basin – tap running, hand quivering, feeling slightly nauseous.

A few minutes pass in considerable discomfort before Vin appears to check on him. 'You'll need to get that dressed, I reckon,' he says, peering intently at the splash of discolouration. 'I'll make up a little ice pack when things slow down a bit and get one of the girls to help you out.'

When Tony fires him a quizzical look, Vin's eyebrows raise. 'They do First Aid at school these days. Saves me bothering,' he jokes.

'Just let me know if you need me,' Tony offers.

'Nah mate. You're right.'

'You sure?'

'Jakey's already onto it,' Vin assures him.

A little later, having fetched a contraption of ice and tea towel, Vin checks the burn again, assures Tony he has seen far worse and, just as he is about to return to the fray, grins at him and says, 'He reminds me of you actually.' And then he winks, all kindness and patience, and gets on with the night, which is still humming.

Venturing out to the rear carpark, Tony props himself on a milk crate and, pressing the crude ice pack gingerly against his hand, listens to the way the busy burble inside mingles with the sounds of the town – cars, distant doof–doof, and a sparkle of voices from the Catchers' Inn. In this unplanned hiatus he is tempted to pick apart the thoughts he had earlier, but instead tries to distract himself by feeling the pleasure of the soft night air and the sting of his scalded skin. To limit his roving mind to immediate sensation. To regard this vignette as simply a small event and not part of a grand, orchestrated plot intended to reveal some heretofore unimagined miracle of enlightenment.

In this, he is fortunate the burn is bad enough to tug continuously at him. He inspects it. The swelling. The sweaty red sheen. This kind of thing never happened on location or in class. Not to him anyway.

Other orders of wounding were more common – injuries to pride mainly. Rejections. Sexual, professional, artistic.

He laughs out loud, thinking how like the straightforward agrarian reality of the Bay it is that his injury should be so instant and physical. So material and matter–of–fact. Jesus, he is thinking, I really *am* becoming a local.

Tempting though it is for him to use the obvious excuse to have a couple of nights off, Tony bulldozes past Vin's genuine concerns and fronts up for his Saturday shift, where one of the waitresses fixes the dressing on his hand and smiles into his eyes. Privately, he will admit that it is worth it just for the brush of her fingers. For the tender nearness of blossoming womanhood.

Despite the awkwardness of the gauze and the pain associated with the inevitable bumps and scrapes of being a kitchen hand, the weekend goes by in a bustling blur. Risk of infection and further injury notwithstanding, Tony is happy to be at work – where he is frequently amused by the differences between the country and the city. While he is ploughing through his list of jobs he spares a thought for his old workplace and its often stifling insistence on Occ Health & Safety. He chuckles to himself, recalling incident reports and compulsory seminars on hazard minimisation and safe work practise. The Dean would be having an apoplexy if she could see him now.

'Don't worry, Vinny,' he jokes. 'I promise I won't sue.'

'Yeah, please don't. The wife will kill me if you do.'

In the kitchen, between the peaks and troughs of the rush, the chefs tell tales of burns and cuts and show off their scars, while Kel trumps them all with stories of death and mutilation from shearing sheds, headers and fishing boats. Only Jake doesn't participate. He laughs on cue but adds nothing to the list of mishaps. 'I got a splinter once,' is all he says, smirking, his distant eyes glinting with secret fires. This charms the crew – who tease him about his baby face and toffee nosed school – but Tony picks it for performance. A line. Quite possibly a lie. It is a front he finds deeply impressive, and he is beginning to see why Vin keeps suggesting the two of them will get along. On the brink of fifty, the poses of eighteen are not just obvious to Tony but, in this instance, a sign of something he recognises in himself.

As a teacher, he is familiar with the ways and whims of late adolescence and early adulthood; that vertiginous bridge between the blasé certainties of the child and the dawning ambiguities of the grown up. It fascinates him. He finds its mix of arrogance and idealism, bravura and underlying vulnerability, compelling and beautiful. In his heart, if not in the more considered hallways of his mind, he is still crossing that threshold himself. Not yet fully formed.

Perhaps this is a corollary of thwarted ambition, a symptom of his stubborn refusal to entirely forsake the teenage dream that lured him from his mother's care. From Christa Bell's sororal but sexual love. He is open to different theories on this, but one thing he *does* know is that Jake and he will form a bond. Of recognition and convenience. An alliance of escapees.

However, there is no time to pursue this in the kitchen, as the weekend trade is hectic.

Eager to take the dollars while he can, Vin pushes front and back of house to keep going past their scheduled knock−offs and everyone thinks of the extra money; except Tony, who is glad when he is the first to be sent home on Sunday night.

He plonks himself, exhausted, in Vin's jumbled office space, signs the time sheet and slugs back his staff drink in relieved gulps. He loves this part of the routine − the glorious slowed down minutes that follow the fast paced hours. The thought of a couple of lazy days without people in his face. It reminds him how he used to feel at the end of a tough teaching week or a troublesome shoot. He smiles to himself, contemplates the now frayed and dirty dressing on his burnt hand and conjures up the stillness that will greet him once he gets home.

There is the small matter of a tired uphill trudge to negotiate before he gets there but, having had his soothing beer and time out, he is ready to make the last effort of the day. As he edges towards the back exit though, he runs into Jake. With only the faintest gesture, the younger man bids him wait, and a few seconds later returns to press a neatly rolled joint into his palm.

'For the pain,' he explains; and when Tony motions to share it, he declines.

'You'll enjoy it more by yourself,' he says, and in this act confirms that he too can sense a connection.

He smiles, holds Tony's gaze firm for a beat and ducks back to finish the rest of his duties.

Not having smoked a joint since the day his mother died, Tony knows how much he will enjoy the sensation. He is salivating already. Promising himself to follow up with Jake.

Thus, instead of going directly home, he buys a lighter over the front bar at the pub and strolls down to the waterfront, where boats bobble and reflected light quivers. He sits on the grassy verge staring out into the black immensity. A surge of memory threatens but he shuts it down and sparks up. The first sweet taste. Rolling it round. Pleasure like a kiss. A lazy ribbon of smoke curling up into the night. Vanishing.

He is in a cloud now. The realm where absolute presence and infinite distance coalesce. He hears the slap of water on fibreglass hulls, the laughter of people spilling from pub and restaurant – yet is miles away.

> *In a photograph with his father.*
> *At a tram stop with a giant glowing version of himself.*
> *In a story he made up about his life.*

Partly, this is due to the marijuana – he knows this – but it is also driven by the thunderous quality of the silence that follows noisy distraction. The revealing absence that comes in the wake of stopping. The truth of empty rooms.

Tony wonders if this is why the common prescription for grief is to get busy and stay busy. To never stop. He can see the sense in it but, by the same token, he can understand why the mystics insist it is better not to start. Despair, he muses, isn't simply a lack, or even a surfeit, it is the tearing wrench between them. The gap between motion and stillness. Wishing and outcome. Youth and age.

Then, with aching body and stoned mind, he contemplates the fifteen minute walk back to the old house and ponders the distance between the two haunts of his mother's ghost. One for starting. One for stopping.

Tonight, Tony has no idea which he will ultimately choose; although right now he is in no rush to decide. Indeed, he is not certain he will *ever* decide. Or if deciding is even necessary.

08. An accidental hour.

A shape emerges from the shadows. A black form in the night, flitting across the road. Skipping quickly through the beams.

In an instant, she knows.

She has been at the pub. Most likely she is a tad over the limit. But she has had a win on the slots, so even if she does get caught – which she knows she almost certainly won't – the fine will be more than half paid. Besides which, she knows the short drive home by heart. Believes she could do it with her eyes closed.

However, the sight of him running into her headlights jolts her out of auto−pilot.

She knows he works weekend nights these days, but still she is not prepared for him to intrude quite like this. It forces a soft, longing sigh from her. An exhalation that is part desire, part annoyance.

How dare he.

She pulls over, blinks her indicators, and throws open the passenger side door. He strolls up casually, pokes his head in − meets her gaze with a tired, satisfied grin.

'Hey you,' she says, trying not to sound attracted.

'Ah bella,' he croons, his voice smoky with relaxed exhaustion.

She smells the evidence. 'Are you stoned?' she smiles.

'Yeah,' he laughs. 'The new kid at work took pity on me.'

She notices the dirty dressing on his left hand and, triggered, her maternal instinct flares into action. Years of scissors have made her an expert at patching up sliced fingers and nicked ear lobes.

'Boiling water,' he explains. 'Wasn't paying enough attention. Apparently.'

She flicks on the internal light and offers to check it out for him but he assures her there is nothing to see.

'Anyway, I got a few days off now so … no biggie.'

'Well, let me give you a lift home and re—dress it for you. Because I know *you* won't bother,' she observes with a knowing laugh.

So he bows to her sisterly insistence and, to her at least, seems pleased to do so.

She has forgotten that in his youth he allowed his mother precisely this kind of licence, simply because it was easier than resisting. Indeed, there are many things about him that the years have smudged. For memory is not only imperfect but pastoral — and prone to being warped by gravities like loneliness, shame, and other self—serving biases.

Though she understands that her recollection is incomplete, and heavily infused with the sickly sweet thrill of nostalgia and the caustic fizz of accrued resentment, she has nonetheless indulged a revisionist desire in the weeks since her adolescent ex came back to town. Reinterpreting, re—contextualising, revisiting old songs and movies.

She concedes the inherent risk but sees the potential benefit. She only hopes she has the smarts to know which is which.

To pretend he is not back, that she is not affected, would be a lie. For this reason she has taken care to maintain a measured distance. Not avoid — but not seek out.

In a small town like Bravery Bay though, anonymity is impossible. Proximity makes collision inevitable. Prurient chatter and bitchy gossip follow shortly thereafter. As the town's nominated hairdresser—in—residence, the topic of Antonio 'Tony' Timone is never far from the earshot of Christa Marie Bell.

From her contemporaries — the women she grew up with, the ones who remember when she and Tony got together and, of course, the way he left — she gets the predictable advice and judgement.

> *Look after yourself, love.*
> *He's still such a player.*
> *I'm sure he's gay.*

They reckon the way he spoke about his mum
at the funeral was disgusting.
Never had much of a career, did he, doll?

Either that or a weirdly girlish glee. 'I saw the way he looked at you, Chrissy. I mean, if you're interested … why not have some fun?'

However, it is the younger women's comments that disturb her most. The ones who never knew either of them back when. Girls like the spunky, pierced, tattooed Rosie Donald from the fancy coffee shop on the corner near the marina.

'You mean, you two were like … *on*?'

'Back in the day, yeah. Before you were even born.'

'He's kind of a hottie really, in like, a silver foxy way. If I were you, I'd totally go there.'

In much the same way, the girls from the restaurant drop hints. 'He's kinda faggy maybe, but also kinda cool. I totally flirt with him and he's always, like, right into it,' they smile – at which point she takes the chance to tear the wax strips from their cute and downy bikini lines with a little more force than is necessary.

The men, on the other hand, spare no charity. Their jealousy loosely mirroring her weakness. Like her, feeling helpless in the face of his crumbling glamour. The allure of his beautiful decline and the novelty factor of his urbane semi–celebrity.

He definitely bats for the other team, darl.
All he's ever done is a couple of fucking ads
and some shitty soaps.
They reckon he's done porno and everything.
He's got an eye for the young 'uns too, I'm told.
Fucken sick, if you ask me.

Christa is not quite as immune to these assaults as she likes to believe. Consciously she combats them, but subconsciously they stir up eddies of conflict – for she is both determined to defend him and, by extension, herself; yet also keen to cut him down. To protect herself from the damage of caring. Of wanting too much.

For in the beating truth of her heart, she has never gotten over the manner of his disappearance. Or rather, the fact that she did not follow.

To everyone else it looked like Tony abandoned her, but Christa knows that *she* was the one who ended it.

With her refusal.

Her fear.

'Let's just go,' he had urged her. Almost begged. 'Nothing's ever going to happen here. I'm not going to be a farm hand or work at the fucking bottle shop all my life. And what will you do? Perms for battered wives?'

God, how she had wanted to run off with him.

Yet there was so much in the way. A big wide world of uncertainty. The fast and nasty city. How were they going to live? They did not even have bank accounts. And anyway, she knew that he tended to change his mind. It could easily be another unrealistic Tony dream. They would get to the city and he would decide he hated it.

Yes, he was her angel – the coolest, funniest, kindest, cutest guy in town – but she knew he wasn't tough. Not inside.

Even when he left, she swore he would come back. A week, a month, a year at most.

Until phone calls every night became once a week. Became silence. An evaporation. Like a dam drying up in a drought. Not even Christmas visits.

She remembers bumping into Gianna one night at the pub and realising that he was similarly distant from her. Maybe even further.

There was a controlled, martyred sadness in the older woman's eyes that took Christa's breath away. 'People say he selfish,' she had said, her accent still strong, 'but they don't know nothing. He don't live for just himself. He live for his dad, and for me, maybe for you. He only do what we all afraid to, or don't have chance to.'

Christa is still haunted by this memory. Gianna was not known for dwelling and brooding. She bore her suffering with stoicism. She was a hard Madonna. Yet her words that night were evidence of something else. The bruises of history glossed over. Things observed but not discussed.

For reasons she still battles with, Christa experiences a shiver of guilt whenever she thinks of it. That she allowed herself to fall into Steve Bell's arms just a few nights later is a correlation that drives bolts of shame through her to this day.

But she tries not to punish herself too harshly for marrying him. For the way she allowed his amorous attentions to over–whelm her better judgement, and for the tricks of thought she played in her head to convince herself she loved him.

Initially, when things started to go wrong with Steve, it was easier to blame Tony. Steve, she theorised, was an available, even innocent proxy. The hard working, down to earth man she hoped would vanquish the ever growing distance between her and the love she craved. Between her and regret. These days, she realises the reasons for the failure of her marriage – and of the carbon copy disappointments of the three short lived relationships she endured thereafter – have more to do with her than either Tony or Steve. Or anyone. She cannot say with absolute certainty what those reasons are and is not confident she ever will. Instead, she has thrown up a wall, if only to ward off the excesses of her own habitual folly.

This, and what she regards as the essentially untrustworthy and shallow nature of men, is what fuels her determined singledom.

> *The male inability to grow up.*
> *Their habit of assuming ownership.*
> *Their pathetic, desperate veil of authority.*
> *The way they beg like dogs for sex*
> *– so fucking see through.*

I'd rather be a sexist than a sucker, is how she reasons this antipathy out.

Yet how she hates herself for wanting them. For the lengths she has gone to. Depths she has plumbed. For the almost narcotic effect of Tony's presence.

Still, she cannot deny that when she had the chance for something different, she had said no.

Indeed, she often finds herself staring into the salon mirrors when the last customer is done, reading the awful lines scratched out by the years, knowing with a thick, inescapable horror that *this* is what she chose. She has never told anyone – but she has cried alone over this caving of will more than she ever has for any man. Tony included.

Because time is a lover that never comes back.

Thoughts like this are fizzing in her brain – a lightning storm, looming thunder – as she sneaks little glimpses at him while she drives, and he burbles warmly in the seat beside her.

She notices the traces of youth that remain. In his jawline and his chatter. In the quirky, boyish way he tilts his head from side to side, as though some kind of dialogue was occurring across hemispheres. Charming though this is, she retains enough of her armouring misandry to entertain the idea that she should have run him over instead. Put the pedal down. A swerve, a soft clump ... and he would be lying there now and she would be nearly home, her winnings in her purse, perhaps a little dent in the grille. Everything not like it is now.

Does he have any idea? she thinks; before the faintest arch of a brow uncannily answers her query with the hush telepathy of isolation – which they both know back to front.

Lonely children whispering in their secret code across an ocean of time. The impossible promise – that all the spaces would collapse to nothing if only they would say it out loud.

But it's not true, and they both know it.

For when they walk in the front door in two and a half minutes, they will *not* be nineteen year old country kids. They will not be boyfriend and girlfriend. Gianna will not be there to greet them, nor little Vinny Carlyle. Christa will not cut Tony's lustrous black hair in the fashion of pop stars. He will not reach

65

out to kiss her. They will not rule the world with their outcast love.

Rather, he will put the kettle on and make them Earl Grey with honey, and she will fetch a clean bandage from the First Aid kit she carries in the car. He will watch her with stoned attention while her skilful fingers go to work. She will hold her breath when he rests his scalded hand upon her knee and look away quickly whenever their eyes meet.

'Are you sleeping in your old room?' she will foolishly inquire.

'Can't quite bring myself to sleep in Mum's bed,' is what he will tell her.

They are in the kitchen, with its kooky mix of retro jumble and expensive modernity. The painted wooden shelves stocked with old ceramic jars that Christa recalls from the eighties, next to the silver grey German sheen of a new fridge and dishwasher. The same cracked, chequerboard lino she used to spill crumbs on – but now a schmick six burner rather than the scratched white stove that used to leak gas and make the house smell. Past and present crammed together. The fragmented stillness of memory mixed with the ongoing momentum of life.

'Shit, I haven't been in here since we were kids,' she declares, giving voice to the sad fact that she and Gianna never managed to feel comfortable in one another's company without the buffering presence of Tony to shave the edges from taciturn rivalry.

'Strange, isn't it,' he acknowledges, as he rinses out the teacups and clinks them into the dish rack. 'It freaks me out every day. Some things different, some things the same. I guess one day I'll wake up and go, 'right, that's it' and change it all over.'

He pauses. Bites his top lip. Closes his eyes.

'But not right now,' he breathes. 'Not quite ready for that yet.'

This is her cue to ask the obvious. 'Is that because you miss her?'

His gaze darts upwards for a second, as though searching for the right answer, before he shrugs slowly. 'Nope,' he says, a curious, vaguely surprised smile creasing his lips.

Christa is strangely impressed by this, despite its apparent callousness. It would have been so easy for him to have said yes. To have played the dutiful son card.

Yet something about his undramatic honesty alerts her. Not simply the lack of sentiment but the backhanded admission of doubt; because in the space where the anchoring spectacles of grief and nostalgia usually play out, she senses that Tony is adrift without coordinates. Not sure of anything. She wonders if this Tony would ever have had the guts to ditch everything and leave town.

Then again, he came back, didn't he?

'So be honest with me, Tone, how *are* you? I mean, living here and everything.'

'Hard to say really. Great one minute, completely fucked the next. I'm smarter and less ... drama prone, I suppose ... but also ... kinda wondering where it all goes from here. Apart from the inevitable, that is.'

'Sounds like getting old to me.'

'Yeah – don't it just.'

'I guess your mum passing makes that more real, huh?'

'Just confirms it really. Can't pretend otherwise now, can I? Not that I ever did. Not much anyway. It's hard not to be aware of age when you spend so much time with the young, let alone look in the mirror.'

As if to underscore the point, he runs his bandaged hand through his hair and she smiles at him, which makes him laugh at himself. 'You reckon I'd look good in a wig?'

'Nah,' she cautions him, amused. 'You'd look like an ageing drag queen.'

'Really?' he says, eyes flashing bright. 'Could be a career in that.'

'Well, maybe you missed your calling – *darling*.'

Though it is clearly a joke – just banter – there is a truth running through it that rings bells for both. Christa detects the quaver in his expression and feels the pinprick on her own skin. It saddens her to see this, but also soothes. Renders him reassuringly human. Neither hero nor monster. For here is something they have in common. Their balancing act. Each teetering on the edge of bitterness. Wondering if the so-called wisdom they have acquired has brought them anything more than a loss of belief.

'Yeah, I sometimes ponder that,' he acknowledges. 'Could I have chased other dreams? Been more sensible? But then, regret is such a useless pursuit. I did what I thought or hoped was best, even if I *was* kidding myself.'

Christa is about to respond when she notices his gaze lingering on her. Tracing her form.

'Don't think I haven't paid a price for it, Christa,' he says eventually, before turning his eyes to the floor and beaming to himself, as if at some private light bulb.

Alive to the dangers of the situation – of how easily things could spiral – she is relieved at the sight of his wistful, still wasted mirth. In turn, she chortles along, and when he looks up again she simply confirms what is obvious. 'We both have, babe.'

In the end she is pleased to have spent this accidental hour together. The ice of mutual awkwardness has thawed somewhat, her wariness decreased several notches. That he elected not to lapse into feeble apology or attempt to justify himself, or worse, to nudge her into sex, has gone a long way to winning her over. She knows she would have – and she knows he knows this. To her way of thinking, he has acted not merely with restraint but with respect.

It is one of the things she loved most about him when they were young; the fact that he viewed her as something more than a vagina on legs.

However, as he walks with her out to the car, she is overcome with a voyeuristic desire to ask him about his love life. She tries to hold it in. It is none of her business, after all. But his guard is down – stoned and tired and relieved not to be working tomorrow – so she guesses he won't resist.

She is almost in the car. The door is open and the keys are already jangling in her right hand. He is leaning against the passenger side, looking contentedly across the roof at her.

'I'm curious,' she says, trying to appear impromptu. 'Is there a special someone? Back in the city?'

As predicted, he offers no defence.

'There was,' he answers with a tiny squeak of guilt. 'But it needed to end. Me coming back here just made it happen sooner.'

What he then proceeds to tell Christa comes as a shock to her.

'Actually, I've never had what you might call a 'relationship' as such. Not like marriage or living together or anything. Just a series of short term things. A year here, eighteen months there. Kinda not really my strength,' he concludes, with an insouciant throwaway.

'Is that because you don't believe in relationships? Too middle class for you?' she teases. 'Or did it just never happen?'

'Probably I was too selfish, babe. Or too picky. Or maybe,' he says, looking back at the house, 'I just didn't have a good role model.'

Though he flips it out with inebriated ease, she feels the wave of generational sadness lurking behind it. His manicured, literary despair and Gianna's fathomless oeuvre of loss; the centuries of grinding peasant woe that sowed it deep into their genes. The history of which Tony doubtless took as his teenage inspiration.

Christa remembers in vivid detail the dark, insistent fires that smouldered inside her once poetic young swain. The good looking boy who thrived on the hormonal melodrama of first love. Who wrote her gushing letters and dedicated songs of heartbreak and desire to her. Who gave her the impression that he would die for her kiss. That the union they shared was worthy of great art.

'And yeah, before you ask,' he adds, half joking, winking sexily, 'loneliness *is* an issue.'

'Ain't it just,' she concurs.

There follows a taut pause, like the yawn of a rubber band, a resolution suspended. They are both holding their breath, wondering which way it will go.

To her relief, Tony once again bursts the bubble with stoned levity. 'Ha! Listen to us. Two lonely old farts reunited after decades apart. Way too fucking corny for my taste, babe.'

Her laughter peals out in the relative quiet of the night, high and immoderate. Pouring from her like birds let loose, fluttering up into the treetops and out across the blackened bay.

'And hey, whatever happens,' he exhorts, 'let's not be a fucking telemovie. We're far too good for that.'

It's classic Tony Timone, and she couldn't agree more.

09. In the presence of others.

Jake Salter is no mind reader but there is something about his father's exaggerated distaste that makes it plain. When he catches the downcast, uncomfortable look in his mother's eyes he feels that his inkling has been confirmed.

'I'll tell you something for nothing,' Jim is frothing, prodding the air with his fork, 'Franco would've beaten ten types of shit out of that snooty little prick. Poncing round town like he owns the joint. Mr High and Fucken Mighty. Treating his mum like shit. You heard the way he spoke about her. I mean, what the fuck was all that supposed to mean? You piss off for nearly thirty years and then you come back and say shit like that. If I was Vinny Carlyle I would have smacked his fucken teeth in.'

The Salters are sitting around their ostentatious new dinner table. It is a hot, dry, early summer morning. The radio is on, aircon humming, and a solitary, fearless fly is buzzing. Outside, beyond the sliding glass, past the decking, the savoury smell of dry grass is drifting up towards the house on the warm breath of the season's first big easterly. Cows swish their tails and seek out shade while raucous birds caw. Up above, the sky is a seamless blue, from which the big white eye looks down. Heedless. The detail of their tiny lives washed out in the awesome brutality of its gaze.

Jake has been back for a week already. The cloistered, nineteenth century kitsch of the school and the garish anonymity of the light speed city seem far off. The rhythm of the country is different – at once alien and familiar – yet it affords him space to think. To be alone. To tinker with his music and count down the days until his one way trip from oppressive fathers and the need to lie.

Listening to his dad's rant, Jake is certain that his expletive poison is really meant for him. All that moralising homophobic anger is the old man's indirect way of telling his son that he does not approve. Does not *want* to understand. Resents the fact that he was even born. The unplanned youngest. Such a scrawny disappointment. Definitely *not* a chip off the old block.

However, what Jake cannot see is what lies just beyond his own egocentrism.

His father's devastating guilt.

In fact, even Jim cannot fully comprehend this — but his wife can.

To her, it is written in blood. It stalks her husband's sleep and taunts him in the daylight hours. It lives in the form of orphans. In the submerged wreckage of unsafe fishing boats. In the memory of widows. No wonder Jake has always rankled him. He is the avatar of his father's culpability. In the dark subsoil of Jim's denial, Jake is the living ghost of a drowned man.

It has taken Shelley Salter years to piece this puzzle together and now, at last, she feels sure enough in her reckoning to tell her son. But she will sit tight for another summer and then, on the morning he is due to fly, reveal all.

Jim, she will never tell, because she senses it would kill him sooner than the cigarettes.

Jake, she believes, will instinctively understand.

'So don't expect me to stand by and say nothing if you start getting chummy with him,' Jim continues, prodding his fork into yet another rasher of shrivelled bacon.

'Does that mean you don't want me doing shifts at Amore?'

'Mate, I'm not saying that — I'm just saying I don't like the bloke and it bothers me that you seem to think he's some kinda cool cat or whatever.'

Jake suppresses the desire to laugh or to erupt into open ridicule. He is determined not to make too obvious a display of his disrespect. So he nods quietly, pretending to take his father's objections seriously. Yet behind his eyes he is thinking archly, *Cool cat! How fucking lame is that?*

'He just seems like a really smart and interesting guy to me. At least he's seen a bit more of the world than most people round here.'

'Yeah, I'm sure he's seen a whole lot of stuff, Jakey – but that don't mean nothing. Don't necessarily mean he's all that smart neither.'

'Sure, I hear what you're saying, Dad … but I'm going to catch up with him anyway, if that's okay with you. Suss him out for myself. See if all the rumours are true or if everyone's just talking shit.'

This tendency of Jake's – to be so calm and clever sounding – annoys Jim intensely. It's not that he doesn't like to see a bit of fight in the boy, but this kind of behaviour strikes him as arrogant and he cannot figure out where he gets it from. His older brothers aren't like that at all. Never were. Not even as young bucks.

He wonders if it's the school's fault – left wing teachers, politically correct curriculum – or if Shelley has been feeding him this nonsense on the sly. Or maybe he's on drugs. Certainly, when he hears the so–called music Jake likes, he is tempted to think so.

Across the table, Jake is expressionless. Acting like it is nothing. In his head though, he is loving every beat of his father's palpable displeasure.

From her perspective, what Shelley sees is two proud bulls engaged in war of attritional vengeance. It breaks her heart – but she long ago learnt that there was little point intervening in male skirmishes. Instead, she keeps her counsel and prays they will all get through till March without tearing one another to shreds.

The advantage of being fifteen years younger than the next brother up is that he does not have to share his space with siblings. The disadvantage is that he finds it harder to evade his parents' scrutiny; but there are locks and headphones for that.

And books.

Jake's room is larger than most teenagers' and significantly more spacious and private than his dorm at school. Indeed, it is his haven. Nothing less than a retreat.

With windows to the east and south it often plays host to the beautiful light. Direct and bright in the morning, reflected and pale in the evenings. Whenever he is home, he makes time to sit and soak it in. It sighs to him. Hints at the possibility of love. Fills him with a longing as vast as the land that stretches, sun–blazed, before his eyes.

This is the nurturing distance he tries to weave into his compositions. To capture with his array of machines.

Synths.
Samplers.
Compressors.
Digital FX racks.

He wants to make worlds of sound as gorgeous as the ones he imagines. As elegant as those he finds in the books he loves. One day too he hopes to find someone who wants to share these light–filled spaces with him.

But not right now.

This morning he needs to be alone, especially after his father's absurd display at breakfast. He needs to re–gather his thoughts. Centre himself. He contemplates rolling a joint but knows that he will risk encountering one or both of his parents on the way outside to smoke it, and so elects to immerse himself once more in Richard Yates. *The Easter Parade.* There is something in the clipped, understated tragedy of the book's heroines, the Grimes sisters, that Jake finds mesmerising. If only real suffering could be that graceful. Instead of so shitful.

This though, is the unmasked Jake – the one who never appears in public – and, catching himself in that fanciful reflection, he reminds himself again to reserve such moments for his room.

The world, he has decided, and virtually all the people in it, would rather subsist on trivia and vanity. Habit and cliché. Fear and smallness. And he will gladly leave them to it.

At times, like now, he is almost overwhelmed by the completist sweep of his contempt; a fact which is beginning to unsettle him as much as any of the flaws he might ascribe to others. He has no desire to be full of hate and anger. To grow up like his old man. Or be cowed like his mother.

He thinks of the few people he admires, looks up to – his two favourite teachers, the tight clique of musos and artists he latched onto in the city, even Vin – and what he sees in them is an inclination to generosity. A tendency to include, forgive, encourage. He hopes that once he has landed in Europe he can find the necessary breathing space to express these qualities himself.

But that is still fourteen weeks away.

✂

After an hour or so of *Easter Parade*, Jake hears his dad's ute firing up and, a few seconds later, the rolling crunch of gravel as it edges down the drive and into the distance. He listens then for other sounds. The radio clicking off. The muffled sound of a shower.

With practised, furtive efficiency he constructs himself a joint and pads softly through the house and out into the building heat of the day. As he proceeds, he hears his mother's sweet, high voice singing and, in it, detects her episodic relief.

By the time Shelley has finished showering, Jake is out behind the sheds, hanging in a diminishing rectangle of shade as the dogs and the flies buzz around him. He leans against the relative cool of a wall of corrugated steel and takes in both the smoke and the sounds of the farm.

It is like far flung music to him. With room enough for truth. For dancing without the threat of stepping on anyone's toes. Were it not for the inching progress of the sun and the high likelihood of his mother poking her head into his room to offer him coffee and enquire after his wellbeing, he would stay out here all day with the incredible cobalt distance. Everything miles off.

Much as he rails against the quarantined, incestuous jingoism of Bravery Bay, he loves the cleansing expanse of the country. Even the air seems to possess a liberating emptiness.

After the mild headspin he gets from the pouch tobacco and the first lurching onset of the dope have settled into the gentle, sustained note of a manageable high, he sprays a jet of spearmint mist into his mouth and starts slowly back towards the house. However, as he is about to make his way up to the front porch, a glint of metallic starburst catches his eye.

The dust and rain blotched 125cc Kawasaki he first learnt to ride as a boy is shining in a razor of sun beneath a stand of English oaks. Exactly where he left it on the wind—blown day he got back from finding Gianna Timone.

He knows he is too stoned to ride into town now but by the time he's cleaned her up, checked her over and made sure she's got enough fuel, he will be straight. His shift doesn't start until six, so he has the rump of the day to go for a ride and hang out by himself. To be in the presence of broad skies.

He will take Richard Yates with him. Roll a couple more joints, grab a towel and swipe a tube of 30+ from the main bathroom. Dig out his old headphones, the ones he is prepared to sacrifice to the abrasion of sand, and go down to the water to chill for the afternoon. Better than having to deal with his dad when he gets back. Or bat away his mother's well—meaning but nonetheless tiresome intrusions.

In Jake's estimation this is a prudent management strategy for an increasingly intolerable situation.

As if to confirm this — a subliminal flash. A few frames of vision dislodged from another verandah.

> *Eyes seeing nothing.*
> *Motorbike waiting, dead on the kerb.*
> *Stilled and unknowing things.*

Then — half a breath later — the crowded and noisy palette of possibility collapses into a splinter of mid—morning light. Like a sigh of completion. A fixed point in a field of uncertainty.

Yet still, Jake finds himself between the end of the end and the beginning of the beginning. With no serious plans for the interim. For the week or even the day. Just plain survival. A linear process. Left foot, right foot.

He pauses under the eaves to let the simplicity of it filter down through the layers. Whenever he conceives of it in this way the churning in his gut and the fizzle of his nerves die down. The pot helps with this; yet Jake has the presence of mind to tag the moment for easy reference.

Thus, when he swishes back into the house to collect his things and let his mother know what his plans are, he does so without lapsing into the faux deference he has adopted as his default setting. He even has a warm kiss for her cheek. A rarity these days.

Both are briefly tempted to open up. Neither does. Too risky.

While Shelley correctly intuits the tenor of her son's prevailing attitude, Jake is still too ensconced in youthful self-absorption to register his mother's similarly bare bones decision to endure. Though she yearns to make this connection with him, she believes that everyone's interests will be better served by a continuation of his measured silence. And of hers.

She does not think that forming an alliance against Jim will help anyone.

Like Jake, she has faith that half a planet and a sustained period of absence will shuffle the deck sufficiently to allow people the perspective they require to see their own imprisoning behaviours for what they are.

✄

Whenever he rides the Kawasaki on the open road, he thinks of T.E. Lawrence and Maurice Martenot, both of whom died in motorcycle accidents.

Jake is not obsessed with death but neither is he afraid of it. Indeed, he is wont to take the occasional calculated risk that most would consider unwise, on the bike *and* off it. Like so much else about him, he keeps these things strictly private. Yet, as he races down the hill and through the gentle chicanes that lead from the property and into town, he enjoys not only the simple pleasures of fast motion and onrushing air but a sense of kinship with the long dead WW1 iconoclast and the French musical inventor.

It is not unusual for him to feel closer to people in books or to dead and distant composers than he does to the people he meets in the gritty procession of everyday life. Because they never judge him. *They* don't have agendas that make things difficult.

For now however, so long as he does not encounter his father on his travels, he will be fine. Hours will slide by in sunlight and solitude before an evening burst of kitchen lackeying will see another day ticked off. Indeed, in the few minutes it takes him to get from home to the parking bay adjacent to Maxi's – the café near the marina that he prefers – his mood approaches elation. The lightness of clarity and the belief that he can stick with it.

For the past few months, as the exams neared and his time at school drew to a close, Jake has been quietly noting the shifts in his thinking. He would not call them profound, or anything that grand, but it is clear to him that the dominant paradigm – his idea of himself as the wronged outsider – is being modified. Not that he is ready to cast off his skin just yet. Rather, he is becoming convinced that one day he will. That he will be able to resist the glare of judgement openly, not secretly.

But this afternoon he will set aside the relentless teasing apart of contradictory thoughts and focus instead on other indulgences. The future, and its attendant uncertainties, will be crowded out by sensations within his immediate grasp.

He will begin with a strong black coffee.

Maxi's is one of the newer additions to the Bay. It sits on the ground level of an apartment block part owned by his family, overlooking the small, lawned 'town square' where memorial statues to dead soldiers and heroic fishermen dominate the foreground of a view across the tethered boats and out to the northern head of the bay. Jake likes it more for its geometric city styling than anything else; and for the way it lets in the liquid light that bounces off the water. The coffee is passable too. Just.

Having ordered, he retreats to a corner and drifts. Quietly, he observes the mix of locals, day trippers and accented, backpacker farm hands – the ones who descend on the town for harvest jobs and visa extensions. He is about to slide deeper into reverie when he sees the suave figure of Tony Timone breeze into the room and saunter up to the perky, flirtatious barista with the trendy tattoo sleeve.

Jake notes how well dressed he is. Just jeans and an off–white patterned shirt, but clearly a cut above chain store horror and deliberately chosen to show off a fine physique. It is a cultured vision. If the practical blacks of the kitchen had previously obscured this, now it is obvious, even with the still bandaged hand.

But Jake doesn't yoo—hoo and wave. It's not his style. He watches instead. Notes the way Tony makes his way to his table, consciously searching for the right vantage. That he chooses to sit where he can gaze into the distance, without the danger of accidental eye contact or the small town habit of forced chit—chat, impresses Jake. He likes it too that there is no recourse to phone poking, newspapers or laptops. When he adds all this to the list of impressions he has already gleaned from the weekend at Amore, and from his memory of the funeral oration, he is convinced that Vin's instinct is right — and that his father's fuming disapproval is all the more reason. He now feels sure that the risk he took sliding Tony a joint on Sunday night will not backfire.

He finishes his espresso and makes his way over, edging into the corner of his quarry's vision. Tony turns with a smile as warm as the day itself. Natural, welcoming, open. He gestures Jake to sit with his burnt hand ... and the next two hours fly by.

✄

Their conversation borders on conspiratorial — like minds with unusual angles, two wallflowers at a ghastly party.

They order more coffees and duck outside to discretely burn down a joint, before returning to swap notes about the things they have in common.

> *Being back in the Bay.*
> *Working at Amore.*
> *Plans for the new year.*
> *Families, fathers, Gianna.*
> *The need to get away.*
> *The confines of expectation.*
> *The unpredictable results of dreaming.*

'I know it probably sounds like some trite middle—aged meme,' Tony says as their table is being cleared and they are preparing to leave, 'but there really is something to be gained from outrageous ambition — and it's not success.'

Although Jake recognises Tony's teacherly habit of encouragement, he also detects the deeper seam he is hinting at —

the obscure and indefinable treasure that emerges from singular deviation, from avenues of enquiry and experience that do not rely on the numbing comfort of reductionist values or the crude commonplace dichotomies that underpin regular conceptions of happy/sad, win/lose, right/wrong. This is thrilling to Jake.

'So let's catch up sometime,' Tony suggests. 'Outside of work, I mean,' he confirms with a coalitional smirk.

'Cool,' Jake agrees. 'Maybe I can even try some of my pieces out on you.'

Tony chuckles. 'In a past life apparently, I was a mouse in a Skinner box, so yeah, I love being experimented on.'

What pleases Jake most about this is not so much the quickness of mind needed to conjure it, but the assumption he would understand. 'Shall I bring a lab coat?' he jokes.

'And some cheese,' Tony adds, rounding it out.

As they shake hands and part, both feel refreshed and enlivened. For Tony it is familiar ground — the kindly mentor thing he has evolved over years of teaching young adults — but for Jake it is almost heaven sent. Despite the teacher/student cliché it is a meeting of minds that until today he never thought likely outside of fantasy. What he likes most is that Tony did not attempt to water down complexities or seek refuge in the lazy black/white cocoon of either/or.

'I was so certain,' he had said at one point, 'that if I just kept at it long enough the universe would provide me with all the answers. That the messiness of stuff would finally turn out to be a form of neatness after all. A kind of secret order. A coded message from God or whatever. *Hey Tony, this is what it's all about, mate.* But I reckon I've recovered from that one now.'

When Jake finally guns the Kawasaki to ride the short hop to the sandy side of the bay, he is jubilant. As he settles himself on the beach and fires up another smoke, he is flushed with the knowledge that this will help him through the ordeal of summer. Will drop him relatively unscathed at the Departures gate.

Basking in the afternoon heat — smelling the salt, plunging his fingers and toes into the warm powdery sand — he allows himself to soften a little further.

Yet there remains a murmuring he is not yet ready to acknowledge in the plainness of language.

> *A sensation approximating happiness.*
> *A tender shoot of hope.*
> *The massing of wild, illogical,*
> *hitherto contained forces.*
> *Feelings until now too dangerous to permit*
> *in the presence of others.*

10. In the ecstasy of emptiness.

Deep in the velvet hush of night, minus the hither and thither of distracting activity, stark light worms its way into overlooked corners. There, the calm diagnostic voice of unadorned appraisal can be heard clear above the quietened channels of daytime din. As though, like some insomniac life coach, it prefers to offer its insights in midnight whispers.

Although Tony is used to this nocturnal practise, he has spent most of his conscious life minimising and explaining away the frank assessments of this plain speaking inner voice. Pretending not to know what he knows.

However, the sleepless voice does not punish him for his refusal; it simply restates what it feels to be the pared down and essential truth. As such, Tony is finding it increasingly difficult to ignore the patient reiteration of in—house counsel. A combination of chronically disrupted sleep and an overwhelming body of evidence are contributing to this.

Yet, perhaps the most striking aspects of this after—dark ritual is that, lately, he has come to understand that all these late night revelations are the result of exhaustive data mining. Findings extracted and refined from the subsoil of memory and habit. Information slowly reconfigured into meaningful patterns, the significance of which are a retro—fit. As though even the dawning of awareness is an act at once natural and constructed. The truth itself an algorithm.

> *Distillation.*
> *After thought.*
> *Archival bastard of language.*

Of the future however, this loop of rumination has nothing direct to say. It deals instead in oblique warning, seeking merely to fuel various determinations. More this, less that.

Or – as is the case tonight – it underlines Tony's newfound attraction to the idea of abandoning previously cherished narratives; especially the ones that have shaped his identity, defined his purpose, and fostered the twin delusions of control and wisdom. Indeed, he feels ready to throw everything away. To shed every skin he ever wore.

It is not so much the perverse dramas of remorse and self–loathing that drive this, nor a yearning for the spiritual, but rather Tony's lingering sense of operating at a slight remove. Of not being *in* the world – and of existing behind a veil of artifice and ego. Though there are times when it manifests as comfortable solitude, aloof contentment, there are others when it feels like loneliness. Like being utterly lost and having absolutely no idea about anything at all. In these moments, he feels he could turn into mist and gently and painlessly be dispersed.

Sometimes he even wishes it so.

As he shuffles wearily from bed to fridge, squinting at the abruptness of cool white light, the voice speaks with calm, compassionate, targeted clarity.

'We've been here before,' it declares. 'Recognise it? We were here at nineteen. Straining at the edges of where we were; preparing the ground for where we imagined we wanted to be. Only this time we have no dream to run to. So the question is: are we prepared to forsake even the act of dreaming?'

Standing in the semi–darkness of his mother's kitchen – fridge humming, an angled canvas of street light stencilled on the worn lino – he tries to pull the question apart. To boil it down to the essential challenge.

> *Replace used up dreams with new ones, like lovers,*
> *or dare to wake up?*

'Now that we're here again,' the voice is saying, 'are we ready for the end of distraction? For the absoluteness of the absolute?'

Whenever the voice speaks like this – which has recently been its habit – Tony is shaken to the core. Somewhere in the centre of his being a bell rings at such an exquisite pitch that it vibrates every cell in his body. The wave is so immense, so indescribably

83

beautiful, that it obliterates distinction, taking him to a place where despair *is* euphoria. Where the ever changing polar dualities of everything become the silent oneness of nothing.

He holds his breath in awe. For now the Eternal is timeless. Here, forever collapses to an instant. Space to a room.

Gianna's kitchen.
3.12am.
The first Thursday in December.

Where an old analogue clock ticks loudly and a lone man exhales a sigh that nobody hears.

He slows his senses, concentrates on background. He wants to see the screen beneath the film.

'Behold the act of beholding,' the voice is saying with kind, remorseless insistence – and Tony cannot escape the implications of this. Because although he experiences a sensation of incredible, exalted liberty and feels lighter than air, in the same moment he is more alone than ever. This, he has come to accept, is where he will end up.

In the absence of everything but beauty.

The clock is now moving on to thirteen minutes past three and he has only ghosts to dance with. No one will ever know that his quiet, slow tears are gathering like diamonds, and will taste like salt on the back of his hand.

As if to compensate for this heightened isolation, there is the claustrophobia of history.

Mum, Christa, Vin.
Maybe even Jake.
The town itself.

The distant city ... billboards glowing.
The enhanced whites of airbrushed eyes.
The student films he watched earlier.

The phone call he ignored.

Her exotic sounding name on the touchscreen.
The memory of her laugh ... and of her long black hair.

It is too late to call her back now, but not for her to press her claim upon his thoughts. Another girl he left behind.

At this, he ruefully smiles. Feels a quiver of shame. Her call has not surprised or alarmed him – although the timing is perhaps a little too coincident for his liking – for despite his desire to divorce himself from the lurid, narcissistic drama of mid–life meltdown, it is impossible for him to deny the fact that he is centre stage in a highly intellectualised soap of balding bachelor ennui.

Twisting the cap from the juice bottle, he laughs out loud, struck by the comical ordinariness of it. He has become the cliché he never wanted to be. There is nothing exceptional about him now. Maybe there never was.

So he takes a few gulps, thanks both the voice and the girl for their reminders, and shambles back to his single bed to make yet another attempt at sleep.

The light comes early this time of year, which means that bird song and a cresting sun are his 5:50 cue for a dawdling, quarter–awake drift toward rising. In this heavy, hazy state, the conscious and unconscious melt seamlessly into one another, while the music of magpies and mynahs, and the rambunctious squawking of cockatoos tumble together in pleasant waves. Somewhere in his slowly solidifying alertness though, a note to self: *call the girl.* For even in hallucinatory drowsiness he cannot ignore what she represents; the fissure she brings into focus.

'Here we are again,' the voice reiterates, before retiring to the shadows for the day.

He is on the porch before eight, sitting where his mother once did. The coffee is black and aromatic. The morning air retains a little of its crisp edge. The bay below is flat. Pale blue satin.

He looks across rooftops to the nestle of the town and realises that he could stay here forever – which is part of the problem.

Since the shock of the tram stop, years of subterranean stirrings have been exposed and are now coalescing into the directness of language. His mother's abrupt demise, and his equally sudden sabbatical, have combined to crush past and future together. Now, after two months back in Bravery Bay, it occurs to him that he could easily follow Gianna's example.

#1: Start the day at glass top table, with coffee from a time–blackened stove top percolator.

'After all, if everything is ritual,' he says to the nearby birds, 'what makes one set of habits worthy and another not?'

They tilt their heads and peer at this new human.

'Is happiness the ultimate deciding factor?' he asks them, and they trill in reply, no such ponderables to bear on their wings.

For Tony, this question is neither banal nor flippant, because he has never been genuinely happy.

He can say this to himself now without fanfare. Minus the judgements of morality and the heroic hyperbole of exceptionalism. Without regarding it as either a catastrophic failure or mental illness; or even as proof of artistic merit and spiritual superiority. Now it is plain fact.

Which is why happiness is fast becoming a serious criteria and – as the voice has told him on several occasions – why it is now clear to him that *he* is the only one standing in the way.

> *His self–talk.*
> *The deeply routined ruts of his behaviour.*
> *An addiction to a vision of self – to the*
> *handsome spectacle of Antonio 'Tony' Timone.*
>
> *Model, actor, screen studies guru.*
> *Lover, loner.*
> *Outcast, orphan.*
>
> *Washed up wannabe.*
> *Self–obsessed fraud.*
> *Total fuck up.*

What the tram stop incident rendered undeniable was that the dream which took him to the city had finally run its course. Not simply that he had failed to achieve what he set out to but that he no longer had the desire to pursue it any further. To be the man in the ad campaign. The one who uses hair dye and wilful delusion to obscure the truth of time. The older dude who pursues younger partners. Who flings himself ridiculously at the clay feet of youth, mortgages his self–respect for pretty faces and firm flesh. The hypocritical cynic still begging for morsels of status and sexual approval. Still doing the same old vanity shit that leaves him feeling sad and alone and useless and old.

Here on the porch, coffee cup resting warmly in his hands, birds twittering sweetly, he is savouring a modicum of distance from the buzzing, busy life he once put so much energy into. He knows that nothing can compel him to return to it, only the fear of change and the ease of the familiar. Dusty things, like duty, like the snide sniping of others, have no power over him these days. Indeed, all the old imperatives – the shoulds, the musts – are hollowing out in front of him.

> *For what power of persuasion can they*
> *possibly retain in the face of the absolute?*

Tony gives thanks for broken sleep and pays tribute once more to the voice that fills the restless hours. Together they have pushed him to the point where an ascetic philosophical nicety has become a useful means of everyday liberation.

Still, he will not be hasty. No rash phone calls to the Dean. No resignation emails.

Not yet.

However, there is one call to the old life he *will* make – because, in his view, the pristine notion of detachment should never be used as a mask for cruelty.

Aneetha may have been naïve, may have had expectations of him that were never going to be met; but Tony will acknowledge that, as the elder, he knew better than she that the physical fire between them would peter out into comfort and ultimately to boredom. Right from the start he understood that the lithe, smiling young woman who cleaned his office and shone her brilliant eyes at him would find it more difficult to deal with the inevitable end of their affair.

Since leaving the Bay, Tony's dalliances have followed this now predictable path. In his twenties he maintained a bullish romantic optimism for something more fulfilling than short lived trysts predicated on mutual lust. For a few years thereafter he nurtured a more measured kind of hope – not so much for a soulmate as a partner in crime. By the time he reached forty however, he had effectively given up, resigning himself to one–off encounters and brief approximations of the love he still yearned for.

If there is any blame to be apportioned for this serial disappointment, he calmly accepts the bulk of it. *His* unreasonable expectations, *his* selfishness and so on.

Therefore, he returns Aneetha's call without either complaint or grudging obligation.

For she is not responsible for his decision to leave the city and sequester himself in a coastal hamlet a day's drive away. She is not the author of his incomplete explanations, nor of his ravenous doubts and growing disquiet. Neither was she as experienced in the illicit business of teacher/student sex. She was just a girl from Chennai on a study visa earning a little extra by taking cleaning jobs. No one had ever paid her the kind of attention Tony did. No man ever found her so attractive.

She was lonely too … and he knew it.

'I'm flying out next week,' she tells him, the tiniest tremolo in her voice. Her course work is done for the year and her family in India are pressuring her for a visit. She steadies herself before adding, 'I'd really love to see you before I leave.'

'That might not be such a good idea – for either of us,' he responds diplomatically. He is trying to say it kindly, fully aware that no matter how he pretties it up it will come out sounding like evasion. This, he knows, is a no–win situation, and his goal is simply to avoid hurting her any more than he imagines he already has.

'Don't you think it would be nice to say goodbye?'

'I just think it'll be better if we meet up when we both get back next year,' he counters. 'That way we'll have a little more distance and perspective on things, and we can take it from there.'

'I don't know, Tony. I'm thinking maybe to change my course. Study somewhere else.'

It takes a couple of seconds for this to register, but in the pause she deliberately observes Tony realises that it is Aneetha who is doing the placating, offering to soften the edges of separation. Now his blood is hot with an instant and wounded desire to drive all day and ravage her like his life depended on it. To savour the silken loveliness of her dark brown skin and the dazzle of her white toothed smile. To hear the depth of her sighs, taste the supple pleasure of her mouth and bask in the validating curl of her slender fingers knotting with his in the bubble of glow that always follows.

Slap!

Now he is reeling. Complacency and hypocrisy in high definition. Loud against the backdrop of her breathing.

'Okay well ... let me think about it,' he says finally, half concussed, suppressing the reflex to protest.

'I fly out next Friday night,' she confirms, her voice now noticeably calmer, with a hint of apology.

'Can I let you know you by the end of the weekend maybe?'

'That's fine,' she agrees. 'But don't think you have to. Only if you want to.'

She says this in such a way that, hearing it, Tony knows at once what he will decide.

He will be tempted, if only by the visceral promise of sex, but he will nonetheless decline. Not out of spite or self–punishing zeal but because she has inadvertently afforded him the opportunity for something different. Just as Christa once did with her surprising refusal.

His challenge will now be to ensure that the window for change does not open again onto more of the same.

In the wake of this cool finality, Aneetha and Tony tread softly around one another for a few minutes more. They swap news, make promises neither will keep, and privately wonder how their once electric passion came to this – to an awkwardness tinged with sorrow and a palpable if unstated relief. In the end, the wrench of farewell is a burden unbuckled.

'I'll let you know about next week,' he assures her.

'Sure,' she acknowledges.

After they hang up, Tony ponders the civilised sidestep of their goodbye. How like an exhausted armistice it was. Once urgent truths not needing to be aired. The shrugging acceptance of bruises.

Yet, shot through it all … the inescapable sense that he first learnt the deft trickery of retreat from his mother. He would like to deny it, but for now at least, if only out of respect for Aneetha, he will allow it air time.

For somehow he always knew what his mother's secret was. She was glad when his father died. It freed her.

She had been *sold* into his purview – concubine, cow, cleaning lady – and his drowning had excused her from all further duties. And anyway, she had already fulfilled her primary function by then. Bello bambino on her hip.

It is mid–morning.

> *Breakfast is done.*
> *Dishes washed.*
> *Emails checked.*
> *Birds going about their business.*

Tony is in the shower, trying to focus on shampoo and conditioner, while countless channels play at volume in his head. A rabble of voices. A ruck of contesting commentaries.

Noises of this nature used to drive him mad but lately he has been practising the art of allowing the cacophony its head without getting drawn into its maelstrom. As each day passes he becomes more aware that this riotous process is simply part of the drama. The introspective scenes, where the hero looks enigmatically off screen while moody music plays. (Or washes his thinning head of hair.)

All these voices, he thinks, who do they belong to? Whose objectives are they pursuing?

He asks himself this because, deep in the scrawl of sound he has become aware of the silence, and thus has begun to suspect that this muted central emptiness is the true wellspring of his being, rather than the hectic phenomenon they call Tony – the socially constructed identity performing externally mandated functions. Indeed, he is starting to understand that the quiet point inside him is not even a some*one* or a some*thing*. It is more like an event than an entity. Absence rather than presence.

Or perhaps a portal overlooking a universe of clamour. A point of observation.

He does not know. Will never know. Yet the mere hint of it is enough to absolve him of the need for complete understanding.

It is a relief. It means that he can go about his day and enjoy the simple things.

> *The time on his hands.*
> *The advent of summer.*
> *The prospect of a casual stroll down to the town.*
> *Things that do not require interpretation.*
> *Moments he will not need to*
> *graft onto a greater narrative.*

He knows his mother would applaud this. Yet whenever he thinks of her, he understands that in order to truly let go he will need to take stock of the load he bears – to recognise that which is his and that which is not, and to identify the cycles at work in his behaviour and his thinking. For he is at last becoming clear about where the lines are drawn between running away and moving on. Between merely ignoring and resolving.

Blindness, Tony now accepts, is not the best way to see.

As he gets himself ready for his daily walk down the hill, he pauses in front of the mirror. His regulation act of vanity. But as he checks himself for stray hairs and other unsightly flaws, he begins to see shadows of Gianna flitting in his expression. He sees her in the shape of his eyes and mouth. Almost feminine. As if she were there behind the bones, looking and speaking through him. He lingers on

91

this, staring directly at himself. Deliberately unblinking. After a few moments, his vision begins to blur and his face distorts seamlessly into a picture of hers – and for the very first time the blunt fact of her death lands without cushioning denial or distraction.

It is a very different kind of silence he is contemplating now.

He bows his head and in a slow, grateful surge his pent up sorrow emerges. Silent at first, then like a siren. Like a howling river stretching back years. To his childhood. To the impossible vastness of a widowed girl's love and the incandescence of her bottled up rage. To the unspeakable dominion of shame and secrets. It is a deluge that hammers down inside him, sweeping away the flimsy tenements of lies and viciousness. It is a flood of redemption and forgiveness, one that is being unleashed for both of them.

The beauty of it is dazzling.

When it finally stops, Tony is drained, emptied out.

Yet, in the cleansed aftermath, he feels that their respective chains may truly be nothing more than a memory of threatening bluster. Relics of fear and control, rusted through and impotent.

> *The cruelty of ownership.*
> *The absurdity of honour.*
> *The vacuity of names.*

'Oh mama,' he whispers to the house. 'It's over now.'

The power of this – so blindingly obvious, so easily mistaken for blithe dismissal – breaks him down again. He sinks to his knees. In thanks. With humility. In the embrace of ecstasy.

When he eventually feels composed enough to venture into town, he floats downhill. The voices in his head offer many takes on the day's events, but the one he likes best is this:

> *I am no longer the bearer of an empty legacy,*
> *No longer the vessel of someone else's meaning,*
> *So now I am free to be.*
> *What next?*

Xmas / NY

11. The end of history.

To Vin Carlyle's way of thinking, something is wrong. Perhaps very wrong. It is not just that Tony Timone has not been himself, or even that he has seemed sadder lately, but that he has become distant to the point of anti–social. Rude. Borderline nasty. With a cynical edge Vin has never seen in him before. He is certain Tony was home the other day – that he was hiding inside, ignoring the knocks, pretending not to hear his voice through the open window. Vin didn't take it personally, but it unnerved him. For a moment he had considered climbing in, before realising how paranoid and ridiculous that would have seemed.

Because, upon reflection, it is most likely a delayed bout of grief. Either that or Tony being dramatic. This, at least, is Vin's wish.

He is not sure he could deal with anything more serious. Not with everything else that's going on.

In the kitchen though, Tony has been sharp. Focused and efficient. Getting through the jobs without undue stress. At times in a kind of trance.

Yet, the entire crew have noticed he is not turning on the usual charm, not even flirting with the girls. Jake Salter seems to be the only one he has time for. However, it has been so busy in the lead up to Christmas that no one has had the time or the inclination to ask. Business has been good and, as Vin knows only too well, this tends to override all other concerns.

Tonight, he hopes, will be different.

It is the Monday before Christmas and the restaurant will close early for the annual staff party. It will turn into a piss–up as it always does, and workaday boundaries will blur in drink and festivity. Embarrassing confessions will be aired and vaguely inappropriate things will doubtless occur in corners and carparks. There will be sore heads and a big clean up in the morning.

Though he recognises the value of the tradition, Vin generally dreads it – but not this year. His intention tonight is to use the occasion to honour Gianna and to find a way to reach out to her son. Quite why this is so important to him, he does not exactly know. He knows only that a deep, tight coil of helpless love and quiet terror are burning at the heart of it. That Tony is the symbol of something fundamental – something he needs to unravel about the way he is, or maybe something he wishes to rescue from the sun–coloured memory of weatherboard houses.

In a strange way, Vin feels as though he is sharing a spot on a metaphoric ledge with Tony; both wondering where they might land after the inevitable jump. He has the idea that time has somehow turned back on itself, bringing them back from the diffusion of decades apart to another finely condensed moment of shared departure.

> *A coach pulls away.*
> *A teenage god waves from the window.*
> *A mother, a lover and a starstruck little boy,*
> *standing in the cool light of a breezy autumn afternoon.*
> *All of them kissing goodbye to the*
> *complacency of nearness.*
> *Drifting inexorably beyond the distance of touching.*

Christmas only serves to amplify this sensation. As though, with its tinsel charade, it exacerbates the gap between fantasy and reality. Between intention and outcome.

Vin's wife and two young girls will be in attendance tonight; but there will be ice in the shape of their smiles. This, as much as anything else, is what will drive him to speak frankly with Tony.

Hank, Clarice and Kel are packing down the kitchen and Vin is out front with a couple of the waitstaff setting up. Antipasto plates have been artfully arranged, gourmet pizzas prepped, formaggi e frutta cut up and fanned out, dolci displayed in a suitably festive way. Glasses are being polished, beers chilled and wines selected.

Vin's daughters are putting Christmas crackers on tables while their mother strings up fairy lights.

The few invited guests – partners and former staff – are already arriving, while one of the waitresses is cueing the evening's playlist. First drinks are now being poured. Pizzas will soon go into the wood oven.

> *Out across the bay a hard, flat sky is beginning to mellow, and the birds are returning noisily to treetops, overhead wires and other vantage points. The cool breath of evening mingles with remnant pools of warm day time air. The streets are busy with locals, seasonal workers and tourists. The light will shortly turn gold and the night will drip down like honey. There is a distinct sweetness everywhere. Summer solstice time.*

> *At the far end of a pontoon, Antonio 'Tony' Timone and Jake Adam Salter share a couple of joints in the company of gulls and bobbing boats. Christa Marie Bell is home alone getting the house ready for her adult children to return from their city lives for their yearly visit. Rosie the barista is partying with backpackers. Aneetha Jharavindra has flown home to India, where she is contemplating her next move.*

Meanwhile, Vin is nervous – wanting a strong drink to calm him. He sloshes a big dollop of Scotch into a tumbler and swallows it whole. His wife has already questioned him about the cost and the wisdom of tonight's event – although his two little girls appear to be having a great time.

He checks the hour on his phone. Tony should be here soon.

When everyone is present and the moment seems right, Vin calls the room to order for a few brief formalities. He thanks the chefs profusely and lavishes brotherly love on Kel before reminding everyone else how essential they are to Via Amore's continued success. A group toast is raised and cheers ripple in a tipsy wave.

'But of course,' he says, 'there's someone who isn't with us tonight. Most of you already know she was like a mother to me, that she taught me everything I know about food, and that she literally helped to make this place possible. Her influence is everywhere here. I don't reckon any of us would be here tonight if it wasn't for Gianna. I know I wouldn't.'

There is a collective hush and Vin feels an ocean rising just beneath the rim of his eyes. His senses are fuzzy. In his head he can hear the echo of her singing. See her hands wiping flour on her apron. Picture the vast and tender sorrow in her eyes whenever she sat him on her lap.

He glances up at Tony. He is miles away. His eyes like hers. Looking across unimaginable distance. Focused on a point so far removed from the tiny details of ordinary existence that Vin can only imagine it to be a source of light.

Where on earth do you go? he thinks – of him and of her. Wishing they would take him with them.

Blinking, he re-focuses on the room, and it abruptly occurs to him that everybody has their own way of disappearing. Some to the busy commentariat of thought, some to the cocoons of fantasy and denial, others to places further afield. All looking for various forms of love and healing and sustenance. All hoping to return to the fray with something to make their journey easier. To make some kind of sense of it all.

He catches Tony's eye – who flicks a minute smile of acknowledgement back at him. It is the merest of gestures, delivered from a great height, yet it is suffused with both fraternal kindness and otherworldly knowing.

Now Vin could cry like a child. Instead, he raises his glass without a word and the room follows suit. 'To Gianna,' he says croakily. 'And to all of you. All of us.'

There is a sizzle of applause and the air fills instantly with a relieved and communal surge of warmth, with an exhaled recognition that will not be put into words but which will be felt for a few happily fed and inebriated hours. It is Christmas, the restaurant is doing well, and Bravery Bay is not such a bad place after all. There is, indeed, much to be thankful for.

The night progresses as Vin predicts. There is drunkenness, amateurish dancing and excessively good cheer. Some ill-advised kissing takes place and a few glasses are smashed.

Although his wife leaves early with the children, he stays until the end. After Hank and Kel eventually stagger across to Catchers' to play pokies and the remaining waitstaff – alerted by insistent phones – drift off to other parties, Clarice, Jake and Tony stay behind to help clear up. They share a joint and another round of shots as they go, and shortly after 1:00am a semblance of order is re-established.

The town is nearly quiet when the four of them emerge into the caress of the night.

> *Only a few young voices.*
> *Scattered, high notes of laughter.*
> *Leaves rustling softly in street-lit trees.*
> *Waves crashing in the black of the bay.*
> *Invisible insects murmuring.*

A few minutes later, Clarice and Jake depart – the latter leaving Vin and Tony with a nightcap – and Vin has his chance at last.

While Tony sparks up, he watches on, trying to read the signs. To work out if his friend will talk. If indeed he has already guessed.

He has. In fact, he begins as though he has already rehearsed.

'Don't stress on my account, Vinny,' he says with a shrug. 'It's just a thing, y'know. Mum and everything. The future, the past and all that. Getting old, feeling lonely, blah blah blah. Predictable really. And Christmas isn't helping. All that fucking family bullshit. So yeah – I'll be okay.'

With this, he passes the joint to Vin and returns his gaze to a point on an impossible horizon.

'I'm not too sure about that,' Vin admits. 'You don't seem so good of late.'

'Well, I'm not about to stick my head in the oven, if that's what's worrying you.'

Vin takes a deep drag and holds it in, all the while watching Tony closely. As he lets it out with a slow, snaking sigh he smiles. 'Mate, if your mum managed to stay around, I'm pretty sure you can.'

This evinces an affectionate laugh from both men. Each in their own way understands the anguish of the late Gianna Sofia Timone. Indeed, they both carry aspects of it with them; although only Tony would be prepared to admit an ongoing addiction to the beautiful mélange of love and agony she bequeathed them.

Like heroin. With its mix of euphoria and damnation.

'Sure,' he says, 'but tell me honestly, how much of her staying here was really out of guilt and fear?'

'What do you mean?'

'C'mon, Vin, she wasn't a saint. Sure, she stayed because she loved us, but also because she was shit scared of what we'd think of her if she did the deed. She just didn't want to be judged. By us, by God, by who or whatever. She was afraid that if anyone *really* looked they'd see who she was – and that they'd come to the same conclusion. That she was weak. Gutless. Stupid.

'I mean, think about it, Vin. Why, when she got off that ship, didn't she just fuck off into the city and disappear? Why did she sail to the arse–end of the world to breed with a man she didn't even know?'

This takes Vin's breath away.

> *The rawness.*
> *The evenness of tone.*
> *Truth accepted without struggle or self–pity.*
> *Without prettying sentiment, or*
> *the tell–tale rust of vindictiveness.*

'I guess I've wondered the same myself,' is all he can muster in reply – and Tony looks at him again with eyes that speak of both affection and cold understanding.

'I don't think it even occurred to her, to be honest,' Tony mutters, taking the last drag of the joint and extinguishing the roach between thumb and forefinger. 'By the time she realised there was another way, she was already a widow with a kid; and that just added guilt and shame to the mix. No way she could top herself then, eh?'

'Nah, probably not,' Vin acknowledges. 'But what's stopping you?' he presses. 'I mean, you got no kids to leave behind. No parents to upset. No wife to judge you. No staff to throw onto the dole queue.'

Tony takes a second or so to consider his reply. 'Other than animal instinct, I don't really know. Maybe there's some optimistic genes in there still hoping I might have a kid one day. Y'know, the reptile part of my brain saying *stay alive, stay alive, just in case.*'

Though he rolls it out it with a practised model grin, Vin detects the forlorn note beneath the cool bluff. A whiff of hopelessness. Bitterness. This too he recognises from the realm of Gianna. Indeed, to Vin, it is as though Tony has come back home to take up the cudgels of his dead mother's lonely crusade. As if they were the holders of a great secret, charged with the task of pursuing an even greater truth across hemispheres and generations.

He understands this apparent compulsion only too well, for it lurks in the middle orbit of his marriage and his uncertainty. It is the awful promise in his daughters' joyful laughter. The kind of gravity that smashes people together, before driving them inexorably apart.

But Vin doesn't yet have language for this – only foreboding. He is half hoping Tony will help him figure it out.

'Never really picked you for the daddy sort,' he observes, after a few beats of quiet.

'I'm sure every man's a daddy sort in his DNA,' Tony chortles. 'Even if some of us do almost everything in our power to avoid it.'

'You didn't ever want kids?'

'Probably wouldn't have mattered if I did. Couldn't ever stay with a woman long enough to make one.'

'So, do you wish you had?'

At this, Tony's eyes drift into the distance once more. A wistful farness. He bites his top lip and pushes out a soft shooshing *huh*, at which his eyes sparkle. He returns his focus to Vin.

'Seeing your girls tonight, playing with them … I was fucking drowning.'

He shakes his head, looks down at the ground, and a bloom of something approaching adoration washes momentarily through his bloodstream. 'But then,' he adds, eyes still downcast, 'the little one got tired and ratty and I was … glad it wasn't me who had to deal with her.'

Vin recalls the way Tony had knelt to be at the girls' level. The way he had shown interest in their prattle. How they had reacted to him with such innocent affection. Even his wife had noticed. 'He's a bit of a charmer, isn't he?'

Yet before Vin can respond, his friend has shifted his weight, shaken off his reflections and shot him a bright, irreverent look. 'Told you, mate – I'm just too shallow. Too many photo shoots and one night stands. Too much time worrying about whether my hair looked good or not.'

Both men laugh knowingly at this. Tony's preening vanity is the stuff of legend. The pretty boy portfolio and soap opera showreel are testament to a talent that went no further than a series of deftly executed poses.

'So there you go,' he smirks. 'No need to fret. I'm far too vain and stupid to commit suicide.'

After Vin locks the restaurant, he drives Tony up the hill and they park, engine idling, outside the old house, where a single porch lamp casts a warm yellowy pool and shadows trace webs across walls and window panes.

Down below, the town is a dotted mosaic of lights. They wink in the mild night, while a waxing moon sits low in the east, casting a silvery sheen onto the shivering black of the sea. Both note with private irony the romantic quality of the scene.

In addition, Vin is wondering if he has pried too much, and he offers his companion an apology.

'It's alright,' Tony assures. 'At least I know you give a shit.'

'Ah look, mate, I just worry about you up here alone in this house. Stuck in this shitty little back water with nothing to do.'

'Apart from working in kitchens, you mean? And smoking dope with the weird kid?'

'And chatting up waitresses young enough to be your daughter? Yeah.'

Tony laughs at Vin's clumsy small town prurience and the passive assumptions behind it. 'Does that really bother you?' he wonders, eyebrows raised.

'I don't know. Should it?'

'Seriously, Vinny, it ain't the girls you need to worry about. They're just fine. If anyone's getting hurt, mate, it's the stupid, deluded middle−aged man, not the gorgeous young women.'

'You sure about that, mate?' Vin asks. 'I mean, I've seen the way they look at you sometimes.'

'Yeah of course they *look*,' Tony concedes. 'They're not stupid. They can spot a sucker a mile off.'

'Prick teasing, huh?'

'I don't think it's *that* cynical. They just think I'm a cute old man or something. Kind of different maybe. A little exotic. Like a cool uncle or whatever. But definitely not fuckable. I can assure you of that, mate. I don't have a ghost of a chance with *any* of them.'

'So why bother flirting?' Vin wants to know, not entirely convinced by Tony's reading of the situation.

'Because they're beautiful. Why else?'

Although Tony tries to obscure the spike of pain that flashes in his eyes and at the corners of his sardonic smile, Vin picks up on it. He does not fully understand the nuances that inform it but he *can* relate it to his own experience − with his wife, who used to make him so weak with desire he could scarcely speak in front of her, and with his memories of a much younger Tony. The one who let Christa Bell give him strange haircuts, and who paraded like a model in the loungeroom in front of his mother.

'*I* might be getting older,' Tony tells him, 'but beauty isn't.'

Again, Vin is hit by the plain, unceremonial nature of his friend's words. 'Far out, Tony, you're not giving up, are you?'

'Tell me honestly, Vin ... when was the last time you ever found a fifty—year—old really sexy? I mean, *really* beautiful. So beautiful you'd do just about anything to be near them.'

The question hangs like thick smoke between them and time itself seems to slow to the pace of vapours.

'I bet you never have. Because I sure as hell haven't,' Tony confesses, his words dusted with gentle self—reproach. 'I mean, I've got plenty of older lady friends, and they're fine, wonderful, kind, generous, intelligent, funny people and all the rest of it. But desirable? Not really.'

Vin struggles to concoct a suitable reply, something that won't sound lame or like a brush off. He knows there is something here for him but it hovers just beyond his reach. Just outside the perimeter of his fear.

'Do the poets wax lyrical for hags?' Tony goes on. 'How many songs get sung for crusty old farts? Look at all the great mythologies; even the gods like 'em young. Because beauty comes with a kind of promise ... and tell me Vin, what promises do old bones make?'

Now Vin is truly concerned. For there is a softly spoken brutality in Tony's voice. An edge that is coolly chiselling away at the stony outer shell of common denial and revealing with each syllable the very brittlest of forms beneath. Perhaps not even that. Just a swirl of dust. Floating in a temporary whoosh of air. Specks in the immensity.

'Fuck mate – are you sure you're okay?'

'What's okay?'

'Like ... wanting to be here for a start.'

'You mean staying alive? I already told you that, Vin.'

'Well, I fucking hope so, mate.'

Reaching out, Tony rests a hand on the younger man's shoulder. Vin feels its weight. Its reassurance and solidity. Its absolute presence.

A catching of breath.
A stifling of sighs.
A single tear – falling cool and slow.
Thirty years – and other things left along the way.
The immeasurable space between loving
and being loved.

'Don't worry about me, mate. Or Mum,' Tony tells him. 'Focus on yourself. On what you *have*. On you and your wife and those beautiful little angels. That stuff matters more than ghosts. Or stupid ideas. Or the bullshit other people tell you about what your life is meant to be. They're only trying to impose their own childish fears on you. To make you dependent on the same ridiculous lies they are. So they can control you. Abuse you. Make excuses for their cruelty and stupidity. Feel a little better about themselves in the process.'

Vin turns to him, smiling now. 'Yessir,' he jokes.

Tony grins broadly in return. 'Yeah, I know ... it's all just hot air in the end.'

'Now that sounds something your mum would've said,' Vin replies – and Tony gives a brief nod to show he agrees, and they say goodnight without further ado.

The effort and emotion of the night have undone Vin Carlyle. As he drives through the darkness to his house on the south–west side of the bay, the sense of looming cataclysm building up inside him since Gianna's passing has become a lump in his throat. Almost impossible to swallow back down. Because now he can no longer deny that it has more to do with him than it does with either of the Timones. Yes, they *are* a part of the picture, but the real clues lie elsewhere. In the reasons that propelled a six–year–old boy to seek refuge in the house of an immigrant widow. In the empty space she and Tony have filled all these years, and the things they replaced.

It is nearly three by the time he crawls into bed. The warmth of his wife's sleeping body and the long sweep of her form beneath the covers provoke contradictory tides of desire and guilt, and make all too real the recognition of patterns. The attract/repulse mechanism at work in their marriage lays unmasked at last. Staring at him in the low light. Eyes unblinking.

While his tiring, splintering thoughts replay Tony's words — and Gianna's bony fingers run though the waxy soft hair of the little boy sitting next to her at the kitchen table, eating biscuit mix from the bowl — Vin begins to believe that the upcoming fork in the road will arrive at a time and a place of his own choosing. That he is not the victim of history.

This is a terrifying idea. For it offers up the prospect that he might get it spectacularly wrong; or that even his loneliness might dessert him.

Then, in the last moments of consciousness, his body as heavy as oceans, this is what he hears: *Because they're beautiful. Why else?*

12. Scenes viewed from above.

One of the things Jake likes best about Tony is that he can deal with silence. Unlike virtually everyone else in Bravery Bay, he does not hide behind the continuous distracting noise of conversation. Indeed, it has become their habit, when sharing joints, to smoke without speaking and to linger in private quiet for a couple of minutes thereafter. Jake feels this repose is something they both require. Or rather, crave.

However, the younger man is in the habit of wondering what the older thinks during these wordless interludes. He is intrigued, although the elder warns him not to be.

'It's nothing really,' Tony insists. 'Just the kind of pondering you might imagine a balding middle—aged hair model might indulge in. Self—obsessed and slightly morbid.'

Though he is impressed by the good humour inherent in Tony's explanation and respects his friend's determination not to either burden him with his troubles or groom him as an acolyte, Jake has found himself caring. This is not something he is used to, and he is not sure he likes it. At times, he has even considered keeping a distance from Tony, if only to render their eventual parting more tolerable.

This uptick in emotion plays neatly into the momentum of developing self—drama. Though Jake gives credence to the idea that he sees in Tony an older version of himself — and that therefore Tony has keys to rooms he is desperate to unlock — he remains wary of letting too much of himself be visible to his newfound friend.

Nonetheless, Jake has discovered a form of sanctuary in Tony's presence. It is nothing less than recognition.

Most likely he will never say this aloud — nor use such language in his thinking — but he is pouring it into his music.

There is a lustrous quality to his latest compositions. His soundscapes have more skin. More blood. There is a sense they are inviting touch; and he is keen for Tony to hear them.

Ideally, he would invite him up to the Salter house to listen to them in his room, with the proper sound equipment and appropriate headphones; but of course this is impossible. As always in the shadow of Christmas, his father Jim's militancy about family honour and proud surnames increases. It does not escape Jake's attention that this coincides with peak season. On the farm the winter/spring crop is almost fully harvested, and down in the town the holiday rentals are filling up and the pleasure craft are booked out. The Salter dynasty, he reflects cynically, is little more than a money–making operation. A greedy and colonial perpetuation of acquisition and dominance.

Jake's friendship with someone like Antonio Timone does not accord with the empire's vision of itself.

To circumvent this, Jake will burn a CD of his work. A few of the best. He knows there is a reasonable 5.1 system in Tony's loungeroom because he wired up the new speakers himself barely a month before Nonna Gianna's passing.

He smiles to himself when he remembers her listening to sixties girl groups in surround sound. A seventy–year–old woman singing *Be My Baby* like a fifteen–year–old girl. Like time and death and disappointment never existed. As though love and hope were still everything.

He cues the tracks, selects the highest quality settings, and hits burn.

As the machine whirs – its low, insect drone hypnotic – he thinks again of Gianna and begins to see how a measure of her doomed girl–pop longing has found its way into her son. And also into him.

He wonders if this is part of what makes them different.

The experience of flight as a precursor to crashing.
Of falling as a means of uplift.
The peculiar romanticism of the solitary.

It is an enticing idea. It feeds into the internal construction of the kind of person he is. Wants to be. It validates his desire to leave home for good. Gives him the little shot of courage he requires to permit himself the belief that he *will* see it through.

> *That he will not look back.*
> *That he will not capitulate to the inherited laziness*
> *of a small town fortune.*
> *Nor blurt out his bile and his secrets*
> *in an undisciplined vent.*

For in spite of his fierce intellect and refined perception, Jake is terrified. As much as he dreams of escaping the confines of village expectation, he fears the impersonal coldness of the wider world, and thus is worried that his judgement may be fatally flawed in this regard. He still needs external anchors to confirm him in his choices. To lay out a pathway.

This is precisely what Tony has been doing for him, deliberately or otherwise. With his kindness and intelligence. His amusing stories and elastic way of thinking. But mostly with the stylish restraint he exercises; for though it is evident he is suffering from a bout of mid–life malaise he is steadfastly refusing to lapse into melodramatic display. Jake's gut instinct is that this has a lot more to do with humility than it does with either bravado or denial. It is a balance that he himself would dearly love to strike.

In the shared idylls of their stoned silence, Jake often finds himself gazing at Tony, tracing his eyeline into what always seems like the great beyond. Whenever he sees this it gives him hope that a state of equanimity is indeed within his grasp. That he may one day make peace with the world. Even if it refuses to make peace with him.

Because, as soon as he ventures from the safety of his room, Jim Salter's glowering scrutiny is in full effect.

Jake can feel his father's eyes locking on as he emerges into the large open living area where his parents are pouring over to–do lists for the extended family Christmas function they will host in a few days time. He tries not to let it affect him but it disturbs the surface of his calm. Like pebbles being thrown.

'Gracing us with your presence, are you?' Jim begins without looking up.

'Not for long,' Jake fires back, trying to keep it light.

'Better things to do than hang out with us, I bet?'

'Totally,' Jake says with a smile he hopes is cheeky and disarming.

'So what is it today?' Jim continues, not cracking, razor gaze over the rim of steel frame glasses.

What Jake feels like saying is: taking amyl nitrate and having random sex with strangers. He toys with the idea for a few beats, enjoying the fantasy of the reaction it would surely elicit

'Stacking dishwashers,' he eventually replies. 'After all, it pays better than hanging about here.'

With that he tries to leave – but his father is not done with him. 'Been racking up a lot of hours down there lately,' he observes with low menace. 'Might have to start charging you board, Jakey.'

Because Jake is confident his mother would scupper such an idea, he can afford to appear flippant. 'Well, as long the rate's competitive,' he jokes.

As he says it, he catches Shelley Salter's eye. She has her usual look of mild alarm. Holding her breath, hoping that by doing so she will be able to contain any conflagrations. In her, Jake recognises the other side of silence. The side underpinned by fear. The kind of quiet in which devious but necessary plans for survival and harm minimisation are hatched. If Jake is ever tempted to regard this as weakness, he quickly remembers how often he employs the same tactic.

There is a minute detail in his mother's gaze. The barest of movements. Beseeching. It is a barely a pip in a stream of noise, but these days he is noticing such things.

As though to reassure her, he mimics her, withdrawing into his own shell. With deliberate slowness he fills a glass with water and calmly consumes it, avoiding any inflammatory eye contact with his father. Starve a fever, he is thinking, as the cool liquid slides down.

'Well, you have a good day, then,' Jim snarls, returning his attention to the Yuletide details.

'You too, Dad.'

At this, both Jake and Shelley know that fireworks have been narrowly avoided. Again. Departing the scene, the young son stops at his greying mother's shoulder, runs the tip of his index finger across it and gives it a little tap. Like a punctuation mark. A high–five.

It is too subtle for Jim to notice. Or so they believe.

The Kawasaki kicks into life. Birds scatter at the sound, wheeling high in a white blue sea. It is a tick past eleven in the morning. Jake has nearly seven hours up his sleeve. A freshly burnt CD in his bag. Some sweet smelling dope in a tobacco pouch. As the bike trundles down the long drive towards the road, bumping gently as it goes, he lets himself shout.

'Fuuuuck yooouuu!'

He pictures himself – belt low and tight, tray table in the upright position – as the plane rolls down the runway. In his gut, the force of acceleration. The nigh sexual tension of escape.

The Kawasaki picks up speed. The Norfolk Island pines flash by. Jake sits up in the saddle. He is flying now, and it is of almost no consequence where he lands.

Provided it is somewhere else.

When he gets to Tony's he stands the bike carefully around the side in the shade. As he rests his helmet on the handlebars and ruffles his hair, he hears the muffled sound of the television inside and smiles at his friend's habit of putting on old movies as background chatter. Jake knows that if he listens for long enough he will overhear Tony chiming out the dialogue in time. This behaviour charms him – stimulates a blush of genuine affection. Like nothing he has ever felt for his parents. Or anyone for that matter.

Then, for a second or two, his heart aches. The plane will fly him far from this.

Tony makes coffee in Gianna's old percolator. Jake sits at the similarly ancient dinner table and rolls a couple of spliffs. On the TV, *Lawrence of Arabia*. 'None of *my* friends is a murderer,' says Peter O'Toole to Omar Sharif. 'You are angry, English,' Tony replies in time with Sharif.

Meanwhile, beautiful summer light pours in through the kitchen window. Aquatint. The colour of liberation. Not unlike the desert sky at Ali's Well in David Lean's movie.

After a few moments, there is a swelling, gurgling sound and a column of scented steam rises as the coffee completes its process. Tony carefully pours the black gold into white cups. This too impresses Jake. He loves it that Tony treats coffee like a lover – with tender attention. He practises putting the very same care into the preparation of the joints.

This ritual has become commonplace. The two men indulging in small delights, in alternating bouts of therapeutic conversation and restorative silence. The one now deliberately seeking courage from the example of the other. The elder now consciously guiding the younger. Both reconciled to the fact they are enjoying their respective roles. Each taking what medicine they can from the exchange.

Only after they are high does Jake confirm he has the CD he promised last week, and they retire to the loungeroom to listen. Upon Jake's suggestion they turn the volume up loud.

'So like, they're not anything at all like songs,' he explains, fetching the remote from the coffee table and plonking himself on the sofa. 'They're not pretty instrumentals either. I kinda think of them as being like paintings in sound. They have a mood and everything, and a texture, but there's no obvious 'story' or anything.'

From his mother's beloved and well–worn armchair, Tony laughs in sympathy. 'You sound like I do when I'm trying to butter my students up before a screening. Like you have to give fair warning. The following content does *not* come with a spoon.'

'Yep, that's pretty much how it feels most times,' Jake acknowledges – failing to keep the flash of disappointment from his eyes.

'Of course it does,' Tony concurs with a flick of the brows. 'Personally, I've always liked it that way,' he adds. 'It helps to keep it special. Like I belong to some small, private club. Makes me feel superior too, I guess.'

Jake nods, getting the point, and Tony smiles, noting that his young charge has understood. 'I know it's hard not to be snobby,' he continues. 'Most people, unfortunately, really *are* stupid. And complacent and selfish and petty and all the rest. I spent a lot of years in denial about that, but of late I'm afraid the evidence has rather overwhelmed me.

'But then in saying that ... so what. You and I are going to be just as dead as the rest of them, and most likely history won't remember us like it won't remember them.'

He throws his gaze around the room. 'I mean, look at all this,' he gestures. 'Is this all that remains of a life? Furniture? Unfinished novels? Grave goods?'

Then, before the air gets too sombre, Tony winks playfully. 'Anyway, I'm pretty sure nothing really matters in the end. Ultimately, that is. That this is all just spectacle. Sound and fury and so on.'

Jake is not sure he agrees, but he thinks he knows where it comes from. The absent presence in the room, and everything her departure represents. He wants to say something about it – to let his companion know he has noticed – but he gets stuck looking for words that won't sound clichéd.

In the space, Tony rounds out his argument, 'So, that being the case, I reckon we're all free to do whatever the fuck we like. I mean, without being total cunts, of course.'

Once again, Jake is disarmed by Tony's wry, whimsical irreverence. He laughs heartily. In a way he rarely does in front of others.

Yet, jokes aside, he appreciates the nuance of his host's contention, as well as the subtle encouragement contained within it. However, what he likes best about this casual mentoring is its sense of allowance. It does not come with the usual layers of value judgement or assume a monochromatic, narrative arc.

'Maybe that could be your epitaph,' he jokes. 'Antonio 'Tony' Timone. Not a total cunt.'

With a big, generous laugh, Tony says, 'If I die before you leave, feel free to recommend it to the headstone guy.'

✂

Jake is on edge as the music plays. Scanning Tony for signs. In a way it is a test, for despite the abstract nature of the compositions, they point at something essential. His longing and his uncertainty. The object of his search and his fear of being lost.

The truth is, he feels exposed. His hiding place revealed.

Nervously, he talks over the top — explaining the origin of samples or describing the blending of certain effects. Though he can tell Tony finds his over compensating chatter distracting and unnecessary, he is unable to stop. Only when he realises that his talking is more revealing than his music, does he find the discipline to shut up.

For the next twenty minutes or so they listen, with buttoned lips, to fluttering, eerie electronica.

On one level it has a dry, architectural quality. A crisp, spatial feel. On another, it has the liquid shimmer of a mirage. The visceral imminence of weather. Each piece is like a scene viewed from above, with the human players as ants. Yet, rather than being regarded as mere fodder for the squashing, or as the experimental subjects of a calculating sonic deity, there is a sense in which they are being considered in the light of their ultimate unity. As creatures propelled by forces beyond the scale and scope of the individual. Everyone alone together.

Towards the end, it is clear to Jake that Tony is getting it. It is more than a simple matter of him liking the music. Rather, that he appreciates what Jake is trying to achieve. Intellectually *and* emotionally. Indeed, he thinks perhaps Tony understands the deeper, oceanic yearning that informs the work.

'Thank you,' he breathes, closer to public tears than he is comfortable with.

Recognising his young friend's sensitivity, Tony assures him he is making remarkable progress. 'I don't wish to bore you with comparisons but … fuck, when I was your age I was nowhere *near* this level. I was just copying things I saw in films; hoping it would make me a better actor. I mean, I'm sure you're imitating people *you* admire, but at least you're getting *this* far. Making your music. Doing your thing. I was just getting free haircuts and posing.'

Flattered though he is by Tony's approval, Jake takes a few moments to safely contain his feelings, and then shrugs off the compliment with a laugh. 'Yeah maybe − but you upped and left all the same,' he says. 'Even if it was just a pose, you still did it.'

'At the end of the day, Jake, all I did was get on a bus.'

Hours later, in the middle of a hectic shift at Via Amore, Jake finds himself returning to this comment.

It is clear to him now that Tony was not simply downplaying or dismissing the impact of his decision to leave home at nineteen, but that he was alluding to something subtler and more profound. That for all the pondering, the weighing up of options and the wondering about what might be, in the end he had left Bravery Bay because he had bought a seat on a Stateliner Express. In its simplest form, the decision was reduced to the ritual of packing a suitcase and to being at a bus stop on time.

In the slam of the kitchen, with the Christmas peak season raging around him − docket rails full, chefs cranky, boss frantic − Jake is able to witness the power of this idea in motion. In the simple, physical act of washing dishes.

He looks not at the pile, concentrating instead on each pan, each plate. Each load being packed methodically into the dishwasher. Discreet tasks happening in a sequence. First, second, third.

'I'm not trying to trivialise what's on the horizon for you,' Tony had said. 'All I'm saying is that a flight has been booked on a certain date. Just be on that plane. All that other stuff − like how significant it all seems and how disastrously it might turn out −

that's just noise. You can tune into it if you want, but you can also turn it off.'

'But isn't that just being careless? Avoiding stuff?' Jake had argued.

'It can be, yes. But then again, if we're afraid, almost anything can be a form of avoidance, including sitting round trying to work everything out ... or pretending there's such a thing as a right answer; when really there's just a choice of roads. All the various ways we can go; and all of them ending up in the same place.

'The point I'm trying to make is that regardless of whether you think you're right or wrong – or you reckon you've got the truth all sussed out – you're going to get there in the end. And then it will all be over.'

As he ponders this, and ploughs through the dishes, Jake begins to get a glimpse of that far off horizon he so often sees Tony staring into. And, in an experience much like epiphany, he realises that it is right in front of him. That, at a certain point, great distance collapses into immediate proximity – as it does in bus stations and boyhood bedrooms – and that sometimes it is only the dichotomy of language that keeps the two points apart. It is why music is his home. Why it sometimes seems like a companion to him. Because in his heart Jake will never be known by the clunky approximation of words.

In the breathless moment following this he is bursting to make contact with Tony. He tries to catch his eye but cannot. Tony's attention is wired into what his hands are doing, in a meditation of simple, repetitive action.

Grinning to himself, Jake blinks to clear his senses, pulling his focus back to the careful placing of a rack of freshly washed glasses on the benchtop. He watches as steam rises from them. He notices that the steam is no rush and that every last plume of it dissolves into the air.

✂

He arrives home well after midnight and, seeing that the lights are off, eases the Kawasaki down and glides to a quiet stop. Only a cloud of dust, briefly caught in moonlight, and a single cautionary bark from one of the dogs will announce his arrival.

The house is quiet, liked he hoped. No talk to endure. No interrogation. He can simply unlace his sneakers and pad softly in socks to his room, where the small click of the jamb will be the loudest sound.

Though he smells of sweat and kitchens and feels in need of a shower, he moves to his keyboard instead. Fires up the machines. There is a song of sorts waiting to emerge. Something simple. A phrase in his head repeated over and over, with only subtle variations. He knows what the inspiration is but is trying not to allow the idea to solidify into direct thought.

In his comfortable eyrie of books and art he has encountered this phenomenon often – always as a spectator. As though it were a beautiful, transfixing and dangerous fire burning in the night on the other side of a mountain. A radiant glow just beyond a dark, protective foreground. An outline.

Lately though, it has been finding its way into his music, and tonight it is an unadorned melody. Keys played in a simple pattern. No distorting effects.

He works on it for an hour, until his head is heavy; but by then he already has the broad brushstrokes in place.

When he plays it back, it is abundantly clear what is going on.

The impact sends him back out into the night, where the smallest hint of damp in the air freshens his skin and amplifies the force of the music. He frantically smokes a joint in the pale silvery light, while nocturnal eyes watch from shadows.

He is in trouble now, there is no denying it.

And once again, when he closes his eyes, he can hear the late Gianna Sofia Timone cooing adolescent love songs.

13. The children of disappointment.

Christa Marie Bell still finds it hard to believe both her daughters are in their twenties. Both graduated and living in the city. Jobs, cars, credit card debts. As though the dusty, salty physicality of their country childhood never happened. Like they were born online, with multiple daily posts as a natural consequence of living. Sometimes their millennial modernity leaves Christa feeling invisible. Left behind by time. A quaint, un−Google−able relic of shameful, Luddite origin. God knows what they think of Steve, she wonders, as she gives the house a final spruce before their arrival.

She does not often think of her ex−husband, but the imminent annual homecoming of their two grown−up girls focuses her mind on him. Like her, he still lives in the Bay, making a living with his hands − building, milking, helping with the harvest − and like her he admits to feeling that his kids tolerate him at best.

'Jeez, Chrissy,' he had said the last time they met. 'It's like they're both ashamed of us.'

'We're probably too yokel for them,' she had agreed, although, when she thinks about it, she realises there is more to it.

Though she does not like the idea, her instinct is that it has something to do with cowardice. Or perhaps even betrayal.

> There is a point at which graceful acceptance lapses
> into fearful settling. She does not need reminding
> which side of the divide she has existed on.

Since the return of Tony Timone, the truth of it has been inescapable. The excuses she used for years − the plausible deniability she clung to, the public misconception she hid behind − have been upturned. The smothered truth, like pink skin after burning, now visible.

Madison and Daria will simply drive the point home further. With their youth. And the way they have of looking at her. Amusement, judgement ... pity.

Then again, Christa thinks, perhaps this is how I see myself.

> *Bright morning, dull afternoon.*
> *Functioning, capable.*
> *Yet, having mislaid or overlooked something vital.*
> *Dreams having yielded to a less dramatic alternative:*
> *the simple progress of hours.*

It is a brute procession, marked by the robotic turning of clocks and calendars. By Christmases – and the steadily increasing distance of daughters.

As she bustles the vacuum into yet another rarely attended corner, she spies her reflection.

> *Tired and sweaty after a full day in the salon.*
> *Hair too dry from constant colouring.*
> *Boobs gone soft.*
> *Single and terrified.*
> *Borderline gambling problem symptomatic*
> *– still hoping for the late day miracle.*
> *So bored sometimes it hurts.*

Though she is used to the presence of mirrors, here she has no public face. No hairdresser role to play. At home, she is neither the popular and chatty ex—wife of dumb ol' Steve, nor the lovely young girl left behind by Wog snob Tony. In this unwiped mirror she is no longer a victim of men. She is a tired mother cleaning up after herself. Trying to suck up the dust of her regret. To hide it from her children. From her own critical eye.

Mechanically, dutifully, she finishes the vacuuming – under the beds, into the difficult nooks of fluff – but, in the blistering silence after the off switch, it is abruptly too much. The brutalism of the self. No soft edges. No prettying, decorative elements. Christa in the raw, as the sum of an unrecoverable past. As a consequence.

She wants to break. To dissolve and be absolved in the grace of oblivion. But she can't. Won't allow it. The girls. Christmas. The utterly ridiculous idea that Tony...

It is at the mere thought of his name – the sounding of the word in her head – that things jolt back into place.

No!

She will not love him. She will *not*. That would be to admit everything. Instead, she says to herself:

> *Madison, Daria – dammit, even poor ol' Steve.*
> *Everything you've ever worked for – your little*
> *corner of the world.*
> *The ninety–eight percent of the time you're okay*
> *– even if okay isn't great.*

This evening, Christa is asking herself a confronting question: do I persist simply because I believe I must? Because it is expected of me?

She is usually alone when she has these thoughts. Often tired and stressed. Like now.

Although her mind is raging with possible answers, she never loses sight of the switch, the one that flicks her into normal mode, where she simply plays the role and things progress as they always do.

'Fake it till you make it, hon,' she says out loud to yet another mirror, as she sprays it with chemical scented mist and wipes off the smears.

This brings a weary smile to her face; and she recalls what the teenage Tony told her when she first asked him why he wanted to be an actor.

'Everyone's an actor,' he had said in his irreverent way. 'Some of us just do more rehearsal.'

She knows this is true. It has got her through years cutting the same people's hair. Enduring constant re–runs of worn out conversation.

What she still finds impossible to prepare for though, is the way she feels around her girls. It is a kind of jealousy. Not simply for their easy beauty – lustrous skin, firm breasts, youthful energy –

119

but because leaving the Bay was so matter—of—fact for them. A decision made without marathon, torturous dissection. Simply an organisational hurdle. A banal and expected relocation. As if any other option were ever realistically possible.

Thirty years ago it had not seemed so simple to her. It was not that there was no precedent; young people routinely abandoned the country for the real or imagined excitements of elsewhere. Rather, she simply could *not* picture herself living another life. She had thrown down roots. Formed habits. Populated dreams. She was clinging to her patch of ground because she knew it would always provide. And anyway, who was she to pit herself against the fast and fierce competition of the metropolis? Maybe she just wasn't good enough.

In the last couple of weeks she has arrived at the view that the stand—offish nature of her relationship with Tony's mother somehow sprang from this. For Gianna, she was a mirror, and for her, the older woman was a warning. Neither quite liked what they saw.

Therefore, it is her daughters' casual freedom that irks her. That sometimes makes her say bitchy things. Pick pointless fights.

Lingering in the shower, she wills herself to let it go. To behave. Because the girls will be here in an hour and none of this is their fault.

Christa wants to ask Madison and Daria why they drive down separately. Is this something city people do? she ponders. Are the close quarters they live in, boxes piled on top of one another, driving them to retreat into themselves? To court isolation as a means of avoiding the inevitable conflicts of being squashed so tightly together?

She muses on this as she watches through the blinds as first one, then the other, pull up a minute apart. Both in neat, compact Asian cars, which they park on the Buffalo grass in the big front yard overlooking the arc of the bay. They briefly confer in the metallic glare of a low slung sun, unload their expensive looking bags, and walk up to the front deck together. Christa smiles to herself when she notices, that for all their city savvy, they carry their father's athletic genes. His strong but heavy–footed directness. The surety of his movements.

Something about this reassures her.

Then there is the sound of their voices at the open door. The word *Muuum* bouncing around the house after so long. Sneakered footsteps on the tiles. She catches the scent of their perfume and the deeper smell beneath. Like milk and blood. The river they all swim in. Even though she knew she would be triggered by their arrival, the power of these details remains direct and instant. Tears rise. Breath catches. Words don't come out right.

Since they left home, Christa has been unable to maintain her tough–skinned bluff around them. The one she still uses so successfully on others. On herself. The very method she taught them as they were growing up. Thus, after the first flush of togetherness wears off, they will fall, as they always do, into lecturing her. Diagnosing her. Then, when they leave in a few days, they will feel exasperated by what they consider to be their mother's intransigence. But for now, all that is over the horizon; and all three of them know it.

Because, in a few minutes — after the girls have unpacked — they will make their way down to Catchers' (in one car) for a couple of drinks and a few pokies. There they will encounter old friends and familiar faces, and for a few short hours the worlds of the guilt–wracked mother and her adult daughters will not seem so far apart.

Christmas, combined with a slightly early conclusion to the harvest, sees the pub full. Townsfolk mingle with suntanned seasonal workers and well–heeled tourists. A bad cover band butchers nostalgic favourites in the front bar, whilst seniors and city folk consume over–priced, aqua–farmed barramundi in the saloon, and the fairground jingle of poker machines spreads out across two large rooms at the back. It is officially high season in Bravery Bay and the Catchers' Inn is at its busiest.

To locals like the Bell girls, tonight's crowd represents both the past and the future of the town – yet, more tellingly, the throng reveals something about the passage of their own lives. This is not the redneck Catchers' that Christa first entered with Tony back in the late 1980s, nor is it quite the bar at which Madison and Daria kissed older boys and got illegally drunk as high school seniors. Indeed, even for the younger women, the inexorable hand of time is evident this evening.

For their mother, it is more obvious than ever. The presence of her babies as grown women, as people she no longer knows like the back of her hand, brings this crashing to the fore.

One minute you have hope, you believe, the next you have memory, and you don't know what to think.

And yet, here she is at the Catchers' again – a routine as familiar as life. Same on the outside; but not on the in.

Much as she tries to sideline these thoughts, and to concentrate on the festive buzz and the pride she feels whenever people compliment her daughters on their maturity and sophistication, they lurk quietly in her knowing. Lodged. A lash in the corner of an eye. A blink from the beckoning of tears.

This is amplified when Steve turns up unexpectedly, and the four of them find a spot in a corner with a bottle of Kiwi Sav Blanc, a jug of Danish lager and a bucket of rubbery calamari.

It has been fifteen years since Christa and Steve split, and he has re-married; so now they can be together without awkwardness or the need to niggle. In fact, the former spouses now have the perspective to see how similar they have become – although their children would not entirely agree.

Throughout their hour together, Christa takes note of the way her daughters tease them. 'Listen to you two,' the elder Madison says at one point. 'You sound like Ma and Pa Amish.'

Younger sister Daria is quick to join in. 'Even if you just did Facebook,' she jokes, 'you could at least stalk us then.'

What lies behind the good natured ribbing is the girls' notion that she and Steve allowed their disappointment in one another, and their shared lack of self-esteem and fear of the wider world, to negatively affect their offspring. In short, that they were prepared to see their own failings reproduced in their kids. Even to engineer it.

Christa at least is not afraid to acknowledge this. Just not here in the pub. When they are meant to be having a good time.

Quietly though, she is dreading it will be said bluntly by the time the girls get back into their separate cars and drive north to their individual handkerchief apartments to resume their private, modern lives on a multitude of social media platforms she will never hear of.

She is turning this over in her mind when Steve grins goofishly and blurts, 'So, did your mum tell you? Her old flame is back in town. The actor dude.'

Though this is not a secret, nor something she is specifically wanting to avoid, it annoys her that it comes out like this. She knows he is joking, trying to keep the conversation breezy, but it puts a spin on it that she would rather it not have, and she cannot understand why Steve would choose to do this. Whilst he had good reason to be tetchy about Tony back in the marriage days, she is surprised to hear him wheel it out now, years later, and in front of the kids. Big boyish smile notwithstanding.

Before she can suppress the impulse, her eyes have shot darts, which only makes things worse. Now the girls are smirking too.

'Ooh, Mum,' Daria coos. 'Revisiting past glories, hey?'

'Well, not exactly,' she says. 'Barely seen him since he got back. Couple of times, maybe.'

'Ah yeah,' Steve jokes, trying not to make it obvious he has been told off. 'Cosy little dinner at the Vinny's one night, I hear.'

'Yeah, about a week after his mum died,' Christa confirms, still annoyed, but going along.

'Wow, Mum, you're not grave robbing, are you?' Madison chirps.

'Even if I was, which I'm not, I think I'm too old for him now. If I still had my twenty−year−old body maybe … but not with a figure like this.'

Though it does not sit well with her, adding a little extra sauce to the town gossip gives the chided Steve a chance to nudge the topic onto safer ground. 'Ah come on, hon, you're still gorgeous,' he winks, picking up.

She is intending to say something polite but instead, arising unbidden from the depths, a sudden impulse to keep the game alive. 'Ah, so that's why you left me, is it?'

There is a short pause, enough for a heartbeat, and for Steve to decide if he wants to keep playing. 'Wasn't it you that dumped me?' he fires back, his smile a little tighter.

'Now come on, you two,' Madison intercedes. 'Remember? Christmas, family reunion, everyone happy to see one another and all that.'

'Yeah, actually your dad's right,' Christa concedes, taking the get−out. 'It *was* me, now that I think of it.'

'Apparently I wasn't good enough for her,' Steve says with a blokey raising of a glass.

She knows he means it − that it still rankles − but she accepts his backhanded peace offering and chinks. It ends with smiles; but both parties are surprised at how quickly they have bruised, and the girls are embarrassed to have witnessed the unexpected skirmish.

Though the rest of the night passes pleasantly and they agree on the timing for their Christmas evening BBQ, there is a sense that disinterred ghosts are hovering. Waiting for their moment.

It is Christa's last full day at the salon before the Christmas break. The first customer arrives at 7:30 and the final cut and colour won't be finished until after eight this evening. It has been like this every year since she opened. Everyone wants tarting up for the holidays. Though it is tough on the feet and even harder on the patience, it is good for the bank balance. Thus, while Madison and Daria amuse themselves, she counts the money and the hours.

Yet, every now and then, she catches herself in the impeccably polished and deliberately soft lit mirrors, as if noticing something in the periphery of her vision. Tell−tale flashes. While her make−up and her cleverly chosen clothes disguise her age and her exhaustion, she detects in the slope of her shoulders − and sometimes in the set of her jaw — a kind of tightness. A general scrunching up. Her defensive wall expressed in skin and bone; as tense muscles and a slight but noticeable bowing. She tries not to let it get to her, to make a drama of it, but she cannot pretend not to have seen it. Felt it.

She tries to convince herself it is just the presence of her kids, or Steve's clumsy joke, but she is too good an amateur shrink to dismiss it as simply an episode. Having practised her people reading skills for more than a quarter century on customers like the one she is working on now, she has accumulated enough tricks of awareness to make dodging difficult. Especially when uncomfortable connections are made.

However — although her unconscious tendency to doubt herself often magnifies and distorts the meaning of her observations — the plain fact is that today is the first day in years she has found herself genuinely wondering if she can keep doing what she is doing. In her gut, a hard blade of unease not felt since the last months of marriage. All she can do is breathe deep and hope it will pass.

But what if it doesn't? she keeps thinking throughout the long afternoon.

What if I can't do this anymore?

She spends the next day, the twenty—fourth, with her daughters. They sleep in, have coffee and toast for breakfast, and trek lazily down the slope to the beach to wet their toes in the crisp surf, before deciding to indulge in a long lunch at the sleek new café near the marina. It is there she points out the figure of Antonio Timone.

'See that guy,' she says, nodding at the haughty but ageing Italian standing aloof and detached at the take away counter in grubby blacks and baseball cap.

The girls crane their necks. To them, Tony is a middle—aged nothing. Someone they would look right through. Though Daria concedes he is in good shape, the consensus is that the legend of their mother's teenage romance is nothing to shout about. In a few unremarkable seconds all the snarky stories their dad told them, the wistful hints their mother dropped, and the shiny and distant glamour of stage and screen have solidified into a bored looking fart in a queue. All that noise for this.

From her angle though, Christa realises he's in standby mode. Preserving his energy for another kitchen shift. It is, she thinks, the most ordinary he has ever looked. She chuckles to herself, knowing how much he hates ordinary.

Nonetheless, she is affected. Not so much by *him* as by the memory of them as lovers, and what it has come to represent. She watches as he takes his coffee and leaves. Traces him across the adjacent rectangle of lawn, past the memorial where his father's name is carved in granite, and off into the indistinct wash of the day.

> *In her already frazzled state*
> *... the sight of him walking away...*

'You really loved him, didn't you?' Madison asks, her voice softened by the recognition of something in her mother's eyes she has rarely, if ever, seen.

'Apart from you two, I never really loved anyone. Not really.'

'Even Dad?'

'I think you both know your dad and I were never really 'in love'. We got along, we fancied each another, there were no other candidates – you know the sorta thing.'

'Not really a great basis for a marriage, is it?'

'No Daria. It isn't. And wasn't. Obviously.'

'Probably not much choice round here though, hey?'

'That's the country for you,' Christa grins, wry and dry, knowing what comes next.

Madison chimes in. 'Preaching to the converted there, Mum.'

'It's not like you have to stay here,' Daria adds, eyes playing, toying with the grenade. 'Unless of course, Mister Tony is a reason.'

'Well, when he goes back to his real job and his modelling or whatever it is, I'll let you know,' Christa replies. 'He didn't hang around last time, so I can't really see him doing it this time either.'

126

'So like, why the hell is he is still here then? Didn't his mum die, like, months ago?'

'I think he's trying to have an 'artistic' mid−life crisis.' Both girls laugh at this, so she quickly adds, 'What do they call it now? Performance art?'

Eye rolls and snorts of derision follow. 'In Bravery Bay?' Madison says incredulously, spreading her hands out, splaying her fingers, as if to indicate how ridiculous the idea is and, of course, to further underline her and Daria's contention.

'Unlike you two, *some* folks reckon it's a pretty pleasant part of the world down here,' Christa counters. 'Or should I say, it's a good location.'

This burst of maternal sarcasm lightens things a notch; and Madison chips in with, 'Ah yeah, of course, he's a creative, right? He's probably, like, getting inspired or something.'

This stings Christa − for she is perversely protective of Tony, whilst reserving the right to criticise him entirely for herself − but she laughs along anyway, knowing that wise−cracking is the best way to hose down the topic.

Just get through, she is telling herself, as her daughters riff cynically on 'pathetic man' jokes.

When they are done, and feeling suitably superior, it is their mother's turn again. She digs a fork into her Thai chicken salad, twists it, and smiles up at her sassy young daughters. 'God help the poor buggers who ever marry you two,' she quips acidly, more than half meaning it − a fact which neither daughter fails to register.

✂

Christmas Day is clear, blue and dry. It smells grassy. Salty. Corellas and seagulls scrawl in the sky, their noisy, cheerful sounding banter oblivious to human ceremony. For them, it is high summer, the sun baking the land, creating updrafts; whilst the tumbling mix of warm and cool air close to the shore gives them plenty to work with, as they dip and swirl in search of food.

Down below, in a house on an incline with a clear view east across the bay, and south to the cosy huddle of the town, the Bell girls have already exchanged gifts and are now preparing to go down to the nearby beach for a picnic.

This is their favourite Yuletide tradition. They all have pleasantly hazy memories of previous years, of beach cricket and sunbathing and feeding leftovers to birds.

Yet Christmas is also a measure of their disappointment.

> *Of accusation and guilt.*
> *Of fine words hollowed out by ill–tempered actions.*
> *Of intentions not realised – or hastily reconfigured*
> *in conflagration.*
> *Each year making it harder to pretend.*

None of them can entirely escape the memory of Christa and Steve's terse and final festive season. For the parents it is a resilient shame, something they would prefer not to look at. Their children are still wounded by the well–mannered violence of that decisive Christmas. For them, it continues to symbolise something fundamental about their upbringing. Something they have fled to a different universe to try and shake off.

> *Maddy and Daria are frightened. Confused. Mum and*
> *Dad are mad. The girls can hear angry voices from the*
> *other side of the house. Beneath the Christmas tree,*
> *brightly wrapped boxes await. They look at them*
> *forlornly, impatiently, while the diplomatic cooing of*
> *grandparents fails to obscure the sound of disharmony.*
> *When they finally emerge, Mum's red eyes and Dad's*
> *fake smile only make things worse. The girls have no idea*
> *what they have done to deserve this. The adults are*
> *ganging up on them. Even Santa is being difficult. They*
> *tear open presents, but it's no fun. Neither feels like*
> *playing now. Their brand new toys gather in careless*
> *piles. Wrapping paper litters the carpet like storm damage.*
> *The sisters agree, this is the worst Christmas ever.*

As Christa drives them downhill to their preferred patch of coast, she is wondering when the subject will be raised. Since the girls left home it has come up every year.

> *Their Christmas from hell.*
> *The divorce.*
> *Her decision to remain.*
> *Her dismal affairs with unsuitable men.*
> *Burying herself in the business.*
> *Poker machines and cheap white wine.*

Every shitty fucking thing. All of it bad, sad, stupid and selfish.

'Okay, crucify me,' she had spat back at them last year.

And that was before Tony, and the subsequent cracking of her usually sturdy compromise.

This year, it is not the girls' damnation she is most afraid of.

When they arrive at the beach though, she is briefly able to forget. The bay is glistening, a light breeze ruffling, the sand strewn with knots of people. Candy−coloured canvas tents and the laughter of children. Gas BBQs and dogs off the leash. The exfoliating pleasure of sand on her soles.

Together they set up their shade, lay down their chequerboard blanket and extract drinks and nibbles from various Eskys and bags. Here they will linger for a couple of azure hours, swatting away flies, waving and smiling at people, and gossiping. Madison will scroll through her travel plans, Daria will post pictures on Instagram and Christa will confess, after three Chardonnays, that she is flirting with the possibility of selling the salon.

'I might just do private stuff,' she elaborates. 'Maybe set something up at home and do a few visits. Set my own hours and all that. Stop paying rent to Jim Salter.'

The girls are clearly intrigued and impressed, which, in turn, adds impetus to the idea. 'What's brought this on?' Madison asks.

'I'm not sure. Maybe I'm just getting tired. And maybe you two are right, and I *do* need to change things up. I'll be fifty next year, so … perhaps it's my cue.'

'Well, you know my opinion.'

'Mine too,' Daria adds.

'So, be honest with me, Mum. Has any of this got to do with whatshisface being back in town?'

Christa can see the danger in Madison's eyes, so she takes a long and cautious breath. Looks away deliberately. Considers lying. 'Yeah sure,' she eventually tells her. 'It's probably got something to do with it. He would say it's really corny and obvious ... but I guess it *has* made me think.'

'Well, cheers to that,' Madison toasts – and three plastic wine glasses are raised to the notion of change.

The sun is disappearing beneath the tree line by the time Steve arrives – a little tired from festive duties with his new family – for their now ritual Christmas night BBQ on the front deck. Though there has been talk over the years of bringing the two families together it has been resolutely resisted by the second wife and her relatives, and so the nuclear Bells gather alone for another Noel.

Without the now dead grandparents for buffering, it is an event suffused with the fallout of history. But at least the girls are old enough to drink now, and so all four edges are blunted enough to allow for a comfortable proximity. To make it possible to execute the familial function.

Ever since the seams of Steve and Christa's marriage began to come apart, the gap between the idealised Christmas of tinsel and turkey and the imperfect volatilities of blood, desire and frustration has been filled – more often than not – with another annum's worth of blame and deflation. Each of them privately wonders why they bother, yet all four come up with the same answer every time.

Hope. And a nagging sense of duty.

Meanwhile, the lovely fragrant sizzle. Onions, steaks, sausages.

Madison and Daria break their diet rules.
Steve banters, beer in hand, about the
foibles of his new family.
Christa circulates with salads and sauces, and
tells stories of difficult matrons and bikini wax mishaps.

Then, as the light starts to dim, a phone rings in the house. A lollipop melody beneath the music. Christa is alerted – curious – but lets it ring off, and the four Bells eat, drink and try not to drift onto touchy topics. Outside, birds come songfully home, invisible critters trill, and the sky moves slowly through gold, red and pink, before settling like warm mist into star–speckled black.

For a while it looks like they will make it through. All of them able to retire to unvoiced resentments. Their powder still dry. Until Christa gives in and checks her phone.

'Well, guess what,' she announces when she comes back from the loo. 'You know Jake Salter? Jim's boy? He's been kicked out of home. Apparently, he just rocked up at Nonna Timone's old place, asking to stay with Tony.'

And thus, the air between them gets goose bumps, and the wave it triggers spreads out in coruscating shivers.

> *There is talk of Jake and the Salters – his strangeness,*
> *Jim's authoritarian conservatism, the family's fingers*
> *in every worthwhile pie.*

> *Then some re–hashed rumours – Jake and Tony going*
> *down to the marina after work, getting high together.*

> *The old joke about Tony being gay.*
> *Christa's reflexive defence of him.*
> *Steve not quite covering his remnant jealousy in time.*

> *Oh come on, Steve – let it go, will ya?*

Daria is the first to pounce. 'Actually, Mum, maybe *you're* the one who should be letting it go.'

'What do you mean?' Christa reacts, loosened enough to be inviting the storm.

'Seriously?' Madison scoffs, taking the hook. 'Come on, Mum, we've been going on forever about you changing it up and getting out of the Bay and now, as soon as lover boy's back on the scene, you're suddenly thinking, *maybe there is something better after all.*'

Christa winces, knowing what her daughter is referring to, regretting she ever let it slip. 'I think maybe you're reading a bit much into that, Maddy. I don't think it's that simple.'

It is a lame defence and they both know it. 'Well excuse me,' Madison continues, scolding and certain. 'You know how much we wanted to get out of here, that we fucking begged you to get us away from this shitty, sexist, bullshit town, and all you could say was 'but the salon, I've worked so hard'. Funny how your own kids can't convince you but some fucking up−himself actor can.'

'Yeah, and what does *that* tell you?' Daria muscles in, hazel eyes focused with bruised intensity. Slits like scalpels.

'Ah jeez, come on girls,' Steve says, sensing that things are about to get nasty. 'Is this really the time for all this?'

'Oh, and when *would* be the time, Dad?' Madison scythes.

She is sitting forward now, her wine glass set aside, her gym−tight frame coiled. 'Let me guess, the time would be never, right? Because that's the good old Bravery Bay way, isn't it? Don't say anything about anything, unless of course it's fucking moronic gossip.'

'Yeah well, you don't live here, so what are you whingin' about?'

'You can't be serious. Or maybe you just don't give enough of a fuck. Gee, I'm sorry I wasn't a boy, Dad. Must've been *such* a massive disappointment to you.'

'Fucken hell, is that what you really think?'

'Why − are you denying it?'

'Maddy, if you don't reckon I loved you because you were a girl then you're −'

'− U−huh, sure Dad. You loved me alright − but it would've been *sooo* much better if I'd had a cock, wouldn't it?'

Christa is about to step in but Steve is too quick. He is on his feet, wiping his hands on the front of his pants, breathing with deliberate, slow menace. About to remind his eldest daughter where she gets her fight from.

'Y'know something, I don't have to stand around listening to this bullshit,' he begins, his voice deeper and more measured than usual. 'If you want to sit around blaming Chrissy and I for everything that goes wrong with your life, go ahead; but if you can't see we did the best we bloody well could for you girls, then you've got a serious fucken problem, Madison Bell.'

He allows the words to hang, sustained and suspended for a beat or two, before re—training his sights. 'You too, Daria.'

'Yeah, run away, Dad,' Madison fires into his broad back as he makes good his threat, departing the scene with slow and surly ceremony.

Without acknowledging the slight, he simply says, 'I'll call you in a day or so, Chrissy. Shout you a drink or something.'

Although Christa sees that Steve's retreat is an act of stubborn refusal — a measured tantrum, a denial forged in a gentle but nonetheless narrow view of the world — she is also aware that it will contain the wreckage. After all, he has another wife to go home to. The son he always wanted. A black and white life of hard work, good money and plainly spoken truths. Not for Steve the torture of reckoning.

'So I suppose you're going to *defend* him now, aren't you?' Madison pushes again, after his growling ute has rumbled away into the cool, silky night.

'He's really not that bad, you know.'

'Says you, who left him,' Daria notes acerbically.

'If I hadn't left him,' Christa corrects, keeping her voice as level and calm as she can, despite fizzing nerves, 'he would've left me.'

'Is that because you were still in love with this Tony guy?'

'I'm sure it was part of it.'

'Part of it!' Madison snorts. 'Fuck, listen to yourself. It wasn't *part* of it, Mum — it was the fucking *cause* of it. You loved some other guy who dumped you and you never got over it and you went and hooked up with Dad anyway … and then, *hello*, you had a couple of kids hoping it would go away but it still didn't, so you fucking gutted out. And all along you were busy showing Daria and I how to have really screwed up relationships with men. Y'know, making like you could do just fine without them, then dropping everything for them like some ditzy prom queen bitch. And then you have the fucking nerve to snitch at *us* about it.'

'Yeah, and you think it's *sooo* fucking funny too,' Daria adds. '*Oooh, I pity the poor guy who gets with you.* Ha fucking ha, Mum. Way to go.'

It is a savage appraisal, and all Christa can do is sit on her hands, look down at the gaps between the slats of the decking and try to maintain her composure. There is, she knows, a lot she could say, but it occurs to her that there is little point. The temperature is too high. The girls too emboldened by alcohol and the momentum of the evening.

And what use are words against the tide of years?

Yet, because she understands that silence too is ill–advised, she attempts diplomacy. 'I'm sorry you both feel that way,' she breathes.

'You're not our therapist, Mum,' Daria replies, her voice low and hard. 'So say what you really think.'

Christa Marie Bell stays head down for a few moments more, before gathering herself up and looking across at her two twenty–something daughters. In their accusing eyes she sees herself. Her own fury in disguise. Their vitriol, she realises, is her self–loathing. Their reigning confusion is her conflicted view of the world and herself.

Somehow, she finds space to wonder whether she has primed them for just this act: to say to her what she would never have accepted if it had come from her own mouth. Or anyone else's.

Then, a beat later, everything turns to fog and guilt again. To a jumble. Except one thing.

'I never told anyone this before,' she says, 'not even your dad; but when Tony left the Bay, he didn't leave me. I left him. He really wanted me to go with him – but I was too scared. I was the one who said no. *That's* what I've never gotten over. *That's* why I went with your dad and *that's* why I was so happy when I found out I was pregnant. It wasn't that you and your dad were replacements for Tony. You were replacements for me. Not the me that Tony left behind ... but the one he took with him. She's the one I lost. The one I betrayed.'

She is on the cliff of tears. The weight of them, like an ocean pressing against a flimsy barricade, is thrilling. The exhilaration of the tsunami is drawing the air out of her, leaving her empty. Ready for the inundation.

'Yeah, pretty speech, Mum,' Madison grumbles – icy, unmoved. 'But like, what the fuck is it supposed to mean?'

'I don't know,' Christa sighs, standing heavily, puffing out her cheeks.

Now she is exhausted. Flattened. Suddenly too tired for the relief of crying. She blinks. Looks off into the night. And there, from the sable air, she plucks an idea.

'It sounds ridiculous,' she says, with a minute shake of her head and faintest exhalation of laughter, 'but maybe he just brought her back.'

14. The rapture of exiles.

There are few opportunities for Jake to impress his father; and though he cares less and less for Jim's approval, he enjoys the small traces of genuine warmth that flow from his timely technical assistance with the Salter family Christmas production.

For the chain smoking, atheist patriarch, tomorrow is less about good will and more about reasserting notions of clan honour and good bloodlines. It is his seasonal gathering of the extended family under the umbrella of patronage and control.

> *A statement of preferred values.*
> *A means of determining inclusion … and exile.*
> *A reaffirmation of clan hierarchies.*

This is the reason Jim pours so much effort into making a show, putting on a nigh heraldic front. It explains the marquee, the hired fridges, the plentiful food and booze. And the PA, which young Jake has rigged up, to enable speeches and other such ceremonies.

'He's even put up lights and stuff,' Jim tells his eldest boy Rob on the phone. 'Some of you youngies might fancy a bit of a boogie later on. Might even have a bit of a turn meself.'

Sitting across the expansive dinner table, beer in hand, Jake maintains his strategic smile. Or rather, tries to mask the feeling behind it. He hopes it projects manly, filial affection, whereas in fact what he feels is little short of outright contempt. He knows that all he has purchased is a brief peace — a rare 'after work' drink. His father was impressed by his display of know—how and masculine efficiency, but Jake is not fooled by Jim's blustery act of mateship.

As his mother finishes serving up the few small dishes that will comprise their quiet Christmas Eve supper, he allows himself to enjoy the temporary respite.

Tomorrow will be a rigorous examination of his resolve.

Brothers, uncles, cousins and others.

Questions and assumptions, but most of all judgement.

While he waits with the quietly deferential Shelley for Jim to wind up his call, he remembers something Tony said to him earlier in the day. 'Be aware that you're doing exactly the same thing to them.'

At first, it was hard to hear but he has accepted the truth of it now.

Presently, he is assuring himself that in ten weeks time, twelve thousand miles away, he will find the distance to see this more clearly, and to consider the ways in which he might change his behaviour. Tomorrow however, his act – and the judgement it implies – will be his shield. For just as his parents will play the part of king and queen for the consumption of the Salter tribe, so too he will perform the role of aloof and difficult prince. The cynosure of all their doubts.

'The one thing I really learned from acting,' Tony had told him, 'was that if *I* believed it so would the audience. Trouble is, it worked much better in real life than it ever did on film. Not so good for my career, but pretty handy all told.'

The point is not lost on Jake. Indeed, it suits his disposition. Helps him stay clear about the task at hand.

> *Don't bite.*
> *Survive intact.*
> *Get on that plane.*
> *Worry about the other side of the world*
> *when you get there.*

His father hangs up and beams at his wife and youngest son. At the head of table, in his refurbished castle, he is Caesar; and all shall render unto him once more. In his tobacco stained, liver spotted pomp he feels proud and very nearly invulnerable. On this occasion, he hopes, he will have neither time nor reason to dwell upon the other Christmas – when he was closer to Jake's age – and men's bodies were being fished out of the bay.

It is late. Jake has had five beers and a sneaky joint. Yet his fingers fall like raindrops. The melody is emerging, a ribbon of jewels trailed across the bubbling surface of the street sounds he recorded the previous night. There is a distance between the simplicity of the repeated phrase and the warm, muffled wash of revelling voices, half heard songs and passing cars. It is a space imbued with melancholy and longing, with compassion and loneliness. With the universal ache.

> *The separation anxiety of I from Other.*
> *The fundamental incompleteness of self.*

This year, he is sure. When he plays it tomorrow it will have an effect. It is less abstract. Some of them might even like it. But it's not that. Rather, it's the beautiful impossibility it points at. Implacable realities that no amount of anger or sorrow or wishful conjuring will alter. He knows that no one will understand it in such explicit terms, yet he suspects part of it will be communicated.

He stops. I could just not do this, he thinks. Just play them something weird they'll never understand. Though this is an option – one he is yet to fully discount – he knows it won't happen. He will try to please them. He will try to smile at the right times. Not be too haughty.

Survive.

It is impossible for Jake to avoid scrutiny on Christmas Day. He is an anomaly amongst robust, broad shouldered and sandy coloured Anglo–Celtic men. A single slender sybarite amidst a crowd of calloused and pragmatic peasants. Against the steadfast canvas of his brothers, he appears especially wanton. Useless.

> *What good's a skinny ponce with fancy talk*
> *gonna do yer?*
> *Nah, Rob and Scotty are the go.*
> *They'll keep the show on the road*
> *when the old bloke carcs.*

He tries to blunt the edge of it by putting his hospitality skills to good use, helping Jim to burn steaks and snags on the big black iron barbie outside, and Shelley to run salads and sides from the main kitchen. In between, whenever he feels he can get away with it, he steals into his room and stands with his back to the locked door, grinding his teeth, slowing his breath and shaking his head in disbelief. He is craving marijuana to put a softening smudge between him and them – but he knows the chances of getting caught are too high and the penalty too much trouble.

Inevitably though, there are confrontations. The alcohol, the hot fly–blown easterly, and the prevailing idea of what a good Salter man should be, have all combined to get the royal family jabbering.

'Mum reckons you aced your exams,' Rob starts off.

Jake had predicted that his 'top five percent' score would likely cause problems once the news got out. Only certain kinds of success are celebrated in a dynasty like this. His mother should have known better than to tell everyone. 'Ah, I just got lucky I reckon,' he deflects with a calculated shrug.

'No way, Jakey,' Rob chortles, prodding him in the ribs. 'You're a little swatter, aren't you? Always got your snout in some bloody book.'

'Or up a teacher's arse,' chirps one of the freckled, dairy farming cousins from a little further down the coast.

'As opposed to up a cow's, you mean?' Jake banters – which makes his brother laugh and slap him across the shoulders; half pissed already.

The cousin chuckles but is less amused. 'I suppose that's it then, eh?' he digs. 'You're going to take your good grades and nick off somewhere? Leave the boys to do all the hard yards?'

Resisting temptation, Jake allows himself a few moments to find a neutral tone. 'Not sure yet,' he says, trying to yield as little ammunition as possible. 'Going to travel a bit first. Then we'll see what gives.'

Scanning the cousin for signs, Jake senses that his non–committal response has done little to dampen the appetite for contest.

For all of Jim Salter's unity talk, the Christmas gathering invariably descends into factional bickering, each year differentiated only by the severity and openness of the squabble. It is apparent to most that the primary reasons for maintaining the festive show of allegiance are money and prestige. To be able to trade on a pioneer lineage stretching back to the 1870s is worth the cost of an occasional blood feud.

However, since the age of twelve Jake has been providing the easiest available outlet for their collective rancour. The entire clan is united in its agrarian disapproval, and because he lacks the physical strength or martial desire to back himself with violence, he is fair game. The ultimate source of authority and respect for the Salter male remains rooted in the solidity of his hands. In his sinews and his sweat. In his willingness to lose and to draw a little claret along the way. It is the same ruthless, Darwinian standard they apply to the cattle they own; and Jake is no prize bull.

In lieu of fists, he has been training himself to subvert persecution and turn it into sport. To channel his hurt and anger into chilled, intellectual defiance. Having realised that this behaviour both confirms and amplifies tribal suspicion, he has opted instead to use it as a form of taunt. For he still has a righteous, teenage lust for vengeance, an adolescent yearning for validation; if not through acceptance, then by repudiation.

'Either way,' he glints at his milking shed cousin with superior relish, 'I'm looking forward to spending Christmas elsewhere next year. Maybe somewhere with less flies.'

As the afternoon progresses and the heat sits thicker on the dry land, the Salter clan work their way through copious helpings of barbecued meat, slabs of lager and numerous bottles of cheap, sweet bubbles. Tissue paper hats and broken crackers are strewn, and shoes are kicked off under tables. Buttons are undone. Ashtrays overflow. Children shriek and fight and fall over. Women clutter in high pitched gaggles to dispense shrill damnation, and men form loud scrums to tell yarns and lies and set the world to rights.

Meanwhile, the dogs are loving it. Scraps and pats aplenty.

Eventually, when the sting goes out of the sun and everyone is sufficiently loose, Jim grabs a microphone and starts the traditional group singing of carols, before reeling off his annual speech and giving both Rob and Scott – his anointed heirs – the chance to 'say a few words.'

Whatever the rivalries of the day have been, this is Jim's way of bringing everyone back together. Of reminding them where the source of their wealth and power lies. Most years it works. Today is no exception.

The stage, therefore, is literally and figuratively set for Jake.

For the first time he can recall, his father is praising him publicly, thanking him for setting up the PA and the lights, suggesting everyone take advantage of the fact and have 'a bit of whirl' to work off the grog.

'Also,' he slurs, 'I reckon he's going to play us one of his tunes.'

To the perceptible groan, he responds, 'Apparently this time it actually has a proper tune. Least that's what the little bugger tells me.'

Amidst laughter, drunken applause and furrowed apprehension, Jake hooks in his keyboard and laptop. As he fiddles with leads, he pretends to be embarrassed – but really, he is savouring their distaste.

'Okay,' he tells them when he is ready. 'I know I've hit you with some pretty weird shit the last couple of Christmases but this year I'm going to try something more …'

The word catches; suspended in his throat.

A note of silence chimes in the cooling breath of evening. There is a flutter of panic in Jake's chest. Like the sound of wings beating around his head. Disoriented for a beat, he wonders if he has the guts.

'Romantic,' he says finally, in such a way that no one can be left in any doubt.

Now there is no shying away. Vapours have coalesced into rain.

Jake closes his eyes, exhales. He can hear his heart pounding, like a muffled drum. He senses a murmur from the crowd; something less than a whisper. Like a portent.

Sitting back in her plastic chair, Shelley Salter's heart bursts. For the arrival of love and the onset of storms.

She sees in an instant that coded looks are being passed between her husband and her eldest sons. Suspicions now confirmed. The trigger for action pulled. It will not be long now.

Shelley takes another drink to steel herself.

Up in the spotlight, Jake buys time, adjusting levels, clicking buttons. When he looks up, his father's eyes are staring hard.

The vespertine air shivers, disturbed by the movement of feathers. Everything is ready.

Jake's index finger hovers. He counts a four in his head and...

Now!

It is a curious scene. A marquee of overfed, intoxicated farmers and their children, reddened by Yuletide excess, gazing at the stranger amongst them. A black-haired slip of a boy. Head down, swaying like a sapling in the lightest of airs, lips slightly parted, moving in a trance. As though unaware of their presence.

And all the while ... a repetitive, circular melody. Like fog on the bay. Hovering. Sensuous.

As if urged by gleeful and fatalistic sirens, Jake performs with untethered intensity. Without the usual barricades. Bloodied and passionate. This is not expressed in volume, nor even in tempo, but rather in the spaces between the notes. For in restraint, abandon. In silence, desire caterwauling.

He brings it to a climax not by addition but by allowing it to dissipate. Until at last all that can be heard is the pre-recorded sound of a summer night, a humid froth of somewhere, sometime. Now lingering like memory.

There is an intake of breath, a droplet of hush.

Then applause.

Unlike previous years, they mean it. Or at least some of them do. Mainly the women. Enough for Jake to sense the difference. Not so much to take heart or feel validated, but to know for sure that he himself has changed.

When he looks over at his parents though, he becomes immediately certain of something else. His mother is holding back tears, his father grimacing, trying his best to smother it with a loud, matey grin. Nearby, his brothers join in the applause but avert their gaze. It is a small town, after all. There is no way he could expect to keep it quiet.

Jake tries to get eye contact. Confirmation. In his synapses, regret and triumph fizz in electric contest, swooshing around one another, vying for the helm. A voice bawls in his head. *Just fucking say it!*

His father is striding up to the microphone now. Clearing his throat. He is about to thank his youngest for the wonderful performance. As he is about to speak, he looks across to his teenage son and shakes his head.

'At least it sounded like actual music this year, eh folks?' he jokes, trying to smother any telltale signs.

While laughter and applause bubble up, he wanders over to Jake, as though in acknowledgement. He places a ruddy hand on his shoulder. He digs his fingers in, presses down, as if wanting to drive his troublesome child into the ground. Make him disappear.

Resisting, Jake stands, grabs his father's hand and holds it aloft. Together, they strike the pose of triumph – but Jim can only bear it for a beat, before snatching his hand away, as if repulsed. It is a reflex many in the marquee note. Jake senses this and, provocatively, blows them a kiss.

Jim Salter's fists clench.

Instantly unclench.

Too late. Jake and others have seen it; and Jim knows he is cornered. Yet, beneath the booze–fired fury Jake detects a subsonic hurt. Caesar is wounded. Another dagger red. *Et tu?*

Before long, someone, probably Shelley, will need to mop up the blood.

The son holds his father's gaze for as long as either can bear. In this, both the distance between them and the ground they share is nakedly revealed. Everything that needs saying is said. No more need for the testosterone spectacle of war.

Jake Salter takes slow and particular care moving his keyboard and computer back to his room. Indeed, he takes time to make sure things are perfectly in place. Only then does he begin to pack.

He is aware that in his absence earnest and frightened conversations will take place. Jim, Rob and Scott will come to a decision. Shelley will argue and this, in turn, will nudge the men towards a softer position. In the first instance they will likely offer exile, if only to protect the tough, hard−working Salter brand from the tittle−tattling locals. They might even frame it as a form of punishment. He will let them.

In the meantime, he waits until the sound of the pop radio playlist gets loud enough and he can hear the pissed ruckus rising in volume. When it feels safe, he exits beneath the cover of this distraction, locking his door with a firm proprietary clunk and making his way out across the wide front verandah and down to where his motorbike stands in the goldening twilight.

Only Shelley Salter notices the beam of white incandescent light as it moves against the screen of straight backed pines. Unlike Jake, she is not so sure things will work out.

'Has the little faggot gone?' her husband snarls at her.

'About fifteen minutes ago,' she confirms.

'Right – well the sooner we get him on that plane the better.'

Shelley agrees. She knows Jake will too – Tony Timone notwithstanding – because he is smarter and stronger than his father. She only hopes that he does not put two and two together. Does not thereafter use the arithmetic to drive the knife once more into the belly of Caesar's shame, to unleash the civil war she is sure would bring the empire down.

At least, not while he remains on *this* side of the planet.

15. A year in the fire of time.

A year ago he was living in the city. On the third floor of a pre—War apartment block, in the same medium sized one bedder he had occupied since his early thirties. With ceiling rosettes and scratched floorboards, pedestal fans and oil heaters, ultra—fast broadband and smart TV. Downstairs, tram stops and 24/7 convenience stores, with his regular espresso haunt nearby and a camp hairdresser with fat white hands who assured him his bald spot was not that obvious.

Elsewhere, his agent had closed a lucrative deal with a men's grooming brand for a sustained, multi—platform, national campaign and his mum had seemed fine. He was secure in his job and philosophical about the creepings of age. The aching bones and stubbornly sore lower back had struck him as normal and manageable. Even his occasional bouts of ennui and despair — an oceanic loneliness and loss of faith that threatened to undermine his long standing motivation and ethic of perseverance — remained in functional perspective.

For the New Year would dawn with the sweetness of a taut young Indian lover. The tan coloured velvet of her form. Her white eyes. Black hair. Her desire.

And his.

This New Year's Eve however, there will be no such sex. Instead, he will sweat it out in a commercial kitchen, helping bad—tempered chefs to send out the kinds of meals his mother used to prepare — when he lived under her widow's roof and slept in the narrow bed that she had struggled to put together from unclear instructions. In which he subsequently dreamt up whole worlds. Entire futures without her.

Sensing this, hoping it was so, his mama had lovingly poured him watered down coffee from the same charcoaled pot he is using now, and she had sat beside him in vinyl covered chairs while he prattled like the dappling light, with all the effervescent hopes of spring. Before the burden of awareness.

She looks at the appointment book. Some local names, some she assumes are tourists, and others she imagines will be getting lucky – the ones booked in for bikini lines and Brazilians. This prompts her to smirk at herself in the mirror. And feel just a little jealous. Her own bush will require no such pruning today, nor indeed at any time in the foreseeable future.

Though she has been invited to a couple of gatherings tonight – politely tipsy, family affairs and rowdier tables of twenty at the pub – she prefers to spend the New Year alone. She can drink all she wants that way. Maybe she will stagger down to the beach to watch the fireworks or perhaps linger in the house vacated by her husband and daughters with the music up loud and the vibrator charged. She can scream it all out then. Start again. Next year. From scratch.

All the arrangements have been made. The kids will go to Nanna's, the kitchen will close at eight, and he and his wife will join a few of their old friends on a boat. They will anchor out near the heads in a sheltered section of the bay, safe from intermingling currents and frothing breakers. They will snort speed and coke like they were eighteen and get loose for a few hours. There will be touching and fucking and squinting at the sunrise with sore heads.

While he shaves away ruddy stubble, he listens to the bird—like song of little angels coming from the loungeroom.

Since his friend and mentor died a few months back, he has found the innocence of his girls almost too much to bear. It is starkly at odds with what he knows. What he fears.

He thinks again of the diminutive Italian zia, of how she took him in and loved him in a way his own parents seemed incapable of. How did she manage this? Why, after everything that happened to her, did she open her house to a six—year—old waif from across the street?

If only he knew how to fill his own terrible absences with such generosity, he is sure he could be a better father.

The slight young man with the deep eyes and full mouth wakes up exhausted in the musty double bed of an old woman whose freshly deceased body he himself had discovered one Saturday on the front porch – but it isn't *this* that spooks him. Nor the ghouls of her dead stare or the feel of her cold, heavy flesh; but the hissing, spitting memory of more recent voices.

His. Theirs. All the cruel things they have said. Playing over and over in his dreams. Truths and exaggerations that will prove difficult to back away from. Promises and threats that will surely require action.

The Rubicon is crossed. Civil war declared.

For the first thirty seconds after waking he feels sick … until he recalls the exultation.

He is free.

It is a light headed, Spartan liberty, at polar odds with the luxuriously appointed captivity he rode away from last week; smoky ribbons of dust trailing behind the bike.

Perhaps they really will repossess his equipment. Hold his books to ransom. Deny him the things that until now he has relied upon for sanity and sanctuary. He is even prepared to countenance the possibility of a beating. Or disinheritance. Because he knows that pride is their pivotal weakness, and that their blunt force will ultimately render his precise incisions all the more effective.

His father and brothers are yet to work this out – but his mother has. Nothing obvious was said on the phone last night, but the icy, ominous slowness of his Pinteresque pauses made it clear. Now she will bat even more doggedly for him. For the few things of value still left to her. Things that mere distance will not allow her to replace.

The wife of the small town alpha bites her nails, while her husband smokes sullenly and scowls at the burnt brown land. She suspects he is watching out for ghosts. For nearly forty years she has been wedded to his guilt – yet the ring on her finger is as much a band of shame as his. Her three boys, all born of compromise, are the only reason she remains.

Now, even this excuse is wearing thin.

She monitors her ruminant husband in the corner of her vision and is reminded once again that she had always known something wasn't right with him. Even before they kissed, she sensed it. His fixations. His tendency to explode. The things he would not talk about.

But there was the lustre of the name. The big house on the crest of the hill and all the money she could ever want. It had seemed like such a big win for the plain looking daughter of an unemployed fisherman, the one the other girls teased for her hand–me–down dresses and scuffed up shoes.

Since then, she has longed for an escape from victory, seeking refuge in shopping, sedatives and other slow forms of suicide. Although the self–help books and counselling sessions she keeps hidden from the menfolk have given her perspective, she remains mutely terrified. So used to silence that she feels unable to breathe a single syllable in defence of the tacit pact that has kept her family from retributive destruction.

Now she will resign herself to the sound of ruptures.

Or to even more unbearable bargains.

It is another sparkling blue day down by the water. The beach is full of schoolkids and other holidaymakers. The bay bobbles with the colourful geometry of hull and sail cloth, and the town is thick with the knot and slither of human flow. People doing lunch. Buying booze. Getting waxed for the festivities. The normally sedate side streets are lined with cars, a high sun dazzling off windscreens, as trussed up police, sweating and surly in bullying blue, strut with side–armed assurance amongst high season crowds.

The air is crisp with sea salt, pierced with avian chatter. Leaves whisper beneath the din. Flies dart and settle, flit again into space. Dogs sleep in cool corners. Talk radio plays in the kitchens of old folks. Sugary drinks fizz on cubes of ice, rattling in glasses. Screen doors let light breezes into otherwise shuttered houses. Ocean waves splinter and broil on the tricky run in to the bay, broken on sub—surface jags.

Above it all, a white star watches — from a distance that might as well be infinity; everything reduced to an atomic unity by its even handed dispassion. For what is a year in the fire of time?

At Via Amore, things are already moving at an intense pitch. The staff work round each other with routine but hurried efficiency, as tables fill and re—fill, and the docket rail runs consistently eight or nine deep.

Nearby, at Equinox, the insect click of scissors and the electric whine of dryers compete with the steady chug of background music and the trill of women. The smells of dye and perfume mingle with the fruity, bubble gum sweetness of shampoo and the damp, earthy bass of sweat and skin.

As the harried and hectic afternoon grinds on...

> *Tony's back and feet start to ache.*
> *Jake rehearses confrontations in his head.*
> *Vin finds quiet moments to feel both the*
> *absence and the presence of Gianna Sofia.*
> *Christa catches her breath between clients,*
> *imagines the pleasure of the first drink.*

They are all sneaking peaks at the clock. It has been a big year for each of them.

Not long now until they can cross the arbitrarily drawn line in time. Its meaning, they realise, is entirely symbolic, yet all are content to accept the fiat of calendars, if only because it permits a kind of breath. Even a tiny distance, measured in seconds, can be enough.

Meanwhile, Shelley Salter is at home in her expensive new kitchen preparing dinner for what remains of her family, certain that a mere tick of a clock will do nothing to save her.

Across the flat back of a desert continent, past the developing monsoon trough, north of the equator on the opposite shore of a rolling ocean, a young woman named Aneetha Jharavindra is sitting in the morning sun on her parents' balcony deciding what she must do. She thinks of her Australian lover – the one her Indian family know nothing of – quite differently now. Regards his seduction through a less romantic prism.

Did he really see her like no other, or was he just playing the part of the attentive, empathic lover?

And the way he desired her – was it really *her* he wanted or, rather, the conquest and vanity of the older man with the younger, less questioning woman?

How things have changed since last year – when she loved him and he called every day. When he turned down a dozen others to spend the night with her. Just her.

Now the phone is quiet. Inbox empty. Weeks have gone by.

At midnight, if she has still heard nothing, the decision will be made. As much by time and silence as by outrage and hurt. As much by him as her.

Tony isn't convinced the party is a good idea, but Hank, Clarice and even old man Kel will be there, along with most of the town's hospo crew. Mainly young. Students, travellers, kids on the run from one thing or another. Cute looking creatures with far too much energy for a man with a tired, sagging body and a head crammed with unknowns and disquiet.

However, Jake has assured him – the rooftop terrace is worth it. Great view of the bay and the fireworks. 'Let's just get high and go for a couple of hours,' he suggests. 'And hey, so what if people see us together.'

Despite his companion's understandable preoccupation, the drama of Jake's family is not the prime motivation for Tony preferring to be alone. He wants to be alone because it is less lonely. Yet he realises his young friend needs support – perhaps even calming guidance – and he knows that *he* is best placed to provide it. Bravery Bay has already stuck its prurient nose into his own manhood and judged him wanting, sent him packing, so he feels that to abandon Jake right now would be to betray himself. To join the snitching, bitching name calling chorus.

Therefore, he will overcome his tiredness and risk the isolating crush of crowds to make it clear to anyone who is watching that he will never slink in the eyeline of casual, groupthink cruelty. Tony is not an especially political man, nor given to the fetish of causes, but this determination is cooked into his blood.

Also, it will briefly distract him from the ongoing and enveloping miasma of mothers and erstwhile lovers, and from the vast and beautiful background he is beginning to recognise as the central nothing by which everything else is finally understood.

He is acutely aware that his recent musings have come at a cost to his mood and sleep and sociability, and that a night of foreground noise will help to ease the ledger back towards some—thing like balance.

When he arrives shortly after eleven, fresh off the back of a shower and two joints, he enters the space with his charm face on. The one he used for three decades of auditions, wrap parties and tute groups. For producers, sex partners and students alike. The cool, worldly guy, using the genetic fortune of good looks to his advantage. The act he himself can no longer believe.

I used to be such an unconscious butterfly, he is thinking, as he warms into his routine, high—fiving with waitstaff, barstaff and baristas. Now I feel more like a bird in a cage. Everything is so *deliberate.*

And yet, the instant he lays eyes on the bright and beaming Rosie Donald, instinctive impulses emerge. A tide of gush, a smile that won't hide, and a node of longing that reduces years to moments. Words to breath.

Without the props of coffee machine and small change between them, they stand closer. In this proximity, despite the spectating of others, he gets a greater sense of her.

Small gestures.
Her manner of smoking.
Her tom boy grin.
Spaghetti string bra strap.
Collarbone.
The very physical fact of her.

Of course he wants to touch her. Adore her.

She lets him kiss her cheek, touch her arm. She puts her left hand flat on his chest. He feels her fingers through his shirt.

All other distinctions are destroyed. Only that which he has always wanted remains delineated. The primal and powerfully present love which only ever seems to hover in the abstract distance. Within the sight of desire, yet beyond the realm of limbs.

Rosie doesn't know it, but he is tearing himself apart in front of her. She thinks he is a likeable eccentric, an old flirt with the gift of the gab and a kindly disposition. She can tell he fancies her and is not opposed to the idea of him looking. She will even allow him to kiss her on the mouth when the fireworks burst. But just once.

He knows this. Does not permit himself a more detailed fantasy. She will only consume his admiration because he is fool enough to offer it. She will dip her toes awhile in the sea of his tenderness because she misses her father's paternal affection, and Tony's is the nearest viable replacement.

When the boyfriend arrives at her side — a tall, scruffy, tanned skater kid with smart sparkling eyes and a sexy, invulnerable smile — there is a savage underlining. The tearing sound of decades. Brute evolutionary mechanics.

The shape of Rosie's lips when she looks up at him.
His arm around her, hand on the curve of her waist.

Tony thinks of a nineteen—year—old boy enjoying his last summer in the Bay before the autumn of the world. Of parties just like this, and a girl not unlike Rosie.

Detaching from the barista and her gangly boy, he circulates. Aside from Kel, he is the oldest. Hospitality is a young person's game and rooftop piss—ups are not the usual haunt of balding has—beens. He tries to act naturally but remains sharply aware of how false he feels. Of what an effort it is to approximate acceptability.

For the last few minutes of the year he leans against the polished metal railings and shares a quiet joint with Jake as he looks across the panorama of the town and the bay and lets the thrum of the night well up and transport him.

Into the future.

To an appointment with a woman who used to smile like Rosie … and a pair of clippers.

Christa never made it to midnight. She is sleeping on the lounge fully clothed. A now warm glass of Semillon Sav Blanc sits patiently on a coaster nearby. The lights are off and the house is quiet, save for the rumble of the town and a sorbet of white noise from waves on rocks. Her phone shows one missed call. When she wakes to discover this, she will hope it is Tony and be disappointed to find a voice message from Steve.

'Hey darl, hope you're not still too upset about all that shit with the kids to be having a great New Year's. I'll be swinging by Catchers' sometime after the fireworks if you're down there. I'll buy you that drink I promised you. If not, I'll see you next year.'

On a rented boat anchored in the bay, almost due west of the sleeping Christa, and in the eyeline of Tony and Jake, Vin Carlyle is trying hard to forget everything for a few blurred hours.

Lines have been snorted. Shots consumed. Shambolic dancing has occurred. Women have taken their tops off.

Overhead, fireworks sizzle and crack. Patterns of light fan out and cheers rise in the warmth of the night. Soft, inebriated lips press against his. He can feel the weight of tits in his hand. The heat of repressed flesh. He is so horny he could cry. As though he will die if he does not soon explode.

Like Tony, Jake is ready to leave the party early. He has done the rounds, shown face, nodded along. Now he wants to sit quietly, savour a night cap spliff and dream about airports.

Together, they exit without ceremony. No last drinks, no goodbyes. Evaporating into January. Unnoticed.

They do not bother waiting for the lift, choosing instead to funnel down the fire escape stairs and out into the narrow lane behind the building, where piss pools and empty bottles have gathered over the course of the night. They spark up a smoke and begin a slow uphill amble home. As they pass revellers they play along with the cheer, but otherwise move in processional relief, both glad to be away from everything.

That is, until Tony notices the car parked outside the house – a figure sitting in the dark.

He nudges his smoking buddy, who takes a beat or two to recognise what is about to happen.

He hands the burning joint to Tony. 'Don't let her smell it,' he cautions.

Forty–seven metres further on, the headlights of a polished silver–grey Korean car wink at them. Instinctively they stop.

Tony pulls in a big toke while they wait for the driver's door to open and for Shelley Salter to emerge. As he exhales the plume upwards, he notices the tension in her body. The shape of her exhaustion. When she draws near, he sees the look in her eyes. A mix of love and fury. Impotence and determination. Collusion and chastisement.

'Yeah, what is it, Mum?' Jake grunts as she comes to a stop, and Tony detects notes of petulance. Impatience. Scorn.

'Nothing really, Jakey,' she sighs. 'It's just that your dad's asleep and your brothers have gone home and I thought … maybe I might find you here.'

'You're not stalking me, are you?'

'If trying to help you is stalking, yes.'

She digs into a pocket. Extracts a single key on a slender ring. 'They changed the lock on your door,' she reports. 'But Jim thinks he's got the only copy. I'll call you when it's safe to come over.'

'And how will you know if I'm available?' Jake pushes.

'You're not in Europe yet, Jakey. People talk in this town.'

She glances over at Tony, narrows her eyes and adds, 'I'm sure *you* know that better than anyone.'

'I also know you can't stop them,' he replies calmly. 'Not even by hiding. Or leaving.'

'I'm only trying to make this as easy as possible for everyone – yes, Jake, including for myself – so if you could just help me out here, Mr Timone, I would really appreciate it. And so will this one. Eventually.'

With this, she holds up the key and Jake steps forward. As soon as they are close, they fold into a tight embrace. Watching on, Tony is awash.

> *Shelley's limitless, maternal love.*
> *Her whispered, pragmatic resistance.*
> *The way she avoids the pose of*
> *either victim or heroine.*

He is not merely impressed but moved. Humbled. It is a grace he himself would like to attain.

As mother and son disentangle, Jake's tears are visible. A glistening, salty film. He holds his elegant, musical hands up to his face and wipes them away. He looks at his tired and enduring mother as if she were a bringer of miracles. It has been years since anybody saw how deeply he felt. Since he himself experienced it like this – abrupt and public.

Although he quickly re–establishes his controlled cool, sucking in gulped breaths to try and right his balance, he nonetheless takes note of the disturbance. Another in a string of recent changes.

Meanwhile, in his palm, a slender promise. A means. He stares down at it while his composure returns.

With one hand still on his shoulder, her fingers still brushing his hair back behind his ears, Shelley calmly asks, 'They're thinking maybe to bring your flight forward. Would that be okay with you?'

A few weeks ago this would have filled him with unambiguous relief. Now there will be a new kind of sadness to add to his existing uncertainties. For his heart has found reasons to remain.

Shelley is not blind to this. She shoots a quick glance across at the older man and he indicates his approval with the tiniest nod.

'Yeah, sure,' Jake breathes, looking first at Tony and then back to her.

'Yep, sooner the better.'

Another summer

16. The consolations of abandonment.

From the distance of forever, an ocean is barely a drop, whilst in the proximity of love the flutter of an eyelid is an eternity.

For thirty years Gianna Sofia Timone looked across the space between her house on the hill and the disembodied places her son spoke of during phone calls – between her care and his other life – and it always seemed unbridgeable. Although, on occasion, she was wont to water the gathered dust of memory with her pent up sorrow, mostly she understood the clean necessity of barren terrain. The glinting beauty of exile. The relentless salvation of time and quiet. Even as she had squinted to make out his face behind the dirty, clouded window of a receding bus, to see his hand waving back at her, she knew it was necessary.

She knew a lot of other things too. Things she rarely spoke of. Secrets not even whispered. Others excluded from the very formation of thought.

People believed this to be a sign of exceptional fortitude. Proof of a down–to–earth, no nonsense approach to life. Gianna was always happy to let them think that, for her tacit under–standing was more than a crude assemblage. More than a cobbled construction of fact and assertion, of fossicked memory and collected revelation. These percolated impressions had formed a kind of coterie. Ideas as invisible companions. The ones who never left. Or forced her out.

It was as if, by keeping them to herself, she would never have to face the prospect of them being abused or diluted. Or sullied by sharing. They would always be wholly hers. Always by her side, as she drank her morning coffee and gazed into the beyond.

Only Tony. Only Tony.

So it was – amidst the scurf of contrary feelings – that she was relieved to see the cumbersome bus lurch around the bend and take him away to the other side of immensity. Leaving betwixt a sea of remainders.

158

✄

It was hot that summer. Dry, dusty and blue. Fly—blown and crow—cawed. Under a scalding orb the town was withering. About to die. Ground down by sun and salt and circumstance.

Fishing boats idle.
'For Lease' signs pasted onto the
windows of empty shops.
The next generation leaving in droves.
The Front Bar propped up by old timers
and boozy recollection.
Streets bleached and quieter than ever.
Places going cheap.

As if in defiant contrast, the weatherboard house was full.

Accidents and outcasts.
Widows and orphans.
The balletic teenage beauty of Antonio and
his cute, buxom girlfriend.
The recent addition of the lost and tender urchin
from a few doors down.
And her.
Mother of strangers.

She fed and watered them all. Enjoyed the company of their youthful noise. The muffled but unmistakable rhythm of adolescent sex, and the high pitched chortle of little boy innocence. She took bittersweet pleasure in their gathering. Was happy to shelter with them beneath her corrugated iron roof.

To squeeze around the secondhand dinner table.
Watch the weird videos Tony brought home.
Listen to his strange music.
Let Christa cut her hair and make her up.
Allow Vinny to fall asleep on her lap.

But when it was just her and Tony there was a quiet pact. As though all that required saying had already been spoken of in the riverine tongue of blood. She could read her story in the well of his gaze. Feel her bruises smarting in the sensual set of his mouth. Witness the theft of her youth in the ebony lustre of his hair. And when he kissed her goodnight – soft lips on upturned cheekbones – she knew that he could taste her resignation. Intuit the nature of her bargain with cruelty and misfortune. With complicity and retribution.

With silence.

It was, therefore, with genetic telepathy that she knew.

He said nothing at first – it was simply a shift in his eyes. A break in the circle of his breath.

Of course, it saddened her; yet she was also relieved. Moreover, pleased. Proud. She had not raised him to stay. Indeed, she herself had not remained grounded for anything less than his eventual flight.

So that he might leave and damn them all with his absence.

She would wear a little loneliness for her measure of this revenge. Cellar their putrefying shame for the thrill of their squirming. Because the power of her stoic quiet was underwritten by their ever–present dread of outburst. Gianna never forgot this.

It was a still Wednesday night and Tony had arrived home from his part time job at the video store with tired, frustrated eyes and a terse mouth. From her lounge chair, she could hear him stomping. The wrench of the fridge door. The scrape of a chair leg.

Sighs.

She gave him a few minutes before wandering into the kitchen to hear it said aloud.

'I reckon I'm going to leave, Mum. I mean it this time.'

She nodded. Smiled. Full of tenderness.

'I'll just work the summer, save up some cash and then...' He looked down. Blinked away the beginning of tears. 'This place is fucked,' he hissed. 'Just fucked.'

He had been mouthing the same bile for a couple of years — always on the brink of adamant departure. Ever more impatient with the claustrophobic cram of the Bay and its narrow, fearful inhabitants. Cousin–fucking, redneck morons, as he called them.

She had been waiting, watching quietly as his retinue of fears and excuses gradually ran out. The comforts of habit had turned into boredom, and the drag of loyalty diminished to the point where the lure of reinventing himself in a world where nobody knew him had become impossible to decline.

'I'll tell Christa tomorrow. See if she wants to come with me.'

Gianna knew this was the reason her son had not already fled Bravery Bay. Christa was the only genuine friend he ever had — and she adored him. And in the glow of her love he had flowered. Grown stronger. Begun to show the first undeniable signs of manhood.

'Suppose she say no?' Gianna wondered, turning over the stone with care.

'Then I'll convince her to change her mind.'

'What if she still say no?'

'Why — do you think she will?'

'I don't know. Maybe … maybe she don't dream like you.'

'Then I guess I'll just book a ticket and leave it up to her.'

It was not the grim metal surface of his words that convinced her, but the wall of sadness they were riveted to. The sense that for every choice there was a price — and that for changing the course of his life he may well be asked to remit the fee with a broken heart. With guilt and loneliness.

For a few moments, mother and son looked across the table at one another. Both allowing stirred up clouds to settle as dust. Gianna reached out and took both of Tony's beautiful hands in hers. She squeezed them lightly and smiled the smile of enormous distance — which was the thing they truly shared.

'Good luck, Antonio,' she said. 'I think is right. For you. For *your* life.'

'And what about you?' he wanted to know.

'Also for me,' she told him — although she never said why.

For Gianna, the weeks went slowly, each day excoriating the thinning skin of her determination a little more. Not long now, she kept reminding herself, not long now – hoping she would make it to the nominated date intact. Having not exploded.

It was not that she wanted rid of him. God no! She loved him with everything left over from raw preservation. It was simply that she wanted him to escape the appalling din of echoes. The clamour of constant reminders. Every time she looked at him she saw his father, and worse, hers. The men who bought and sold her. The ones for whom honour and breeding were more important than her wellbeing – mere girl, slender and lovely object of exchange.

A lithe vessel of pleasure.
A comely trophy of ownership.
The indentured womb of petty fiefdoms.

And right alongside her immolating rage, the shame of chains. The ones she had lumped all the way from Italy to Australia; that she could still hear clanking about her ankles on bad days. Because, in those frightful moments, she was even more scared of the alternative.

The big world. Freedom. Responsibility.

Just go, she kept thinking whenever Tony spoke of leaving. Take their bloody name and go to where they'll never find you.

Never get their hands on you.

All through summer ... nightmares. Dark figures breaking down the door. Carrying off their prize. Their prince. As though he was theirs all along, and she was just minding him. She never admitted it but every morning when he emerged barefoot and bleary into the kitchen, she was relieved. Another disaster averted. One less turn of the clock.

From the moment she realised he was growing inside her she had determined to keep him from them. To deny them the fruit of *their* hubris and *her* weakness. When Franco drowned amongst the white caps within clear sight of land, she renewed her vow with the black steel of a young widow's loss. It is why she encouraged her son's feminine side. Allowed his sensitivity to develop. Applauded his teenage outsider pose. Anything but the doppelganger masculinity of simpleton brutes.

Antonio 'Tony' Timone would never be the son of habitual cruelty. And he never was. He was her beautiful, skinny boy instead – the one who would never be satisfied with the calloused crumblings of a peasant kingdom. Who could never be the robot cipher of custom.

She loved him with a battering intensity; and across that drawn out and flinty summer it would gather to a crescendo of white light and noise. A near ecstatic cacophony of promised quiet. Of which she never breathed.

She did not need to. He already knew.

He would look across from her to the playful figure of Vinnie Carlyle and understand that, for her, the presence of this bruised, adorable child was a chance to love without fear or guilt or vengeance. For though the blood of her suffering was scarlet and strong inside him, he would forever be wrought from the sinews of tyrants. Forever the scion of viciousness. Product of her capitulation.

Summer burned into mid–March. The town sagged under the weight of the heat. Cattle roamed drier and hungrier over the baked and fissured ground. Flies hovered in blanketing clouds, hot air somehow amplifying their drone. Crows watched on – black sentinels of opportunity. People scanned the forecasts for autumn. Looked south–east to the sea for the rolling advance of storms.

Tony still had not convinced Christa. Nor she him. Her loving, her young body, their outsiders' union – none of these would cause him to stay. The seat was booked. The money saved.

163

A stall at the Saturday market arranged – the props of boyhood no longer required. Saleable objects; priced to go.

> *Books, records, cassettes – hundreds in all.*
> *Most of his videos – save a few favourites.*
> *All his neatly rolled up movie posters.*
> *A desk, a beanbag and a beaten up bicycle.*
> *His barely touched guitar – strap, case*
> *and tuner included.*

As Christa stood next to him that morning contemplating the pile, Gianna observed the space slowly opening up between the two lovers.

The calcifying quietness of finality replacing their erstwhile volubility.

The hard edge of imminent separation chiselling deep into their youthful dream of unbreakable partnership.

The sexual shine in their eyes dulled by the sad dawning of fact.

Sharpened to a point of resentment that neither wished to express.

Only once his girl had gone home, did he voice it. 'I'm not going to force her,' he declared. 'And she's not going to guilt trip me either. So yeah, it's pretty fucked.'

All Gianna could do was to offer him the arms of wordless consolation. The gentle kiss of forbearance.

Though his heartbreak was turning a knife – triggering maternal reflex – she knew that the momentum of his decision to leave had long passed the point of reversal. He had staked so much, so publicly on it, that it would seem like abject collapse not to get on that bus.

Like cowardice.

Or the acceptance of slavery.

It was the same for her. If, in her desire to hold him close, to never let him go, she forestalled or prevented his departure, she would never be able to escape the idea that she had handed a kind of victory to those who had laid claim to her. Thus, in the last few days of Tony's childhood, she battened down her mothering impulses and carefully retreated.

She couched her love instead in the restraint of immediate practicality. In an envelope filled with fifties.

In new shoes.

A bag of toiletries.

In the carefully bottled sauces she made for him to sell at the market.

Years later, she would recall that last Saturday on the parched and flattened buffalo grass of the town square – in the shadow of the monument with her dead husband's name – with a torrent of emotion she had refused herself at the time.

Franco Timone in granite relief. Just letters in stone. A name stripped of context, reduced to the spectacle of martyrdom.

The blotched, sun ruddy faces of the locals who once rejected her, chirping and smiling as they bought her thick red passata for two bucks a pop. As they shook Tony's hand and wished him luck – their dishonesty and ill–feeling palpable beneath their practised country folk geniality.

The slowed down and detailed memory of Shelley Salter, the true meaning of which took years to unpick. Her gaze like the sound of fire. The way she looked at them both – especially Tony.

How careful she was not to use the name of either husband. Nor even to grant them the acknowledgement of breath.

Some nights Gianna would dream of that bright sky morning. Would hear her son's voice next to her, calling out the price tags of his youth. Would turn around and…

... He would be gone.

Later, on the front porch, with the coffee and the birds and a view of a wide blue arc, she would smile to herself.

For it is done – and she is free at last.

Australia Day weekend

17. The king of history.

It is the fourth consecutive night of a January heatwave, the darkness muddied and perspiring, the air heavy with expectation, like the strain before breaking. Every door, every window, flung open – yet still the weatherboard house sighs with baked exhaustion, melting on the anvil of summer.

In the lounge room, with a whirring pedestal fan for company, Antonio 'Tony' Timone is streaming videos on You Tube. Clothed in sweat and headphones, he watches a man he used to dream of being lip–syncing songs he used to know by heart.

In the nineties, when, like the video singer, he was young and beautiful.

He had bought their records and worn a blood red t–shirt with their name emblazoned in stark white, lower case lettering. He felt so cool when he wore it, like a member of an exclusive club. And when he listened to their songs, he believed he understood – and was understood in turn by the glamorous man at the microphone. Their records made him swoon. Pine. Feel exceptional.

Yet, it is tonight's digital reunion that is the exception; as Tony is not normally prey to the lures of fiftyish nostalgia. It was triggered earlier. By chance. A backpacker. A kid with a languid slouch and a faded secondhand tee. Someone Rosie Donald knew.

Tony and the boy had talked at length – the songs, the albums, the singer.

'He's still really good looking,' the younger had said.

'Lucky him,' the elder had replied.

Watching the slender frontman now in the solitude of a sweltering night, Tony is reminded again of irrecoverable belief.

Of pride, delusion, optimism.
The melodrama of self.

The quiet, inexorable entropy that is undoing everything.
The way in which even the revelatory
is fast becoming the mundane.

For it is the singer's beauty that most makes him wince. With an absurd longing.

His feline, rockstar swagger.
The aloof and ambiguous sexuality.
The narcotic and impossible lustre of him.
Gorgeous black hair falling that way – like a girl's.

At the age of twenty–five Tony had modelled himself on the singer fantasy; which in truth was a theatrical extension of who he wished *he* could be. The beautiful boy siren wrenched from ordinariness – poetic and unknowable – silencing the doubters, crushing the bullies with his enigmatic allure. So much more than a walk on part in a prime time soap or a bisexual pout in a hundred fashion mags. Better by far than an overpaid clothes horse.

Although Tony is acutely aware how ridiculous he is being, he is learning to accept these occasional shortcomings. His periodic lapses into purple narrative excess. He also understands that the self–scorning voice trying to mock him into walking away from the screen is simply the internalised, constantly criticising drone of others. The truth is plain enough. He does not need to be reminded by the stinging monologue of judgement.

There is no hit song of his on You Tube. No immortalised scene, with Brando–esque 'contender' moment to inspire every wannabe on the planet. No TedTalk, no million hit viral sensation. Just a middle–aged guy watching videos on a laptop, sweating in two dollar undies, midriff blancmange, caught somewhere between despair and acceptance, erstwhile beauty and future decay. Between laughing out loud and drowning himself drunk in the ebony waters of the bay that took his phantom father nearly half a century ago.

Tonight, he is a man on the brink of cliché. The B grade actor in the pilot that never got picked up.

Part of him *wants* to give in, to allow the music and the memory their magic effect. To make the shabby spectacle somehow literary, and to lend his corny introspection an element of the grand. To pretty—up the dismal.

He hits replay on his favourite video and is about to slide into the familiar storyline when … the sense of another, soft footsteps nearing, his headphones being lifted.

Jake. Joint rolled. Crouching down behind him. Assessing the scene in a blink.

'Hey old man,' he says. 'Smoke this instead.' And he places the joint with sensual deliberation between Tony's lips, motioning him to stand. 'You've got the rest of eternity to travel back in time.'

Jake Salter has been sleeping under his roof for a month.

In Gianna Sofia's bed.

Together they have smoked over a hundred joints, watched a dozen or so movies and talked till daybreak most nights.

In turn, Bravery Bay has been talking non—stop; a fact which continues to amuse them. Indeed, it has been their sport to tease and provoke, if only because Jake's departure is days away and Tony has little to lose.

'By the way,' Jake tells him after the smoke is sparked, 'I spoke to Mum earlier and she reckons Friday might be a good day for it; while everyone's doing their flag waving thing.'

Tony takes a drag and nods approvingly. 'Clever,' he says, picturing the upcoming Australia Day ceremony, with its speeches and jingoism — and Jim Salter pressing townsfolk flesh as the pre—eminent good ol' Aussie bloke. Big fisted heirs and frightened, furtive wife as lieutenants, with their boxing kangaroos and Southern Cross stubbie holders.

'After all, it's not like Dad wants me round to queer his pitch,' Jake adds, brow arched, eyes spiked with a shot of hurt and vengeance. Bruised adolescent scorn bristling with damnation.

In this, Tony sees a vision of himself more honest than the approximation of lead singers.

170

✂

The daylight, when it arrives, is bleached. Nearly white with heat. The air is dry, spiced with the scent of warm sea, baked earth and thirsty eucalypt. Another hot morning rent by crow, fly and gull.

In the kitchen early, having given up on meaningful sleep, Tony tamps the coffee into the percolator and counts the days in his head.

Seventeen.

Though he will never tell Jake, he cannot wait.

For everyone's sake – especially his own.

As Shelley Salter had predicted, her son's departure has been brought forward. Swift exile agreed upon as the least damaging strategy. Hands mutually washed. Bloodletting minimised. 'I just want him to go and for everyone else to calm down,' she had confessed. 'And give me some bloody peace.'

For the last couple of weeks Tony has been taking secret calls from her. She has all but broken his heart, not merely with the details but with the sorrow of her telling and the urgent, unexpressed guilt he detects in her voice.

It is not hard for him to guess the source of this – but he is in no hurry for confirmation. The ghosts are numerous enough.

While he waits for the percolation process, he takes a slow breath to centre himself in his surrounds. To focus on the light and the air and the ruckus of birds and, in doing so, to disentangle himself briefly from the web of phantoms.

It may be a new year but it has begun in the thrall of the past. In an old house with a pretty young boy who reminds him of himself. With old songs and repeated motifs. Former lovers and familiar cooking smells. Like a movie remake; something he might screen in his class.

In truth, it is grinding him down. Hemming him in. There are moments when he just wants everyone to fuck off.

> *For Jake not to be so obviously in love.*
> *Christa not to be so torn between blaming him*
> *for everything and hating herself.*
> *Vin Carlyle not to want some form of rescue.*

Shelley not to be seeking his forgiveness
and permission.

It is his mum all over again – and, by default, his absent father. The drowned fisher he was somehow meant to replace. The tyrant/martyr/bully/victim. Tragi–hero of town cenotaphs.

Am I simply the king of history? Tony has been asking himself lately. The puppet of a thousand cruelties, re–enacting the classics and modelling the ancestral robes for a new generation. Simply a mouthpiece. An iteration.

Inside the swelling dome of the steadily gathering morning heat, as the coffee bubbles on the stove, he feels small and unimportant. Or rather, *wants* to feel that way. To vanish into insignificance. Melt into the background. To rise like a speck of dust into the bright awesome sky of oblivion.

And in this moment, he hears the calm inner voice gently intoning. 'Don't worry, Tony. It will all be over; and there will be a silence … and it will be the most beautiful thing you ever heard.'

He exhales. His shoulders drop. His head lolls to the side. Now there is only breathing and the smoky joy of freshly brewed coffee. Everything else can wait.

Meanwhile – outside, oblivious – the magpies are carolling.

He fills his cup and walks towards their lovely chortle. He sits at the old circular table and floats into the vastness of summer's blue tinted cauldron. It brings a broad smile of gratitude to his face and he murmurs out loud, 'Seventeen.'

Before the sun renders it unwise, he is dressed and striding down the hill. As he descends, the bay sparkles, handfuls of treasure scattered by light. The air is hot and salty, parched and clean. The tarmac exhales, sweet and chemical. The sound of sprinklers and flies blends with the low, sporadic growl of traffic and the disembodied voices of neighbourhood kids in their final week of summer holidays.

Tony registers all this, savours it. With age, he has learnt to find the beauty in such things. For just like the distance, the simplicity of everyday backgrounds have become a form of retreat. Available healing so near at hand. Like the captured sounds Jake weaves into his music. The banal as profound. As liberty.

He is thinking about the paradox of this – the sheltering distance being so immediate, a form of absence achieved in presence – and he thanks Jake for sharing with him the wordless wisdom of his compositions.

> *Like scenes realised whole – without recourse*
> *to the distracting focus of detail.*
> *The silence inside the clamour.*
> *The stillness that follows the fever of doing.*

Here again … things carried forward from family. The legacy of repetition. The dissociative, imaginative mechanisms of survival – remedies sought by children and honed to an artform by the adults they become.

He thinks of Gianna and is reminded once more how he first witnessed the path out of peonage being hacked from the thickets on the ledge of her knee. With her rage – which was not unlike Jake's – and an earthy acceptance which he himself is still trying to learn.

Then, with the swing of a door and the smile of a girl, his attention is pulled back to the present.

Sexy Rosie.

God, how he wants to love her. Touch her, fuck her. But won't.

Aneetha, and all those before, Christa included, have taught him not to seek solace and completion in the sex and admiration of others.

Better just to look.

Nonetheless, Rosie's beaming eyes, and the flirtatious move of her shoulders … playful invitations he is not ready to resist.

The firm and supple shape of her loveliness and the teasing mischief in the soft, parted set of her lips shatter the surface of his middle–aged reflection, calling him into the realm of female beauty, with its promise of harbour and deliverance.

'Hey there, beautiful girl,' he chirps.

'Hey there, handsome man,' she coos.

Tony and Rosie have now perfected their mildly sexual game. It shines a little light into each of their days. She likes that he likes her – wants her – and he is grateful she trusts him enough to allow him scope for fantasy; in which he most certainly indulges. Both realise it adds spice to the rumours; for Rosie, like Tony, is wont to toy with what she regards as small town pettiness.

Thus, she makes a point of bringing the macchiato over to his table, making others wait at the counter while she exchanges a few words with him. 'You behave yourself now,' she says with a wink, before sauntering back to the coffee machine.

His smile is reflexive, like a blush. Her youth, her intelligence and humour, the hope implicit in her manner – he could get high on these things. Then crash. For there are many flowers, yet there is always autumn.

He laughs at himself. At his predicament. He thinks of the singer in the video, frozen in time, and of lines around eyes and irrefutable bald spots. Of being twenty like Rosie. Of fifty in a few months.

As he watches her go about her routine, it occurs to him; the academic year will start soon and the Dean will be on the phone. Rooms full of kids just like Rosie will be waiting – looks and dreams intact. And his agent will push him to audition. Indeed, she has already told him that another hair colour campaign is on the cards.

Then, in the wings, Aneetha Jharavindra. *Back in a couple of weeks*, her email said. *I'll come over and make dinner if you like – but only if you like.*

Shortly, the world outside the aquatint bubble of the Bay will press its claims on him.

'Same old, same old,' he mutters out loud, with a tiny shake of his head.

Following the thought through, Tony draws another parallel. It has a satisfying, storybook neatness. He would flinch at it in his screen studies class.

Obvious.
Contrived.
A convenient reduction.
Serve with a bucket of sugar.

Yet, in the circumambient swirl of self–drama, it is clearly appealing. As he finishes his coffee, he turns the idea over, teases it out.

'Maybe one last time,' he says to himself, and promptly strolls over to the counter, where he orders another long mac and asks Rosie if she thinks he would look good bald.

18. The last summer in shitsville.

She is mad at him now. He should know better. Toying with people like that — rubbing it in their faces like he was nineteen. Like he used to when she was his girl, and they didn't give a fuck about anything but their own crusade; and the old woman was around to back them up if things went pear shaped.

She understands why the kid is into it. He is young, his dad is a tyrant, and he is way too clever for a dumb arse town like Bravery Bay. Just a bit of summer fun before he jumps on a plane. A middle finger to those who gave him hell about being different and wanting something more than a surname and a sun−bleached fiefdom.

But Tony...

Surely, he can see Jake is besotted with him? Or is he lapping it up, playing mentor for the impressionable boy, sustaining himself with the fantasy that he is still the sexiest thing on Earth?

Christa Marie Bell has contemplated calling her ex on more than one occasion but has held fire. She knows her chance will come. Wait until Jake has gone, she tells herself. No need to involve him in her and Tony's leftovers. For this is what her anger is truly about. She knows this.

If not for her pent up frustrations — and a note of discomforting jealousy — she would be cheering them on.

However, making matters worse is the constant chatter she endures in the salon.

> *A man of his age — it's outrageous.*
> *Bloody socialists — they think they can*
> *tell the rest of us how to live.*
> *It's a wonder Jim don't take a shottie to both of 'em.*
> *Jake's an ungrateful little shit — but your mate Tony*
> *should have a bit more class.*
> *If I had my way, Chrissy, it'd be illegal.*

Initially, she tried to combat it. Now it has worn her down. In fact, it has started to reflect badly on her. 'How can you defend a man like that?' one of her regulars scolded, eyes accusing.

However, the situation only became *genuinely* intolerable on the morning Shelley Salter turned up for her six weekly colour re-touch. Instantly, all eyes were on her, all conversation turned down a notch. The background music abruptly seemed louder, its poppy vanilla brightness awkward and out of place. Scissor clicks and drier drone began to grate. There were deliberate coughs. Throats pointedly cleared. The sunburnt gap year kid Christa hired to help during the holiday rush shuffled nervously in her sensible shoes, stealing furtive glances at her tight lipped boss. Hoping her elder's eyes might contain both clues and reassurance.

Yet, when it was her turn, Shelley came calmly to the chair, aware of but unmoved by the presence of radar. Her tired, polite smile told Christa that she, for one, was not looking to make a scene or indulge the newsfeed of scandal.

Indeed, as Christa applied the colour with careful attention, she noted the black around her client's eyes. The sadness. The sense of grimly hanging on.

'So when's the big day?'

'Feb 10,' Shelley had said.

'I guess you'll miss him, hey?'

'I imagine so … but he's been missing for years already.'

At that, Christa felt a fist tighten around her heart, a sudden withdrawal of oxygen. For a moment she was spinning. Vertiginous. The salon seemed to lurch, the hair strewn floor moving anti-clockwise beneath her. She had to step back for a second. Compose herself.

In the mirror, Shelley's gaze found her – and amongst the whorls in her eyes and the knots in her brow … space for compassion. Maternal. Sororal.

It was a look that said, *it's okay, I'm used to it.*

The gentle hand Christa then placed on her shoulder confirmed what they both understood; and she finished the colour with calm and practised precision, in near silence. As bitchy eyes watched on.

Only later, at home on the decking, barefoot, tipsy, sweating in the relentless January heat, did her tears come down like the relief of rain.

That was last night.

Today, Thursday, her blood is heated — hot like the dry air. She is ready to burn; yet praying for a change in the weather. Hoping nobody stirs her too much about Tony.

Meanwhile, she consoles herself. At least the busy season is nearly over; just a few more days until the kids are back at school and the city folk return to their real lives. She will take time off then, thank the hired help, Yvette, for her much needed assistance, and try to decide if she really does want to close the salon.

As the door chime announces the first customer, she composes her chatty hairdresser face and sets about her business, falling back on decades of experience to help combat the mounting boredom and give her clients what they pay for.

The day is grinding much as any other when, shortly after ten, she notices a figure passing in front of the shop. At first, she does not register who, until she looks up from the head of hair she is part way through cutting and sees him standing a few feet away.

> *Take away coffee in hand.*
> *Cool shades in place.*
> *Raffish off—white shirt.*
> *Top three buttons undone.*
> *Understated cologne.*

'Any chance of fitting me in today?' he asks, his smile familiar and playful.

She wants to say something but her mouth is dry, thoughts boiling.

Yvette, who has been in town long enough to guess, has traced her eyes over his form in a flash and is looking at Christa with her own smile, also playful.

'I thought maybe we could bring that appointment forward. Get it done right now. If it's not too much trouble.'

By the time the words are out he has ascertained Christa's explosive disposition and is shifting his stance, taking off his sunglasses. He looks across at the young assistant instead. 'Perhaps if you're booked, she can do it. It's only a shave.'

Although Yvette is clearly agreeable, Christa is not.

Drawing a tense breath, she pulls up her shoulders and apologises to her client, a summer tourist she will likely never see again. 'I'll just be a few moments,' she says. 'Yvette, if you could maybe make some coffee or something, and just let people know.'

With a scowling nod she bids Tony to follow, which he does – knowing exactly what he is in for. She leads him through the back of the shop and out into the glare of the rear carpark, where the oven dense heat hits them. After a few moments, they settle into a wedge of shade and her eyes lock firmly onto his.

In their steel: history, heartache, and a measure of open scorn.

She has so much to say but does not know where to start. She wants to explode. Erupt. Accuse him of everything. Vent all her issues with men.

'Is this a game to you?' she begins, holding her hands up like claws, lacquered talons glinting.

'Is *what* a game?' he asks annoyingly.

'The whole fucking charade. Coming back here, fucking around with Jake, sleazing up to every starry eyed slut in town. *Oh Tony, you're such a hunk for your age.* And this pathetic sad man act of yours. This bullshit head shaving thing.'

'Is that what you really think?'

'Don't fucking talk to me like I'm one of your students, Tony. At least spare me that routine.'

'What is it you want me say? That I'm sorry? That I hate myself? That I wish I'd never left you all those years ago; even though it was *you* who left me? You want me to take the blame for everything, Christa? Is that it?'

This sears her. Catches her off guard. She was not prepared for such careful, even toned, laser guided thrusts. For him to state it so matter-of-factly. She swallows her breath, purses her lips.

'Go on then,' he taunts, on a roll. 'Why not complete this little scene by slapping me or breaking down or something. There must be some dramatic gesture you could try that would make me realise how absolutely right on all counts you are. Then I can do my bit by skulking off to indulge in a fit of white, middle class guilt. I can curse the fact that I inherited a Y chromosome from my dad and wish that my karma had been good enough for me to have been born a woman. Sure, it's a lame and predictable whinge that changes absolutely nothing and leaves us both feeling like shit … but if makes you feel better…'

She flexes to berate him – irritated by his habit of talking about things as though they were a film. His fake intellectual pose. But she catches the first syllable before it emerges, as it occurs to her that the wound his act masks is real. Most likely still bleeding. Like hers.

It is clear that he has risen so quickly to her combative pitch because, like her, he feels encircled.

'I just don't know why you're still here, that's all,' she says, changing tack. 'Why would you want to spend any time at all in a town you so obviously couldn't wait to get away from?'

'Or is it that you just don't want me around?'

She lets it pass – but it is a good question. 'I just don't want people coming up to me every bloody day and bitching about shit as if *I'm* supposed to do something about it. As if letting Jake suck your dick is *my* fucking fault.'

Tony shakes his head, expels a tight jet of air. 'Please tell me you're not serious.'

'Well, it's pretty obvious he loves you.'

'Yeah, no fucking kidding – and you think I'm not hanging for him to leave?'

Now it is Christa's turn for a disbelieving shake of the head. 'Oh come off it, Tony. Admit it, you love the attention. Having somebody want you, hanging off every word, thinking you're *sooo* amazing.'

'Yeah, I know I'm shallow, Chrissy. We've established that fact already,' he retorts. 'But at least I'm not a vicious, narrow minded tyrant.'

She takes his point, yet feels impelled to ask, 'So why are you encouraging him? Why make such a show of it?'

'What am I meant to do? Punish the kid; deny him his little moment in the sun? He's barely eighteen, babe. Beating his chest, testing the limits – and so he should. If people can't handle it, that's their fucking problem.'

Despite the tension, Christa smiles at his passion. For a second, she sees him as he was, the determined teenage hair model who loved her. Who pleaded with her to follow him out of the Bay. To risk everything for the chance of something other.

'Look, I'm sorry if you're copping the backwash,' he tells her. 'Obviously, that's *not* what I intended.'

'Yeah I know – I just wish you didn't feel the need to ... *taunt* people.'

'As opposed to joining the abusive, homophobic, sexist cunt club, you mean?'

Again, she gets his point. Agrees almost entirely. But she is tired. Perhaps even profoundly exhausted. 'Please don't make it any harder than it already is, Tony. That's all I'm really asking.'

Sensing the nearness of tears, he relents. 'Okay, sure.'

She closes her eyes, tries to right herself.

Right now, she could drop everything. Not even go back into the salon. Just jump in the car and vanish.

She also wants a hug from Tony – yet *that* is a risk she will *not* permit.

Instead, she focuses on her breathing, and lets the wave of the moment pass through her.

'I better get back,' she says, and he bows his head, deferring.

'Okay well ... if the snitching gets too much, just send them over to me and I'll deal with them.'

Christa laughs. 'If I decide I want to lose all my regulars, sacrifice my business and get run out of town, I might just do that.'

Their conflict resolved – or rather, put on hold – the two old flames stand quietly in the thickening heat looking at one another; and once more both are struck by how strong their thirty–year bond remains. By how little some things have changed, and how others have altered beyond recognition.

'If you really want that shave, maybe just give me a bit more notice next time,' Christa smiles, before landing the barest of kisses on his cheek and walking back to a half–finished haircut.

The salon is closed tomorrow, so Christa takes herself across to the Catchers' Inn after work, not so much for the convivial buzz of a hot, high season evening but to round off the edges of the solitude that awaits her at home. In her empty nest. The incessant echo chamber of years.

Also, she needs to defrag after the Tony incident. Did she let him off too lightly? Is it her own complacency she can no longer tolerate?

As she cashes in a hundred and hefts her bucket of gold to the pokie lounge, she thinks about the usual suspects: fear and procrastination.

She remembers a scene from thirty years ago, when Tony first told her.

'Let's just work our butts off over summer,' he had urged. 'Let's make this the last summer in shitsville.'

What she has never forgotten, nor been able to deny, is that she knew right away she would not join him. Though she spent the remaining months trying to convince herself, and hoping he would think of something to make her change her mind – or his – she nonetheless felt a distinct note of relief when he pulled out of the Bay in the clunky old bus, and she was left waving from the roadside.

'He'll be back,' she had said to Gianna, hoping to render the turmoil irrelevant.

'No he won't,' the old woman had replied.

The irony of ultimately being proved right is not lost on Christa Marie Bell. For there is no victory – merely fact.

Mechanically, she funnels dollar coins into the slot, hoping the machine will consume her uncertainties, if not deliver a jackpot in the form of clear decision, and the self–belief to act upon it.

Come morning, she is poorer and has a headache. But she will not need to be on her feet all day. Cutting and colouring. Straining to keep herself from stabbing people. The relief of this helps to make the continuing heatwave more bearable.

Throwing on her baggiest outfit and scruffiest sneakers, she ties her hair in a rough top knot and decides to treat herself to breakfast in town.

She has forgotten that the official national day festivities will be taking place in the square. Thus, when she finally gets a table for one, she has to wait twenty minutes for her coffee, and endure a playlist of kitsch Australiana blaring from the PA on the lawn.

But she is cossetted in a corner with a view, hidden behind shades and left alone to wander in her thoughts. A few locals say hi but no one steps in to engage – and for this she is thankful.

By the time her poached eggs and 'smashed avo' arrive, she is ensconced in crowd watching. She has already spotted Steve and his second wife, their cute little boy in tow, and noticed Vin Carlyle's missus circulating without daughters or husband. Then, she sees the unmistakable figure of Jim Salter, his Akubra hat and rolled up sleeves signifying his masculine, Aussie primacy. He shakes hands and slaps backs, the idealised totem of larrikin bonhomie. Meanwhile, Shelley hovers, looking distracted, searching the throng with nervous eyes, as if scanning for trip hazards.

However, as soon as the ceremonials commence – Jim on a makeshift stage waxing about what Australia Day means – Christa spots Tony.

He has materialised at Shelley's side. She notes the way they talk, their body language, and it becomes clear that whatever the Salter family's public position is regarding Jake, the two of them have made a pact. The fact that Tony melts back into the crowd before Jim has done pontificating strikes Christa as significant. Everyone knows Shelley keeps herself to herself; that she is an isolated queen without visible confidantes.

Although Christa is once again miffed and jealous to observe the easy intimacy Tony seems able to form with almost anyone – baristas, backpackers, black sheep – she is nonetheless reassured. It seems to prove something she has always doubted. Not everything about him is an act. Nor a provocation or stubborn refusal.

Somewhere in her heart she has always believed he only left the Bay because he had backed himself into a corner. He had made such a deal of it. Been so adamant. Not to leave would have proved everyone right. He had, she suspected, chosen the pose over love, and that therefore she had mattered less than his teenage vanity. Than his ridiculous fantasy of self.

Now, in a flood of electricity, the fine hairs on her forearm are standing on end and, in a beat, she knows with near certainty that her love for him was *not* constructed out of nothing. That he had torn himself apart to leave her. That, like her, he had never found another love. And that all the replacements were proxies for despair. The sorrowful traces of her doubting.

She is shaking, fork unsteady, as she finishes her breakfast. The tough and wise-cracking Christa exterior is fissuring, but she holds it together well enough to negotiate the scrum of bodies and move out into the scorch of the day.

Before she makes any rash decisions, she has to know for sure.

Jim has finished his speech, a line of people have taken their citizenship oaths, and the national anthem is being played poorly by a gaggle of schoolkids. The flag hangs, barely ruffled, in the thick blue heat. Most people are still, a public display of legislated respect; yet Christa is arrowing through.

She finds him beside the monument. His gaze out to sea.

She watches him for a moment, until he senses her presence and turns. In his eyes, she believes, is something akin to what she feels. It is something both distant and near. Ever present, yet irretrievably lost.

A sadness that takes the form of euphoria.

Christa knows at once. This is as close to confirmation as it gets. No other symbolic gestures or forensic unearthings are required. Nevertheless, the anthem plays out and they stand quietly in the sightline of the blazing eye. It is the perfect disguise.

184

19. The absence of objects.

Jake is confident it will not be regarded as stealing. His mother has given him the keys and it is *her* car he is driving up to the big house. Nonetheless, as he inches to a stop a few dusty metres from the wide brimmed verandah, his heart begins to thunder.

Stepping up to the threshold, he peers through the broad, mullioned windows into the interior – newspaper spread out where his father would have taken breakfast, twin bowls and mugs on the dish rack – and he thinks how sparse and cold it looks. How like a house without love. An object of power and display. A castle for a hollow kingdom.

The key turns smoothly in the lock and the door pushes inward.

There is a smell of wood and flowers. Of fly spray and tea towels.

He hovers – calculating the time he has and the tasks he must perform. There is no break, he reasons, only entry.

The last month has been difficult for Jake Adam Salter. Like coming apart at the seams.

> *Head and heart.*
> *Present and future.*
> *The promise of escape versus the inevitability of loss.*
> *The unknown chasm of the world*
> *and the predictable void of the village.*

And Mister Timone – sleeping in the next room, wrapped in a towel after showering, seeming to understand everything.

Including the perils of desire.

Though frustrating, he is grateful for his friend's restraint. Jake knows a few weeks of ardour will not compensate for any delay or derailment of planned departure. This, he reminds himself, is just another summer. When what he really wants is another life.

Entering his old room, the coolly considered plan of attack is upended. Scanning the racks of studio tech, especially the keyboard, he realises at once. The idea that he would simply take a few books and other small items no longer seems feasible. Now, the music will take precedence. It is, after all, nothing less than his voice.

He calculates the practicalities – family occupied with obligatory Australia Day routines – and powers up the system. He listens with quiet delight as the machines hum. In his own tangled circuitry there is a parallel tide, likewise electric, and as he sits down to play his whole body is running at a higher click, thrumming like the wakened speakers.

It has been weeks. Indeed, since Christmas a part of him has been muted. His only outlets have been late night laptop tinkering and sporadic field recordings; but now there are octaves before him and his heart is in flight. He closes his eyes, slows his breathing. His slender fingers hover in space.

Now the music flows – a riverine tendril. A surrender to desire. It emerges effortlessly, like wild running.

Thought, in the guise of words, is momentarily blanked out by the purity of sound. All arguments settled. Irrelevant. While he plays, he is both the song *and* the dance. No more dichotomy. No longer the secret.

This is what he came for.

When it is over, he releases a shuddering breath. He is exhilarated. Flushed. He laughs out loud. At himself. At the situation he finds himself in. And then, just for a moment, he allows himself the nakedness of unbidden tears.

> *Sadness.*
> *Relief.*
> *Love.*

For Jake has never needed to contemplate the notion of heartbreak before now. Of finding someone and then losing them. He has read about it, but this is different. Now it is an idea in human form, realised in blood and hormones and a relentless craving deep in the fibre of muscle.

The keys, compressors and fx rack are merely the syntactic devices of a language he has devised. A tongue that both masks and reveals the complex simplicities of elemental hunger and, by extension, the obverse dividends of their denial.

Collecting himself, focusing on the immediate, he rises to start the process of hauling things to the car. As he methodically breaks down the studio, he finds himself thinking firstly of his mother, then of Gianna. The overlap soon becomes clear, if not in their respective biographies, then in the shape of their strangeling sons.

In the manner of their love and their sacrifice.

At this, tears well again. He bites hard on his bottom lip. Scrunches his eyes tight. Just get it done, he tells himself. Lose it later if you want. On the plane maybe.

To this end, he reminds himself of the clock and steps through the process – stripping the room that used to be his haven, leaving behind its lovely light and an increase of echoes. Another dorm departed.

> *A cube with a bare bed and*
> *windows in need of a clean.*
> *Leftover furniture and items of discarded clothing.*
> *A jumble of books on an undusted shelf.*
> *Three old posters – stuck yet sagging*
> *on white washed walls.*

Pulling the door to, he wonders what his mother will find when she peeks inside. How long it will take his father to realise. He imagines the fight that will ensue when he does. The loud and bullish bluster that will surely turn to a coughing fit. The taciturn perseverance that will outlast all such quakes.

A minute later, sitting in the car, he is sending a simple text to the two who need to know.

Half time.

Then he is driving, and the house is receding in the mirror, misted in a tail of dust. Only the dogs are noting his departure.

It does not take long for an edge of panic to set in. What will he do with all this stuff? There is no way he can take it to Europe; and putting it on eBay would be foolish. Can he really expect Tony to babysit it for him? And for how long? Perhaps he has been rash after all.

Jake is not used to acting this way – feeling like this.

He is watching himself with mild alarm. This is not the calculating hauteur that has kept him safe all these years. This is more like crude reflex. Blunt and unexamined. A kind of hot, sweating haemorrhage, like madness seeping crimson from the pores.

Transferring his furtive cargo from car to lounge room, broiling in the high oblivious sun, hoping that snooping eyes are not lurking behind the tremble of curtains, he murmurs a puffing supplication to unspecified gods. *Help me make it to safety in time.*

Then – as boxes, bags and expensive equipment mount in clumps on the floorboards – he is reminded, by their incremental gathering, of a conversation from the previous night; one that had taken place in this very room.

It was late, after their shift, and he and Tony were winding down, as usual, with stubbies and smoke.

'I've been thinking about all this *stuff*,' the older man had mused, waving at the space, his late mother's possessions still very much as she left them. 'By which I mean, what am I going to do with it all – what to keep, what to throw, where to put this, that or whatever. In one way, I'm just fretting about ultimately meaningless objects ... yet I can't help but see a kind of truth in it.'

Jake had smiled with stoned affection at him. 'Spoken like a true critic, mister.'

'Yeah, I know; over–analytical wank.' Tony had acknowledged with an arch of the brow. 'But seriously, we do all this rearranging, all this moving around, and what's it all for in the end? It's just re–configuring the same basic things into slightly different places; like shuffling a deck of cards. Nothing *really* changes. Only the surfaces. Even if I strip this place top to bottom and completely re–fill it, I'd be going through almost exactly the same motions as Mum. Like a re–enactment.'

He had paused then, perhaps to finish a thought in silence. 'I don't know, Jake, maybe we just get fooled into thinking we're any different.'

Now, with the heavy lifting almost done and the tension of the moment waning, Jake takes a few seconds to ponder the import of his housemate's words. By the time he closes the car boot and activates the lock, he is once more marvelling at the way Tony seems at ease with ambiguity and uncertainty. He appears to resist any temptation to reduce himself and others to simple, linear encapsulation. It is the kind of quality Jake likes to believe he himself exudes; an intellectual and moral discipline that marks him out from countless others. From most everyone, as far as he can tell.

And yet, he is cognisant too of the subtle warning his friend has given him.

✂

When Shelley texts him he steels himself for the last act of the day's subterfuge.

Like her, he is taking pains not to get caught. Both know his father's pride would drive him to turn the screws, and each is acutely aware they have a substantial amount to lose. Shelley more so. Therefore, though part of him wants to gloat – mock, humiliate – he stays true to the practise of faux deference that has worked so well for him.

But he is also heeding another of Tony's more explicit warnings. 'Remember Jake, when you're safe on the other side the world, she'll be left here to deal with Jim.'

He had wanted to argue the point – her silence was more than failed peace keeping, it was outright complicity – but he could see in Tony's eyes that he was not simply excusing her, nor minimising her role in the ongoing fracas. Neither was he appealing to strategy or pity. Rather, he was imploring him to permit a measure of compassion. And not just for broken mothers.

So he had held his tongue, and will continue, as agreed, to uphold the pact of prudent collusion the three of them have devised.

It is the best way to make it to Feb 10.

Consequently, when he drives the compact Korean car back down the hill, he makes sure to skirt the busy cram of the square and the eyeline of Maxi's, and instead brings it in behind the boat tour shop and unseen into the rear parking bay at Via Amore.

Where his mother already awaits.

There is a sturdy impatience about her. She wants it over.

'I hope you didn't make it obvious,' she says.

'Not a trace,' he assures her.

'Because your brothers are coming over later and I don't need a scene.'

'None of us do, Mum,' he echoes – and as he does, he takes on a little of her tiredness. It is the exhaustion of survival.

'Okay,' she sighs, neither convinced nor prepared to contest. 'I'd better be going. Your dad will be wondering where I've gone.'

At this, mother and son embrace. Tentatively at first; but soon with the tension of clinging. Both are emotional but trying not to let it overflow. Yet still Jake's eyes fill with tears. The third time today.

> *She feels so frail in his arms and he so brittle in hers.*
> *There is a warm, motherly smell about her.*
> *Hers is the very flesh from which he was made.*
> *This is the raw fact of touch.*

'Not long now, Jakey,' she soothes.

Which is just it. He will leave – and the distances will be even greater. Anchoring routines will be removed. The comfort of well rehearsed roles will be disrupted. His heart will stumble at the idea of Tony. Falter at the way intimacy transitions, in banal sequence, to fractional traces.

Though Shelley correctly interprets the numerous signs, she says nothing of his teenage infatuation and the inevitability of its dissolution. Instead, she fixes him with a direct and gentle stare, which he holds for a few beats before they back out of their hug and compose themselves for the next phase of operations.

When – after a sweating walk beneath a glaring sun – he has re–ascended the hill, he rolls himself a joint in the kitchen and wonders where Tony is. He could call him, message him, but is aware his friend is most likely taking the chance to be by himself. Jake imagines him sitting at his favourite table, maybe flirting with Rosie, lingering over a macchiato. Doing his vague–out thing.

'I'll smoke this one for both of us then,' he says out loud, enjoying the compact perfection of his handiwork. For though he will admit a note of hurt, he takes great solace in the similarities between them. Indeed, Jake finds their likeness validating. Vin Carlyle had been more right than he imagined – it was not simply that they got on, it was that Tony provided a mechanism of proof.

With the stone coming on, he meanders into the lounge, where his rescued stuff is piled.

> *Cold.*
> *Dead.*
> *Objects in stasis*
> *Awaiting the resuscitation of meaning and purpose.*
> *Like words in the absence of voice.*

It is in the precise aftermath of this thought that Jake first gets the idea.

Now, out of nothing, there will be a reason for song. Many reasons.

Inspired, he packs clothes and other items into Gianna's room before gathering leads and plugs, rigging up a quick approximation of his more elaborate bedroom studio, and patching it into the sound system.

It is while doing this that he stumbles across an old CD in a scratched jewel case and this, in turn, takes him back to the day last year when he had listened to its now departed owner singing along.

He knows in an instant what Tony would make of such serendipity. How much he would revel in the symbolism, in spite of his more post—modern pronouncements. Indeed, there is an aptness which even Jake will not deny. A music so direct and plaintive, a fever so blissful and dishevelling that it resides in the bones and emerges through the viscera, salty and satisfying. It is a euphonious yielding to primitive improbabilities.

So, won't you say you love me ...?

And even though he knows Tony will never utter the phrase – and neither, he suspects, will he – Jake plays the song several times over, each time singing with abandon.

By the end of it he is flat on his back, glad of the fact that his love has chosen to avoid him for an afternoon. For in the absence of its object, Jake's passion has been truly present; and in this he realises that while things and actions may change colour and shape, and the names we apply may differ, desire remains the same.

At last, if only in this, he is no different.

20. The ambiguity of survival.

Having worked so hard to contain the various tensions, Vin Carlyle is now forced to admit the storm has broken. All other explanations would be disingenuous at best, if not flat out denial.

With the end of the summer tourist season just days away, he is exhausted. Nerves fried. Cranky. No longer sure he can make it through. The business is fine; everything else is screwed. Home especially.

Amanda Carlyle is furious with her husband. Mad, jealous and losing patience. Although he can sense it, Vin feels unable to still the momentum. Worse, his efforts to do so have largely backfired. Indeed, she has interpreted his attempts as further proof of what she now regards as his weakness and serial lack of understanding.

'You've got no fucking idea, have you?'

Vin conjures biting replies but chooses to hold them in. His problem is that he has far more idea than his wife will ever concede. He need only note the bewildered and frightened looks in his daughters' eyes. The way they hold onto him, their skinny arms wrapping him with all the force they can muster. The accusing stare the eldest gives him.

So too the way Amanda now sleeps with her back resolutely turned, or that their sex has become rare and robotic.

Once again, he will beat off in the shower before sliding into bed next to her.

He will try to remember, for the umpteenth time, what brought them together, what it was she expected of him, and how he failed, so spectacularly, to deliver.

The restaurant is clearly the main issue. She has been complaining about it for the last couple of years; accusing him of using Via Amore as an excuse to avoid her and his responsibilities as a father.

'I thought you would have known better,' she has argued more than once, 'than to abandon your own kids like your parents did you.'

It is a fair point. He acknowledges this. It is why he previously agreed to close for two days rather than one during quiet times, why he took Clarice on to back up Hank, and why Kel is still on the pay roll. It is the driving reason behind his decision to take an unprecedented ten day break after the long weekend.

Yet, initially, his industry and passion for the business had impressed her. She was the blue eyed, honey blonde country girl thankful to get a front–of–house gig at Bravery Bay's best new restaurant, who found her employer's energy and drive attractive. She had admired his loyalty to Gianna Timone, especially in the face of ungenerous whispers, and she could see how much their bond meant to them. From Amanda's perspective, this cast Vin as a man of commitment, honest hard work and vision. He was cute too.

Sometimes he thinks of this Amanda in the shower, of her curves and her horniness. Her breasts so full and glorious as they were unhooked from their C cups. Her belly, her hips, the sigh she exhaled when he entered her for the first time.

And when he is done with these fantasies, he recalls the enduring significance of those early amours. Before her, sex had been simple role play, acting out the standard routines of porn – flirt, suck, lick, fuck. With Amanda it felt more like love. In *her* arms he could be himself.

Aside from Gianna, she was the only woman he could bring himself to trust.

Now he is back to square one on this front, having lost both.

As he tiptoes through the house, perspiring in the incessant heat of yet another unbearably hot night – plonking a couple of ice cubes into his pinot – he is a man bracing for an explosion. He can hear the ticking yet does not know when or where the inevitable detonation will occur.

Perhaps the dynamite is strapped to his midriff, a suicide vest awaiting its one way mission. Indeed, Vin is sometimes afraid he might be one of those murder/suicide types. The cracked husband. The bloodied residue of his silent captivity making a gory splash on the news.

At times like this – in the after midnight hush, sitting foot sore and shattered on the lounge, lights off and lonely – he contemplates the possibility of the deed. Only little girls stand in the way. Only their big eyes and how they absolutely crush him.

He thinks of the conversation he and Tony shared on the topic before Christmas – of bargains made with time and knowing – and once again he finds himself wishing that Gianna Sofia was still around. She might not have had her son's way with words but she would have offered up other forms of solace and clarity. Of rescue.

She wouldn't let him drown.

In the morning, still weary, he snoozes through the early bustle. He can hear his wife and daughters – their high voices, the rattle of breakfast and the chatter of TV – and it sounds so pleasant in his tired cloud that he rolls over and lets heavy lids droop down. He floats, half awake, for an hour or more, dreams merging with kid squeals and adult instruction. He is only pulled up to the surface when he hears the shower. Amanda getting ready.

Dawdling into the bathroom, he takes note of his wife's naked form behind the dimpled screen – and of her palpable anger. It emanates in quiet, seething waves. Hits him like a wall. Yeah, good morning, honey, he thinks to himself.

'Hey darl,' he says out loud – more in pre–emptive defence than greeting.

'Awake, are we?' she responds, in no mood for pretence.

'Almost,' he answers her.

She pokes her head out from behind the glass, hair flat to skull, and asks him whether he has forgotten what he promised the girls. He tells her no, although in truth he has. Foolishly, he tries to cover. 'Insane shift last night,' he tells her, searching his memory.

'Heard that one before, Vinny,' she snarls. 'Why not try some other bullshit instead?'

Perhaps because he is tired, unhappy and frightened there is, out of nothing, a slam of steel. His head snaps around, eyes drilling. 'And what makes you think it's bullshit, babe?'

His voice is louder and more menacing than she expects from her drowsy husband. By instinct she flinches, rocks onto the back foot.

'Do you want to count the takings just to make sure? Or maybe you can call Clarice to check up on me.'

Amanda holds her breath. She scans him for a second before retreating to the shower, pointedly closing the screen on him. Even his anger fails to convince her now, so she just mutters to herself. 'Yeah, whatever.'

This, at any rate, is what Vin believes he hears.

In a beat he is wrenching open the frosted door and pinning his wife to the caramel coloured tiles. Before she can scream he has his hand over her mouth. Now her eyes are wide.

'What the fuck is it you want from me?' he bawls in her face, clearly very awake.

Her reaction is to bite.

Hard.

And then she is gone and he can hear her screaming at him – calling him everything under the sun. He is looking down at his palm, oozing with blood. At his feet, the floor is already dotting with red.

He turns off the pelting stream and backs out onto the bathmat, where he stands for a moment, soaked and wounded. A blink later he hears the girls start to cry.

That's right!

He was meant to take them to Maxi's for baby cinos and banana bread and let them experience the crowds in the square. He had bought them little flags.

The next few minutes go by in a distorted fog of fury and disorientation. The children try to intervene as their parents launch into a high volume cataclysm of insult and accusation. Nothing gets smashed, no physical blows are landed but things are said that neither will forget.

'Of course I'm angry. You do anything and everything for some old bitch who isn't even family but you can't even take five minutes to be with your own kids.'

'She was more bloody family to me than anyone else. At least she gave a fuck.'

'Oh really – and I don't?'

'Ah sure, babe, you care alright. Care about money. Care about yourself and what a fucken hard done by perfect little mummy you are.'

'At least I'm *capable* of caring; not like you.'

This stings him. Touches an exposed nerve. For a second, he wants to drive his bloodied fist into her, devastate her smugness, but he catches himself. 'Oh, poor fucken Amanda,' he snarls instead, hoping to land an even more telling blow. 'What a bloody saint she's becoming these days. A real fucken nun.'

'Yeah right, Vinny – because why the hell would I want to fuck you?'

And so it goes, lash for lash, until the eldest daughter, just turned five and ready to start school, is pulling so hard on Vin's bitten hand that he is jolted out of red mist. The reset button is hit. His eyes alight on her and there is no way he can continue.

Seeing this, his wife spits, all acid and pent up disappointment, 'Tell you what, why don't *you* be good cop for a change.'

Then ... a crash of doors and a rush of dressing. A grab of keys and a grumble of engine.

In her wake, silence. Like the drop of an anchor. Stillness like the freeze of winter.

The whole house and everyone in it is concussed. Not quite able to take in what has just happened.

Spinning, Vin takes stock – or tries to.

> *Tooth marks in his left palm.*
> *Scared children begging him to make it right.*
> *A wave of grief rolling inexorably towards*
> *the moment of crash.*

The urge to flee to higher ground.

But his little angels are pressing themselves against him, their screams now rhythmic sobs against his thighs. Wet eyes buried in his saturated dressing gown. He crouches down to their level and holds them and, while they cry, he tries to think of a way to make it easier for them.

A few months back he would have called Gianna.

Today – though it is yet to occur to him – he will call her son.

After patching up his hand and booking in to see the doctor – because he has heard that human bites can be dangerous – he prepares toasted sandwiches for the kids and tries to settle them down by watching cartoons. He does his best to answer their questions honestly and tries not to make promises that will not be kept. Yet, all the while he is listening out for Amanda, checking his phone for messages, both dreading and hoping to hear.

As much as he is angry with her and thinks that she is a petty, mean spirited, guilt tripping bitch, he knows in his heart that the basis of her argument is sound – and that his earlier eruption was splenetic acknowledgement of this. The two girls on the sofa with him *are* in danger of being orphaned, of being effectively abandoned by adults too wrapped up in their own agendas. Yes, the restaurant is part of the explanation. The easy part. The part that could be put on the market or farmed out to competent management. The deeper reason is the one Vin shudders to think of: that perhaps he does not even *know* how to care. That this facility has been frozen in him and that Gianna Sofia Timone may have played an unwitting part in this.

It is early afternoon and the heat of the day is bone dry. Even the normally vociferous birds have retreated to the siesta of shade. Up above, the sky is streaked with pale, brushstroke cloud. The sharp azure of morning has baked to a hazy, crackling blue. Out of the sun, the girls play in the inflatable wading pool and the dog barks at the splash, snapping droplets mid−air.

Meanwhile, Vin watches the clock. His appointment is not far off. Via Amore is due to open at six. Another night of solid bookings. Soon he will need to decide.

He digs his phone from his pocket and taps the icon to speed dial Amanda. It goes to voicemail. He says nothing – even though he has the contradictory urge to both vent and beg.

He looks over at the kids, listens to the peal of their simple joy. Although they are distracted for now, he does not fool himself into thinking they have forgotten. Or indeed that they *will* forget – particularly the five year old.

After all, he did not forget when he was her age.

In an effort to divert himself, he fills a tumbler from last night's leftover pinot and paces around the kitchen, head full of monologue, heart full of dread.

> *Another nervous check of the time.*
> *Another glance across at the girls.*
> *Another cube in the wine.*

Head bowed, hunched and frazzled, he is watching the ice melt − surface smoothing, corners rounding − when he gets the idea to call Tony.

It rings off and abruptly he is at his wits end, whispering to himself − 'fuck, fuck, fuck' − when Tony calls back.

'Sorry, Vin − had the phone on silent. What can I do for you?'

In a flurry of words, rushing and frothing like white rapids, voice accelerated by the near panic of imminent cliffs, Vin unloads − and in doing so is relieved to discover that he has made at least *one* right choice today.

Tony steps up, slowing him down, making him explain in a clear sequence, ascertaining at once what comes next. 'Mate, I'm round at Chrissy's at the moment. Why don't you bring them over here?'

Before long, his daughters are dressed. Spare clothes, toys and books are thrown into an overnight bag, the dog's bowl is filled to the brim, and the car is winding its way a couple of kilometres north, tracing the lip of the bay.

Pulling into the drive, Vin's heart lurches when he sees Tony and Christa together on the porch. In his chest he feels the pressure drop. Time splinters and it is 1988. He is nearly seven and they are still lovers. Inside the weatherboard house the kitchen will smell of deep red sauce and black coffee. Of sanctuary.

Yet, in the mirror – in the hard shatter of the present – beautiful children wait in the back seat. Uncomprehending. Trusting. Utterly vulnerable. Like he was. Still is.

For a moment he is paralysed. Pinned into position by the weight of everything. By the memory of a frail little kid seeking refuge from the chaos of grown–ups. How quickly and easily he had transferred his loyalties. With ruthless child logic, he had abandoned blood for love.

Perhaps this is what scares him most: that his girls will just drop him. That an animal core of self–preservation will override all attempts at fine point explanation. Because, ground down, the truth defies excuse, and all but the most resilient details dissolve in the downpour of years.

He thinks of his parents, and for a drumbeat his heart is breaking for them … because, unlike him, they did not find a way to survive the maelstrom of demons. There was no kindly 'zia' waiting up the street for them.

But these, he realises, are thoughts for later turning. Right now, the urgencies of the day require his attention, and he reminds himself not to shy from the risk of choosing. He need look no further than the approaching figures of Tony and Christa to understand the cost of doing otherwise.

It is only while at the surgery, wincing as his wound is being cleaned out with a syringe that he decides. Something about the doctor's warnings – hepatitis, tetanus – puts things into perspective.

As soon as the dressing is in place and the follow up appointment made, he calls Tony again and asks him if he could manage opening and closing over the weekend. 'Just get a couple of extras in to help out; maybe someone who's good behind the coffee machine. Pay them cash – thirty an hour if you have to. And take a grand out the till for yourself.'

Then he texts the wife.

> *Taking time 2 think. Kids @ Chrissy's. Dog fed.*
> *Work dealt with. Call if need. Bk Monday. Take care. X*

He laughs at the banality of it. Just like walking across the bitumen to Gianna's.

Can I come in please, Aunty Gigi?

Only when he is a hundred and thirty kilometres away, watching cricket in a motel room, does he think, *fuck, what have I done?*

In the short ad break between overs his thoughts rush forward, a crowd pressing.

> *Marriage, kids, livelihood.*
> *Past, present, future.*
> *Guilt, love, blame, forgiveness.*

He wonders if this is his fate, a lesson he is meant to learn, or if this is the price he must pay for running away – from his parents, from the mess he is in now.

Yet, in the deep quiet, he already knows. It is grief and all its seedlings. Not so much the feelings, as his failure to feel them.

Later tonight, safe from view, and a little too tired for the incessancy of analysis, his beer–smudged musings will centre on the vision of a sandy–haired child, a boy who used to cry too much.

The other kids are laughing at him.

Carlyle's a pansy. Carlyle's a pansy.

His folks are no use, in fact they are the primary cause; so he escapes to the Timones instead, and they defend him. The son with his cleverly worded swagger and willingness to front the bullies, the mother with her stoic, less spectacular, long game.

Be brave, Vinny, be brave.
When they are all dead, be alive.

Tomorrow he will wake up late – no wife and kids to rouse him, no promises to forget or fulfil – and he will eat a dull breakfast in a non–descript café to the drone of aircon and strangers, and it will occur to him as obviously as the cobalt glare of summer that plain survival is not necessarily brave; nor indeed does it represent clear cut victory. Indeed, there are many forms of survival, some of them little better than the alternative.

21. The form of the good.

'What a fucking crazy weekend,' declares Antonio 'Tony' Timone as he walks away from the now darkened restaurant with sore knees and a thousand bucks in his back pocket.

He is exhausted, glad it's over, but also rather pleased with himself. His organisational nous, his people and time management skills – honed in countless classrooms and staff meetings – have been put to the test and deemed adequate. In fact, first rate. Even if he does say so himself.

Yet, the best thing about his brief elevation to responsibility is the change in mood. More than mere distraction, or simply being too busy to think, it was the feeling of being useful, of repaying Vin's faith in him and, in turn, of confounding the expectations of others. Especially Christa's.

And then of course there was Rosie, and the believable excuse for enjoying extended hours in her presence. For them to flirt. Steal the faintest of touches between orders. For her to share joints with him and Jake after work, and for him to indulge in the absurd but nonetheless reviving fantasy of youth.

Now, instead of quietly dreading it, he is looking forward to being back in the city, to weekdays filled with young people.

Any thought that he might stay in Bravery Bay has been put to rest. He makes a note to thank Vin for the accident of clarity.

'Think I might go to the beach tomorrow,' he burbles, apropos of nothing. 'Maybe do something indulgent and anachronistic, like read.'

He pictures himself taking one of his mother's partly read books from the shelf and starting from where she left off.

Meanwhile, next to him, Jake Salter is laughing gently. 'At least there'll be no bloody tourists,' he observes.

This brings a smile to Tony's face. 'Hearing you say that – *tourists* – reminds me how much this place has changed since I was your age. Or should I say, how cosmetic the changes are.'

Both men ponder this for a moment while the younger lights up. 'Well, not long now, I suppose,' he adds, taking the first lungful.

Tony raises his eyebrows and a note of wistful departure vibrates the warm night air. It is a moment they do not need to sully with further words. Instead, they walk up the hill in consentient silence while they burn one down, observed only by the whispered breeze and the far off stars.

Only when they are home – beers cracked, feet up – is their quiet momentarily disturbed.

Tony checks his phone. A string of messages from Shelley. Sent, he guesses, in a burst of cortisol earlier in the evening. He reads them without reacting, sipping his beer, shaking his head.

He looks over at the keyboard and other gizmos Jake has wired into Gianna's sound system and says, 'Apparently you grabbing all that gear wasn't part of the deal.'

Jake flicks dark eyes at the offending stack of expensive equipment. Shrugging his shoulders, he replies, 'No, probably not.'

If he is expecting Tony to admonish, he is relieved his friend simply purses his lips and puffs. 'Well, your mum is predictably furious. Actually, probably more just panicked.'

'So I'm guessing she checked my room and now she's freaking out about what Dad'll do?'

'I did say predictably.'

Jake muses on this for a few seconds, playing out scenarios in his head. 'I just couldn't leave it.'

Tony understands. Music is Jake's lifeblood; not merely his passion but a locus of meaning. Like acting was once his – before harsher realities drove him towards the practicality of teaching. He knows too that Jake's art is more than a conduit of expression or signal for attention. Less about the vanity of authorship and more about the process of making. Perhaps, he wonders, it is akin to the Platonic form of the good. Something at once impossibly vague, stubbornly abstract, and yet always within easy reach. An obscure source known only by the advent of its many rivers. A point of eternal mystery hinted at by the emanation of waves rippling outwards from an unmappable centre.

> *It hovers in the black of the young man's eyes.*
> *Murmurs beneath his breath, in a*
> *barely audible tongue.*
> *The calm eye in a cyclone of longing.*

Tony has been mulling on this for decades and, after much reflection, has settled on the idea that for people like him and Jake the act of their art — the creative 'flow' moment — is an example of what he likes to call an entangled awareness. He is not sure about the terminology but he knows the experience. That it involves, simultaneously, unity and duality. Total focus and yet, in the same space, witnessing the act from the outside. Of being both self and other. Maker and watcher.

And somewhere — is it the middle? — the enigmatic meet point.

Because he still has a penchant for drama and flourish, Tony imagines this node of synthesis as beauty itself. For in beauty, he tells himself, everything is transformed, understood afresh, and easy distinctions like good/bad, happy/sad are blurred out.

However, he knows Jake does yet not have such language, and has no wish to impose it upon him; so instead he smiles raffishly. 'Yeah, I reckon I would've done the same,' he assures him with a larrikin lilt. 'Tell you what, let's just say it was my idea. Something plausible; like I pestered you about recording a voice track or something.'

It comes out naturally, so without fuss that he catches himself. His weekend as Vin's stand—in has defragged his thinking. He understands that it's a temporary high but he is enjoying it nonetheless — and he can see that Jake loves the idea.

In fact, his eyes are on fire. 'Whoa, you're in the zone, old man,' he jokes, his voice teetering into the coquettish.

'Must be all those drugs you keep feeding me, boy.'

'So like, are you serious? Do you really want to record something?'

'How many days till you fly? Twelve, thirteen?' Tony gestures, holding out his hands. 'Plenty of time. Then we wouldn't need to lie to your mum.'

'Cool,' Jake nods. 'Because I already have an idea.'

'As long as it doesn't involve singing or reciting shitty poetry, I'm in.'

It is nearly 2:30 by the time Tony gets to bed. For once he can contemplate the prospect of easy sleep. Although he has outgrown the aching single bed that squeals whenever he turns over – and, since Jake moved in, feels slightly cooped up whenever he shuts the door – tonight he senses a sweeping tide of relief rising from the soles of his feet, as he lets the last of his clothing fall away. Exhaustion will soon override the lifelong habit of shallow, punctured nights. Of repetitive thoughts and nagging spirals.

He regards himself in the window, by lamplight reflection. A naked middle–aged ghost hovering in the warm black like a see through peeping tom. Gazing in, appraising itself of its more corporeal twin. Slumping shoulders, slackening skin, softening midriff. The frailty and ordinariness of the body when compared with the vast dramas of self–important imagination. Meat hung on bones. Not moral, not poetic, not immune. An electrified, homeostatic, chemical soup. At once indistinguishable from the sea, yet still a defiant island. A paradox sculpted in flesh and memory.

Tony smiles sardonically at the mirage and hears again the low toned calm of inner counsel. 'This is the primary act of consciousness,' the voice is saying with unhurried assurance. 'Self observing self in the flow of becoming.'

Because he is too tired to tease the idea out, let alone argue, he simply jokes, 'Ah yeah, it's all about me, clearly.'

He chuckles to himself. The ironies of his vanity are manifold. 'You're such a poser,' he winks at the reflection, automatically assuming one of the model stances he has had so many years to refine.

Tummy held in.
Right shoulder forward.
Lips slightly parted.

Ah yes, he thinks, beauty … and its passing.

So he kills the light, and the vaporous Tony blinks away. Only his outline remains, etched in noir. Meanwhile, his silent echo reverberates in the heaviness of limbs, and in the deeper archive they embody. His own tiring, crumbling physique.

And that of Jake, mere metres away. And Rosie. Both so firm and lustrous. Muscle elastic, skin aglow. The scent of vitality. Time's largesse unspent.

Like Aneetha and the numerous others. Like the Christa Bell of yore; the girl who used to squash into the narrow bed with him thirty years ago.

The satin gravity of sex and its concurrent animal flight.

Now his cock is hard. Urging him.

He masturbates, conjuring the curious melange of sexual fantasy; a blur of replay and invention, of disembodied scenes played out in his head, starring phantoms with names and those he simply imagines. He comes in a writhe of tension and collapse; then allows the curtain of satisfied fatigue to draw down. The show at an end for another night.

It will be noon before he wakes, having had his best sleep for months – since he found himself waiting alone at a tram stop in last autumn's drizzle, staring into the illuminated eyes of airbrushed illusion.

Eventually, heat and a repeatedly vibrating phone alert him, and his eyes open to a room bright with midday. He rolls onto his back and tunes into the world. A sheen of sweat and a need to pee. The sound of Jake pottering, his music playing softly. Flies and birds and, in the background … is that the sound of waves on rocks? Of a break in the weather?

He sits up, considers checking the phone, but takes a sip of water instead. His body is still paying the price of a strenuous weekend, in the stiffness of his lower back and the bearable but constant pain in his heels. But so too he is enjoying the afterglow.

He is feeling less hermetic. More like bothering with the world.

When he eventually attends to the phone, he is not surprised to see missed calls from Vin and Shelley – their respective missions urgent – but he was not expecting to see Christa's name on the list.

'Hey, bella,' he chimes when she answers, and he can hear right away a kind of song in her voice, a tripping lightness he seems to recall from forever ago.

Her wall against him has been breached. He had sensed this – or rather, hoped it was so – at the base of the monument on Australia Day. But now he knows for sure. Indeed, he thinks she may even be happy, not merely affable.

'Amanda wants me to mind the girls for a few hours. I thought I'd take them down to the beach and I was wondering if you might want to hang out because ... they seem to like you.'

Though, by reflex, he shrinks from the mummy/daddy double act she is suggesting, this afternoon he is ready to allow it. It is, after all, simply another role. One of many. His caring, capable guy act. As long as she likes it, and it helps him feel good about himself, he will play it to the hilt for the benefit of all, and for the disarming delight of sparkling, child eyes.

Also, he divines the context. Vin will be driving back from wherever, and he and Amanda will need time. Thus, there will be another part to play later in the day. Reliable rescuer. Solid, dependable man.

As he is getting ready, he ponders the ensemble of public and private persona.

> The co-conspirator routine he uses
> with Jake and Shelley.
> The evasive ex role he plays for Aneetha.
> The ageing diva thing he sometimes does
> to annoy his agent.

The urbane critic of the classroom
— so suave and worldly.
A silver fox for tattoo Rosie.
A missing son for a dead mama.

A billboard role model for countless greying dreamers.
Yet another second rate actor — scouring the lines
for something indisputably real.

Once dressed, he attends to matters at hand. The insistent phone. He paces, almost professorial, as he skillfully placates and reassures Shelley and Vin with his maturity and understanding. That done, he wanders back to the bathroom to check himself in the scratched oblong of mirror. There, he fiddles with his hair, examines his complexion and says to himself, 'Antonio Francesco Timone: balding pantomime horse. Giddy—up there, boy.'

These things play over in his mind as he makes the first coffee of the day and appraises Jake of his conversation with Shelley, and of his revised plans for the afternoon. Noting the young man's responses — gratitude and relief, followed by a scintilla of jealousy — it occurs to him how easily he could exploit juvenile fervour. How he could manoeuvre Jake into almost anything. Sex, servility, supplication. Or indeed any number of irrational explosions. This further reminds him that, despite the convenient play acting that informs notions of character and morality, when viewed up close, human beings find themselves engaged in a game of exchange with consequences far more potent than the carefully crafted pay—offs of a three act structure.

Not that he really needs reminding of this. Not in his mother's house.

However, sharing the coffee with Jake, counting down the minutes until Christa arrives to take him away for a day of playing happy families, he thinks about the part he would like to enact for himself. What version of Tony will walk him through to the final scene? Who will *that* guy be?

The man who yields the man.

✂

It is obvious to both Christa and him that babysitting the girls — holding their hands while they wade in the shallows, building sand castles with them — is a window into a world that could have been theirs. As such, neither can resist the available jokes, nor entirely deny the twinges they privately feel.

'If I'm not wrong, this is the scene where we express our profound regrets, realise the error of our shallow ways and fall at long last into one another's arms, thereby reasserting middle class norms,' he announces, eyes running all over her.

'If that's your way of asking for a root, it isn't working,' she smirks in reply, keeping her voice low enough to avoid alerting the eldest girl's curiosity.

Having heard her say it, Tony thinks for a beat about fucking her. They both know it would not take much. Time and loneliness, sentiment and opportunity; perhaps with a chaser of booze. Or even a joint.

He imagines her wandering tipsy into his room. Sitting on the bed they lost their virginity in.

'Maybe I was just being clucky,' he diverts. 'You know the kind of thing — childless fifty—year—old has epiphany and realises how empty and selfish his life has been before foolishly over—compensating by having children to fill the void.'

'Ah come on, Tone — surely you know I'm way past all that now.'

Despite their banter and the protective apostasy underpinning it, both are entranced by the tumble and whirl of children.

If their riffing is cynical, their focus on the girls is instinctive; and Tony is no longer too proud or determined to refute this. For just as Christa is radiating motherly lumens, so too he is loving the run and splash. The cherubic faces. The blonde curls. The sight of sand on fat little feet and the sound of sibling chatter. He is human after all. Programmed to partner. Wired to father. Thus, in between the adult commentary, he is happily engrossed in the immediacy of cute kids. In being Uncle Tony and, in discreet corners, permitting himself the fantasy that they are his.

Seen from without, he realises Christa and he would look like carbon copies. One of billions of mortgage belt mamas and papas. Mister and Missus Ordinary. This forces a wry laugh from him.

'I'm pretty sure there was a time when neither of us would've been seen dead doing the kid thing,' he says.

'Speak for yourself,' she contests, eyes still teasing and lively, despite the truth she is alluding to.

'Really?' he asks, not sure how serious she is.

'You're the one who always wanted more,' she answers him. 'I didn't really know what I wanted. That was probably the big difference between us. You were sure. I didn't have a clue.'

'Jesus Chrissy, I wasn't *that* sure. I just told myself I was. Really I was shitting myself.'

'So was I.'

He takes this on board; not merely the fact of it, which he had long ago surmised, but the equanimity of the admission. Seizing the cue, he tells her he never understood why she stayed. 'I had my theories but at the end of the day, given that at any time you or I or both of us could've just got the bus back, I still can't say for sure.'

'Me neither,' she tells him frankly, shaking her head. 'I guess I didn't really trust you. I know I didn't trust myself. Maybe I thought you'd just meet some hot babe in the city and I'd be like the dumpy high school sweetheart you'd be ashamed of.'

She tries to say it with levity but the weight of it strikes him. He thinks of how fickle his attentions have been over the years – how even Aneetha's adoration had soon bored him – and in his blood he knows that Christa is probably right. How easy it would be to indulge the idea that it would have been different with her, how crass to appease her with revisionist platitude.

He is still trying to frame his next sentence when the boisterous interruption of Vin's daughters burgle the moment.

Now he is wondering if this *would* have been a better bet. Not to take on his mother's tragedy, but to knuckle down to the unassuming struggle of family with the one woman he has managed to love for more than five minutes.

But then he catches himself. Reminds himself how good it has been over the last few days. Active, decisive, sturdy.

'Well, I promise not to ask you to run away with me this time,' he half jokes, thinking of the spare room in his apartment, and of the camp hairdresser friend he could introduce her to.

'That's a pity,' she shoots back. 'I might finally be ready now.'

For the rest of the day Tony tries to talk himself out of tempting Christa to the city. He understands things are different now – matters of practicality – but also that the psychology is still fraught. Fifty, he realises, offers no more protection against delusion and need than nineteen. He remains as prone to the comforts of the known, and to the lure of surface storybook symmetries, as any teenage fantasist.

His normally nocturnal inner voice pipes up, 'The alignment of stars is simply a consequence of viewpoint. It neither proves nor disproves.'

The drama of the moment, he remembers, as he is watching it unfold, is simply noise. A spectacle of gesticulation. The raising of voices and the flapping of hands. Not to mention the plural lies and their numberless justifications.

All of this is running round his head as Amanda and Vin arrive at Christa's to pick up the kids and retrieve the keys to the restaurant.

It is an incredibly awkward scene. Only the youngest – not even three – seems untroubled by the dense, charged air. Her parents hover like giant, patched up combatants. Figurative blood having been spilt. They move with ginger motion; exhausted figures bandaging their wounds while the ceasefire holds.

Tony catches Vin's eye and notes in it the same punch drunk, startled pleading he first saw in the tear–streaked expression of a six year old boy.

Back then, he had jumped at the chance to play older brother/protector. Just as his mother had stepped in to play her part with gusto.

Without it ever being said, both took to the urchin Carlyle kid to prove a point; that for all the country folk blabber about caring and community it took a wog widow and her effeminate strapling to step up. To provide the shelter. To do the loving.

Except that he had abandoned his role. Left Gianna to hers. Vin to his.

And Christa Marie ...

He glances across the room at her — watches her as she mums the little girls and sisters Amanda — and he remembers that she too was there when Vinnie turned up, and he flew away. Now he is wondering if it was she who bore the most honest love.

Or maybe, he thinks, I'm just romanticising, and there is really nothing to see.

> *No great unfolding.*
> *No vision revealed.*
> *Simply people getting by – or failing in the attempt.*
> *Making it up as they go along.*
> *Hoping they are doing the right thing.*
> *Or that they won't get caught.*

In the meantime, the story is playing out. Amanda is thanking Christa, who is insisting she does not require thanks. Minding the girls has been an absolute pleasure for her. Meanwhile, Vin is manfully embracing Tony, delighted and reassured that his childhood hero was able to save the day.

'Even Clarice thought you were a natural,' he says.

'Ah, it's just organisation,' is Tony's reply.

'I don't know mate – you might just have a real talent.'

'Yeah ... and look how far it's got me.'

Tony watches as a flinch of discomfort darts across his friend's face, signifying that Vin has taken the comment as a slight against either him or the town; and this underlines once more his reasons for choosing the cosy anonymity of the city.

'Well, if you need a gig next summer, you know where to come,' Vin recovers. 'And it would sure help me out,' he adds, indicating the wife with child now hoisted on hip, her scathing eyes driving home nails.

Seeing this, Tony offers a little hope. 'Let me think about it.'

'If it makes any difference, I'm sure your mum would've approved,' Vin suggests, trying to appear casual.

'Somehow I don't think it's mum's approval we have to worry about.'

Again, Tony takes care to observe the perturbations in Vin's expression. The licking of dry lips. The eyes darting down. A scratch behind the left ear.

What he observes is not merely the clichéd cringe of the pussy—whipped husband but the subtler seismology of grief – and, as he watches his friend fidget, he tunes into his own responses. He wants to know if his mama's ghost is still alive in his veins. More than that, if pop—psych notions like 'getting over it' and 'closure' are in any way valid. If indeed recovery is simply a matter of looking at something else. Of tactical avoidance. A mode of forgetting.

The sun is a quarter hour from setting before Tony gets away.

Christa offers to drive but he elects to walk.

She watches him from the deck as he trundles down the incline to where the bay has just started rippling, mussed by the welcome arrival of cooler air from the Tasman Sea.

He can feel her gaze on his back, on his bald spot.

This sets off a chain of reflection.

He drifts back decades, to when she used to cut his hair, and little Vinnie watched on. Music would be playing loudly, aerosol mist filling his nostrils, and Christa's warm torso would be brushing against his. Sometimes he would get so horny he would make up errands for Vin, to send him happily scurrying. She would kiss him voraciously in these moments – all tongue and saliva and soft, breathy moans – and he would cup his hands under her breasts and their bodies would crush together.

When he arrives at the shore, he reflexively turns to look back up the hill, as if trying to pick her out amongst the coloured jumble of natural and manufactured shapes. As he does, he wonders who else might be detected perched on the branches and the guttering.

As if in screeching reply, birds are wheeling in. A rush hour of magpies and corellas. Crows, gulls, and the soaring laughter of kookaburras. It is a metaphor for the scratch and scrawl of memory. A chaos equation of sound, movement and probable return. Tony watches, listens, loving the loud melee of their instinct, and the deep and silent organising principle beneath it.

He walks on, tuneful splatter in his ears, following the rim of the inlet as he tracks anti–clockwise towards the town. After a week of heat the south–easterly breeze, at last, is cooling. The sweating veil that has hung over everything is being swept back.

'Clear air,' he says to himself as he savours the breeze.

Soon though, the evening commences its slide into night, and the blue bay starts morphing to black. Artificial light begins to speckle the hillside and the huddle of the township glows brighter and brighter. By the time he finds himself at the corner of his street, a red/gold dusk and a post–holiday hush have descended. Only the pub shows signs of life.

He briefly contemplates going in for a beer but decides against it, if only to keep his promise to Shelley – not to provoke back–water bitching.

And this reminds him that in less than a fortnight he will be driving Jake up to Sydney. That he will wave him off as others once did him.

He walks the remaining distance to the old house ruminating on this.

> *The ambiguity of loyalty.*
> *The strong yet tenuous imperatives of love.*
> *The endless dream of leaving.*
> *The inevitability of homecoming.*

When he gets to the house, he stops out front. He can hear Jake's music. Pictures him crouched over his keyboard. Guesses he is waiting to pounce the moment he walks in.

Perhaps I never really left, he is thinking as he walks up steps to the porch. Maybe I should contemplate trying.

Or maybe …

He looks at the glass top table, visualises her sitting there in the chiaroscuro, welcoming him like she used to when he came home from school, looking out to the bay that took her husband and set her free.

The screen door still creaks whenever it is opened.

The house still smells of her.

Another festive season

22. The will to remain.

It was inevitable, the old timers said. (After the fact.) They shook their heads, tut—tutting in their beer. The decision to go out that day was pure madness. Everyone had read the forecasts and, suitably warned, were staying ashore.

> *A writhing sky.*
> *The heaving, spitting sea.*
> *A bristling, muscular southerly.*
> *Dark grey, forbidding bay.*
> *Two days till Christmas.*

Besides which, the long term outlook was clear.

> *Good catches harder to find.*
> *Costs mounting, returns dwindling.*
> *The big boys slowly killing off the family firms.*
> *The town's main industry dying of strangulation.*
> *Of progress.*

Why risk it in a storm like that? What was he trying to prove? These were the questions that exercised the minds of astonished locals.

Yet, Big Jim Salter had either assured or harangued those who mattered. His more cautious father, Clem, had trusted his judge—ment in the end, despite misgivings. Meanwhile, the boat's veteran captain — a wiry, barnacled man who knew a lot more about storms than Jim — and the young migrant muscle who hauled the nets were in no position to argue with the fiscal certainties of the situation.

'No catch, no cash,' Jim had cajoled; and they had looked at the blackening sky, felt the holes in their pockets.

Deep beneath the bluff reasoning though, Jim was not so concerned about fish. He had seen the rude maths of the business and heard rumours of rivals wanting to sell out before the numbers turned terminal. The boats, he believed, were unlikely to survive the decade. The world was turning its back on towns like Bravery Bay. On men like James Reginald Salter.

Nevertheless, he was there before dawn in the unseasonal wind, whipped with heavily salted spray, taking command on the weathered old jetty. Head still fuzzed from another long night at Catchers' but determined to prove to his father and everyone else in town that *he* would be the last man standing and that, when all the others had buckled, *he* would profit from their lack of fortitude. He would save the Salter millions. Resurrect the Bay. They would surely make statues of him one day.

Although Jim would never fully acknowledge the underlying rationale for his decision that day, he would pay an early price in noisome scandal and, thereafter, in wordless knowing. In a quiet, background sense of scurrying panic that never quite went away, and in the fact that he would never again be able to look certain people in the eye.

And – because in his gut the knowledge of his error could never be denied – he had agreed to the secret terms of a defiant and surprising pact, one sealed with blood money and mutual silence. With ongoing shame.

For Gianna, it was just another morning in a cramped, untidy house full of men. Making Franco and his two fisher buddies their breakfast in a kitchen rented from their Aussie boss, while baby Tony cried from the bedroom, and a summer storm rattled every beam and bone of what she now called home. Where the shiny trinkets of Natale, the household's reminders of a now distant Italy, trembled in the bluster.

How could she possibly have known that these were the last fried rashers of mandatory service?

She was too tired, even for the rattle and sizzle of portents. Too disappointed in herself to allow scope for the luxury of dreaming.

Time was her only hope. Years would pass and things would get easier.

To her grateful surprise however, Franco had noticed. He had seen the deep fatigue in her eyes, observed the trudging perseverance she dragged through the days. Could hear in the dull rote of her words that he was *not* the man she hoped for. Knew, as she did, that they were wedded to an awful compromise; and that their crying child was now their innocent accomplice. He had been promising her – *when we save up enough, we'll move to the city.* There were better jobs in Sydney and Melbourne. Or so it was said. And lots of Italians. They would not feel so alone then.

But Gianna was not worried about being alone. It was people she had become wary of, Italians included. Thus, when the men strode boisterously downhill to the boat and the baby finally settled, she wandered into the bathroom, a dazed automaton, to stare at herself in the inadequate mirror. She saw a young woman in her physical prime; already showing signs of wear.

> *Maid.*
> *Milking machine.*
> *Muted object.*

She thought again of the long journey from a cobbled village; and of the girlish hope and adult dread that had corralled her around the globe and into the obscurity of a sunburnt fisherman's bed.

Still, with the men at sea and the young one sleeping, she was able to draw breath.

Despite the wintery firmament, she aired out the house as usual, hoping to extinguish the stench of fish and men, and the cloying vapours of her own folly. Looking out from the porch, she noted the seething sea. Saw how the rain on the horizon was falling at a severe angle.

On the days Franco worked it was her habit to walk Antonio down to town in the cheap and rickety stroller she had found in the charity shop. There she would choose whatever looked half decent from the grocery store – which was never much – and practise her English by reading signs, buying secondhand books, and taking the opportunity to talk with other mums.

Were they taking pity on her? Were they wary, keeping tabs on their diminutive and shapely Mediterranean competition?

Either way, she always stopped to say hello. Tried to learn their names, remember things about them. Invariably they would tell her how adorable her little man was. Would coo over him as though he were an item of exotic European beauty.

Then, as the months went by, they began, one by one, uninvited, to whisper daring sexual confessions to her over tins of baby milk powder and loaves of bleached white bread. Their fancies settling upon one of the twenty or so lately arrived Latin work horses — all single young bucks tumbled from packed migrant boats to land feet first in lowly paid labour; and now furtively revealed as the irresistibly attractive objects of bored Anglo–Celtic fantasy. Drafted to give small town fishers the lifeline of cheap hands, the scab wage imports had instead sent a hormonal shock wave through the town. Female feathers were ruffled. Male domains challenged. The subsequent import of shapely, olive skinned wives like Gianna was therefore viewed with an unmistakable measure of relief. The wogs would surely stick to their own kind now. No climbing the fence.

That morning, a band of hard needling rain had blown in from the Tasman Sea. It was lacerating the land, turning the unsealed roads to slick, sloping tracks, and the churn of the ruffled bay to a thrashing spasm of pins.

Gianna was half way down the hill when the squall hit.

Her first instinct was Tony; strapped in, quickly getting soaked. She tried to shelter him; prepared herself for the wail of his displeasure. But he didn't cry. His big eyes simply fixed on her. And in the summer rain she crouched down to his level and kissed his chubby wet cheeks; and for a few seconds they lingered on the street, hiding beneath an inadequate umbrella, watching the scene turn to watery murk. Not minding at all.

At least, this is how she came to remember it in later years.

She was not alarmed when none of the men came home that afternoon. Drinking, she assumed. It was not that she particularly missed or especially wanted the malodorous pleasure of their company, but she did wonder about the promised savings going over the bar.

Thinking of it − knowing it − made the brute fact of her situation undeniable. She was a captive. Living at the behest of others. With Franco, the husband she barely knew, in charge of the key. How could she ever have believed it would be otherwise?

Six men died that day − but there was only one widow.

The press, with its instinct for carrion, swooped into town hours later. By sundown, the tempest had eased, and by midnight the first helicopters were arriving. Sounding like a cataclysm of mechanical bees.

By daybreak − on a becalmed yet storm−damaged Christmas Eve − the news crews were roaming the streets, vultures questioning bleary−eyed fishers on the slime smeared docks and filming police divers as they slithered ominously into guilty waters. Later, they were on hand to capture the stream of shell−shocked locals, as they gathered to throw flowers from rotting wooden jetties onto the eerily benign, leisurely rolling back of the 'day after' bay. Meanwhile, TV people filed their reports from the decks of commandeered boats and reporters from big city papers waggled chewed biros and scrawled shorthand in tattered pocket notebooks.

Before long, word was out that Big Jim had found himself on the wrong end of several microphones. His story smelt of too much booze. Of profit over people. The rich owner from the proud pioneer family sending his poorly paid minions to their deaths on an outdated, unsafe vessel. It made Salter Jnr the ideal bad guy. The man who killed Christmas.

Predictably, the news people also came knocking on Gianna Sofia's door.

Her part in the drama was that of the brave, black—maned young widow with the big—eyed baby on her hip. But she was not prepared for the ugly and intrusive directness of the man who turned up on her verandah that evening, and after less than a minute of his bullying vulgarity she had slammed her door on him and his photographer. He called out his insistent questions through a sliver of open window but, upon being ignored, retreated to the roadside to keep watch and smoke cigarettes for half an hour before disappearing.

What Gianna had quickly grasped in the first seconds of doorstep harangue was that everyone expected her to be the model of grief. Leaden, like the storm swathed skies that had sent her man to the bottom of the sea and left her high and dry on a eucalypt hillside. It was only natural she should be distraught and terrified.

So young, so far from home.
With a little one to feed.
The noble and bereft paragon of female,
working class martyrdom.

Yet, she was afraid her relief might show. For how long could she hide the guilty, serendipitous fact? She felt lighter. Reprieved. Very nearly cut loose.

That night, while journalists and well—wishers came in dribs and drabs to her door, she hid in her kitchen ignoring their knocks, and sat at the newly emptied table with her beautiful, dreamy looking boy. While the radio played, she drank the rest of Franco Timone's Cinzano Rosso, sliced off thick wedges of salami and panettone and opened the ghostly presents. At some point, well after dark, she realised that for the first time in her life she would not be attending midnight mass, and that no one would be around to castigate her for this flagrant breach of the rules. Then, as she finally settled tipsy into her bed, his smell on the linen, she felt the enormous unburdening of knowing that she would not need to wake early to cook breakfast.

To be a servant.

Even so, when it dawned, it was a brash and sudden Yuletide.

A baby crying.
A kind of silence in the gaps.
The house seeming like a vault.
Cleared out.
Excavated.

'Buon Natale,' she said to the unwashed dishes.

'Have a happy Christmas,' in her stumbling English to the balls of scrunched up wrapping paper.

Later that day a thick set policeman would arrive to let her know her husband's body had been recovered. With a mewling Tony in her arms, she would make her way to the officer's car, past a clutch of zoom lenses and shouted questions. Minutes later, she and her child would peer down at the rigid and discoloured flesh of an erstwhile father and husband. Once, not so long ago, he had been a strong–boned man from a neighbouring village, a distant cousin from a good family who had fled the impoverished post– War countryside north of Venezia with everything he owned in a secondhand blue/grey suitcase. Now he lay flattened out like ocean catch – a man–sized fish hauled from the waves and wrapped in a tarpaulin.

Meanwhile, perhaps triggered by unconscious animal understanding, Tony's crying became deeper, more baleful. It rang out across the bay, seeming to swathe the whole town in a miasma of unspoken lament. It made grown men look down at their shoes, hold their breaths. It sounded like the universal sorrow of remaining – the ancient exhalation of unfathomable loss. The cry of the briefly and tenuously known, waiting at the gates of eternal mystery.

Even the stolid copper was forced to swallow a rising shudder of pain.

But not Franco. Like a sentinel, his witness silent. Comfort everlasting.

Then, as the embarrassed rookie officer drove her back uphill, Gianna Sofia's own tears had finally flowed, jolted from behind their dam of shock.

For she had woken abruptly from the surreal blur of events to find herself nakedly alone, and before her, in merciless definition, she could see exactly what the terrain of sudden liberty entailed.

The hovering cameras recorded it as a widow's heartbreak – but inside it was more like a deluge of terror. The sickening, unbalancing spin of violently imposed newness. The vassal child's disoriented stagger into unplanned adulthood. More than once that night she would dream of throwing both mother and son into the same broiling sea that had so thoroughly and summarily pardoned the father.

Only the departed, she thought. Only the departed are truly excused.

In the strange and brutal light of her predicament, what Gianna failed to count on was the response of the town. Because tragedy, she would soon discover, makes saints – and hindsight, especially when mixed with the odour of complicity, clamours for the cathartic theatre of justice.

Help came her way in the form of a thousand unbidden favours. All manner of once withheld kindness was extended effusively at every turn. Indeed, as if somehow purified by the extremes of widowhood, she was magically recast as a genuine south coast heroine. Truly one of us. No longer the mail order bride of snide dismissal. Suddenly so much more than just another blow–in dago.

Everyone soon agreed that Jim Salter's actions were careless. Possibly cruel. Definitely criminal. They knew in their hearts that her husband's drowning meant the end of the boats. And everyone, it appeared, thought that the empire owed her. Owed them all in fact.

It was old man Clem who read the mood of the district best and – advised by shrewd city solicitors – decided to act before the toxic effects of official inquiries and wrecked livelihoods could mount any lasting threat to a century of accumulated, hereditary prestige.

Jim, however, was in no condition for such arrangements, to make any sort of public gesture – and so it was Salter Snr who made the first approach.

A note, on gilt letterhead, slid under her door within seventy–two hours. An offer to pay funeral costs and, tucked inside the cream coloured euphemism of a condolence card, two crisp fifty dollar notes; the first she had ever seen.

With her piecemeal English and upside down world, Gianna was never quite able to follow Clem's precise meaning but, over the course of subsequent meetings, she began to intuit from the texture of his gaze and the manner of his generosity that he wished her no harm. That, in fact, he meant what he said.

Indeed, to this day word persists in certain circles that Grandpa Clem became immediately and hopelessly infatuated with the beautiful young Italian castaway, hence the easy terms of his largesse. The weatherboard house he signed over to her in his will was, for many – Jim especially – the final proof of a shame–fired and unrequited love. Gianna always scoffed at such talk, though she fancied it might be true.

When Jim Salter appeared at Franco Timone's funeral, on a warm breezy morning in the first week of January, his face was set in grim steel. The knot of his tie steadfast and tight. But behind his protective sunglasses all he could see were bodies being dragged from choppy waters.

> *Dead men, heavy and damp, laid out flat on sheets.*
> *With tags on them.*
> *Being photographed.*

It was not his first encounter with death, but it *was* the first time he had been made to answer such direct questions about it. In his heart he would never be reconciled with what he knew to be the answers.

His own culpable hand. His pride.

The sight of baby Tony, with his round eyes peering widely at the commotion, perhaps only vaguely aware of its significance, drilled further holes through Jim's girded composure.

And the mama − comely peasant girl, widow of his hubris − how she drove the hammer home. Her very existence. Her being there in Bravery Bay. The shape of her scrutiny, carving him out, and the grace of her sorrow; its quiet presence denying him the laziness of mitigating excuse or the pity seeking indulgence of collapse.

'I know you no bad man,' she had said, her accent still so strong that he struggled to hear her properly. 'I know is accident.'

In the end, that was what Jim could never get over. Her behaviour that day − and the way his father treated her. The way *everyone* treated her. As though he had died with the deck hands and then, in an awful twist, been sent back as punishment to live out his second chance life in a world of entirely scrambled allegiance.

There was a quality about her he knew he did not possess, and it had conferred upon her an aura of noble untouchability. Her naturally occurring goodness, he believed, was something he could only ever imitate. He would never know what it was to *feel* good.

Yet, what would linger most in his mind from that glum morning in the glaring sunshine, was the image of her looking back from the front row of the pews, finding his eyes in the crowd, holding his gaze for the length of a breath. For Jim Salter, the mystery of this gesture is still to be resolved.

Gianna Sofia Timone did not have the right words on the day − she was simply guided by gravitational impulse − but in later years she would find an explanation she could live with.

Some days she would take her morning coffee and amuse herself with the idea that, if Jim ever deigned to ask, she would tell him she was trying to strike a bargain with him.

'I'll cry your tears. You feel my guilt.'

No one else remembers that moment in the Federation–era church. Except for a young girl, barely twelve, who saw it from the corner of her eye. Shelley Jean McCartney – shy bookish girl that she was – could never forget a thing like that.

Years later – lover, bride, mother, nanna – Shelley came to understand that it was Jim and Gianna's shared and stubborn pride that allowed things to settle back into place. For the rupture of tragedy not to derail the slow glide of a coastal community. For individual shame and secrets to be safely stored. For decades to pass. Things to get better. Become more manageable.

February

23. The bell of forever.

He winds down the window. She leans in and kisses him. There are still tears in their eyes. Still so much unsaid. So far to go. But for now, the angled light of the morning, shot through with ocean blue. The looming heat of another summer day rising from the tarmac. A dry, dust scented nor–wester. The whirl and cry of birds. The breeze shivered trees, their leaves gossiping in ruffled whispers. *Oh look ... he's finally leaving.*

As the low drone of the engine kicks in, she steps back. A wave is rising through her body from the sun–browned lawn; like the mechanical unfolding of mere inevitability. The moment now here. These the final fractions. Two more breaths at best. His gaze clings to hers. The cord is stretched. There is an invisible, choreo–graphed movement of finely machined parts, and the black tyres inch forward. Then, just like that, it is done.

7.56am. February the tenth.

> *Shelley will treat herself to breakfast at Maxi's,*
> *maybe go for a walk on the beach.*
> *Jake will experience a brief but*
> *nigh orgasmic rush of relief.*
> *Tony will drive to the bright new servo*
> *on the outskirts of town and buy supplies.*

Meanwhile, in the salons, bars and bedrooms of the Bay, the chatter will bubble up, like water tumbling on rocks, into a kind of collective judgemental splattering – none of which will particularly bother the protagonists. For theirs is now the village of distance. The clean and curious intimacy of time and miles.

Jake is not surprised by the bittersweet taste of liberty, by the churn of his contradictory feelings.

His books, his music, the few people he has allowed close; all have served to prepare the ground. This moment, he realises, is part of the beautiful complexity of human experience, the vast yet molecular event of self—identification that doubles as life. As Tony wheels the car out onto the highway and Bravery Bay begins its steady reduction to a dot on a map, to selective revision and flawed memory, Jake closes his eyes and lets the alpha and omega percolate together.

> *Triumph, loss.*
> *Vindication, guilt*
> *Lightness, terror.*

However, there is something he has not yet reckoned with. The wild, insurgent clamouring of his desire. Its brutal insistence and ruthless impelling. Its conquest of other fantasies. Its colonisation of his thinking.

Jake is no virgin – but sex and love have never coupled, and the experience has left him shattered, almost degraded. He looks across at Tony driving and he knows that he could easily have begged. Could still do so. Could drop his head into the older man's lap and...

They could stop somewhere, get it done and still be at the airport on time.

> *But no. Too late now.*
> *And anyway ... having made it thus far.*

As though by erotic osmosis, Tony detects the ripple in the waveform. His sideways smile is knowing. Gentle, compassionate, respectful. Jake thanks his friend once more for his adept discretion. For his quiet, undramatic discipline. For not taking advantage of him.

Rather than the convenient outlets of sweat and semen, Jake is grateful they channelled their respective longings into the relative safety of recorded sound. Of pristine digital information. Ones and zeroes.

There is a nearly complete composition filed away on a ten terabyte hard drive; and this is how he plans to both consummate and exorcise his love.

A few more hours of post—production on a laptop in a cheap hostel in another hemisphere.

Everything that ever was between them — an entire summer — will be compressed, however enigmatically, into twelve minutes of spoken word and electronica.

Desire as data.

Without it being explicitly intended, the piece evolved over several iterations from wistful pining and simple romantic melody to a multi—layered wrestle of hunger and fasting. Of embracing and letting go. Refusal and acceptance. Now it feels more like a dialogue, like call and response.

If, in its pared down and rarefied way, it has come to evoke their shared experience, the detailed process of its creation was more like useful distraction. The quarantined focus of its making proved to be a carefully constructed and plausible refuge from the predictable high volume chaos that, in the last fortnight, had threatened to consume their attention.

Pondering the fallout of recent family dramas, Jake leans into the rushing current of hot air pouring through the open window, and in the buffeting of its car—sped blast, he feels the empire's hold on him being loosened. Like nails prised from rotting timbers in high winds. Once solid structures creaking apart. With each kilometre, their threats of violence and disinheritance recede.

Or rather, his caring about them diminishes.

Before the day is out, he will be beyond their reach.

Then, a day or so later, he will carry most of his remaining possessions through customs and vanish into a foreign metropolis. Only an empty room remaining, resounding with the echo of failed dominion.

His heart won't break for *them* though — only for himself. For the handsome Italian at the wheel and, now that she is safely behind him, for his stealthy and understated mother.

He pictures her alone in the big house with her brood of hard labouring men and her tactical silence, playing her carefully plotted long game. Executing the slow salvation of haunted Caesars. Waiting patiently for the chance to escape the expensive confinement of her own corrosive malaise.

'I have something I want to tell you,' she had said in the minutes before he drove away. 'Call me from the airport.'

Judging by the slight and involuntary upturn that had creased Tony Timone's lips, Jake is now sure that she has already told him – and he wonders what else she has been saying. And what has been said in reply. Indeed, he is beginning to wonder if he has been carefully manipulated. Stage managed. For whose benefit? he asks himself.

He watches the man he loves as he concentrates on the road. Eyes ahead, shoulders tense, two day stubble, fingers drumming the wheel to the tune of private musing. Is this my future? Jake wonders. Is this my past?

'Mum likes you, I reckon,' he says.

Tony's focus is elsewhere – as ever, distant – and Jake has to repeat himself a couple of times before the elder can respond.

'She trusts me,' he confirms.

'What – to keep her secrets?'

'To understand the need for patience. To have some idea what it feels like for her,' Tony explains. 'And anyway, they're not really secrets; not if you really think about it.'

The direct and sustained look Tony shoots him unnerves Jake. Rankles him. Spikes of jealousy and adolescent indignation pierce his lovely skin. For a beat, he is scornful.

'Are you goading me, old man?' he asks, throat clenched to dampen sudden rage.

'Why, do I need to?'

Jake's practised reserve nearly desserts him. 'Ah fuck, puh– lease,' he bitches. 'Don't give me that shitty menopausal 'voice of experience' bullshit. Not today.'

Sensing his passenger's combustible mood, Tony nods and acknowledges the overstep. 'Yeah, sorry,' he soothes. 'Lame arse, middle class advice is pretty fucking pathetic; but that wasn't my intention.'

'Okay, so what is it that's so important that she had to run it by you first?'

'Again, I'm sure you can probably work most of it out, or get Chrissy or Vin to fill you in, but I don't think that's really the point. It's not so much the information, or even her interpretation of it – which, granted, *is* pretty astute – it's more the fact of her *telling* you that matters. It won't change your life, Jake, but it might just give her the chance to change hers.'

Jake is rolling his eyes and shaking his head before he can censor the impulse. 'Oh gee, the pathos is killing me. Really, what next?'

If Tony is tempted to bite, he holds his tongue. Tilts his head back, looks down the line of his nose. However, Jake senses he has left a little bruise on his companion. That things could easily spiral from here. Partly he wants them to. Wants the volcano of repressed sex to erupt. His bookish, defensive calculation to disintegrate. To fight, to fuck, to fly away ... and leave it all in flames.

> *The wreckage of dorms.*
> *The emptiness of anonymous cock.*
> *The conditional, abrogated love of*
> *honourable families and small towns.*

Indeed, he is red with tension by the time Tony brings the car to a halt on the roadside, leans across him and flings open his door.

'Feel free to hail the next bus,' he hears the older man say, voice like dry ice.

A short while later they are seated in the pre–fabricated, cartoon coloured interior of a freshly refurbished roadhouse. Black coffee in paper cups, lukewarm chips in a plain white bowl, a plump and smiling teenage attendant with a name tag – Brady – asking them if everything is okay. Jake lets Tony do the talking. The charming. Brady giggles. Returns with a replacement round of long blacks. This time, not so hot.

Meanwhile, Jake broods in shame and heartache. Exhausted and abject. He has screamed and yelled at the first person who ever truly offered sanctuary and recognition. He has cried like a child in the arms of this man. Behaved in a weak and juvenile fashion. Shattered the armour plating of his studied cool.

'Fuck it, Tony, I love you,' he had burst. 'Can't you see that?'

'Of course I can,' Tony had said, mustering all the diplomatic gentleness he had learnt in classrooms.

'Sure – but you don't love me back, do you?'

'Not like that, no.'

And then Tony had held his breath, and his eyes had focused once more on an elusive horizon. 'I probably haven't loved anyone like that. Except maybe Christa.'

Hearing that – and the plain, unsentimental way it was said – allowed Jake the break in momentum required to return from the fog of tantrum. Now, quietly swirling the black aromatic liquid in front of him, he understands why Tony refused to apologise for his lack of ardour and why, by extension, he himself has no cause to feel guilty for the tenor of *his* feelings.

He smiles, still embarrassed, and as he takes his first sip, he remembers something from Gianna's funeral.

'I would never say sorry for loving someone,' Tony had told the rows of mourners. 'And it's been a long, long time since I apologised for *not* loving someone. I'm pretty sure Mum would've approved of that.'

Looking at Tony now, Jake wonders if he has finally ascertained the underpinning point of their connection. Neither of them love who they are meant to. Both can perform the rituals, yet neither can be bothered. If anything, they are both, in their own manner, slowly refining the art of being alone.

They reach the ruck of the city without further incident.

It is early afternoon and the grid is hot, a bald sun glaring down. The expansive light of the country has diminished to stabs of white from tinted windscreens and reflected oblongs thrown from the sides of glass clad buildings. Generous coastal horizons have contracted to the fumes and squawk of a teeming, geometric maze.

While Tony tussles with traffic, Jake thinks of school, and of the furtive weekends he spent coursing through the wires of the big smoke.

> *Like minds, private functions, obscure venues.*
> *Drugs, illicit fucking.*
> *Anonymity.*

He thinks of the two thousand year old town waiting at the end of his flight – even bigger, even further way – and he imagines a reinvented young man. One scrubbed clean of farmer boy stink and dumb cousin assumption. Released from the burden of a venerable surname. A solitary particle in super–position.

It is both an enticing and terrifying prospect. For a chain is also a safety net. A locus of blame. An excuse.

When he mentions this, Tony chuckles knowingly and gives a small shake of his head. 'Failure is its own kind of freedom,' he says. 'It's like, the moment I finally accepted I was nothing more than a balding hair model, all bets were off. Sure, it was unpleasant at first, but now … now in a way it's almost like I've been given permission to accept myself. So I guess what I'm saying is … it doesn't really matter what *happens*; whether or not you find an audience for your music, or you just fall in love and live in a flat somewhere. Or even if you come back home with your tail between your legs. Maybe if I'd known this at nineteen, twenty, thirty – fuck it, even at forty five – I would've enjoyed things a whole lot more. Might even have made me a better actor. Who knows.'

This is not quite the response Jake was expecting. 'So like, what are you saying? Not to give a fuck, not to even try?'

Once again, Tony laughs to himself and his eyes sparkle with kindness. 'Just because it doesn't really matter doesn't mean you shouldn't care.'

Now it is Jake's turn to smile and arch brows. 'Ah, so right after you drop me off at the airport, you're going to enrol in a Life Coach course?'

Taking his young friend's point, Tony grins broadly, nods appreciatively, and fires back, 'Okay, so rather than dispense any more hackneyed menopausal wisdom, how about I just say that I'm pretty confident you're smart enough to work it out yourself.'

In one sense this is exactly what Jake wants to hear, yet he also suspects that Tony is obliquely pointing at something more elemental than the culturally approved virtues of risk—taking and self—determination. Something wilder, braver, more sinuous, less linear. Not restricted to the easily commodifiable outcomes of masculine endeavour. Not a hero's journey or an Aristotelian arc. Perhaps not even a journey. Indeed, he is beginning to wonder if what Tony is hinting at is already present. A shifting and subtle enigma, so palpably absent from his upbringing.

As if in answer, at the next set of lights, amidst the rumbling discontent of automobiles, Tony gazes at him with a look full of years, with a compassion Jake has never known.

And in that alchemical mirror … *is that me in thirty years?*

> *The moment moves like a shadow of the future, flitting across the surface of an ocean made from sadness and exultation. Like a still point in a desert of activity.*

The lights change. Impatient horns blare. The rush begins to surge around them.

They sit unmoved by the furious urgency of the city, simply looking at one another. It only lasts a second; but for now it is enough. It says all that can be realistically said.

Jake Adam Salter has known it for weeks … yet now, in the throng of the airport, there is nowhere else to store this knowledge. It is like flight information. A departure time glowing on an overhead sign, an event in a sequence of events. Waiting in the queue for oblivion. And all the while … earth turning, human beings going about their business. The living and the dying. Emerging and vanishing. The import of the day crushed beneath a cosmic banality.

Yet, for all that, in a few minutes he will bid farewell to Antonio; most likely for good.

This is not the way he imagined his final summer in Bravery Bay would end. He was supposed to save money, stay out of the firing line and fuck off to Europe. Done and dusted.

But then, before its advent, who can ever truly imagine the tectonics of love?

His books did not prepare him for the visceral experience of earthquakes.

He reflects on his earlier, irrational behaviour, his intemperate roadside outburst, and it occurs to him that such lengths, such extremes, are not the sole preserve of art and explanation, and cannot always be distilled into the beautified representation of music or the sculpted reflection of dry ideas. Perhaps, more often, love resides closer to militant distemper, to the bloodied and unsightly honesty of hunger, than to the disinfected elegance of intellect and artistry. Desire, Jake realises, is not a composition. Will not sit like a polite child in the silent imprisonment of digital memory; not speaking until spoken to.

As the minutes trickle by, he sits in a row of hard plastic chairs and unfocuses his gaze. The scene becomes a wash, individual details merged into a larger flow. A union of colour, sound and scent. Then, as his breathing slows, a distinct sensation starts to form in the vapour, like a silhouette appearing on a line of horizon.

Next to him, Tony curls an arm across the back of his shoulders. Jake feels the unambiguous warmth of his body. The solidity of its presence. Its strength and utter fragility.

This is just a man, he thinks. That's all.

And he remembers again all the seeming madness of summer – his father's stormy bombast, the inscrutable machinations of his mother, Vinnie Carlyle's crack up – and he begins to allow the idea that he may just have joined their fevered ranks.

His eyes focus, unsated, on Tony once more. Shabby, etched, old. Bald patch obvious. The granite remains of a once supple boy. Not so pretty these days.

Nonetheless, Jake leans in and kisses his favourite spot, above the left brow, his lips pressing with slow and deliberate attention. Isolating a patch of still smooth skin, tasting the remains of loveliness on the end of his tongue, and, in the process, stealing the confirmation of touch from the indeterminacy of solitude.

While close, he catches the disinterred whiff of a ghost. Hears her heavily accented voice in the busy kitchen. Feels her dead weight on the porch. Eyes fixed on infinity. Seeing the nothing that comes after everything.

He breathes in. The air tastes soft. Now, for a moment at least, he will know precisely what made Gianna Sofia sing. His body will electrify. A cold, sensuous wave. An entire ocean moving gracefully through him. The bell of forever. The sublime and tiny majesty of human desire. A hand held out to the immensity, reaching into the magnificent blackness. The sheer euphoria of the despairing gesture and the boundless, transcendent beauty of futility. And there in the light, a frail migrant widow crooning in a weatherboard house.

> *So, won't you please...*
> *Be my little baby?*

Jake swallows. Blinks. Tries not to dissolve. Takes a long breath to return to the room.

This is an airport. I am here to fly.

The clock ticks, the queues shuffle, and the PA sounds. Jake is back now – and Tony makes sure to catch his eye. To anchor him. He gently hovers an index finger above his young friend's forearm just to be sure all the hairs are standing. Abuzz.

'I know,' he breathes. 'I know.'

At which he simply stands, kisses Jake's forehead, strokes his hair, looks for an unfaltering moment right into him ... and then walks away.

Jake watches his back, follows him as he is consumed by the swirl of the crowd, and is very nearly in a state of awe. It is the most impressive act he has ever witnessed. Exactly, he thinks. Why bother with goodbye? Why not just leave?

24. An autumnal condition.

In a multi—storey airport carpark, he sits exhausted. At last it is over, he is thinking, listening to the sound of jets. *At fucking last.*

Tony slumps in the driver's seat and drinks down huge breaths. He rolls his head, loosens his neck and shoulders. Sighs. Verges on laughter.

It is the first time he has been alone since Christmas.

The last fortnight has been especially intense, but it is done now and the exterior cladding he has been wearing in public flakes off. Now there will be a cleansing episode of silence. A catharsis of relative isolation.

> *Boy gone.*
> *Carlyle mess under control.*
> *Christa's hackles down.*
> *Next few days to do as he pleases.*

The mix of accrued tension and overdue release remind him of his other life; of the last day of term, when the constant questioning ends, when the pressure to be on call recedes for a week or two. When he does not need to be anybody. Give anything.

Right now, freed from the act of caring, he is looking forward to a night alone in a hotel room with a harbour view and a couple of Jake's perfectly rolled joints.

Maybe then he will return Aneetha's call. Welcome her back to the country. Check in. Decide if he wants to catch up when he arrives in Melbourne.

At the thought of her — the memory of her touch — his fatigue resolves into an abrupt ardour and he realises that, buried beneath the scrawl of the summer, the sexual availability of Jake and Christa and the flirty temptations of Rosie have stretched a band of savage yearning tight in his bones. In his gut, hunger flares.

Starvation in the form of gravity. A deep, earthy wrench. He briefly contemplates wanking in the car but defers to the privacy of the twenty–third floor room that awaits him.

Or then again, he could just sleep.

Gunning the motor, he steels himself for another fracas of traffic and, as he inches the car out of its spot, the thunder of overhead aircraft remind him once more of the great cycles of departure and return that have marked his life; and of the stubborn stillness chosen by his mother. And by women like Christa and Shelley. As if, like trees, anchored and sustained by a solitary patch of fertile ground, they undertook their epic journeys through the rotation of seasons, their circumnavigations powered by rhythm.

Sun, rain.
Seed, flower.
Growth, decay.

Crawling through clogged streets towards his hotel bed, Tony wonders if running and standing still, going and staying, amount to the same thing. If only the years are traversed, and that the act of journey – the noisy spectacle of self and life – is a supreme banality. An artefact of the data, emerging from the ordinary function of constant flux. The simple existential two step of order and chaos. The event of being.

This thought pleases him immensely and, as the rush hour writhes around him, he begins to feel the particular lightness of futility. It is a vast and encompassing compassion. The final irrelevance of judgement. The liberating tabula rasa of point–lessness. And there, in the absence of meaning and purpose, he experiences something he will later come to regard as pure beauty.

So he drives in a line – wheels roll, tides heave, sun sinks – and he shudders with the sigh of unburdening as he inches his way. No longer reined to any great end, least of all enlightenment.

He wakes early. Watches the morning as it glitters on the harbour. The promise of another hot blue day beckoning. The thought of great distances. The slow-roasted land between Sydney and Melbourne. Rooms he has not seen for months.

It occurs to him that he used to hate long road trips. Today, he can barely contain himself. What if I just keep going? he thinks. What if I take a random turn-off and disappear down a dirt road into the ancient vastness of the inland?

He laughs at the lyrical folly of it, partly because he knows he won't do it.

Despite the attraction of more poetic choices, he remains a bedroom fantasist, dreaming up action for a hero Tony. The beautiful enigma, entrancing to behold. Ever the intoxicating vision.

Yet in his heart he knows he is re-enacting his mother's journey from servitude to untouchable refuge, from the prison of heritage to a porch overlooking a bay.

Tony may not have been the most loving son but now, finally, he sees the emancipating expanse bequeathed him. Without pretty language or high ideas – or ever saying it directly – she has shown him the trick of transformation. Her means of morphing the apparent tragedies of circumstance into the gift of permission. The way she allowed an orphan boy to be free from the dead weight of fathers.

History, family, his Italian identity ... these are simply names carved in stones. Monuments. And in time, the blind equality of wind and rain will render even these conceits as dust.

'Everything remembered will be forgotten,' he says to the air, as he casts a final glance around the room and prepares to travel back to the life he left behind in the spring. To the inner urban Tony who teaches, models hair dye, and still turns up to auditions.

By the time he opens the door on the unmistakable scent of gathered dust and stilled air, it is night. He has a sore back, tired eyes and the jittery tightness of too much caffeine. Snapping on the light, the living room bursts into his senses, its familiar contours somehow strange. Everything where it was, passively in place, and yet not, as though time itself had suffered a hairline fracture. Like a continuity glitch. The slightest of jump cuts.

For a moment, it is both home and elsewhere – and he is both who he was and someone other. Clever replacement. Inexact replica.

As though he were entering a stranger's house, he pokes his head into every room. Appraises the amenity and the décor, forms impressions based upon the array of objects. And as he does, he slowly begins to recognise himself. To understand how he ended up in a high ceilinged 1930s apartment with visible cracks and a distinct lack of female presence. To know why, soon after waking tomorrow, he will resume his morning practise of nudging his comfortably worn Barcelona chair into a pool of sunlight and gazing out the north facing window into the cobalt sky, nursing a mug of strong black espresso.

Tony has not so much come home to a building as to a notion of self. To the ongoing story that *is* his life.

Now that he is back in town, he turns his attention to practicalities. He makes appointments – agent, work, accountant – and steels himself for the inevitable reunion with Aneetha Jharavindra.

They agree to meet in the city. At a steampunk café they both love; an airy, old world space in a converted factory overlooking an alleyway. The room in which they shared their first kiss. He would have chosen somewhere else, but she has insisted, thereby telegraphing her intent.

Though he could easily refuse, he acknowledges her need for a scene, for the ritual of it, and he allows the young woman her moment. It is, after all, only fair.

Nevertheless, as he sits on the tram, he pictures dainty white knickers and golden brown thighs. And the curl of her toes. He conjures the urgent press of her unleashed desire, its weight and warmth upon him, even though he is determined not to go there, and is equally certain she will have locked the gates.

This is what you get for running away, he tells himself.

Therefore, if he must bear witness to her scorn, he will do so with grace and politeness and allow her the last word.

She is waiting outside when he arrives and her beauty smashes him on sight. Her shape, her smell, the fire in her eyes.

The way she refuses touch.

He follows her up the stairs and over to a sturdy timber table. That he is the oldest in the room does *not* escape his attention. The rest could be in his class. Groovy, earnest undergrads borrowing the nostalgia of dead generations, somehow at home amidst the pre−TV industrial kitsch of the room. For them, he realises, (for people Aneetha's age), the past is an aesthetic, an academic curio and fashion statement.

For Tony, it is more like memory. More like an object his mother once held in her hands. Something once touched.

Like the gorgeous Indian girl piercing him with the iron of her gaze. The one whose sweat he has worn. Whose lust he has tasted.

'I don't think we will see each other after today,' she tells him flatly, as if reading out the findings of an inquiry. 'I have transferred to another school and I will delete your number as soon as we finish here.'

He nods, lets her know he understands. Does not offer argument or defence. 'So, can I ask, do you regret it? Us, I mean.'

'No.'

'You sure?'

She ponders for a beat before answering. 'I'm upset, I'm angry at you, disappointed in myself; but I'm glad I know what I know.'

'Which is what?'

'What you taught me.'

Tony laughs, impressed. 'That is a wonderful answer,' he says, and does not push her further. Does not need to. Her tone, her body language … they are enough to signify the nature of her discovery, which is not so far removed from plain disappointment.

> *The shine coming off.*
> *The fallibility of humans.*
> *The inevitable cost of loving.*

'And what about you?' she wonders.

He contemplates the simplicity of plausible evasion – finishes his lukewarm coffee to buy time – but decides instead to say what he truly feels. 'In my experience, what begins as regret often ends in forgiveness, if not acceptance.'

Aneetha's eyes spark. 'What have you to forgive me for?'

'It's not *you* I'm forgiving.'

This intrigues her. 'Does that mean you think what happened was wrong?'

'Not so much *wrong*, Aneetha ... more like the same old pattern repeating. Dreaming the same dream and waking up in the same bed. The same bed I've been making forever.'

'So ... was it a mistake?'

'Only if you assume that all repetition is automatically a mistake,' he replies. 'Anyway, is it a mistake to want to be close to someone? Is it wrong to risk heartbreak for the possibility of love?'

'No, maybe not,' she concedes. 'Maybe just stupid.'

When he reflects upon this later – after the diplomatic farewells and other gestures of conciliation – what strikes him most is the absence of self–pity.

The alluded stupidity, he guesses, is his; and a small note of concern is duly lodged.

In the meantime, he puts the phone on silent and drifts around, a holiday at home. He goes to the cinema, eats out, reads. Masturbates. Walks to the beach in the evenings to watch people, especially the backpacker kids – whose casual, semi–naked, volleyball laughter resounds in the chamber of his longing. Their sand covered limbs and the manner of his increasing invisibility brings a bittersweet smile to his face.

Soon, he knows, he will be free – even from sex.

The only interruption to his comfortable, rambling solitude is the long conversation he has with his accountant. Inheriting his mother's house has come with a raft of tax implications. Does he sell or rent it out?

'Or do you lease your apartment here and retire to the country?' the accountant says.

'Is that really a possibility?' he asks her.

'Financially, yeah,' she assures him. 'Unless you have expensive habits.'

'Depends what you mean by expensive really, doesn't it?'

✄

The following Monday, yielding to his agent's increasing urgency, he visits her high–sheen steel and glass office to confirm the details of a new campaign deal she has negotiated on his behalf. It is easy money for a morning in the studio; except that he is now wary of the dissonant effect of the illusion, the jagged edge between the two dimensional model and the flesh and blood reality of every day.

'Just to let you know,' he tells the surgically smoothed go–between who has represented him for more than twenty years, 'this is the last time. I'm shaving my head next month.'

When she makes to protest, he cuts her short. 'Come on Sharon, let's not be ridiculous. I'm too old for the whole pretty boy thing now,' he says, ruffling his once proud mane. 'Anyway, it's unbecoming; pretending to be important, carrying on like selling hair colour actually matters. It's an insult. A barefaced lie. I'm hardly anyone's hot young thing anymore, and I'm certainly not emerging talent, so why would I bother with all this?'

'Having an attack of principles, are we?'

'I'm not sure I'd call it that,' he replies. 'Where is the so–called 'principle' in recognising that you're wasting time on a dream that's never going to come true? Isn't it really just a matter of growing up and getting over yourself?'

Sharon scrutinises him through designer frames. She has heard this kind of thing before from actors who never quite made it. From those who wished they were big enough to be *real* divas.

'I know what you're saying, Tony,' she allows, lowering her pitch to seem more soothing. 'But look, even if that big part never happens, there's still a few more years of low hanging fruit out there for you. And hey, there's tonnes of less attractive people in

246

the biz who'd love to get *half* of what you're going to get for having your photo taken. Maybe this is just one of those First World problem things.'

Though he cannot deny the basic sense of her argument, he remains unconvinced. His disquiet has gone beyond the coolness of monetary consideration or the crudity of Sharon's guilt trip. He thinks about trying to explain but – noting the expensive detail of her cosmetic refusal to acknowledge time – he pretends to be swayed. Plays along, signs the contract, agrees on a shoot date. Promises not to do anything drastic with his hair until the artwork is finalised.

'Don't go Buddha on me, Tony,' Sharon cajoles. 'Not until the client signs off anyway.'

He raises a sardonic eyebrow. He does not say it, yet he knows that what she means is: *don't shave until the money's paid.* Moreover, he knows that she knows this is what he is thinking, and that she simply does not care. His pay cheque is her ten percent. Simple as that.

Both are too experienced to believe there is any other reason for their continued association.

Again, briefly, he flirts with the idea of explaining. He wants to let her know that his unease is more than mere snobbery, more than disappointment or bitterness. Yet, he realises this would be pointless – not because she believes the industry's notoriously breathless hype but because she does not. What is on the table is a deal, nothing more. The signatories could be anyone. She and Tony, even the client, they are simply placeholders. Examples of a market mechanism.

> *Product, model.*
> *Payer, payee.*

Ah, so *that's* it, he thinks, penny dropping. The inherent dehumanisation. The reduction of a life to a rectangle.

He wonders if this is why the sight of himself flattened out – cropped, colour–corrected and centred in the glowing frame of a billboard – had proven so disruptive. Because, in that accidental mirror, he had seen something pivotal about his mother's experience. The shrinking of a woman to a uterus for sale. The sacrifice of a peasant girl's teenage naiveté to the stoic grind of grown–up survival.

Widow to martyr.
Siren to shipwreck.

Now, as he watches Sharon's lips moving, Tony hears the calm and resonant inner voice. 'When you saw that poster you thought *that's not me* – and so the obvious next question was: *then who the hell am I?*'

He nods, acknowledging, and thinks of country towns and inner suburbs.

Washing dishes and taking classes.
Young lovers and old girlfriends.
Model looks and male pattern baldness.
Acting and watching.
The conflagration of making, and the ashes of undoing.

'So is that a yes?' Sharon is asking, looking over the rim of her glasses, wanting to seal the deal.

Later that day, as arranged, he arrives at the college precinct – a mis–matched gaggle of constructions spanning almost a century of architectural vogue – to be greeted by students and colleagues alike. It feels like homecoming, the comfort of the known, and he is uplifted by the youthful energy, the high–fives and the handshakes. Despite the perturbations of recent months, this is his domain; the cosy, bounded world of art and film and the character he plays within it. The regular wage and the sense of solidity. The authority he draws from his stature.

Tony does not beg for a role here. The stage is his.

However, amidst the bonhomie of welcome and the easy fit of familiar shapes, he soon observes a hard node of dislocation. A feeling of whispers steadily getting louder as he nears the red brick admin building. By the time he has swept up the main staircase to

the senior management wing there is a distinctly refrigerated edge
in the air.

> *The taut expression and off—ish stance*
> *of the Dean's normally effusive secretary.*
> *The formality of switching their*
> *appointment to the boardroom.*
> *The crisp lines of the Dean's outfit, reeking of power,*
> *as she emerges from her office.*

She beams her best smile but it barely covers her agitation.
Beneath the cloud of her scent there is a whiff of ambush.

As he follows the tempo of her heels along the corridor to the
fusty, wood panelled, inter—war room where board members meet
beneath portraits of famous alumni, and ministers and money men
are schmoozed for cash and favours, Tony forms the impression
that he is about to be fired.

If he is crushed, it is only for a moment.

Around the table with the Dean, the black clad and bearded
faculty head, and the immaculately shiny HR guy, he feels almost
giddy with the relief of a fait accompli. The anxiety of decision,
and therefore of doubt, excised.

Expensive habits indeed, he thinks; and the idea forces an
audible chuckle from him.

In response, the Dean tightens her lips and holds her breath.

'I'm not quite sure how to say this, Tony, but —'

'— you've spoken with Aneetha, I take it?'

'Unfortunately yes,' the Dean confirms — and this is all Tony
needs to know.

Everything else is standard issue shock and disappointment, a
show of predictable disapproval and judgement. He could save
them the bother, say it all himself; but opts instead to let them
suffer through the motions. Allows them to squirm.

'I'm sure you understand the College's position,' the waxed
and pruned HR guy contends. 'Even though there's no illegality
involved or even any question of harassment, per se, things like
this are definitely inappropriate and, of course, don't align with the
message this institution wants to send.'

'Which would be what?' Tony inquires.

'That we have zero tolerance for sexual misconduct of any kind.'

'So, where was the misconduct exactly? Or is it just that it *looks* like misconduct? Older white male, younger brown female. Rich man, poor girl and all that. Patriarchal, capitalist oppression.'

At this, the faculty head leans forward, hands folded in front of him. 'Don't be facetious, Tony,' he intones. 'You knew all the power was yours to begin with, you knew she was naïve, maybe even starstruck; and I'm sure you also knew that by the time the gloss wore off you would already have had your way.'

The directness of it — especially coming from a man he has known and worked alongside for years — stings. Even though Tony already knows this about himself, hearing it said so calmly sets him back on his heels.

Is *this* who he is?

The handsome Svengali who wangles impressionable under-grads out of their underwear.

'Isn't that why you kept it all hushed — like a dirty secret?'

Tony looks away, deliberates for a moment before responding. 'Not entirely,' he maintains. 'But yeah, maybe that *was* part of it.'

The Dean — who seems more upset than anyone else — is next to speak. 'Oh Tony,' she sighs, 'everyone knows you've got an eye for the ladies, particularly the young ones, and we all know they've got an eye for you. We just didn't think you'd be silly enough to consummate it on campus.'

'And now that Aneetha's spoken up I guess you can no longer pretend not to know?'

'We just can't take the risk,' the HR guy states. 'Not in the current climate.'

'So then, this is really about ... what ... politics, brand integrity, media management?'

'What kind of college condones fifty year old lecturers fucking twenty-one year old students? Even if she gave her consent, which she freely admits she did, we can hardly be seen to encourage that kind of thing. Surely you understand that.'

Tony bites his bottom lip, looks down, shakes his head. Aneetha has indeed had the final word. *And how!* He is pleased for her. Admires her savvy, the sheer poise of her vengeance. He thanks her in the privacy of his thoughts for her tactical intervention. For now the possibility of denial lies in total ruin – as if it were not already a crumbling façade.

He wonders aloud what happens next and the answer is as he expects. Officially, Antonio Timone will simply not return from compassionate leave. Nothing more needs to be said.

'Any outstanding entitlements will be paid and, should you wish to pursue opportunities with other education providers, fair and reasonable references will be provided,' the HR guy informs him with decorous efficiency.

'None of us have any problems with your teaching,' the faculty head chimes. 'In fact, it's obvious most students really respect you. They certainly seem to love your courses.'

Hearing this, Tony feels a bloom of tenderness and regret. He looks away and his head fills with the sound of the young and the eager. It is the reverb of youth's retreat, the delicate and shimmering coda of an erstwhile faith. This, he accepts, wincing, is the autumn of his condition.

'I'll be sorry to see you go,' the Dean adds – and Tony can hear she is genuinely sad. Maybe even let down. Over the years, their association has warmed into comradely affection, and it strikes him now that more than being sacked, he is being compulsorily de–friended.

For a few awkward seconds there follows a shuffling silence. The room, with its decades of cellared air, appears to exhale, as a gallery of glorious graduates avert their ossified eyes.

It is as though the truth, once glimpsed, must at once be turned away from.

Yet Tony does not judge this propensity; guilty as he is of the same reflex.

Somewhat shell–shocked, he makes his way in the sundried afternoon light to the rooftop bar where he used to meet furtively with Aneetha on Friday evenings – where he bought bottles of wine and ordered tapas plates, and they kissed in the glow of the skyscrapers before cabbing it back to his apartment to make love and promise one another miracles.

He nestles into the shade beneath an umbrella and, cold lager in hand, peers over the ledge into the street below. Watches the anonymous to and fro. The seeming chaos and branching net-works of a city, the circulatory system of human society. And in that ruck, he thinks, every kind of person. All manner of desire and every shade of denial. The lovers, the liars, the lonely. The cruel, the kind, the undecided. Those with mad dreams, others with broken hearts. And the stubbornness of hope, carrying on, making its way to somewhere. To its next appointment.

Looking across the thoroughfare at the towers opposite, he contemplates the many windows and ponders what might be happening behind the glass. *What the fuck are they all up to?*

'And meanwhile, I'm here, doing this,' he says to no one, sipping his beer, narrowing his attention to a fine point, thereby enabling a weighty cluster of forlorn self-regarding to dissolve into the simplest kind of freedom.

> *The absence of presence.*
> *The immediacy of distance.*
> *A horizon beyond the horizon, located in*
> *the exquisite realm of the near.*

Now the dramas of his past are momentarily on pause, all his fretful futures collapsed to the cold sensation of amber liquid and the gentle caress of warm air on his skin.

The now is forever. Eternity … infinitely … tiny.

But then, jolted, he remembers Aneetha; and in his heart he apologises.

How confusing, how distressing it must have been for her to witness her lover recede, to go from the terrain of hot muscle to the coolness of blue hills. The peak, once climbed, left behind. If only she had known what he did – that he would burn like an urgent star and fizzle out.

252

The faculty head was right. Yet also wrong. Tony had not set out to hastily consume the moment of another's sexual awakening, nor had he gorged in the certainty of the famine to follow, but rather he had reached out in the unreasonable hope that the light would shine without eclipse and that when the darkness finally arrived he would go there with her.

With *somebody*.

It is a dream he is slowly teaching himself not to entertain.

So he sips his beer, closes his eyes. Focuses on the toasted breath of summer. And he is a boy again, holding his mother's hand, walking down the hill on a bright morning. Trying to count the jewels on the body of a deep blue bay.

25. An offer too good.

Christa can tell Tony is not thinking straight. Despite the surface calm, she detects the submerged ruction in his voice. It is a note, she feels, of something nearing panic. The rendering of a crude dislodgement. The flailing uncertainty of a life stripped of predictable routine. He talks of freedom and opportunity, yet what *she* hears is the sound of once useful maps being ritually burned. The man she is talking to tonight reminds her of the disoriented Tony who arrived on the tide of his mother's passing, who made moving eulogies and did not bother with lipstick smears. Vulnerable orphan, suddenly adrift, compass confiscated, clouds obscuring the guidance of stars.

'So,' he asks, 'would you consider it?'

'Well, I'm not saying no,' she replies.

'Could be just the break you need,' he argues – and she knows he is right.

> *Get out of town.*
> *Take it easy for a while.*
> *Do a few temp shifts to keep her hand in.*
>
> *Shed her immaculate Bravery Bay disguise.*
> *Find out who she is – or wishes to become.*
> *Get to grips with the pokies.*

Her daughters would approve, and it is unlikely anyone in town would especially miss her. Not even Steve. Indeed, the ease and convenience of it is undeniable, its pragmatism appealing; and if the salon *were* to sell for a reasonable sum, she would not need to worry about money. Almost a no brainer.

Yet, for all the calm mathematical consideration ... nestled deep ... the faintest murmurings of reflexive dread. The hair trigger of her comfortable reluctance.

As always, her omniscient doubt.

Him. Her. Everything.

'Or maybe you could just come home,' she counters, trying to contain the onset of tremors. 'Do your Zen thing, help out at the restaurant, tease the yokels. Maybe you could even do some hair modelling.'

'Or perhaps we could just take turns,' he suggests, letting the tease pass. 'Rotate between houses; city, country, a bit of work, a dash of whatever. We could do the grey nomad thing. Have the best of both worlds.'

She laughs at what she regards as his surprising naiveté − as if everything were that simple. Then, when she remembers the risk taking, teenage Tony, the one who laid the whole world at her feet, the faintly romantic timbre of his urging makes more sense. Once again, he is promising her everything for the price of a punt on the unknown; like coins in a slot machine. In a way it is touching. In another, a confirmation.

'Okay, so what are we suggesting?' she jokes. 'A business deal or a divorce settlement?'

'Actually, I was just trying to be practical,' he says, still not taking the bait − though she can hear the playful smile broadening in his voice.

'Vinny Carlyle reckons you're pretty good at that,' she fires back. 'He's determined to get you back in as manager.'

'Trouble is, I can't really see myself in hospo. Not long term, and certainly not back in the Bay.'

'Why? Is it beneath you?'

'It's not that. It's just that we're not getting any younger,' he reminds her. 'And we both seem to be toying with the idea of changing things up. Breaking the old routines. I just thought maybe we could help one another out with that.'

'Alright,' she concedes, 'I'll definitely think about it.'

And she will. Right after she gets off the phone and has a couple of calming drinks. Later, when she finds time to slow down her thinking; and for the small but tightly clenched fist of anger in her abdomen to relax and unfurl.

Once again, Tony has broken into the private space of her compromise, sneaking past her defences like a figure in a dream, moving effortlessly through walls. Magically materialising in the cell of her secrets. The ones she tries to obscure from herself. That she only ever acknowledges when she is put on the spot. When she feels compelled to say no to him.

For now however, she will indulge the voluble fantasy of living in his apartment. Of a different life. A menopausal reprise of a youthful drama – with the middle thirty years having been edited out. The bumpkin hair cutter and the failed artist, surviving on a carefully portioned diet of memory and forgetting. Disputing the facts, yet quietly agreeing on the omissions. An informal contract between honesty and make believe.

Because some lies, she reasons, are kinder than their blunt alternative.

Therefore, she laughs in time, expresses her gratitude, shows him ample affection; if only not to blurt the truth and have it become irreversible.

She remembers the night it first occurred to her – or rather, coalesced into the clarity of constructed thought.

They were out, loitering late, down at the beach gazing up at stars; strewn as they were like toy crystals from a child's playbox, scattered like surplus jewels. He was pointing and naming – a newly inspired, library book expert – showing off his powers of recall and his recently acquired enthusiasm. She was pretending to care; all the while thinking how beautiful he was. All the while wondering.

If. When. How on earth.

'I look at the sky,' he had said, 'to remind myself how tiny things are down here.'

She had always loved his way with words. His flights of literary fancy. They were his way of remaking the ordinariness of things, and of offering up his better, more beautiful world for her delectation. Her role was to accept the various gifts. Or decline them.

'Down here, we shove everything into boxes; but these guys,' he expanded with an upward flourish, 'these guys work in huge cycles. The scale of it is magnificent.'

In that moment she saw it all. Tony's vaunted beauty was as fragile as the night. Too easily subsumed in the glare to come. Burnt off. Cauterised. Medicated. Exquisite, hand—wrought detail reduced to the standardised flatness of a machine made surface. He seemed to her not properly built for the jungle. Not suited to the inevitable compromises of accrued disappointment that, as a nineteen—year—old girl, she had come to regard as the assigned lot of adults.

'It's given me the guts to stop putting things off,' he continued, his tone coming back to earth. 'It's like, even my worst doubts are trivial in comparison ... so I finally went in and booked my ticket.'

Before she could muster more than a dropped jaw by way of response, he had filled in the key detail. 'March 21. Equinox. Y'know, the line between summer and winter. Half way between the light and the dark. Seemed like an appropriate day for it. Astronomically speaking.'

'Wow,' she had eventually exhaled, jolted by his calm execution, wondering if he had rehearsed it that way. 'So you're really going to do it?'

'Yeah, Chrissy, I reckon I am.'

Back then, she had not known how to react. A chorus of voices were screaming conflicting instructions in her head. A cacophony of sorrow and fury, disbelief and desperation. There was even a channel for scorn. And another for the punitive, domineering drone of self—loathing.

While she reeled, concussed, he moved with a muted assurance. Cool and methodical.

'I know for a fact there's still plenty of room on that bus. I'm pretty sure there'll be loads of seats for you to choose from,' he said, looking directly at her, leaving little latitude for sideways manoeuvre. She had never before seen him wield such obvious steel.

He was leaving. That was that. The rest was up to her.

But of course she already knew. Had always known. She had simply gambled that he would never ask, and therefore, that she would never be called upon to answer.

✂

She *had* loved him. Absolutely. Of that there was no doubt. She had yearned for him night and day. Taken refuge in him. In his wordy hauteur and defiant refusal.

Yet, she had also taken care of him. Stood in his corner and kissed it all better.

She had consumed him too, ravenous, and in turn had surrendered to his version of her hunger.

And he had loved her back. Maybe even more so.

It was generally assumed they would get married. 'Two strange birds,' people used to say; and they were happy to be considered thus. The fixing scrutiny of others, the moat of their judgement, served only to reinforce the castle walls. Make them stronger. As such, theirs was an unchallenged domain – a circle of exclusion drawn around them – and, in the confines of that adolescent idyll, they had both been found. First by the other, then in the mirror. All they had to do, it seemed, was name the day.

Voila! Equinox.

A cool day as it turned out.

> *Sky hazy, light flinty.*
> *Trees in a rustling kafuffle of ocean–chilled breeze.*
> *The bone dry blade of summer having*
> *cut the furrow for a bloodless autumn.*
> *The town dusty and desiccated,*
> *a stale overcooked shambles.*
> *More For Lease signs, more taped up windows.*

Into which lurched an old coach liner, its livery dated, with fat tyres and a cloud of diesel fumes. The rumble of its engine low, like the groan of the Earth on its axis. The sound of inevitability.

She watched as the driver heaved Tony's bags into the hold and checked his ticket. Then, their fingers unlocked.

The look of sorrow and wildness in his eyes, like a child unmasked and afraid, had made her want to take it all back. To wrap him up and hunker down in their hand–hewn cave and watch the world from the safety of a voluntary exile. From the sanctuary of one another.

But no. They had decided. The last summer in shitsville was over. He would climb aboard, the pneumatic doors would wheeze shut, and they would wave as he was driven away in a billow of fuel scented dust. This was their final promise.

'Please don't try to persuade me to stay,' he had begged her. 'And I won't try convincing you to come.'

Christa has since made a million vows involving both the real and imaginary Tony – mostly in the vapour of her thoughts, sometimes in the water of her tears – but she has long known the hard facts. When he offered her the means to fly, she pledged her troth to the ground. Not convinced by his hopeful show of feathers. Or that hers were truly wings.

At the time, all she could say for sure was that flight involved the prospect of crashing. That hope was the engine of disappointment. That being in love implied the possibility of falling *out* of love.

This, she will now confess, is what she had feared most. The day that Tony – eroded by the harsher rub of the real world – became *un*–remarkable. The morning she woke up in a sterile marriage. Her love no longer believable. When she became her mother. Just another cherry gone bitter. Every man a bastard. Every dream a lie.

She had studied him in great and deliberate detail that night at the beach, watched him carefully as his eyes once more distracted themselves in the firmament. She had traced the delicate features of his movement, noted the meter of his breathing. Drank in the lovely particulars. That was when she allowed the thought to be heard.

She would always prefer him as he was at that instant.

Tony the untarnished. Looking up at forever, scanning the heavens for beauty. Like a hero in a 'coming of age' sub−plot. The gorgeous boy who would never let her down.

She would always love this Tony. For what possible reason would such a Tony ever have to leave her?

Christa sits on the decking, rugged up against the crisp mint night air, wondering if now is the time.

> *For the truth of him.*
> *For the risk of them.*
> *For the uncomfortable bareness of self.*

She finds, in the star−spattered sky and the yawning rhythm of the dark and rocking sea, the safe distance required. Now she can look back fearlessly and acknowledge the historic traces of her own misjudgement. Antonio Timone's failure to make the A list was always the most likely outcome in the lottery of fame − but that he had survived his predictable mediocrity, that he had proven so enduring and resourceful, and that he never crawled back to the Bay, has long annoyed Christa Marie Bell. As if to say: *how dare you not be crushed.*

Maybe, she muses, this was the real issue with Gianna. The old girl's refusal to lose it. To wilt in the face of massed expectation. To play the assigned victim role. Yet, whereas the widow's resistance was couched in the sturdy act of remaining, the orphan's rebellion was the trick of disappearance. Both were a response to a form of grief that others could not − would not − comprehend. Both were a kind of absence.

Christa is not sure she ever resisted anything. Neither, she now admits, did she find room for genuine acceptance. She simply bumbled along. Cut it how the clients wanted.

Tonight she wonders if these too were forms of absence. Her distance from herself. From the phantom Christa who rode out of town with her lover on that wind−blurred afternoon. Who held his hand clasped in hers as the bus rattled up to the main highway and turned right.

Will it be *her* waiting in the city, welcoming her to his apartment? Will she be recognisable? Likeable?

The one who said yes.

Catching herself, she laughs aloud, and carefully begins to disentangle herself from the whirl of her second guessing; instead, taking stock of what he had said to her earlier.

'It's not like we have to decide right away. After all, there's a still a few weeks till our appointment, so we can talk about it then.'

'You're going to look so strange without hair,' she had replied, picturing the clippers, his black mane in soft clumps at her feet. Ready to be swept up and binned.

'Well, feel free to point and laugh,' he had assured her.

'Shave and shame, huh?'

'Sure, why not. You can even call me names if you want.'

'You just want the attention really, don't you?'

'I'm merely providing a public service,' he says. 'Giving people something to gossip about. Validating their assumptions. It might even make me popular. People love it when you tell them they're right.'

Yes indeed, she is thinking now, how very annoying it is when someone refuses to stay in the box we make for them. And how we punish ourselves for picking the wrong box.

Before his latest departure, he had entrusted her with the key to the weatherboard house. 'Maybe just air the place out a couple of times, chuck out any junk mail,' he had requested, and she had readily agreed. Today, she will finally make time to go over for an hour or so.

With salon duties trimmed to a more tolerable, off–season level, and Vin and Amanda's child minding requirements tapering off, Christa has found herself with the rarity of free time. Slow mornings and ambling afternoons. Home cooking. Gardening. Waxing, plucking, taking naps. Still, the thought of being alone in Gianna's house, with its spectral shadows, its history of imperfect love and irredeemable loss, has kept her away until now.

She enters. Gingerly at first. Tiptoeing. Only the dust is disturbed by her presence. The silence remains, an unresponsive witness. The one jarring note is the tower of Jake's equipment, stacked and wired up in a corner of the lounge room.

The rest is a domestic museum. The old woman's things still largely in place, with only a smattering of her son's recent imprint overlaid. And Christa's own memories, shuffling in their corners. Still waiting for the hero's return.

She moves with care, as though in a gallery, through the lounge, into the kitchen, and left into the cluttered laundry. There, she turns the old latch and opens the back door. Dry February air, scented with salt and eucalyptus, coloured summer blue and sprinkled with bird babble, flows in. It fills her lungs and, a moment later, she can smell the shifting of years, the whispered and inexorable motion of the seasons as they move through the rooms and winkle out the ghosts. Christa hears their laughter, their footsteps running across the floor, the chink of their cutlery. She catches a whiff of Napoli sauce. Of coffee and hairspray. Of Gianna's old lady perfume and of Tony's teenage lust. His sweating weight on top of her.

She remembers movies on VHS, music on cassette. Vin watching cartoons and licking biscuit mix from wooden spoons. Tony putting on eye liner in the bathroom. Gianna imploring her not to let herself get pregnant.

Taking the opportunity, she snoops. Open doors. Cupboards. Drawers. Unearths old pill bottles. Discovers unused vouchers. Runs her hand over folded piles of modest, practical underwear. Smiles at the highly ordered stash of Jake's stuff – books mostly, sorted by author – at the foot of Gianna's old bed. Feels a wrench of longing when she wanders into Tony's room.

The band posters are gone. So too any sign of boyhood detritus. There is only a single bed with crisp, obviously new white sheets and one small, clearly ancient bedside; on top of which is a scented candle and a CD with a handwritten title in black felt tip.

First complete demo (needs mix).

The candle smells of soap and star anise.

The bed smells of him – and of time.

Christa lies down, embraces the sensation, even as the bed springs yelp beneath her. She closes her eyes and before long, within a handful of breaths, she is with him once again, curled around his slender body, naked and safe. The heavy sweetness that comes after fucking enfolds them. All other sounds blur into the dapple of background. Decades reduce to the Rothko colour of cloudless evenings. Loneliness somehow becomes togetherness, and they are covered head to toe in sweat and union. As though the stars had instructed him to stay – or given her the strength to leave.

Without noticing, she slides into a half sleep, dreams mixed with semi–conscious awareness. She drifts like this for a couple of hours, and by the time she fully wakes the light has changed and her hair is badly mussed.

His bed bears her imprint. Sheets warmed by her body. The evidence of her passing.

She thinks about straightening. Decides to leave the tangled clue.

While she fixes herself in the bathroom mirror, she imagines the poetic Tony encapsulating the afternoon. She feels sure he will enjoy the symbolism of her asleep in his room. That he will appreciate the signs. A rumple of bedclothes and a few stray hairs. He will know it was her and be glad of the fact.

'All of this,' he had said at the funeral, opening his hands wide, 'is a symbol. Us all being here. Her bundled up in that box. Me doing this eulogy. This is like a shadow of a wave passing through. But it represents something we all value, even those of us who trample on that value and exploit it for the delusions of personal gain. This is a proxy for our love. Not so much for the love we give, but the love we withhold. Nor even for the love we receive, but rather for the love we miss out on.'

In her heart, Christa knows the truth of this. Although she still does not know if she will take him up on his latest offer.

26. Skin without scars.

Vin Carlyle has fallen into the habit of visiting Gianna Timone's grave.

Unlike her husband, she is not buried in the small Catholic cemetery but in the larger, civic plot on the north side of the bay. With the town's war dead and football heroes. With farmers, fishers and family members.

There, his own parents have a Spartan, neglected memorial in a shady corner. Bright young lovers burnt out. Blurred shapes in awful memory, hushed to sentinel granite.

Greg & Monica Carlyle. Tragically taken July 10, 1992.

He had stopped living with them by then; having traded them in for Zia Gigi. He remembers their funeral. How it seemed to him they were strangers.

It sends a shudder through him when he realises that he is now older than them.

Since the dust—up with Amanda, Vin has been drinking himself to sleep at night. He has passed out on the lounge a couple of times, crawling into bed in the early light, heavy and seedy. Dreading the idea of another day. Of the obstacle course his life has become.

The only certainty is that things will never resume their old formation. The restaurant – open again after a post—season break – has become a symbol of everything that irks his wife. Her jealousy, her fears, her sense of isolation and confinement. Vin sees all this but is not fooled. Via Amore, he knows, is a stand—in for their shared regret. In his heart he can finally admit he wishes he was not married to her, and he suspects Amanda wishes likewise. They have been a great disappointment to one another. Both turned out to be merely human.

Nevertheless, he has been occupying himself with accountants and business plans.

Does he sell a half share?
Should he poach one of the smart young kids
from Maxi's to run the place?
Could he ask Tony to take over?

He is also contemplating the idea of putting it on the market and leaving town. He thinks perhaps he might move to Melbourne, maybe even crash at Tony's until he gets set up. He could do something simple – a hole in the wall on a cool strip somewhere; soups in winter, burgers in summer, pump out take away coffees all day. Just him and a cut price backpacker. No wife, no ghosts, no table numbers.

Yet, his girls make it hard. Nearly impossible in fact. They never asked to be born into their parents' turmoil.

He thinks of their eyes, of their skinny little fingers twined in his, and he wonders why Greg and Monica were not similarly moved. How come his sadness was not enough for them? Why did they never kick in Gianna's door and demand she give them their boy back?

The obvious reflex – to blame and vilify – has long since ceased to satisfy and, over the years, he has been drawn to a subtler yet more seismic explanation. Amid the blur of their self–destructive behaviours, they had loved him with force enough to let him go, to understand that he was better off in someone else's care. Now he thinks he knows why Gianna never joined in the town's chorus of disapproval, and why she scolded him whenever he expressed such easy sentiments.

He recalls that it was *she* who had seemed most affected by their passing; and that she had soon delegated the tending of their modest grave to him.

But of course, she never said as much directly. It was not her way. Her methods were silent, whispered at best. Gianna Sofia Timone moved beneath the glassy surface but, unlike Franco, she did not drown.

She was taking her morning coffee when *her* moment came. Alone on a porch with birdsong and a bay view on a brisk September Saturday, having worked her regular shift the previous night and kissed her adopted son 'buona notte' in her usual fashion; as though moving from life to death without noticing. Just a sharp hiccup and a hot knife moment. A blink into blackness. No fuss. No conspiratorial rancour. Content to be discovered, stiff and already smelling, by the skinny scion of the red–faced plutocrat who sent her husband and five of his peasant friends to their storm riven end.

And all while Vin slept in.

Standing before her headstone now, he takes a moment to enjoy the cool shifting of the sea air and the panorama that encapsulates his whole world; and as he does, he imagines the bigger arena. The one beyond the south coast. The one that does not include flawed parents, sour spouses and replacement families. The realm that Tony took a bus to.

But then he remembers that Gianna too had taken a one way passage out of an enclosed village. Had followed the heady scent of an exotic promise, only to find the same kind of walls in place in her new world. Because prisons are not always cast in stone, and distance does not always fulfil its promise of liberation.

'I was bored, Vinny,' she told him once, when he was old enough to insist on more than platitudes. 'I see this big, beautiful world in movies, these wonderful handsome men, and big houses and jewellery, and I tell myself this is what I will find if I come to Australia. I am a child. I have no idea. I do not know what 'go to other side of world and good looking man will marry you' really means. I just want something that is not in this little town in Italy. Something I find for myself, not something others give me.'

Another time, when he asked her why she had not left the Bay, she had said, 'Everywhere is same.' Then she had rested her open palm on his chest, feeling his juvenile heart robustly beating, and added, 'Here is the only new place you can go.'

Though he now suspects some of it was mere sentimentality, and still more a mythology designed to opiate an otherwise intolerable suffering, he understands the realpolitik of it. However else he might configure it, Vin never forgets that she found a way to survive and, having done so, tried to help the wounded souls in her care to do the same.

As he crouches to wipe the salt and dust and bird shit from the rock bearing her name, he notices a recent addition. A simple white coffee cup. Sitting in its chipped saucer. Nestled there amongst wilting flowers. Placed with obvious care.

Tony.

He only has to say the name in his thoughts and, as though it were a form of permission, it triggers a shuddering and shaking stream. A soft and private downpour that, in spite of its melancholy, contains the mineral evidence of an undiluted rage. Of a manifest unfairness, rankling and scything, spitting like a cornered animal. Teeth bared.

After which, in a calmer, clear sky moment, he knows precisely what he wants to do.

Though he will not use the same devices as Gianna, he will act in the same spirit. *This* is what he can do for his shell—shocked daughters: he can help them survive the orphanage of adult fallibility.

'If you don't mind me saying, you look like you've been crying,' Christa says softly, discreetly, as she watches him in the mirror while she trims and neatens his already short, ruddy brown hair.

There is little point lying, so he smiles back at her reflection in confirmation. 'Anything you want to talk about?' she asks. 'The kids maybe?'

Though he feels a little uneasy about broaching the topic in the fishbowl of the salon, with prying eyes and ears just metres away, he takes the opportunity. 'Yeah, it's the kids ... but also ... the old girl and everything she represents. And Amanda, of course. And Tony.'

Christa draws an involuntary breath at this, which Vin notices. 'Anything else I can do to help?' she offers.

'Mate, you're already helping plenty. Amanda and I can't thank you enough – and the girls really love hanging out with you.'

As he speaks, he sees a vision of himself, a six—year—old with kid—blonde hair, going straight to the Timone house from school.

Not bothering to let his damaged parents know where he was. Leaving them to destroy themselves. He remembers getting free haircuts and how, after a few visits, there were always *five* chairs crowded round the kitchen table. Always a little treat set aside for him.

'The thing is, Chrissy, what's really fucking with me, and maybe has been for years – at least since the kids were born – is that I can't decide if Gianna rescued me or stole me.'

'Whoa Vin, that's crazy.'

'Is it?' he wonders, hoping that Christa's wide eyes might hold a clue. Or that his direct stare may serve to chisel loose a long secured secret.

'Look, I've got my own issues with Gianna, but seriously … even if she did play mummy, you were … I mean, what else was she to supposed to do? We all loved you, Vinny. Not just her, but me and Tony, and we loved having you round.'

'Yeah, I guess I was a cute little plaything, huh?'

'That's bullshit, Vin. You know it wasn't like that.'

'I don't know, Chrissy,' he exhales, shaking his head. 'Why would anyone just let some kid move in? Why the fuck would someone like Tony, who totally couldn't wait to fuck off out of town, give a shit?'

Cognisant of others in the room, Christa leans in close and says, 'Okay, maybe you're onto something. I guess you took our minds off things. And yeah, you were probably a whole lot easier to love than pretty well everyone else in town. So … okay … maybe we *were* just being selfish.'

From her tone and tense posture, and the palpable hurt in her eyes, he intuits a deep unease. He senses that she feels accused, not merely for her past deeds but for doing the same with *his* kids. Siphoning them away from blood. With something more closely approximating love.

'Mate, I'm not accusing you of anything, believe me,' he says earnestly, turning from the mirror to face her, to underline his point.

'Well, I hope not,' she replies, trying to cover up the bullet holes, mindful of other customers waiting their turn, returning her hands to the immediate task.

Following her lead, Vin lets it go; simply smiles and nods and says nothing more until, at the register, he tells her that his daughters have been wondering where her husband is.

'And they don't mean Steve,' he reveals.

Freshly shorn, Vin wanders a few doors down to begin preparing for what he hopes will be a solid Friday night's trade. Mild weather should help with this and, if the rumours of big city corporates coming south for a fishing weekend are true, Via Amore's reputation as the Bay's best restaurant should swell the numbers. Despite residual tiredness, he welcomes the potential distraction.

However, as soon as he slides the key into the lock he is reminded that the band aid of busyness will not obscure the real task at hand. For Gianna Sofia is everywhere; her authorship evident in every important detail. In the very fact of him being in the restaurant game. Of him knowing anything about food in the first place.

Bustling through the opening routine – security codes, lights, coffee machine, etcetera – it occurs to him that the business represents a later, less personal incarnation of the weatherboard house. A beacon for a vessel wondering which way to turn.

He was in his late twenties when Aunty Gigi first suggested taking over the lease. He had studied and travelled – working hospo jobs as he went – and had found himself back in the Bay. At a loose end, staying once more under her roof, sleeping in the creaky single bed. His intention had been to linger for a few months, no more, pick up casual shifts at Catchers' and finally decide what he might like to do with himself.

Moving through the restaurant, with its overt Italianate aesthetic, he wonders if Gianna made the choice for him.

> Had she sets her sights on him, believing him
> more likely to remain than her son?

Was she looking for any reasonable means
to keep him near?
And why did he agree?

These and other imponderables crowd his thoughts, hold his heart in a heavy fist, squeezing it till his chest hurts. His whole body feels leaden. He moves, as though through syrup, only by an effort of will, following the tracks of a long established routine. Executing the function with as little energy as possible.

Yet, by the time Hank, Clarice and Kel arrive to get things motoring in the kitchen, Vin feels that the day's events may have delivered at least one note of clarity. He is now convinced he is nearing the end of grief, and that the final part of letting go is the accounting of sins. Madonna Gianna, saintly mother of exiles, has long gone – now he must look into the eyes of the broken and terrified widow. Of the calculating and vengeful bride, who, in having her faith destroyed and her self–worth undermined, inadvertently poisoned the well for everyone.

Such that he internalised her elemental disappointment and made it his own.

He realises too that he must account for his own culpability. Selfishness, subterfuge, lies he has told himself. The way he has played the helpless urchin card, as both child and husband. His unconscious habit of setting up heroes, only to enjoy the perverse relish of their downfall and his subsequent letdown and sense of righteous vindication. As if to be betrayed is to be confirmed.

See, I told you.

As the time nears for the first customers and Vin settles into his corner, ready to pull coffees and pour drinks all night, he imagines a philosophical conversation with Tony – running the tape of it in his head as his hands make sure everything is ready for what he hopes will be a steady flow of orders.

'After we get over the shock of it, after we get used to the space left behind when someone dies, we're left with ourselves – and I guess that's what *I'm* really grieving. For me, that's the saddest thing of all. The bloke looking back at me in the mirror and the shit he's still pushing uphill.'

270

Of course, Vin would never say it so plainly or succinctly; nor would he wish to court another of Tony's daunting intellectual appraisals, but he enjoys the sound of it in his thoughts. It makes him believe he is ready.

To stop crying.

And then the door chimes and happy voices fill the room, followed soon after by the rich aromas of northern Italian cuisine and the chink of coins in the tip jar.

When he finally gets home, shortly after midnight, Amanda is on the lounge in track pants, channel surfing. Her voice acknowledges his arrival politely but her eyes are still honed, her body language forbidding. There is no kiss, not even the standard peck of coupledom. Both feel safer this way.

Still, his gaze lingers on her, as he twists the cap from a bottle of American Honey and pours himself an anaesthetising drink, which he swallows in a beat before topping up his dimple bottomed tumbler and settling onto the sofa; making sure to leave a judicious space between him and her.

'Good night?' she asks.

'Yeah, real good. Got smashed at one point.'

She looks across at him, and for a moment her eyes are shot with agony, with a pain bordering on uncomprehending desperation. He catches his breath, waits for her to speak. Time slows. They hover on a precipice.

'Okay, well, I'll see you tomorrow,' she mutters – and the fissure closes up. Her face resets and he goes back to being a housemate. A bill payer.

As she scuffs off, he watches her and, somewhere inside him, the man who still loves her takes stock of her exhaustion. Like him, she wears the mantle of defeat. It hunches her shoulders, slackens her skin, dulls her hair.

And there, in her grim survival, he sees tiny traces of Gianna.

'Just so as you know, I'm taking the girls to Mum's this weekend,' she informs him. 'It's her birthday on Sunday.'

'Sure,' he agrees. 'It's good for them to have nanna time. I'm sure they'll love it.'

'We'll probably leave around ten, so maybe don't drink the whole bottle if you want to see them off in the morning ... because I know they'd love to see you.'

Vin takes on board her well intentioned advice, as well as her undisguised scorn and diaphanous attempt at blackmail. He raises his half empty glass and promises her. 'Tell you what,' he smiles, 'I'll cook you all breakfast.'

Although Amanda does not believe a word of this, like him she is too tired to fight – so she flashes a thin, unconvinced smile and leaves him to it.

He kills the TV and listens for a few minutes while she potters, picturing her as she cleans her teeth and climbs into their sexless bed. So familiar is he with her, he can imagine the precise cadence of her routine, the exact shape of her body under the sheets. Even the way she tucks her chin into her shoulder. And the slow circles of her breathing.

He waits until he is certain she is asleep before grabbing another drink and moving outside for a smoke.

There, he pulls up a chair and sits in the light of the waxing moon. The sounds of the night surround him.

The deep shoosh of the sea.
The furtive rustling of foliage.
Isolated gull cries.
Invisible insect clicks.
An incongruous engine snaking up the hill.
Headlights sweeping clockwise,
like searchlights above the shadowy tree line.

Before long, he finds himself peering through the darkness, eyes vaulting over the township and across the bay to the opposite headland, where other bodies sleep. Only then, in the solitary lunar quietude, does it become clear. At least to him – although he wonders if others, Amanda especially, saw it months ago.

Years ago.

His challenge now is how to address it.

He ponders phone calls and other forms of reckoning but defers to the relative safety of the written word. I'll get it all out that way, he tells himself. Without me stuffing it up. Or him interrupting.

Though his first instinct is to wait till morning he overrides sensible caution and fetches his phone.

Vin knows that in matters of this kind he has too often remained silent, constrained by fear. Afraid he will be discarded. Sent out to play, only to have the door locked behind him. For his knocking and screaming to go unacknowledged.

Squinting at the small bright screen, he fumbles with the miniature keyboard, prods out his message. While he types, he thinks constantly of deleting, knowing that nothing will be real until he hits send. However, despite a fizz of nerves, he persists.

> *I know this might seem weird but when i saw the coffee cup at the grave today & i knew u put it there it suddenly made me admit something i been trying 2 hide. When yr mum passed & u came back i was mad as fk with u & her coz i was jealous. I was mad at u for just waltzing back & taking over. I was pissed with her for not seeing that i wanted 2b the one who did all that stuff. Sounds pretty fked i know but i guess i just wanted 2 say goodbye to her like i never did to my folks. I wanted 2 feel like i really fkn mattered 2 someone & that i wasn't just a guest or a refugee or a sweet little cry baby with druggy parents. Its like i just wasn't gd enough – like even my tears weren't as gd as yrs. It was ok for u guys 2 luv me but not for u 2 let me luv u back. Thats how it feels anyway. Just had 2 get that off my chest. Sorry mate.*

He knows he will regret it in the morning but sends it anyway. Even if it is embarrassing, it is the truth, and knowing it – saying it – seems to part the clouds.

Slumping forward in his chair, he lets out a huge sigh. He accepts that nothing is solved or decided but hopes this moves things forward. The dust, at least, will be swept from its corners. Shutters thrown open. Furtive whispers spoken at a volume that will force people's hands. Now, perhaps, their colours will be revealed.

273

Honesty or denial?
Love or tokens?
Respect or pity?

Swirling the liquid in his glass, slugging it back, he hopes he is prepared for the possibility of life outside the House of Timone. Of skin without the mask of scars.

It is the song of the girls' voices, like a falsetto trill, that stir him, calling him in from head fog and half dream, not caring if they are sirens, or if crags are waiting beneath their sweetness. Or if he ends up in the bay like Franco. Drowned and memorialised.

He can tell, even through crusty eyes and vertical blinds, that the morning is bright, the bleached colour of summer just beginning to yield to the deeper blues of autumn and beyond.

To his wife's surprise he holds to his promise. Gets up and gets breakfast – moving around the kitchen with the efficiency of restaurant years. Poached eggs on toast for everyone. Coffees for the grown–ups, smoothies for the kids.

It is an act, and Amanda knows it. But it is not for her benefit. Nor his.

He keeps his attention on the little ones, not wanting to give even the smallest sign. They burble happy nonsense for the length of egg and toast, and then he kisses them and waves them off.

'Bye daddy,' the youngest one calls from the back of the car.

'Ciao bella,' he smiles in reply – and she giggles, bathing him in sunshine.

Meanwhile, inside, on the kitchen bench, his phone is vibrating, Tony's name illuminated. It rings out before Vin can get to it.

However, by the time he has seen Amanda and the girls off, had another coffee and a smoke, masturbated in the shower, and dressed himself, his stomach is churning at the prospect of talking to his boyhood hero.

Noting that he now has *two* missed calls, he is satisfied that Tony has seen fit to respond in good time. Vin will get back to him later.

After a few minutes though, curiosity gets the better of resolve. He opts to risk the voicemail, just to be sure, shaking visibly as he presses the appropriate button, mouth abruptly dry, throat clenched.

'Hey mate,' his friend begins, his tone calm, perhaps a little sorrowful. 'I hear what you're saying and ... yeah look, it's nothing I haven't thought myself. I mean, I felt like a bit of a fraud during the whole mum dying thing. I was always a bit part player; not like you. So like, how the hell was I meant to do the grieving son routine? I still don't know. But look Vin, these things are always pretty messy. None of us is a saint or the devil incarnate; so yeah, if you want to call me back you can ... but maybe this is something for you and I to talk about when I get back in a couple of weeks. Just let me know, hey. I'm here either way, Vinny Carlyle. Please don't ever forget that.'

Trouble is, there remains a lot that Vincent James Carlyle can't forget.

'Yeah,' he mumbles, 'maybe that's my problem.'

Other than a short text to thank him for responding, there is no further communication between Vin and Tony. They will talk next month, after the latter's photo shoot.

Nevertheless, Vin ruminates obsessively, trying to weigh up his options, to pick a clear path through the noise and scrawl, to find a viable way to feel better. Aside from the distracting routines of work and the hiatus provided by booze and sleep, there seems no escape from the sheer intensity of it.

Yet, dense and turgid though things are, he feels the beginnings of lightness. Not so much in articulated thought but in his body. Something is dawning, even if he does not know what.

It is a beautiful Tuesday morning in late February. Sea flat, sky crystal cerulean. Air gentle, verging on cool. Magpies whistle musically. Raucous corellas yell.

The wife and kids are occupied elsewhere and Via Amore is closed for the day. An ideal opportunity to walk the dog, whose upright ears and smiling eyes seem to be making the same point.

Vin bundles a few supplies into the car – sunscreen, water bottle, dog treats – and sets off. For half an hour he lets the dog loose on the beach and stands shin deep in the shallows while she bounds in and out of the clear, calm water and runs her big wet nose over everything in sight. He loves the way her body moves, so unfettered, and her sandy, salty exuberance. Indeed, in a roundabout way, it inspires him, as if her careless play were a call to action.

Rather than going straight home, he diverts to town, ducks into the hardware store and buys a hardy looking pot plant from the gardening aisle. He requires something low maintenance, something tough, for what he has in mind.

From there, he drives a few minutes north to the headland cemetery. He tethers the still wet dog to a fence post in the shade, leaves her nibbles and water and kisses her salt–flavoured head. Her eyes linger on him as he makes his way, plant in hand, to his destination.

His parents' modest grave is untidy. Unloved. There has been subsidence. Weeds have sprouted. The headstone is titled.

He spends a few minutes cleaning up – uprooting, wiping down – and then places the plant with ceremony in a central spot. He waters it from his drink bottle and wishes it well, hoping it can endure the elements it will be exposed to. That it will indeed be sturdy, just like the man in the shop said.

Thereafter, he stands in repose, gaze focused on their carved out names.

Greg. Monica.

He does the sums. They would be in their early sixties had they lived. In their mid–twenties when he was born. Their accidental child.

It strikes him how quiet they now seem. How restful. Not at all like the volatile, conflicting people he remembers; their shouting, tempestuous war against the world and each other having ended on a highway bend. In a clapped out Ford Cortina.

All that turmoil. Over just like that.

'Thank you, Mum. Thank you, Dad,' he says, by way of simple offering. 'I'll see you soon.'

A few minutes later he is at Gianna's graveside and the contrast could not be more obvious. He counts all the reasons she had to crack; and wonders why *she* endured and *they* did not. It occurs to him in a flash. It is not an entirely new thought, but its startling and unambiguous quality is. As is its lack of judgement.

She had taught herself not to care.

In an act of raw survival, she had detached and – in order to pass muster – had honed an approximation of caring. Reducing her love to the practical; to repeatable and visible tasks. To the safety of action. And in turn she had passed this knowledge onto her son, and thence to him.

This, for her, was the best of love.

Indeed, to love truly was to offer up for others the possibility of liberation from the burdens of loving – and because she had loved both him and Tony with all the power of her broken heart, she had unconsciously schooled them in the salvation of distance. She may never have prayed, yet hers was the god of silence.

The divine absence.

But unlike her wordy, flighty son and his tear–stained replacement, Gianna's act of faith was a tangible and rhythmic persistence. The simplicity of routine and refinement on one hand, point blank refusal on the other.

Make it to the end of the day.

Vin thinks of his daughters and of their mother. Of the orbit he has placed them in. He wonders if this will make it easier on all of them when they finally decide to throw him out. To lock the door on him.

Lifting his gaze to the fuzzy line of horizon, to where blue meets blue, it occurs to him that it doesn't have to be this way. He thinks of something Tony said one night as they shared a smoke with Jake on the pontoon. It had been addressed to the younger man and uttered half in jest, yet it had stuck with Vin.

'When I was your age, Jakey ... I used to think my life was a movie, like it was leading to some great point. Y'know, with the big pay—off for the audience and all that. Now I reckon it's more like some kind of semi—improvised, durational theatre piece that just carries on until everyone stops watching and the actors walk off stage. Or maybe like a Jackson Pollock painting. Could be an ugly bunch of splodges … or it could be the most beautiful thing you ever saw. Just depends how you see it. Point is, you're free to deviate from the plotline any time you like.'

Recalling this, Vin is prompted to swing his gaze to the right, to bring the microcosm of his life into view.

> *The snaking line of the coast stretching south.*
> *The parabola of the bay and the town beyond it.*
> *A shawl of hills speckled with trees and houses.*
> *The bell curve of all he has ever known.*

He realises how easy it would be to turn around and walk back to the car. To drive home with the dog and resume his role in the upcoming rupture. All he need do is apply Gianna's template.

> *Be there in body.*
> *Say the words.*
> *Make appropriate gestures.*
> *Appear to be present.*
> *Yet truly, covertly, be elsewhere.*

This, he knows, is the tithe to be paid for the right to remain. The performance required for audience.

He draws in a deep breath, feels vertiginous. He is on a cliff top now. At the completion of a cycle. Once more the sandy—coloured kid, arriving home from school, standing in the road and listening to his parents scream at one another inside the house. Thinking to go inside and try, again, to break up the fight, as though he were responsible for its outbreak. And then deciding against it. Knocking on another door instead.

So now, in the eyeline of the sun, with the buried past all around him, the time has come.

To choose how it ends.

Autumn equinox

27. Acts in the likeness of life.

'Well,' she insists, 'did you or didn't you?'

He is surprised it has taken her so long. Then again, perhaps not – for to ask is to risk reply.

Tony is in his late mother's kitchen, stirring a thick tomato based sauce, watching over the penne as it softens in the bubbling water. He steps back from the stovetop and finishes pouring the red, plummy wine into the glasses. Nearby, Christa is smiling at him; but he can tell she is serious.

Therefore, instead of answering right away he takes stock, allows his memory to wander back.

> *Did he always know, deep down, she would refuse?*
> *Was it not clear to him, even then, that he would*
> *prove unworthy of her love?*
> *So much easier to run away.*
> *To let time and distance do the unravelling.*

'It very nearly killed me when you refused.'

Her eyes widen. 'Really?'

'Really,' he confirms. 'I guess I knew it wasn't the idea of leaving town you were saying no to, it was me. I suppose it was your means of rejecting me; or at least that's how it felt.'

She is stung by this. It shows in her voice; the smallest of tremors. 'Is that why you stopped calling?'

'I knew that if I did – I mean, if I heard your voice too often or saw you – I would be tempted to come back; and I knew that wouldn't have been good for me. Or Mum.'

'So, be honest with me … doesn't that mean whatever you were chasing out there was more important to you than what you already had back here? Than us? Than me?'

Again, Tony pauses, feeling for the line between truth and respect.

He hands her a glass to buy time. Sangiovese. A leftover of Gianna's he found in a cupboard. A blood coloured offering.

'It wasn't *more* important,' he tells her. 'It was *as* important.'

✂

The reason Christa is visiting Tony on a grey, southerly chilled evening is that, as she predicted, he had cancelled his appointment at the salon. However, before her victory could be fully enjoyed, he had said, 'I reckon maybe it'd be better if you did it up at the house. I could cook dinner. We could make a bit of a ceremony of it.'

She had laughed. 'Ha — typical you.'

'I know it's cheesy,' he had confessed, 'but if it's okay with you, I think I'd prefer it that way.'

'I suppose it'll be like old times then, won't it?'

'Yes and no,' he had replied

Though it would be a *physical* re-enactment, a routine familiar, each actor taking their cue, it would also be an entirely re-drafted scene. Reduced to its two principals. Same stage, same action, but no bit parts. *They* would only be present in the shape of their absence. In the spaces between lines. Via the chimera of memory.

Believing she had understood his allusion — though she had not — Christa concurred with a flick of the brows. 'I guess we're too old for that now.'

Reacting to the sparks in the hazel of her eyes, and to the sensuous shift of her frame, Tony had responded in kind with a sculpted male model grin — white teeth, playful glint, quick wink. 'It's only a shave I'm after, babe, not a happy ending.'

✂

A few hours earlier — day breaking sharp with the first teeth of autumn — Tony had brewed a pot of morning coffee and, as agreed, logged on to Skype with Jake. His young friend had tried to sound blasé, to maintain his armouring cool, yet the signs of his relief and excitement, the adrenalin of novelty and uncertainty, were obvious. He was a world away from small town scrutiny. From dust covered legacy and guilt stained dynasty.

It reminded Tony how *he* once felt, of the breathless moment when he moved into his first rented room in the city, when he truly begun to understand that he could be an entirely different Antonio; and that the blunt instrument of miles had effectively liberated him, cleaving him from the accumulated history of a svelte and soft orphan boy. He was no longer Gianna's fatherless brat. Or cute Christa's undeserving lover. Neither was he the faggot queer, snob prick, wog weirdo. Nor indeed anything. All previous labels conveniently sealed in the vault of a dying fishing town. He was just a man child from the sticks. In a room without furniture. A blank slate with pretty boy looks for sale.

Noting the way Jake's eyes had beamed at him from the screen – so young, so ensconced in the drama of seeking – Tony could virtually smell his friend's sense of freedom; that tipsy concoction of fear and jubilation, self–doubt and vindication. And, while Jake babbled, effervescent, he had thought again of his mother. Of the space and time she had left behind for him to fill, and of the particular geography she had willed him. Her slender, elevated niche; the one from which she could behold the various oceans. The salty *and* the psychological. The depths she had so doggedly manoeuvred into place between herself and them. The shining seas of her disobedience, in which, one by one, she had methodically drowned all those who wished to claim her.

Then, in the midst of Jake's youthful and verbose unknowing, he too had glimpsed a body of water. It was the same silver–blue expanse upon which Gianna Sofia had once deliberately set her only child adrift, lest, in her anger or heartbreak, or in an act of blind repetition, she herself had raised the tyrant's flag of possession.

Tony's heart had just about burst at that point. A wave of electric ecstasy, bordering on tears, had surged through him. Like everything and nothing all at once. Like love in all its blind egalitarian vastness. Compassion without caveat.

Through a laptop aperture on the other side of the planet, even Jake had noticed. 'You alright there, old man?'

'Yeah, just a thought,' Tony had stammered, clutching at the prop of the coffee cup.

'Anything interesting?'

'Ah y'know, just putting the pieces together. As you do.'

At which Jake had smiled, wistful and understanding – long suppressed tenderness surfacing, beautiful like a bruise. 'For the better, I hope.'

'I guess one day we'll find out,' Tony had replied. 'Although, really … it could just as easy be nothing.'

'Is that really what you think though; that it's all just nothing?'

There was a note of such obvious hurt in the young man's voice that the elder had quickly relented. 'Sometimes it matters like life and death,' he had said. 'But I guess I've just come to accept that in the end I really *can* let everything go … if I want to. Before it gets taken away, that is. For me anyway, Jake, that's pretty huge. I suppose you could call it freedom.'

'Does that mean you're going to let the hair go soon?' Jake had teased.

And Tony had laughed, delighted by the young man's directness. 'Tonight,' he confirmed. 'Equinox.'

After the call, Tony had lingered in front of the bathroom mirror, running his fingers through what had once been his prize asset. His father's midnight mane. That sensual and sable laurel of virile manhood. Of potency and power.

He pictured himself on new billboards. A giant Tony Timone. Abstracted into an anonymously perfect form. A cipher for a soul.

Would Aneetha, he wondered, ever pause in front of his picture? Would any of them – the string of sex partners, the alumni, the cast and crew? And what if the ghosts of Gianna and Franco stopped by? What would his stilled and magnified eyes reveal about the man they had made in their image? Or would they, from the tower of oblivion, see only ink on paper?

> *Dots in the shape of a child.*
> *Incidents in the form of a narrative.*
> *Acts in the likeness of a life.*

Minutes later, in the pelting shower, his thoughts returned to the sea and, without him having bidden it, the gentle and resonating inner voice whispered to him in a tone as deep as the tide.

You are home now.

And now ... Christa Marie is at home with him, sitting around the table that is now his, enjoying the pasta he has prepared, drinking the wine he has poured.

She is impressed. 'I never knew you could cook,' she says between mouthfuls.

'I didn't spend the last thirty years living entirely on pizza,' he jokes. 'I realise that as a single, white, middle—aged man I'm meant to be a useless and stupid creep with no taste but, hey, I was never one for ordinary.'

Despite the inherent criticism — she knows she is more sexist than him — Christa is charmed by his continuing refusal to allow others to pin their assumptions on him. Though she wonders if it is simply a refined adult expression of a reflexive juvenile pose, or merely his jaded and more contemporary spin on Gianna's legendary stubbornness, she is at peace with it this evening. If faux rebel vanity is his worst sin, she can well forgive him that.

Indeed, she no longer cares to analyse his reasons for the head shave because she has finally allowed herself to enjoy the renewed pleasure of having him around. Her daughters would be hurt to hear it so readily confessed but Tony's return has worked a kind of mechanical magic: that of raw disruption.

For his part, Tony is not so much disturbed by her presence, as re—anchored; especially now that his teaching contract has been torn up and his fading genetic glories are starting to look inescapably sad (and unsaleable). Though he has engineered for himself almost all the liberty he could want, and is steadily transforming the freeze of loneliness into the quiet bask of solitude, it is Christa's remnant doubt that affords him the best measure of surety. For the fissure of her disbelief is the fulcrum of his many—headed mythology. The dissenting reminder to look up. The shrewd and respected critic of an often gaudy and self-performative spectacle.

It is not that he swallows her savvy like medicine, but rather, that he enjoys it. Chooses it. And so, to an extent, does she. If this is going to be their game, he thinks, gazing across the table at her as she eats, they may as well play it with gusto.

After all, they're here now.

He smiles at the idea, before adding, 'Of course, if ordinary suddenly became the new exceptional, I might well make an exception.'

'Oooh, I like the sound of that,' she says, before raising her nearly empty glass and adding, 'Here's to being exceptionally ordinary.'

They squeeze a chair into the bathroom, set it in place. She asks if he is sure and he gives her the thumbs up.

'It's not like it's irreversible,' he observes.

'Sure, but it could be ugly,' she teases.

'I'll just cut some holes in a bag and wear it over my head if it's too hideous.'

At which she laughs, as if at some private thought, and starts the clippers buzzing.

It is with some amusement that she notices his eyes are scrunched closed. Like a child about to get the needle.

In the chair, he breathes slowly. Focuses on the cool glide and vibrating hum of the cutter, as well as the warm proximity of her body. Her skilful hands, tender upon him.

He does not look until it is done. Until she has planted her lovely soft lips on his newly naked crown.

The mirror provides a shock. The shape of a human head.

> *Ape-like skull covered in pinkish skin.*
> *Pale, simian reality.*
> *Ears jutting, eyes looking smaller, more recessed.*

Lips thinner, teeth more savage.
The lines of age now deeper and more defined;
the high contrast crags of time.

Somehow, he looks brutish and fragile at once. Just a wedge of hard bone between being and unbeing. A quarter inch layer of padding to differentiate the now from the never.

All Tony can do is gasp and laugh at himself. Run his hands over the revealed cranial fact. His head feels wet, like he forgot to rinse out the conditioner. It is a strange and unexpected sensation. Like an abrupt kind of nudity. A damp unveiling. As though the soil has just been turned.

Is that me? he wonders.

Over his shoulder, in the splotchy mirror, Christa is grinning ear to ear. Laughing, but trying not to.

Meanwhile, on the chipped tiles, grey and black evidence, ready for the bin. All ceremony, all grand gestures and fanciful invention, all higher meaning … rendered mundane. Carried off shortly by dustpan and brush. Leftovers vacuumed. Already memory.

Just like everything else; waiting in time to be forgotten.

'I wouldn't worry too much, babe,' Christa cajoles, stopping his train of thought. 'Mirrors never really tell the whole truth.'

Tony turns to look directly at her and shrugs, 'Oh I don't know, Chrissy – I sometimes think we only ever see ourselves in reflection.'

It is the morning after equinox. A grey–blue gauze of mizzle is drifting along the coast. The thirsty earth seems to sigh. Summer is over. The holidaymakers are back at work and Rosie Jayne Donald has left town for good. Soon the ground will smell wet. Before long, the breath of the cows will steam in the dark, musty fields and the birds will look fatter with feather. In a few weeks a bald man will turn fifty.

Tony steps out of the house – skinny black jeans, tight fitting long sleeve top, aviator shades – and feels the autumnal air more than ever. A dewy shiver, almost minty. For a moment he thinks about fetching his black and battered kitchen hand cap but decides to brave it.

He knows he could hide in the house but that is not the point. This is.

> *The visible show.*
> *The act of social unmasking.*
> *Doing it in front of others, and thus before himself.*

He walks calmly down the hill into the off–season quiet of a drizzly Thursday morning, where only locals remain to greet him with big eyes and wide smiles, with wise–cracks and selfie requests.

> *Wow, so you actually did it.*
> *Well hey there chrome dome.*
> *I have to say Tony, it makes you look*
> *a lot more manly.*
> *Nah really, it suits you, mate.*
> *You ripper! Chrissy owes me twenty bucks now.*

At Maxi's he orders poached eggs and smoked salmon and makes small talk with the new barista before settling into his favourite corner, where he gazes out to the white caps that snared his father and counts down the minutes until his breakfast date arrives.

She enters furtively and they go through the pantomime of pretending not to have arranged their rendezvous. His shiny nude head helps with this. Shelley Salter is genuinely taken aback. However, although struck by how pleased she is to see him, she refrains from any displays of affection. Instead, she takes a seat across the table, orders a juice, and keeps it strictly business.

They talk about Jake and Jim, and Tony hands her a CD. 'It's the piece we recorded,' he tells her. 'He asked me specifically to make you a copy. He thought you might like it.'

'Why, is it any good?' she asks him, smiling – but he knows what she really means.

'I might be biased but I think it's quite beautiful,' he answers. 'It's less forbidding. Gentler, more humane. More vulnerable. More forgiving.'

Shelley ponders the implications of this before thanking him profusely. 'Not just for this,' she says, waving the disk, 'but ... for letting him love you.'

Rather than brush it off, Tony gratefully acknowledges, if only because it is clear how significant it is for her. As it is for him.

And, by extension, for Jake and Gianna; and most likely for Jim. And, of course, for Vin, whose love is still dammed – poised – and for his adorable girls and stranded wife. Indeed, if he is honest, for most people he has ever known.

He holds his next breath and, for a tiny moment, his eyes turn once more to the swollen sea so that, in the brief silence, he can catch its murmur. *For who shall not drown in the echo of their love?*

'Tell me, do you think Jake will ever come back?' Shelley wants to know, her voice reeling him in from the wavetops.

'It's possible,' he concedes. 'After all, I did.'

After breakfast – when he and Shelley have fixed their public faces back into position – he makes straight for the salon, unable to resist the temptation. There, Christa greets him with her warmest eyes, running her hands gleefully over his slick head. The ladies present join in a chorus of appraisal. It is precisely the amicable scene he predicted. The jokes, the photos posted online, the games of flirtation.

'And to think, you used to be *sooo* pretty,' Christa teases.

'Back in the day I reckon I was prettier than half the girls at school,' he camps, playing along. 'And I definitely had the best hair.'

In response, Christa high–fives him and they fall into a matey hug, at which one of the customers – old enough to remember them as teenagers – says, 'Actually, you two were quite a hand–some couple in your day.'

Now their embrace is a notch tighter, deeper, verging on language. He feels the unmistakable presence of love in her fingers and she recognises the same in the tightening of his arm around her waist. Nothing more needs to be expressed, nor does it need to be acted upon. For it is unambiguously known, as it was when they invented it back in high school; and this, they believe, will be enough to sustain them.

'So come on, Tone,' Christa nudges, enjoying the play fight, 'how does it feel not to be so beautiful anymore?'

'Sure, the mirror was a little more ... *vexing* than usual this morning,' he parries, doing his best bon vivant routine. 'But hey, what is beautiful anyway? I mean, perhaps beauty is really just a way of responding.'

The room fills again with laughter and camaraderie and everyone present is charmed – cosy in their coastal corner of the world.

Encouraged by this, Tony concludes, 'If the rumours are anything to go by, at least people will take me more seriously now that I'm not so cute.'

All the women raise their eyebrows and nod, and he knows that at least he has *that* to look forward to.

A short while later, as though to confirm this notion, he gets a text from Christa.

> *Btw – still thinking about your offer –*
> *if you're still serious that is.*

He goes back to Maxi's and orders a take away. He wants to amble awhile inside the veil of showers that are folding themselves gently across the shoulders of the bay. To embrace the soft, cool promise of autumn. To ponder the richness of damp ground and the Earth's implacable cycle of growth and retraction. For he is starting to like the way his shaven head feels. Its exposed sensitivity to the air; a clean membrane of contact between him and the rest of everything.

It is as though an obscuring layer has been peeled back, not simply from a skull but from a life. Yet the revealed truth is nothing like the explosive drama of revelation. More like unfussed acknowledgement. A plain and emergent acceptance. He will be fifty in a few weeks. His pleasing looks, which he has clung to as if they were his identity, will fade into the wrinkled shrivel of age. And his bones will follow a similar path. He will walk, inevitably, to the same door as his mother and sink with little trace into the same chill waters as his father. For all the self—applauding noise he has made, he too will go in silence, surrendering memory to the culminating quiet.

The simplicity of it. The equality. The absolving brutality of fact.

He takes in his surrounds — a huddle of humanity on the rim of the sea — and it fills him with both relief and pleasure. Today, the old town feels welcoming. More than that: like plenty. Now he believes he could look out across the bay every morning and not wish for more. Even if there *is* better and wiser and more dynamic out there, or if staying in Bravery Bay represents an excuse to withdraw from a world fast becoming too much. Or indeed, if his long—winded homecoming can be coldly categorised as an admission of defeat or deficiency. These, he realises, are the pejoratives of judgement, the bullying sneer of pass/fail, the crude economy of either/or. What use has he now for such bankrupt mantras?

As he walks on, he turns these things over in his mind and the more he teases them apart the less urgent they seem. And in this autumnal calm he is able to take pleasure in normally overlooked acts.

> *Breathing.*
> *Sensing temperature.*
> *Working the muscles.*

Making his way up the incline, he tunes his happy senses into the birds, whose song and cry and arc and whirl happen without his intervention. Regardless. To them, he is but one of many land bound figures, a slow moving creature somehow denied the practicality of flight. They only care to know if this lumbering thing will offer them sustenance or danger. There is something in this animal logic that gladdens him.

Then, as he enters the house, taking stock of its patchwork of objects and aromas, and of his mother's face in a frame on a bookshelf, he recalls a few lines from her funeral, the ones he had re—imagined for Jake's composition.

> *She never said much, only enough – enough to make a spark. I used to think she kept secrets but it wasn't that. She wanted me to know, not just be told. To find the truth, not just receive wisdom. So she cleared the space for me to enter, left a silence for my voice, made an ocean for all of my waves. And now she leaves an empty house, vacates the garden of years, and I have only dust and traces. Clues, not chains. Tomorrow, not history. Beginning, not ending. That's why she kept it so dark. So that I could find the light by myself.*

He remembers the way the gathered mourners had squirmed in their chairs, their evident discomfort, and how much he had enjoyed it.

Gianna Sofia would have loved it. Of that he has no doubt.

So now, after all that has been and gone, Antonio 'Tony' Timone has room for something else. For there is an ageing, post—War weatherboard house, with its clutter of stuff, and the unknown time remaining. But there is no mission, no audition, barely any need for mirrors.

He wanders over to the bookshelf, smiles at the proliferation of bookmarks – mostly scraps of paper, old receipts stuffed between pages – and he knows right away where he would like to begin. He laughs out loud at himself, at his defiant penchant for neatly symbolic symmetries. It is a hangover from adolescence and an ultimately pointless gesture. But that is why he likes it.

He gets the percolator going, rustles up a few snacks – mostly hard Italian cheese and black olives – and drags his mother's favourite chair into a pool of light nearer the window. Then, while birds sing at him from the porch and waves turn to froth on offshore rocks, he closes his eyes and runs his fingers across the spines of incomplete books.

When it feels right, he slides one out. Presses it between his palms until he is sure. Opens his eyes. Notes the title. It is not something he has ever heard of nor, judging by the cover, would it ever make his reading list. But it is today — and there is a plush and comfortable seat waiting.

Wedging himself into position, adjusting the cushions, making sure the coffee and nibbles are within easy reach, Tony flips the paperback open to where Gianna left off … and, without even the tiniest glitch in the rhythm of the stars and the rocks that twirl around them, the story continues.

About the Author.

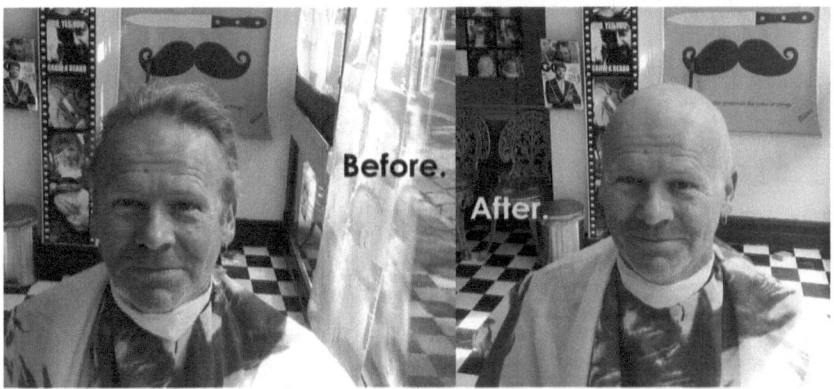

Before.

After.

Above: author Paul Ransom in March 2017

Paul Ransom was born in Brighton, England in 1965 and moved to Adelaide, Australia in 1972. After growing up in outer suburbia he studied to be a teacher. Thereafter, he worked briefly in the disability sector, taught Drama to kids, and Maths and English to prisoners in a maximum security gaol, before switching to find work as a rock journo, film critic and magazine editor. He also worked short stints as a nightclub DJ and band manager, in addition to writing PR blurbs and directing a film festival. In the early 2000s Paul was a lecturer in the media/arts sector. However, after his marriage ended he absconded to the tropics, where he edited local publications for three years, before relocating to Melbourne to successfully complete a mid−life crisis and become an award winning independent filmmaker. To date, he has published hundreds of articles for various publications, made four arty rock videos, written reams of copy for countless clients and created a blog consisting entirely of love letters. In 2019, his non−fiction work *The Pointless Revolution!* was published by Everytime Press. He currently lives in a low rise 1930s apartment building in Melbourne, where he 'plays' two guitars, feeds birds on the back porch and contemplates the void. If prevailed upon, Paul would most likely describe himself as a durational performance event.

Also by Paul Ransom.

https://everytimepress.com/everytime−press−catalogue/

The Pointless Revolution!

The Economics of Doing Whatever You Want

978−1−925536−74−4 (paperback)
978−1−925536−75−1 (eBook)

If all you really have left is time − how will you spend it?

The Pointless Revolution! is the ultimate lifestyle heresy. It turns economics, self−help and philo−sophy upside down. It promises neither enlightenment, salvation or utopia; nor does it require purity or genius. Yet, by striking a new bargain with time and re−evaluating our most primal fears, it paves the way for everyday freedom and genuine self−authorship.

Audacious and counter−intuitive, this personal and cultural revolution overthrows commonplace fantasies, fairy tales and addictions. By switching off the legislated lifestyle megaphone and challenging the authority of gods, brand ambassadors and social norms, *The Pointless Revolution!* is pure existential weight loss, an intellectual and spiritual de−clutter that will get you spring cleaning your entire life.

The revolution may be pointless − but it will sure feel good!

About Truth Serum Press.

Established in 2014, Truth Serum Press is based in Adelaide, Australia, but publishes books from authors in all parts of the English-speaking world.

Like sister presses Pure Slush Books and Everytime Press, Truth Serum Press is part of the Bequem Publishing collective.

Truth Serum Press has published novels, novellas, and short story collections. We also publish smaller, shorter poetry collections.

Sometimes, when the mood strikes us, we publish multi-author anthologies. Generally, we publish fiction ... and sometimes (just sometimes) we publish non-fiction.

We publish in English, and we would gladly publish in other languages if we understood them.

We like books that take us to new places, to new experiences and inside new minds and hearts.

We also like to laugh.

Visit our website at https://truthserumpress.net/.

Also from Truth Serum Press.

truthserumpress.net/catalogue/

- *The Last Free Man* by Lewis Woolston
  978−1−925536−88−1 (paperback) 978−1−925536−89−8 (eBook)
- *Filthy Sucre* by Nod Ghosh
  978−1−925536−92−8 (paperback) 978−1−925536−93−5 (eBook)
- *How to Catch Flathead* by Peter Michal
  978−1−925536−94−2 (paperback) 978−1−925536−95−9 (eBook)

- *A Short Walk to the Sea* by Eddy Knight
  978−1−925536−01−1 (paperback) 978−1−925536−02−7 (eBook)
- *Easy Money* by Steve Evans
  978−1−925536−81−2 (paperback) 978−1−925536−82−9 (eBook)
- *Square Pegs* by Rob Walker
  978−1−925536−62−1 (paperback) 978−1−925536−63−8 (eBook)